To Andy + Jolene,
Keep up the
good work or else!
It won't get done!

Dajeany

In Pluto's Shadow

by *Dagaan Galakticos*

In Pluto's Shadow by Dagaan Galakticos
Is the First Book of the Trilogy Ixtellaria Druidda
bluestarwheel@Gmail.com

Copyright 2017
All rights reserved
Use of sections for quotes in reviews
and publications allowed.

This is a refined edition formerly titled
The Alphabet Trees

Glossary of Names at End of Book

"The greatest art of the Devil is making us believe he doesn't exist."
                Baudelaire

"Sheila knew that the way was prepared before her because her god was Oval."
          'The Robber Bride' by Margaret Atwood

'A compromise with evil is not possible; evil must under all circumstances be openly discredited.
          Hexagram #43 I Ching - Chinese book of changes

'Let us dare to read, think, speak and write.'
          John Adams 1775

'I regret I have but one life to give for my biosphere'
Paraphrasing Nathan Hale, Teenage Martyr in the American Revolutionary War
and a Junior High School in New Britain, Connecticut.

"It is not a God, just and good, but a devil under the name of God, that the Bible describes."
                Thomas Paine

Contemplation of the One is Creation of the Self -
                            Extra Terrestrial Koan

Chapter One

A rose phosphorescence glowed on the underbellies of fat popcorn clouds as I drove east into the Sangre de Cristo Mountains. Rusty shades of red stained the weather blasted hills and hundred year old adobe ruins along the potholed highway out of Jaconita, the centuries old village in New Mexico where I live. The road winds through the village of Chimayo and then twists up into the mountains, through Truchas and Taos.

The setting sun threw blue shadows across the ground from the pinon pines and junipers scattered across the deflated hills looking like dark, grazing sheep. Between the trees and the ugly little cholla cactuses, jewel-like pebbles in every color of the rainbow glittered in the sandy earth - the last remains here of the mighty Rockies that have slowly disintegrated during New Mexico's fifty million year long siesta.

I'd seen this supernatural sunset happen dozens of times in the seven years I've lived in the Southwest. Yet the wonder I felt from the sea-shell pink glow of earth and air got to me just as much as it had the first time. It's like being on Venus or something. This time it made me feel a lonely ache that I had no one to share it with.

'Isn't it beautiful honey?' I asked aloud in the empty cabin of my truck as it hummed along.

The wine stained mesas, windblown infrared canyons and cracked, cactus covered beds of arroyos I passed by were like a dream seen through rose-colored x-ray glasses. These famous sunsets are the color of blood with sunshine passing through it.

With the valley plain here between the Sangres and the Jemez Mountains to the west at 7500 feet, we live as much in the sky as on the earth. At this altitude, outer space is visible to the naked eye as a dark hollow behind the baby blue and there's a feeling of something out there - breathing.

I saw some tourists pulled over on the side of the road taking pictures and gazing idiotically at the horizon with the temperature out there just above freezing. But I'd done it plenty of times myself and might have done it again but for this intense anxiety I was feeling. I really needed to see my friends, Spencer and Lena, which was why I was risking a speeding ticket. The loneliness and turbulence I felt that evening are clearly imprinted in my memory because it was the last normal evening of my life.

Feeling depressed while surrounded with such beauty was so contradictory, but the worst seemed about to happen. It was two days before Bush's re-election and a bass drone feeling of dread lay on the land, if not on the entire planet. It seemed something terrible was about to happen.

Everyone I knew felt physically ill from thinking about the election for the last six months. I'd watched some of the debates on TV and read stuff in the papers and magazines - probably to see at just which point a congressman or some prominent individual might stand up like Washington in the rowboat crossing the Delaware and shout 'THIS IS A FUCKING LIE!'

Expecting the double talk and misinformation to stop and real words be finally said, I actually started listening to the evening news on the radio again. I'd broken the addiction after the first election was stolen. How could there be real news after that? But all I learned from the radio was that things could either turn out bad or they could turn out worse. The first election was won by a judicial coup d'e-tat. It was as though Y2K had actually happened. Evil machines had taken over democracy.

With these thoughts grating in my head I didn't think twice about a strange car parked in Spencer's driveway. If I'd seen Yvonne's old tan Volvo instead of a blue Subaru she'd borrowed, I would have spun on my heel and gone home to feed my dog.

Like a lamb to the slaughter I followed the sound of voices into the dining room and locked eyes with Yvonne who practically arched her spine like a spooked cat on seeing me. I was shocked to speechlessness. She nearly hissed. It was Halloween night and though I'd intentionally avoided all the goofiness, here was a black cat crossing my path anyway.

I shouldn't have been that surprised to run into Yvonne there. She and Lena had become close friends during the two years Yvonne and I had been together. We used to go over there all the time. The women had lunch regularly now which I'd get from Spencer when he worked with me at my landscape construction business.

Yvonne and I had broken it off in a basically hostile way after I'd caught her spying through my window one night. It was the night Esteivana, a folk dancer passing through Santa Fe with a Brazilian performance troop, was giving me a private demonstration of a folk dance from the province of Bahia that dancers do real fast called Samba de Fuegi.

And to be fair, that was only Yvonne's retaliation for finding out that I'd watched her necking on her living room couch one evening, well, a little later than that - maybe eleven - from my truck parked across from her condo - with, yes judge, binoculars. She had hooked up with this New Age prophet after the lecture and book signing of his best seller - "Pleidian Angels and the Wings of Economic Opportunity" - or something like that. So, you can see that the trust had kinda broken down between us.

I had laughed about what had happened so many times - Esteivana and her amazing, jiggling rack and the Pleidian shmo with his blond ringlets, and holier than thou nose stuck on a cloud, that I couldn't take it seriously anymore. That said, I still felt betrayed by how Yvonne had changed horses in midstream. Esteivana was just an accidental incident I thought.

It's true that we had both regularly stepped back from the relationship. And it's true that I was stepped back when she hooked up with Goldilocks. But the truth was that our relationship had gotten kind of iffy and only the inevitable had happened, I thought. I was sure she felt the same way. Still, the parting had left jagged edges.

The two of us being suddenly in the spotlight in front of Spencer and Lena, close friends to us both, somehow brought back all the ins and outs of our relationship. They had witnessed the full spectrum of our emotional changes. From puppy love to rabies. Suddenly, between two heartbeats in the dining room doorway, there it all was again.

On seeing me, Yvonne became very polite, formal - and cooold. And this made her so sexy! All that heat and femininity locked up in the compressed lips and the elegant figure held erect as steel. But I knew how she felt - I didn't want my still unresolved feelings pulled out of my chest like the gooey strings of over cooked spaghetti, only to be held hostage to her etheric New Age evasions and her astounding presumption that she had deciphered the 12th Insight while I hadn't yet got through the introduction to the book.

The particular shade of her dark silky red hair, now sheared to extend the line of her lips along her strawberries and cream cheeks hit me like a cigarette burn to the heart as I rounded the corner into the dining room.

Yvonne's suspicious smile at me as I stopped dead in the doorway, making me feel like Curly about to get it from Moe, didn't take away from the sweetly familiar lines of her shoulder blades or make her green gaze less than something I would like to be cherished by again. For a moment, desire and mistrust had a head on collision in my chest and my concerns about global fascism shrank to nothing in the face of real and immanent danger - the wrath of Yvonne.

'Joe! Great to see you!' Lena - quick, short, wide hipped and vibrant with her sad Madonna face that bursts into a crinkly eyed smile at the least provocation, had felt the shock going through Yvonne and me when our eyes collided. She used her professionally bright nurse's voice - taking charge of the guy on the dolly with his throat slit. She got up and gave me a big hug and a loud, smacking kiss, demonstrating that I was a real friend and belonged in the house as much as Yvonne. The three of them were sitting at one end of the long oak planked dining table Spencer and I had built a couple of years ago. The untouched dishes of steaming food before them, the orange and black napkins with little witches on broomsticks flying around the margins and little cardboard jack-o-lanterns with devotional candles inside them all said a cozy little Halloween dinner party was about to begin.

The last of the sunset shined directly into the room bathing us all in vin rose - like a daguerreotype of some other incarnation. Their brain waves were still connected around a conversation they'd been having when I'd interrupted. Me - Joe Soloski - the intruder.

An oddly long and thick hardbound green book lay open on the tablecloth between Spencer and Yvonne. Yvonne was impatiently kicking her streamlined legs under the table while her face held a patient - and fake - polite smile, barely hiding her resentment at my interruption. I'd felt the hairs bristle on the back of her feline neck as I'd crossed the threshold and imagined her cat-like claws sliding out of their sheaths.

But Spencer and Lena's place is almost a second home to me. The glossed adobe walls, exposed logs in the high ceilings, the pewter lamp sconces I had put up with Spencer gave the room a Spanish colonial look reminding me of the house where Zorro hid out when he took off his mask. Spencer's house is at the back of a dirt road off the old stagecoach route into the 250 year old village of Chimayo. Everything out there is ancient. The orchards and irrigation canals, the houses and the fence posts.

Spencer is a dropped-out professor of linguistics and cognitive science from Berkeley who decided he couldn't stomach the radical pretensions of Berkeley academics whose radicalism never seemed to leave the coffee houses. He dropped out of school and started a web site to track the doings of the World Bank and the IMF and with Lena now raises chickens and quail and teaches Permaculture. The two of them helped organize the Internet coverage of the Battle of Seattle a while back. Lena is a nurse practitioner who did her first nursing out of the back of a van during the Chicago Seven riots in the Sixties. She now works in the clinic at San Juan Indian Pueblo just up the road. They're political activists to the core, now entering their silver years.

Lena had jerked back one of the tall pine chairs for me. It clunked loudly in my favor against the saltillo tile floor and put Yvonne in her place. So I hung my coat on the back of the chair and sat down.

Yvonne and I both knew we were trapped. There was too much goodwill in the room to get snippy. We were gonna have to make up, we knew it, there was no way out.

'I've made a huge eggplant casserole and there's more than enough and you *must* be hungry,' Lena commanded me through a steely, slit eyed smile that said - start a fight and you're both road kill! She turned her attention to the entree - Eggplant Parmesan casserole - that almost-food dish in honor of vegetarian Yvonne no doubt.

Yvonne, who has no problem expressing herself and is pretty quick on the draw, looked silently into space, her eyes glittering dangerously. Her silence was like an incoming tide, gathering depth and force. She had subtly hunched her shoulders, dropped her chin and was holding a tight, sour little grin. I used to tell her she looked like a cobra when she did that.

But this was a new, very feminine and sexy cobra. With the short, stylized haircut, a dark red, knitted skirt and a tight, short sleeved peach angora sweater with garnet earrings and a lipstick that matched, she looked so elegant, modern and professional. Even hunched up like a cobra. With her long, naked limbs, silky girlish shoulders and the full, ripe bosoms I once knew so well - she looked smashing boys.

I was used to seeing her in big loopy, earrings with lots of necklaces and bracelets and flowing, flowery dresses with tight bodices and compressed cleavage - a gypsy St. Pauli's Girl. It had been her image of a mystical Tarot card reader - something she used to do, sitting at a table for two in front of a New Age bookstore at a Santa Fe mall on Saturday mornings.

The corners of those spacey green eyes were watching me closely out of what I knew to be a deceptively innocent face. The sarcastic remark pursed on hold in her pouty little smile wasn't something I needed to hear to know was there.

Spencer - a shaggy blond bear in a wrinkled Hawaiian shirt - big blue-white eyes, expanded by too much information in a thick Nordic skull and Lena - spiked, black Argentine hair and black feral eyes she says come from her Polish grandmother - who is known to have shot a Cossack, point blank in the face as a teenage girl just after the Second World War - were both holding their breath and watching us. They felt the electrical suspense between us and were trying to neutralize it with big generous smiles and over loud voices.

'Spencer, pour Joe some wine and let's eat! I'm starved!' Lena said, flashing her brilliant I-dare-you smile around the room again.

'Did the rest of the lumber come?' Spencer asked me in a pretend dumb voice, letting me know he was still my ally and letting me know he was no less trapped than me. Spencer was helping me build the frame of a stucco wall around a Santa Fe nouveau mansion for some very successful child custody and divorce lawyers. He knew damn well I'd ordered the rest of the materials for the next morning, which was a Monday. He worked with me because he needed the cash but felt that all we were doing was adding on to Babylon, which he found depressing. Spencer could care less whether the lumber ever showed up. He filled my wine glass to the top with an almost black Rumanian wine and in a ceremonious gesture of compassion, passed it across the middle of the table to me with both hands. I was sitting next to Lena and catty corner to Yvonne.

'Hi Yvonne,' I said, sort of smiling at her, surrendering to the inevitable as I took the wine glass and sat back in the tall chair. 'Nice colors.' I said, vaguely waving my glass at her pretty clothes in an offhand tone that came out kind of choked because she looked so sexy. It's true. Cuteness rules the universe.

'Thanks Joe,' she said brightly, expelling the extra breath she'd been saving for her scorpion sting, her eyes still glittering enthusiastically.

'I like your look too,' she added with pursed-lip emphasis, waving her hand royally in my general direction.

There, she was saying, we've made public peace. And there also was her never distant sarcasm. I was wearing faded jeans and a dark green T-shirt - what I usually wear - and which, among a lot of things, Yvonne had tried to upgrade.

'Yeah it came,' I said to Spencer, acknowledging his show of friendship and ignoring Yvonne's slice of humor.

'Thank God it's finally cooled down!' Spencer said in his booming voice, expressing real relief that the hanging-by-a-thread suspense in the room had eased up. 'Working in that sun was just too intense this summer.' He gulped his wine.

'I saw a report on heat related cases from Albuquerque General at the clinic for last year,' Lena said, keeping it chatty. 'The incidence of severe sunburn related cases was three hundred percent higher this year than last!' She dished up some eggplant and handed me the plate with a congratulatory smile. 'Sun burn, heat prostration, sun blindness, cataracts - stuff that I've only seen happen occasionally all of a sudden was an everyday thing.'

'The ozone hole in Antarctica opened up the second widest it's ever been recorded,' Spencer said. 'And there's one of those holes over the Rockies you know. At this altitude and with this drought, there's less of an atmospheric shield so we get huge amounts of solar radiation. I felt like my body was cooking from the inside out.'

'Well according to this report honey, it was!' Lena said as she chopped her eggplant into bite sized pieces.

'The hens were acting funny all summer - molting irregularly, the eggs coming out watery - weird stuff,' Spencer said and sipped more wine.

To avoid making eye contact, Yvonne and I were staring back and forth at Lena and Spencer like they were playing Ping-Pong.

But what they were saying was true. I'd worked outdoors all summer with Spencer helping me out some of the time and we'd talked about it then. It had been hot but there was something else going on because I felt like I never cooled down. It was like I had a fever all summer and it took unusually large amounts of cold beer at the end of the day to feel normal again. Ordinarily the temperature drops twenty to thirty degrees at night in the high desert but for two weeks during July it stayed in the nineties day and night.

'In Phoenix, Albuquerque and Salt Lake they were getting some kind of Geiger counter readings off the sidewalks!' Lena said. 'And there was a twenty six percent increase in cataracts over the average.'

'This is creepy!' Yvonne said with her low, sensual precision. 'I noticed something going on with my clients this summer.' She was a partner in a physical therapy practice. 'A lot of my patients are seniors and they would come dragging in and flop down on the table like steaks. After treatments they were worse. I had to call relatives to come get people a couple times a month. I thought it was odd at the time. I really wasn't aware of the bigger picture!' Yvonne cut a tiny piece off a slice of eggplant and brought it to her lips without bending her spine one millimeter.

'And now the Fuehrer wants everyone to stop thinking about global warming, the AIDS epidemic and starvation in Africa, Prozac in the groundwater and concentrate on a Mars landing!' Spencer shouted in disbelief. 'Are these people even human? And does the media point out this obvious distraction from the war for oil?'

'Maybe it's not a distraction - maybe they're serious Spencer,' Lena said soberly.

'Serious!? Lena! It would take trillions to pay for something like that!'

'So what? They just spent a trillion on Iraq. With that kind of money they could have just bought Saddam's Army. But maybe they think they can double their money before global warming gets out of control.'

'Get serious Lena. Why would they want to go to Mars and how could they possibly live there - there's no air!'

'O.K There was a Life magazine article a few years ago that detailed how they could build these huge plastic domes on Mars big enough to contain towns and grow a massive amount of trees in them, start farms, set up solar collector factories etc. So - they build a certain amount of these domed towns all over the planet - and remember Mars is smaller than earth - then, when they gauge that they have the right amount of atmospheric density trapped in the domes that would be held by the planet's gravity, they open all the domes and presto!'

'O.K. Kind of far out. But O.K. But why do all that instead of fixing this atmosphere that's going bananas and developing cancerous ozone holes and force five hurricanes smarty pants?'

'Well...' Lena thought for a moment. 'You have this mass consciousness that has been deeply imprinted - and for two thousand years! - with the idea that they are going to heaven for going to church on Sunday. Heaven is up...Mars is up...'

We all burst out laughing.

'Lena wins!' Yvonne said, raising her glass. We all laughed and toasted Lena.

'So what's the book?' I asked trying my best to surface from the dark dread that had brought me there and fit in with the jolly mood. Spencer held up the abnormally long, dark green book for me to read the spine as he masticated crusty, melted Parmesan. It said; 'The Fairy Faith in Celtic Countries' in snaky, silver lettering.

'It's about the folk religion of Europe before Christianity. I've heard about this book for years but never could find a copy. It's very rare. A guy who owns a bookstore in Berkeley found it for me. It was the Oxford thesis of E. Evans-Wentz, the guy who translated 'The Tibetan Book of the Dead'.

'He describes how the monoliths of pre-Christian Europe were connected by ley lines and that a grid of electromagnetic energy was activated through Druid rituals on the cross-quarter days - the original holy days - and that a dimensional portal opened and people from a parallel world crossed over and that Humans made babies with them.' He said all this rapid fire and then scraped a wad of melted cheese off the casserole top and flopped it on his plate.

'Damn!' I said. 'How come I'm always the last to know?'

'So what's a ley-line?' Yvonne asked Spencer, subtly turning her perfect posture away from me with compressed lips and returning to the conversation that had been going on before as though I'd never sat down.

'Ley-lines were lines of vertical stones embedded in the ground connecting one circle of stones to another across a grid that covered whole areas of Brittany and the British Isles. In modern times it's been discovered that many of the circles of stone were built over underground aquifers and that the ley lines connecting the different stone circles were placed over subterranean water streams. Water conducts electricity. The rocks themselves have quartz in them which also conducts electricity, so that the rocks above ground mirror watery, underground electrical grids. These are perhaps natural electrical bio/grids formed as the Earth's crust cooled. They may have something to do with maintaining a biodynamic electrical charge between the electricity in the earth and the magnetic aura of the biosphere connecting the earth to the sun.'

'Auras huh?' I said bitterly, sensing that any minute we'd be into Pleidians. Lena snickered catching my drift. Spencer ignored me. Yvonne re-adjusted her attitude with a little downward smile like I had the brains of Scooby Doo and needed that little extra bit of compassion.

'The Druids performed ceremonies at the main stone circle sites at the exact hour of the equinoxes and cross-quarter days by reading solar calendars that told them the exact moment when there was a perfect balance of electromagnetic energy that could be somehow manipulated. This is what is supposed to have made a hole, or passage between the dimensions. Kind of gives a different sense to the word 'holy' doesn't it?' This was too much, my Richter scale went off.

'Oh my God, I've stumbled into a voodoo cult in progress haven't I?' I was remembering how Spencer and Yvonne loved to get into these vague, mystical ponderings that led to impossible concepts that were conveniently un-disprovable. I was just putting up some pre-emptive defenses in case it got too far out while I was still in the room.

'What's a 'cross-quarter' day?' Lena asked.

'It's the halfway point between an equinox and a solstice - actually - like Halloween is the halfway point between the Autumn Equinox and Winter Solstice. Hey! This is a holy night! It could happen right now!' Spencer giggled gleefully. Lena and I zapped him with death rays.

'Each date marks a forty five degree advance of the earth around the sun,' Spencer went on undisturbed. 'It's mathematical. Sacred Geometry. The original religion of Europe, Joseph, was a shamanic based interaction with nature that had never been interrupted by the theoretical abstractions of the Human mind. Pagan shamanism is only a set of words for the unbroken tradition of consciousness that goes back to single celled organisms.' When Spencer called me Joseph I knew he was pulling rank. He is nearly twice as old as me and three or four times more educated. Yvonne, a meticulously polite person, glared silently at me for having interrupted the great professor.

To achieve just the right proportions of haughtiness and dignity in her glare, Yvonne dipped her chin and arched her spine a couple of degrees which made her eyes tilt up and her boobs stick out so that I felt compelled to look at her with more attention, the result of which was a deeper burn from her sage green eyes. She was killing me. I jerked my head back at Spencer.

'Early humans existed halfway between the intuitive animal and the evolving rational human mind.' Spencer lectured on as I snuck glances at Yvonne. 'Whatever their experience of the world of the living - and of the dead for that matter - was practiced and refined for hundreds of thousands of years. This was the Garden of Eden where people were as innocent as plants. This was the folk culture of Europe and the Western World - that Christianity took over. For a million years these early Humans were experiencing the mysteries of creation without mental interpretations. Their interaction with the dead, with angels and demons is beyond our knowledge since history got rewritten by the Church and the monarchies.

'Just as the planets materialized out of the molten solar mass, biology materialized along the lines of the Earth's - and the sun's magnetic lines. The magnetic aura Joseph,' he said, rubbing it in. 'Organic life is the result of the shielding of the cell from harmful solar and cosmic radiations by duplicating this magnetic encapsulation. The planet is a microcosm of the Sun, as cells are a microcosm of the Earth. Just as the Earth separated from the Sun, actual dimensions of time/space could have separated from one another as dimensions individuated.' Lena and I nodded at each other. So there ya go.

I tried to look interested because it was growing on me just how sweet Yvonne looked. I really wanted to engage this new Yvonne in some meaningful conversation so I tried to bring the cosmic jibber jabber in for a landing.

'Are you saying that before Humans evolved and the Earth achieved this particular atmosphere that there could have been a... dimensional ecology?' I thought that sounded pretty spiffy and looked around the table for concurrence.

A corner of Spencer's lip tilted up. He knew that my sudden interest wasn't for any pre Human dimensional Genesis. Narrowing his eyes, Spencer shoved his reading glasses up off his nose and buried his face in the long book. Lena, who knows me well and, seeing how fetching Yvonne looked, was smirking with veiled eyes. Spencer looked up at the ceiling.

'In the eighties Joseph,' Spencer took a deep patronizing breath - a breath he was going to regret when I had him back on the job tomorrow morning; 'There was an interview in Omni magazine with the Army Major in charge of closing the Air Force Blue Book project. The Blue Book project was a collection by the Air Force, of all known reports about UFO's from 1945 to 1967.

'They had tens of thousands of reports collected over forty years of research from which they culled any information that was unreliable. They favored reports from military personnel, cops, professionals and airline pilots. After they'd got rid of all reports that raised any doubts - they still had thousands of reports and decided that these reports had to be accepted as having potential military importance.

'So - this Major getting interviewed goes on to say that they had to accept that something was being seen and by reliable witnesses. Now - since there's been radar all over the planet since 1945 that could track a basketball coming in from outer space to within a hundred feet of where it landed - it stood to reason that whatever was being seen was not coming in from outer space since it wasn't showing up on radar. So they hypothesized that; A. reliable witnesses were seeing something real and B. it wasn't coming in from outside the planet. So the conclusion they came to was that there must be a parallel dimension and that the things being seen were coming from - right here!' A kind of long silence happened. I felt goose bumps crawl up my arms.

'Woho!' I said.

'My God,' Yvonne's eyes became saucer-like as a little girl's as she looked around excitedly. "So it could be Fairy People in the UFO's?' She tilted her head to the side, clasped her arms around her middle so that her layered hair, red as a red setter running through autumn leaves, swayed, brushing her cheek delicately as the peach angora hollows of her shoulders became accentuated in the candle light. I tried to get a grip on this conversation and drank more wine.

'What Evans-Wentz is saying in the book is that in pre-Christian times the Fairy people - or fiery people - were a dimensional as well as a biological extension of Homo Sapiens, and humans were meeting them - in the flesh - out on those planted fields in Brittany and the British Isles. And they weren't just exchanging recipes - they were getting it on! And this isn't totally supposition. The circles of stones are there to this day. A lot of work and thought went into making those circles. It isn't like the people of those times had nothing else to do. There had to be a payoff!'

Yvonne's posture made the spherericity of her breasts express themselves laterally and I became determined to get more New Age right away. I tried to make my eyes vacant and dreamy like the Pleidian Goldilocks. I let my head sway at the wonder of it all.

'Didn't the Irish believe that Fairies kidnapped children and mutilated cattle?' Lena said dryly.

'Well, yeah,' Spencer said irritated at being pulled back from dreamland. 'There were good ones and bad ones! Sometimes when people were murdered or just disappeared it was said that 'the Fairies took 'em'. And folk beliefs don't just spring up under cabbages you know.' Spencer laughed at his own joke.

'So when the door between the worlds was opened, both good ones and evil ones could come through?' Yvonne asked, alarmed, sitting up even straighter.

'Why not?!' Spencer said.

'But why just Europe?' Lena asked. 'Wouldn't a parallel world include the whole planet?'

'Well, every culture has folk stories about Jinns and goblins and ghosts.' Spencer said leafing through the book which I noticed didn't have any helpful photos. 'American Native folk tales are full of Star Maidens and Katchinas.'

'Imagine that - evil green eyed Fairy thugs wandering around Europe on unicorns way-laying people,' I said in a floaty, breathy voice. 'Maybe they could come through on Winter Solstice and stick around 'til the doors opened again in spring! Wow, three months of murdering and kidnapping!' Somehow I wasn't doing it right.

Yvonne ignored me, looking exalted. She just believes everything that comes down the pike. If it's written in a book it's already true for her. Yvonne has a personal belief system that includes astrology, yoga, geomancy, fung shoe, angelic guidance, past life alliances, Mayan calendars, spirit animals - you name it and it's part of her system and if she's never heard of it she just pries two beliefs apart and sticks the new one in between. For her there is this universal networking army of angelic beings trying to help people evolve into happy smurfs. On the other hand she has an uncanny ability to ignore the self-evident and when challenged becomes passive aggressive and manipulative to the extent that we often became alienated because I wouldn't float around with her in unicorn heaven. To her, my pragmatism was a failure of faith. For me, her etheric glee was a barrier to human intimacy.

For her, the happy ending began with being happy regardless of realities. For me, there is the paper-bosses who keep the working poor so tightly enslaved to making their daily bread by adjusting the interest rate against them that they can't afford to know what's going on because they have no time or energy left to do anything about it! Meanwhile, the rich rape the ecosystems and generate wars for cheap resources and new consumer markets on which to unload disposable plastic crap.

Spencer and I agreed on the hard realities of the sinister intelligence scams of the corporations though he also believes the aurora borealis, for instance, is a bridge for angelic beings to return to earth in winter - when the Hopi Katchinas come back from the stars. In the South West you hear a lot about this. Lena, more reasonably, believes that most people are in the elementary stages of spiritual evolution and there is a long, long road ahead so that the most important thing to focus on is health. 'You can't have a revolution if people can't man the barricades,' she liked to say.

We four had played all these ends against the middle without getting anywhere so many times that we'd learned just when to cool it. Usually Lena and I teamed up to gasp in disbelief at Yvonne and Spencer's willingness to just leave orbit. Our silences spoke volumes to one another. I had to remember, looking at the curve of Yvonne's graceful spine that I hadn't been invited and she, the Fairy Princess had. So they unraveled the universe while I kept my mouth shut by pouring wine down my throat. Her inaccessible loveliness just made the ache of loneliness in me worse. And no one was talking about the unbelievable re-election.

'Well if Fairy thugs could come through - Human thugs could go through too!' Lena said later when Halloween being a pagan holy night came up again.

'Why are you all so obsessed with the thugs?!' Spencer said. 'What about just regular farmers who would be dancing around the Maypole giving the eye to a Fairy girl whose prancing around in her new spring dress. Imagine these lovers from across a dimensional warp walking in the woods, colored ribbons floating from her hair as they lay down in the flowering clover. They only have a couple hours before the dimensions close ... time is short ... the bees are buzzing in the flowers...' Spencer laughed. What an image!

'Boy that sounds like something worth getting dressed up for!' I said, meaning the opposite. Yvonne snorted. Probably at the idea of me getting dressed up.

'In physics,' Spencer said clearing his throat dramatically, irritated at my sarcasm - 'for every atom of physical matter there has to be an atom of anti-matter. It's an electromagnetic balance in the energy context of the universe. Without the one there can't be the other. So - maybe these beings are anti-matter people. I mean, it's kind of naive of science to make all these observations about time warps, worm holes, energy morphing and synchronicity and still hang on to the idea that there is only this one dimension where people struggle to eat and stay warm and then just die like dogs.' Lena waved us all off and cleared the dishes off the table.

'O.K. picture this,' I said. Spencer's description of the Fairy maiden, her cleavage beribboned in the colors of the rainbow bouncing along as the shadows of the sun dappled forest played across her flower patterned dress bright in my mind.

'What if this Fairy maiden was running through the dimensional hole just as the time warp ended and her foot was still sticking through! Would her leg be in one dimension and the rest of her in another?' I asked innocently. Lena laughed. I was brought up Catholic and we used to have so much fun with this kind of stuff.

But these guys were too serious. Yvonne and Spencer just ignored me and leafed through the book with creased foreheads. Lena finished collecting the empty plates, giving me with her sad Madonna's smile and dished up frozen apricot slices from the trees on their land. Yvonne surprisingly refilled my wine glass. We smirked at each other.

'You're a bright kid Joe, I don't know why it's so hard for you to stretch your imagination to include what's outside the box.' Spencer said finally.

'Joe's left brain needs to learn how to dance!' Yvonne primly stage whispered to Spencer. These clichés!

'Yvonne's right brain needs to learn how to walk!' I stage whispered to Lena. Yvonne went 'sssss' with quiet intensity and wobbled her head sarcastically at me.

'Ach!' Lena said in warning.

I realized nothing tangible was going to come of this patched up good will between the lovely new Yvonne and me and, realizing I was getting pretty drunk and to show my contempt for their sloppy thinking, I got up to go.

'Well, I'll leave you phairies to your phantasies as my pumpkin awaiteth me and I must goeth,' I said, tossing an imaginary cape over my shoulder with a flair as I grabbed my jacket. Goeth got kinda slurred into goth.

'Happy trails pumpkin!' Lena said with a big grin.

'I'll see you at the job Joseph,' Spencer said soberly looking up momentarily and giving me the hairy eyeball as he searched desperately for *proof*.

Yvonne didn't even look up as I left. She was asking Spencer something, her eyes quizzing and intent on his flipping through the pages of the Fairy Book but as my gaze brushed across her corner of the room, she slowly scootched forward in her chair so that her skirt slid up her thighs, her legs entwined like lovers writhing in bed.

With my eyes glued to Yvonne's thighs I stumbled against the leg of my chair and lurched for the door. I glanced at Lena who had seen Yvonne's maneuver and had raised an eyebrow above a pitying smile that seemed to say; 'You don't have a chance against us mortal.'

I went for the outside door at the end of the hall rather than walk all the way through the house so that I came out into Lena's kitchen garden. The sudden cold made me snap to attention.

With a waning moon above the mountains, the stars were brilliant in the frosty night. I felt the cold freeze-dry my nipples and zipped up and shoved my hands deep in my pockets. A breeze rustling the stalks of corn in the fenced garden caught my attention and I looked to see the scarecrow Lena had made out of straw stuffed into a thrift store tuxedo complete with tails and a squashed top hat. She'd cut out a cardboard fiddle and tucked it under its arm and made two cricket antennae out of coat hangers with bobbing cotton ball ends that stuck up out of its head. The fiddler-cricket stood shivering beneath the huge boulder that sticks out of the hill. The moon was rising above the boulder and a hump of quartz crystals towards the top of the boulder sparkled in its light. Subtle lines of crystal light radiated from the quartz and for just a moment the entire boulder seemed to become transparent. I saw little Hansel and Gretel cottages making up a little village with warm, orange, glowing lights on in their windows. I blinked and the mirage was gone. My gaze shifted to the rows of straw piles covering carrots and turnips in the garden that hadn't been harvested.

I walked inside the open gate and stood drunkenly next to the scarecrow. We looked up at the stars flickering away in Morse code. The stardust of the Milky Way trailing off to nearby galaxies. I felt just as lonely and angst ridden as I had when driving down the highway at sunset. The image of the beribboned medieval girl laughing and prancing through the sunny forest vivid in my mind. The crackling cosmic electricity in the horse-trough of brilliant stars up in the sky looked so thrilling, virgin and vast. I put my arm across the scarecrow's skinny shoulders, looked up at the lonesome slice of moon above the boulder and made a drunken, deeply heartfelt wish - that I could stand gazing at all this with someone who knew what it was worth. It was the next morning that I fell off the ladder.

Chapter Two

'But that's not my point Joey. It's not about you and becoming famous. My point is that what has happened is rare in the extreme and keeping a diary about it could help you keep track of what's happening!'

Yvonne was sitting across from me at my kitchen table, her green eyes flashing, silky red hair swaying as she rocked side to side while strangling her mug of tea with evangelistic fire now that we were into the mystical mysteries that were her home ground. It was a week after the dinner at Spencer's. Bush had been re-elected and a dead numbness hung in the air.

She was wearing jeans and coincidentally the short sleeved, peach angora sweater that had tortured me at Spencer's. The fuzziness of it made my hands itch to pet it like a kitten. When she'd called to say she was coming over, I'd put on a green plaid flannel shirt over a dark red T-shirt so that I wouldn't incite her wrath over my WalMart dress style. Too late I noticed that I matched my tablecloth.

'Isn't a diary what girl scouts keep about their ponies Yvonne?' I grinned sarcastically. Yvonne had heard what had happened to me after the fall off the ladder and she'd come over with a video - 'The Commitments' - and a six pack of my favorite beer to interrogate me. The movie was about a bunch of Irish kids that start a soul band. It was great. While the video played she'd actually cooked us dinner - garlic breaded tofu in cabbage diapers - yum! ...and generally demonstrated real warmth and concern. I soaked it up.

She'd heard it through the grapevine - meaning Lena - the experiences I'd been telling Spencer and she'd come over to see how I was handling it.

But the idea of a 36 year old guy keeping a diary of his dreams made me feel ridiculous. That was for her New Age pals with their pie in the sky eyes and tarot cards that made confusion romantic. I'd resisted all that hocus pocus this far and wasn't about to cave in now.

'Diary, record, journal, whatever. God, the way you react to words is like you're straight out of the Fifties.' She strangled her cup some more.

'Yeah - when men were men!' I said this knowing it would be a stinger to her. Half our arguments had always taken place around gender fencing. But also half our fun. She snorted.

'My point Joey, is that people need to know such things are *possible!*' her voice was like velvet with a daycare kind of tolerance, trying to make her point to the problem child. I sniggered. One of my main problems with Yvonne is that she always has to make points. Though, on the other hand, when I put it that way, Yvonne has a couple of really nice points.

'Write it down while it's still fresh in your mind!' She was getting exasperated and looked out the window into the back yard where the setting sun was peeking through a line of purple clouds on the horizon making my cholla cactuses cast long violet shadows across the yard. In the distance, the Black Mesa badlands skyline towards Los Alamos looked violet and powdery through a purple cloudburst. My dog Neutron was staring in the bay window at us, tilting his head side to side as though he wanted the volume turned up.

A couple of pallets of adobe bricks that would eventually be a wall around my cactus garden was developing dark brown spots as the rain hit it. A pile of blood red flagstone that was piece by piece becoming the patio floor was growing maroon polka dots. I'd read a book when I was a kid called My Secret Garden and had always wanted one.

It had got chilly. The cold has a stupefying effect on us here in the Southwest after endless months of cloudless sunshine and radioactive heat. We become like lizards in air conditioning, slow and dopey. I had the oven on with the door open because Yvonne looked chilled in the short-sleeved sweater. With the cold rain spattering the windows her peachy presence warmed the whole house.

'I just don't have time Yvonne,' I whined. 'When I get home from working for that yuppie bitch I feel like my jumper cables are fused. You know what she said yesterday?' Yvonne groaned into her cup of tea. 'That I owed her for that three days it rained last week when I couldn't work! Does she realize that if I'd had the concrete truck go across her front yard while it was all muddy there'd be tire tracks a foot deep that would have stayed there for five years? Nooo.' Yvonne was practicing yoga breathing.

'She said to me – 'a professional would have found some other aspect of the project to work on!' She said those very words! Like I was a high school kid. Does she know anything about building?' Just thinking of the tall, skinny divorce lawyer and her pinched, snippy voice still rattles me.

'You're not writing the script to the Titanic deary.' Yvonne completely ignored what I'd just said and stayed on her mission. 'Just take a half hour here and there to put down the facts as you would tell them to me.' She made her voice low and breathy to imitate me; 'I went out of my body again last night. I woke up standing in the dark. The clock said two fifteen. I went to the fridge. Got a beer.'

I noticed that when she imitated me she used the same voice she gave to Neutron planning his day; 'First I'll pee on the latilla fence on the corner. Then I'll scare the shit out of the cat. Then I'll go over and eat the Corgi's breakfast...' I laughed. Once. The lawyer was stuck in my throat.

'Yesterday she said I should pay for the speakers and wiring I added because now they're part of the wall and should come within the original bid for a wall! Can you believe that!? All of it was extra, none of it was in the original bid and she knew this when she agreed to have me add it on! I swear they teach these people to screw you. That's what college tuition buys these days. They think spontaneity and human warmth are vulnerabilities - red flags telling them where there's blood to suck!' Yvonne was rolling her eyes, hugging herself and rocking side to side in melodramatic anguish.

'Here he goes,' she said rolling her eyes to heaven. This was like old times.

'Well this lawyer is only following the lead of the corporate elites and the politicians isn't she?' I asked Yvonne. 'Look at America - we use fifty percent of the world's resources and only make up six per cent of its population. Don't you think the other 96 per cent of Homo Sapiens has an opinion about this? They know their tungsten or bananas or oil is being hijacked to America through some puppet government that lives in an energy sucking mansion surrounded by CIA trained commandos - Venezuelan mothers see Pamela Anderson on satellite jumping out of a sports car and running down a beach laughing with her well fed tits bouncing as a weight lifter chases her into the sand dunes while that mother doesn't have food or medicine for her children. Don't you think those children are going to grow up with an attitude of revenge?'

'My god how you exaggerate things to protect your opinions!' Yvonne said. 'If 94 per cent of Humanity felt American politicians were unjust they would report it to the United Nations who would let the American people know and we would do something about it!'

'Yvonne, your awareness of political reality is the same as how bourgeois Nazi's felt while Hitler was killing off his rivals. Good people can never believe there is real evil in their midst because evil lies with such conviction!' Yvonne pouted and rolled her lovely eyes some more. 'The same corporations that place puppet governments in places like Guatemala to control their bananas and Uganda to control their rubber own the radio and television stations that broadcast news to us. We know what the corporations want us to know and no more. Do you know why there are ten thousand millionaires in America?

'Past life karma?' She looked a little doubtful saying this.

'They have it because the poor, landless, uneducated underfed masses don't have it!' I said glumly.

'You have an absurd sense of the dark side of life Joe! And it's the result of your not dealing with your own dark side. You choose to identify with poverty, limitation and lovelessness and so you manifest bitterness and dissatisfaction in your life. If you would just let your right brain talk to your left brain once in a while you could start some internal relations!'

'Yvonne - your version of life is so buried under sparkling saccharine sprinkles that you can't see murder happening under your own nose. If the corporate elite can manipulate half the countries of the world to steal their resources don't you think they're gonna use economic pressure on the working classes of America to keep us in our place?! The corporations have hijacked America! They don't care about democracy! They just want power!' Yvonne put her palms together and looked up to heaven for help but that didn't stop me. 'America has become a country of the elite, for the elite and by the elite. Working people - people who labor - carpenters, nurses, farmers - the same people who snatched America out of the teeth of predator kings - are today looked on as inferior peasants rather than as the backbone of their own country! How is it that one or two arms manufacturers and a handful of oil and pharmaceutical companies are more important than a two hundred and eighty million workers?' Yvonne blew out all her air.

'Deary, you've got to lift your mind above these things. Money is just energy. People get what they need to fulfill their karma. You create wealth in your mind.' Yvonne had her angel look on - infinite understanding and compassion as she delicately arched her spine.

'So this yuppie bitch deserves a house that covers three quarters of an acre and vacations in Nepal and Bali because she's so spiritually advanced?' I asked reasonably.

'Maybe.'

'Maybe!? I can just hear her talking with her friends! "You look kind of unhappy Harold. Maybe you need a divorce. Why don't you call me at the office?"

'I don't know how it is that you always attract these women that want to test you!' Yvonne has an electric femininity. Magnetic waves of it were pulsing out like radar and activating my sonar systems. She was framed inside my fading, dusty, black and white poster of Emilio Zapata on the wall behind her. I could see the ruby reflection of her hair in the glass when she tossed her head so that her hair bounced when she emphasized her points.

'I didn't attract her!' I said, exasperated. It was like two people talking on cell phones to other people who weren't present. 'I gave her the best of four bids plus she knew someone I'd built a car port for.' I sneered at her.

'Well, you still attracted her! You were brought together for a reason!' My God she sounded just like a prissy schoolmarm from 'Little House On The Prairie' saying 'do unto others as you would have them do unto you.' This party line liberalism is its own kind of fascism. Why was such a fine woman wasted on this oatmeal mush mentality?

'Oh my God. Now here she goes.' A smile escaped me as I said it. I really liked having her in my kitchen.

'Of all the people I know who should suddenly start astral traveling, it would be a beer swilling construction worker who still builds model airplanes!' She put her hands behind her head and arched her spine so that her breasts pointed at my third eye.

'Oh my back!' she moaned.

'I think you mean a landscape contractor - not a construction laborer - bit of a diff there sweetie. And your spiritual pals with perms also live in houses you know.' I said. 'Someone has to build them.'

'He had naturally curly hair and we only knew each other for a week and that was an eon ago so why don't you drop that one or do you want to discuss Es-tey-fana the topless dancer from Rio?'

'She wasn't a topless dancer!'

'She was when I saw her!'

'Well you had your new squeeze so I got one too. So ...' I ran out of arguments.

'Well, we weren't married.' She said the word with an Old English aristocratic accent. Mahrried.

'Married!?' I choked out the word. Why had we split up? Why we had got together in the first place? It was all a confusing mess of contradictions to me now. But having Yvonne sitting across from me at the kitchen table, her lovable smile, the warm peach colors of her with the cold gray wet sky outside, steam rising from the tea kettle on the stove, the homey warmth of the oven drifting over us was stirring loving memories.

'Baby let's not go there O.K.?' she said. 'I think something serious is happening to you,' she said, petting the checkered table cloth.

'You mean like insanity?'

'In this book...' she said, tapping the book she'd brought over that sat in the middle of the table. '...after he starts having OBE's, Monroe gets scared that he's going insane and goes to a psychiatrist.' I looked at the book; 'Journey's Out of the Body' by Robert Monroe.

'Hmm,' I grunted. This thought had sort of crossed my mind. I was putting up a good show of unconcern about it to Spencer and Lena and now to Yvonne; but ever since smacking my head on the flagstones I'd been floating out of my body and flying around seeing things and having intense dreams. Lena gave me her nurse's opinion that it was a mild concussion and that I should stay home and watch videos for a week. But I couldn't abandon the job when we were so near completion. But I was afraid I could float out of my body while say using a table saw. Or what if it happened when I met a hot babe?

'You know - if you're going crazy, keeping a record of the events could help someone figure you out if you suddenly became catatonic. It could be cheaper than say, a full frontal lobotomy.' Yvonne embraced herself as she leaned her elbows on the table and gave me her practical look. 'Have you any idea what lobotomies run these days?' she asked in her no nonsense voice as she bounced against the table. She sat back and ran a finger along the green plaid tablecloth caressingly. Her beautiful hands and gentle, feminine motions reminded me for a moment of how much tenderness we had shared.

'Can you still get a driver's license after you get a lobotomy?' I asked, swallowing involuntarily. I couldn't quite meet her eyes. She knew me too well.

'Oh sure. The way people drive?' She got up, walked around the table, came up next to my chair, shoved the table back with meat of her butt and sat on my lap. She knew me all right.

'Is it cheaper to get a partial lobotomy?' I asked, wrapping my arm around her hip and kissing her protruding lower lip.

'Sweetie you already have a partial lobotomy, you're a male!' She laughed and kissed me back going for the full honest territory in the middle. I used what was left of my partially lobotomized brain trying to pull her sweater up out of her jeans as she tucked her elbows in to make it more difficult.

'Just try and write some of it down while it's still fresh in that pretty little head of yours will ya? Huh?'

I tugged. She pouted. And arched her spine so that she was taking it away and pushing it forward at the same time as she let me kiss her.

'You little witch!' I said sort of fake snarly - still tugging.

'Is that a yes?' She made her eyes wide like Little Red Riding Hood.

'Yes,' I said like a zombie in a trance looking into those beautiful, familiar cat eyes and feeling the warm, dense weight of her on me. She raised her arms high over her head, wiggling all her fingers and gave me her biggest smile.

Chapter Three

You really are a witch to make me do this Yvonne. I woke up before you yesterday and watched you sleeping - you looked like a porcelain doll.

O.K. A deal's a deal - here goes. And remember you promised! No spelling corrections!

11/04/04   7:26 A.M.

Oh my god! My right brain is wiggling! It tickles! It's doing the hootchie coochie or something - I remember that the 1st of November, All Saints Day, was a Monday. I was in a rush to get to the job for the bucktoothed, cross-eyed, anal retentive, obsessive compulsive, homophobic yuppie lawyer where my crew of three noble working class heroes were waiting for me.

Before going to the site I had to pick up Spence because Lena had their truck so I was in a hurry. We were in the last stages of putting the frame down on a footer for the stucco wall around the palace of the sainted lawyer while Emillion and his crew were about to begin slathering on stucco. I'd driven halfway down the block from my house when I realized I'd need my 100 foot extension cord and went back to get it.

As I pulled into my driveway, I saw Neutron chasing my neighbor's cat, Precious across the front yard. The cat jumped up into the tree in the front of my house and climbed out on a branch and dropped onto my roof. Then I knew I would have to haul out the ladder and get Precious down or my next door neighbor, the fierce old Senora Lucia, would get hotted up, call the dog police and then I'd have to tie Neutron up for a week until things cooled down and I hate doing that because you know how he can lie there, at the end of his chain, with his head in his paws groaning and sighing. Senora Lucia, who is just five feet tall, once got in an argument with the manager of the WalMart about the return of some item. He kept pointing at her with his index finger and she kept telling him not to point at her until she grabbed his finger and dislocated it! She's no one to mess with.

So I climbed up on the roof, grabbed Precious and was getting back on the ladder to go down when the cat squirmed in my grip, slashed my face and jumped into the tree. I reached for it but lost my balance. The ladder skidded off to the right and then wham! I hit my head on the flag walk and floated up in the air over the house.

I could see my body lying there on the ground, and I could see the cat was running back to Lucia's house with Neutron happily chasing it right in front of Lucia's big bay window.

I felt totally normal. It was like looking through barbecue fumes but otherwise it was real. I was up over the roof and looking down I could see this patch I'd put on the roof last month and I glided over to check on it. It was well done. So then I remembered I was in a hurry to get to work and floated down towards my body. I don't know what I was planning to do - knock on my forehead and say 'can I come in?' But all of a sudden I was sitting up and feeling really weird. I looked around in a daze and then threw up my breakfast burrito into my lap. I could see bits of green pepper and onions - I hadn't chewed the tortilla very well. You said to put details in it Yvonne!

I felt a lump growing on my head and saw a little blood on my hand. I was feeling nauseous. I called Neutron and went indoors. I put on sweat pants and lay down on the couch. Later I went to the job. And that's how it started Yvonne. And Yvonne I was going to ask you - does an angora sweater, you know, tickle?

11/06/04

O.K. So that night, Monday, I was lying in bed and thinking about sex and wondering what it was like Vonnie, when I started drifting to sleep and thought about the feeling I'd had when I'd been floating up over my body lying on the flagstones. I'd felt like I'd swooped up out of my actual body like a slow swarm of buzzing bees. As I concentrated on remembering that feeling, there was a kind of jerk, a pop and then I was floating up over my bed.

The lights were off in the house but I could see whatever I wanted to! When I focused on something, like the biplane on my bureau or the mirror on the wall, I could see them without turning around to do it. It was weird. I was particularly curious about my own body which I could see plainly there on the bed with its eyes closed and breathing. The body looked like a sick caricature of me. I looked like a Walt Disney pirate - lantern jaw, hollow cheekbones like an Old English peasant, cadaver-like straight hair and amazingly long toes sticking out from under the covers. It all looked animalistic, thick and corpse-like. Does that confirm anything for you Y?

It made me feel a little sick to think that that's what I look like. It wasn't the features - the long noble Polish nose, deep set uncannily perceptive hazel eyes, the rich, dark complexion, the high intelligent brow and handsomely squared chin; it wasn't the rich, floppy brown hair, the whipcord physique, the long silhouette of my crotch under the sheet - that's not what I noticed Vonnie. It was the density of the skin and the sense of this dark animal breathing there in my bed. It was like seeing my face on the body of an orangutan. Really gross.

I looked around my room - at the two maple bureaus in the corner. The Spitfire hanging from the ceiling, the aquarium on the bureau with its green nightlight glowing in the water, the corals and the sleeping fish. I looked out the windows at the back yard. There was moonlight on the rock garden. I felt an itch on my leg and scratched it. This woke me up and I found myself scratching my leg.

11/07/04

I felt perfectly normal the next morning and went to work. Sometime during the morning I was loading up wood scraps when I felt really dizzy and sat down on the ground. I closed my eyes and floated up over the lawyer's house and saw the whole property and the neighborhood houses. Then I blinked and was back inside my own body again. After a while a felt O.K. and went back to work.

We had the radio on and heard Bush making a speech in that dark, menacing voice of his as though we are all his enemies.

That night, curious as hell if I could consciously have an OBE again, I concentrated on the buzzing bees feeling and swooped up and out of my body. I tried to see where I was but everything was hazy and vague and I wondered if I was just sleeping. But then my sight became clear and I discovered I was standing in Lena's garden under the big boulder with the hump of quartz on it. As I stood there I felt an intense shock, like an electrical shock. Everything became intensely focused for a second - the garden, the big boulder, the stars in the sky and then I woke up in bed.

That night I dreamed thousands of pterodactyl birds were flying in black waves over the land coming from the west. I awoke with this sick feeling of intense danger.

11/08/04

The next night, as I was drifting into sleep I thought about doing it, (I mean having an OBE! Really Yvonne - control your mind!) The buzzing bees started up. There was the swooping feeling and a pop or two and then I was standing next to my bed. I could feel the texture of the rag rug under my feet. I walked into the kitchen and then went to the living room. I looked out the living room window at the street lights shining on the parked cars. I walked through the house.

A funny thing happened when I tried to open the back door. I wanted to go out to the back yard to see if Neutron could see me. When I tried to grab the doorknob my hand went right through the door! So I just walked through the door like it was a hologram. It's like I'm in a dream but I know I'm dreaming - oh a dream door! and I just move on through the dream. Neutron was lying there half out of his little doghouse. I petted him but he couldn't see me or hear me or anything.

A glass I'd left by the pallet of adobe bricks reflected the thin moonlight. I couldn't tell at first just what was magnifying the light and was curious. Before I'd even decided I wanted to go over there, I was right next to a half glass of water I'd left out a couple of evenings ago.

I looked at the sparkle of light and sort of automatically looked up at the moon which was causing it - as I did this I started flying or floating fast up into the sky - I looked back at the house getting smaller and smaller and felt a wave of fear - because I thought I was about to shoot off into space. There was a jolt and the next thing I knew I was opening my eyes in bed. The sudden shift was strange. One minute I was accelerating through the night sky and the next I was sitting up in bed. There was a kind of hiss I could hear or feel - or maybe it was just the intensity of the sudden, total silence.

11/09/10

I was heading for the moon, flying naked through the air - Yvonne you should 'a been there! - I guess I was naked because my body in bed had the sweat pants on. It was a fascinating feeling. The entire Western Hemisphere looking up and seeing my skinny white ass flying to the moon!

While I was working that day I'd remembered flying towards the moon the night before and wondered if I could actually get there. So that night as I was going to sleep - when I got to the right point of relaxation and awareness - it's a kind of fuel/air mixture - when the proportions are right, I start to feel the buzzing bees and I can just swoop up and out. So I did that and walked through the bedroom wall into the backyard. I looked up at the moon and whoosh I was on my way. And then there I was - standing on the moon looking at the earth and it looked just like the pictures except for the barbecue fumes that are like optical distortions. I walked around a bit - it was like walking on baby powder but there are dark rich colors instead of just grey. I seemed to be wearing an opaque kind of robe. I looked for footprints and space junk but I didn't see any.

When there was nothing more I wanted to do I looked at the earth down there and picked a spot that was in the sunshine and sort of aimed myself at it like a slingshot. I think I'd picked India. I pushed off and landed on a hillside overlooking rice paddies or lagoons - and it was daytime, the sun was shining. It was like a hazy dream. Then I felt I was about to sneeze - ah, ah - and then on the choo I woke up in bed sneezing.

11/13/04

O.K. The next time was on Thursday the 11th. But I also went out again last night but I'll put them down in order. I buzzed, swooped up and out and then immediately was flying over Santa Fe. Below me was a blur of street lights and car lights. I was pulled to a car parked on a dark side street. There was a guy, a teenager, Hispanic, standing next to the car. Inside the car was another guy who had been shot and was dead. The guy outside the car wanted to get into the car but he couldn't and he was confused and scared. I realized this guy trying to get in the car was the spirit of the guy who was dead in the car. He was kind of stuck - he didn't know what to do next and he couldn't go back into his body.

He saw me and said; 'Yo dawg, help me get this door open my hands be slipping.' He was near panic and trying to act cool. He couldn't get a hold of the handle. I was paralyzed for a moment realizing this guy could see me and that I could hear him - that he could talk when he was like that - a spirit next to his own dead body. He became aware that our looking at each other was weird, different, and he got distracted from trying to get a hold of the door handle. Then we both started floating upwards and a feeling of mixed sadness and wonder was shared between us. At some point he vanished and I woke up in bed. The feeling of sharing his death was really strong and I stayed awake a long time thinking about him and where he'd gone.

11/17/04

Yesterday morning as I was loading up the truck to go to work, I saw this beautiful woman come out the front door of Lucia's house. She had shoulder length black hair and was muy *guapa* . She was Hispanic and had the classic kind of Indian/Spanish beauty you see in old National Geographic pictures of South America - full, high cheekbones, wide, luxurious mouth, the full figure and teased up oiled hair and though she was just wearing jeans and a white blouse and not some exotically colorful dress, I felt, when our eyes met, that I was looking into the eyes of the Indian soul. A little charge of attraction passed between us and then we both looked away. Almost immediately Yvonne, I swear. She took off in a huge old maroon Impala with skinny low rider wheels and I drove off in my truck.

That night, I got the fuel/air mixture right and felt the buzzing. I swooped up and out and saw that same woman from the morning standing at the foot of my bed.

I said; 'I saw you this morning'. She said 'Yes. You live next door to my aunt,' and before either of us could say another word we were kissing and holding each other and having sex. It was really beautiful, tender and sweet. I didn't try to make it happen or even think about her when I was going to sleep. When it was over I woke up in bed and thought about it. O.K? You said to tell the truth and put in the facts.

The next day, when I got back from work, I saw the Impala was gone and I went over and asked Lucia who she was. I wanted to tell that woman I'd dreamed some silly dream about her to see if she had also. The woman was in fact Lucia's niece who had been spending a few nights but had now gone back to her husband in Albuquerque. Lucia sort of stressed the husband part and I assured her that I got the picture.

11/22/04

I went out again last night. I was really tired and just went to sleep after watching a video. I woke up out of body. I flew into this strange house and the Hispanic woman was there waiting for me at the front door. She was dressed in a heavy, floor length gown - thick as a curtain. I couldn't see any part of her body. She had a dead pan serious face and said; 'I am with Ornefio'. And this clinched it; subject closed. She was not available. I just drifted away and found myself in my garage, feeling kind of rejected. I looked at the model airplanes hanging from the rafters for a while. Then I just woke up in the morning normally. I never noticed when I went back into my body.

11/23/043:12 A.M.

The dashboard glow on the instrument panel of the Spitfire was so real! The look of my gloved hands vibrating on the controls was so familiar. A drone like thunder rumbled on below me where clouds hid German bombers. Searchlights streaked through the fog and blimps and patches of London showed up in the searchlights. The melody of a popular song kept going through my head - 'Death where is thy sting-aling-aling'. Two hundred Hurricanes and Spitfires surrounded me as we headed west, descending through the fog over the English Channel onto an incoming formation of German bombers flanked by Messerschmitt 109 and 110 fighters headed into London.

There they were below me as I broke through the clouds. My machine gun was going all out. I'd strafed across the top of a bomber when a Messerschmitt came up on my right-rear. Rounds went into me like warm fingers under the skin and then I was floating up over the bombers as they went by. My plane fell away into the English Channel and I woke up ten minutes ago.

This was more than a dream. Every detail was graphically real. The instrument panel of my Spitfire was so clear. A crack in the Bakelite frame enclosing the altitude dial where I remembered banging my head on landing once - the picture of a dark haired girl in a nurse's uniform with a familiar sarcastically sweet look was so familiar. In the dream I remembered her name, Kelly - as I awoke I could still feel the cold steel of machine gun handles vibrating in my hands.

11/24/04 1:43A.M.

I was flying over the Cerrillos Avenue drag where I used to go looking for a date sometimes when I'd first moved to Santa Fe. I was bar hopping. Investigating. It was really eerie. Inside the bars people looked like corpses drinking green, bubbling poison. Their skin was thick and oily and these big, black amoebas or spiders were crawling on the walls and sitting on people's shoulders. I saw this woman in a short shiny dress backed up against a bar stool playing with the straw of her drink. A man stood in front of her talking. There was this elongated triangle - like a broken shard of glass - sticking out of her into the man and globules of crystal light were trickling out of him along the triangle of black glass and into the woman - the whole time she was giggling and he was laughing.

There was a dance floor and people were dancing all tangled up in cobwebs and shooting things into each other. It was very weird and it made me tired and depressed and I decided I wanted to go back to sleep.

Instantly I was in my bedroom. But when I tried to get back into my body, the spiders were floating around my body on the bed and they would grab me with their slimy tentacles and prevent my going forward. I couldn't get back in my body. I got really scared.

As I got more and more scared these things came closer, touching me with tentacles that burned cold. I became desperate at one point and made a dive up and over them and got back into my body and woke up. When I was awake I could still see them faintly, hovering around the bed in the dark. I got up and turned the lights on and walked around the house until they vanished.

11/26/04 9:12A.M.

The business with the spiders really got to me. I was too nervous to try and get out for a few days. But I had very curious dreams. In one dream I was standing in a transparent dome on the bottom of the sea. Outside the dome, on the ocean floor, there was tall grass waving in the current and two white angora buffalo grazing as their long hair drifted with the current.

In another dream I was piloting a UFO. The control panel took up the entire width of the ship behind the windshield, which curved and angled downwards. The ship was huge - as wide as the wings of a 747 and extremely powerful. I was flying along fairly close to the ground and fairly slow - I could see a wide river below. On either side of it were roads with the high speed traffic of a modern city. I could see telephone poles and wires and office buildings. The dream was very brief but so real that I lay thinking about it for a long time after I woke up. The density of the physical ship, the immense power in its engines was so real I felt sure I really had just been somewhere in another reality.

In another dream I was in a moving elevator, lying on an operating table and five or six people in white cloaks stood over me and aimed a kind of x-ray machine into different parts of my body. I wasn't scared and it felt really good. They were healing me somehow.

In another dream Yvonne was dressed in a peach bikini, snapping her bra straps and dancing at the foot of my bed saying 'Joe wake up. Joe please wake up!' Ha ha... Just kidding Vonnie!

11/28/04 7:23A.M.

I've finished reading the book Yvonne gave me. 'Journeys Out of the Body' by Robert Monroe. Incredible. He was having the same experiences as I am! And this was written in the fifties!

It's amazing. His experiences are so much like mine. I can't stop reading the book. Yvonne said there are two more books of his. I'm going to get them.

11/28/04   2:52A.M.

I can't sleep. I'm feeling depressed. Yvonne and I aren't going to get it back together. She's being nice to me because she's a 'good person' and being nice is what good people do. We're old friends and I'm a great lover. She told me so once. Maybe she said the same thing to Goldilocks.

I'm so sick of getting up and going off to build yet another roof, or wall, or car port. The world is such a mess. Politicians are just waiters for big business. Mussolini makes his diatribes from the White House and radio personalities discuss what he said because that's their job. There's so many poor people who work and work and get nowhere and live in dives. I'm one of the one's that hires them but I can't pay them any more than my competition. If the top cats gave up even ten percent of the interest on their billions, the whole of America would be uplifted. I wish I could do something that was actually useful for this world.

Chapter Four

Nov/29/04

Before going to sleep I re-read the part of Monroe's book where he describes going out of his body by turning around 180 degrees inside his physical body and going out the back of his head. This leads him to this place where there is a world much like ours and people who are very similar to Humans. This passage has stayed with me and I've been wondering if I could go there.

So when I got the buzzing feeling going, I turned around carefully inside my body and went forward cautiously. With a sudden rush I spurted out the top of the back of my neck and was suddenly shooting through dark space. After a bit I was gliding through the tall waves of a blue mist. It was like an ocean of dense dark blue vapor and the waves were incredibly tall and moving in very slow motion. There was a very soft and continuous thundering and hissing like the sound of the ocean in the distance. A dark, rich perfume filled the air like a garden of lavender at night. I felt an emotional tenderness so powerful that I'd forget I was on a mission - to duplicate what Monroe had done – to reach this place. I had to make the decision to investigate the blue waves at another time and with a great effort pushed on.

I came to an opening in the darkness like Monroe describes - it was an oval, rounded opening like a cave. Its rim was bordered with the same cobalt blue light as the waves that were still moving in a ghostly kind of majesty behind me and stretching away for what looked like forever. In an alphabet I had never seen but easily understood, curled letters that resembled the snaky curves of the waves spelled AOUVWHUAALLA around the rim of the entry in some ancient language that I seem to know. As I was reading these letters a magnetic force overwhelmed me and sucked me through and I was flying slowly over a huge city.

At first I just saw hundreds of winking lights as though through barbecue fumes. Then the shapes of tall office buildings came into focus below me. Some of the buildings were very modern and some were old fashioned buildings made of cut stone as I've seen in war pictures of Berlin and Paris.

Images of the city were vague at first but as my sight became more focused I saw people walking on the sidewalks and vehicles on the streets. UFO's were floating slowly and silently over the airspace of the city. When I experienced this at the time it didn't seem so extraordinary because when I'm 'out' everything is like a dream. But now I'm wondering – what was that?

I continued to glide over the city, pulled by some force or purpose I don't fully understand...I passed beyond the city and then drifted slowly over a dark rural countryside. I clearly saw the constellations of Orion and the Big Dipper. I automatically found the North Star and acknowledged that the stars must be the same as ours.

I was being pulled along by a sense of direction that I wasn't choosing but which I felt compelled to follow. I drifted down over the tops of tall, evergreen like trees towards some small, straw thatched cottages separated by hedges and trees. The countryside looked like England or Germany as they appear in the paintings in history books in the 1700 and 1800's before the industrial revolution except that everything seemed curved and elongated in an odd way. The shapes of the houses, the gardens, the farm fields all had these elongated curves to them. I guess I was looking with the eyes of a builder and these lines were illogical to me because there were so few right angles. Elaborate little fenced gardens were next to each house. Each garden was carefully organized into different sections. There were few leaves left on the trees and plants so that the season seemed to be about the same as New Mexico. The rich, tangy green smell of evergreens filled the air in a comforting and familiar way.

I noticed little, economy sized UFO disks of different colors, like large glistening M+M's parked in most of the driveways of the cottages. Between the houses were the oval farm fields. The broken stalks of corn registered in my mind as the source of a dry, warm dusty smell mixed with the evergreen smell.

With the shapes of the Blue Waves fresh in my mind, I saw a resemblance to them in the shapes of the farms and houses. And though it was night, I could see the essence of the colors - particularly the evergreen trees, which were a dusty, powdery, soft and glowing shade of dark green. This green glow of the trees gave me the strange sensual desire of wanting to eat them or kiss them. I wanted to lick the needles. It was as though they were food. There was a gentle, thrilling energy coming out of the trees.

I was pulled down towards one of the gardens and found myself standing on the ground. To my right I saw a boulder sticking out of the side of a hill that looked very familiar and I was drawn to it. Then I saw the clump of quartz crystals near its upper rim and realized it was just like the boulder in Lena's garden. The hump of quartz crystals sparkled in the brilliant moonlight. The now nearly full moon was floating above the top of the boulder - almost exactly as I'd seen in Lena's garden the night before I fell off the ladder!

This garden was more lush than Lena's and the plant stalks unfamiliar. The fence around the garden was in a different shape and made out of wood where Lena's is barbed wire but the slope of the land was just like Spencer and Lena's land!

As I looked longer, and became accustomed to the different sense of color and the elongated lines of the houses and breathed in the smells of the night, I realized there was a different radiation to life here. Matter was inherently, atomically different than Earth. It was like the inexplainable difference a male or female feels toward the other sex. And yet this difference felt strangely familiar. An intense wave of goose bumps traveled up my arms and neck at the alien familiarity I experienced. My heart began beating violently as though something tremendous was happening. My 'body' felt completely at home there but in my mind I was going through the mother of all deja vu's.

The leaves left on the trees had the same elongated curves as the blue waves. These were echoed by the shapes of the gardens and farm fields and on the cornices of the cottages and in the silhouettes of UFO's. There was no resistance to flow. There were so few right angles or the intersections of x's. This unresisted flow created a sense of moving energy. When next to a tree or a plant, some of its color came off into my breath. I was breathing colors. It was eerie but I also felt happily drunk.

There were no telephone poles or electric wires anywhere and the few streetlights cast lights of different colors - an orange one followed by a pink one then a bright green one etc. In the distance I could see the city lights twinkling.

Next to the garden there was a cottage with its lights on and I felt drawn to go into it but began to feel overwhelmed with the odd uniqueness of it all. My eyelids began to droop with sleep and I was pulled back to my body. I woke up in bed in the stillness and silence of my room. I heard the gurgling of the fish tank and saw its green glow. I felt a warm happiness inside and reviewed pictures of what I had just seen for a long time before I turned on the light and wrote it down.

Dec/2/04

As I went out the back of my head I felt a brief thrilling vibration. It was a silly feeling, like when I was a little kid in the back of a car going fast over a hill and felt like I was going to pee in my pants. The place where I 'went out of my head' was very specific - it was at the base of the skull at the top of the neck. I then passed through the huge blue waves of the gaseous liquid and again felt a deep heart centered tenderness and wanted to stay there but felt a sense of mission to be on time somewhere. I came to the oval opening and passed through.

Instinctively I seem to travel stretched out with my arms forwards - just like Superman. I flew like this through the night sky over the same countryside of oval fields and groves of trees and came to the thatched cottages and farm fields below me. The rich smell of evergreens surrounded me with a feeling for the power of the life in the land. I landed in the garden with the boulder with the crystal hump. In the distance I saw the lights of the city as before. I felt pulled in that direction. I became intensely curious about the look of the buildings and began to float towards them. Then I was flying low over the city. There were tall buildings of steel and glass. The newer buildings were mostly made of glass in fluid designs. Some were water green, others blue, dark gold, dark red. UFO craft were flying silently and slowly in single file air-lanes going in different directions and at different elevations over the city. Between the buildings there were gardens with miniature greenhouses and orchards planted in neat rows.

Between the buildings and passing through the gardens were grassy paths with stepping stones and people walking along on them. Of its own accord my body assumed a standing position and I joined the people walking.

When I was on the ground, I noticed window boxes attached to the buildings with flowers and herbs growing in them. These were lit softly from above. As a man walked by one of these boxes, he stopped, put his briefcase down and pulled some weeds out from between the flowers, then picked up his briefcase and walked on as though this was a perfectly normal thing to do. I noticed that he had oddly elongated, peaked ears but other than his having a long and narrow face, he looked human. This made me curious about the appearance of the people and I watched as another man walked by.

He also had the long narrow face and peaked ears. His features were sharp - a defined jaw, prominent brows, a strong down sloping nose. The rest of his body was unremarkable because it looked like any human's. His hair was remarkable in that it glowed with health. His whole being glowed with health. I mean he really glowed - some kind of actual light seemed to illuminate his features from within.

As I continued to walk along, the rich smells of the garden boxes on the sides of the buildings and along the walkways rose up to meet me. A woman and a man came around a corner laughing and talking in a rapid fire - like Puerto Rican but with a lot of vowels - it was a sing song way of talking as their voices went up and down in melodies and there were actual long notes. They had the sharply defined faces and chins, large eyes, peaked ears and the incredible glowing hair. I followed them and we came to a large brightly lit portal that led into an indoor shopping area and I entered behind them.

I should say, no one paid any attention to me. I was as invisible as the air. And while the sights and smells and physical presence of the people around me were real, it was also like watching a movie at a distance.

We had entered an indoor sort of farmer's market. There were booths and hundreds of people shopping and talking loudly. Everyone was dressed colorfully and with conviction. These felt like city people, proud, defined, energetic, busy.

I became fascinated with the clothing people wore. It was unique, colorful and stylish. Many had jackets with theatrically exaggerated lapels or flared sleeves and cuffs, elegant dress gowns with long sleeves and gloves - different shaped elf-like hats - knee high boots. I saw two serious young men who looked medieval. Their coats had cuffed sleeves and they wore pantaloons. Each also wore a short sword in a scabbard at their side. I noticed then that a number of men wore swords whether dressed stylishly or not.

Being surrounded by these people in a large group like that I felt the intense presence of a collective kind of mental intensity. Their minds felt intensely, even painfully aware. Their physical presence was unique as well. They were like dense holograms of flesh but not flesh like Human flesh. Their biological flesh seemed to be almost semi-transparent. The mental intensity and the peculiar energetic of their bodies seemed to go together somehow.

I became aware of an upward pull that 'we' were all feeling but also consciously resisting. The sky, the Universe, was pulling everyone's minds upwards like a magnet. Anti-gravity? It was some kind of social code to pretend this wasn't happening. Why?

The vegetables in the food stalls were of odd sizes and strange colors that I had never imagined existed. Red oblong beet like things, things that looked like huge, semi-transparent grapes, slabs of flat, juicy leaves that looked like a kind of fruit. There were all kinds of oddly shaped and textured leaves of many different colors - red, violet, green, yellow - that were displayed as food for sale. There were an unusual variety of shades of green. The color green in particular had an iridescent shine to it. There was also normal and abnormal looking poultry and fish on ice for sale. The food, like the people glowed with an inner light. The presence of the vegetables and food was very exciting to the people milling around the stalls. People were continuously pointing and exclaiming about the food.

The continuous sense of an upward pull began to fizz and wiggle like Alka-Seltzer in my brain and I looked up. As I did so I noticed that most people in the market were also looking up. A kind of astral fish or serpent with colored fins swooped down through the ceiling and then went back up leaving a trail of shimmering colors behind it. Everybody oohed and aahed and then nonchalantly went back to picking through the vegetables. They had all looked up at once, sensing the thing together. It hadn't made any sounds that I could hear, and yet we all looked up at the same time. What was that?

I heard a burst of girlish laughter and singing and turned to see three college age girls walking with their arms tightly linked together. They each wore pants but were bare breasted with their blouses and sweaters tied around their waists. They had gleeful, defiant expressions on their faces and were singing in the vowel filled language. I clairvoyantly understood the words of their song through the mental vibrations of everyone around me.

'We are Ovvalan women from Saala!
Our breasts give life to all!
It is not our fault you find them irresistible!
It's the milk of God within them that you love!'
Be happy you aren't dead yet!
And leave us to our own freedom!

A hush had come over the crowd as the girls sang and then wild and happy laughter burst out when they finished. A number of older women yelled out - 'Karoolia!' and momentarily lifted their blouses at the girls who laughed wildly and yelled 'Karoolia!' back in a chorus as they giggled and laughed and ran through the marketplace. The two serious young men took out their swords and slapped them noisily against their metal scabbards, smiling proudly at the running girls who smiled coyly back.

I mingled with the crowds leaving the market area and went out into the street where there were people sitting at tables and chairs eating and talking as waiters brought food. A block away silent, squat, wide buses stopped and people got on and off. As one of the buses, which were completely silent, turned a corner I could see the lighted insides. There were seats with a central isle. Each seat was capable of seating five or six people.

There were window boxes along the buildings bordering the outdoor restaurant and dwarf fruit trees growing out of ornamentally bordered areas in the sidewalks. The inner glow of vitality in the trees and the people moved like a light green mist between everyone carrying the smells of earth and plants. Was it only me who could see the colors drifting through the air because I was out of body? Far overhead, the UFO's streamed silently in traffic lanes.

I sat down in an empty chair at a table with two women and a man using laptops. They were oblivious of me. The lap tops looked just like ours except that the characters on the keys were in a Cyrillic kind of script. Sitting close to these people, I felt the glow of health that radiated out of them. It activated my own sense of healthy well-being.

When I've been in the astral around humans, the vibrations are steady and regular. But Ovvalans are different - the vibrations are fast and erratic. I felt waves of subtle mental intensity coming off these people.

Their skin fascinated me. It was made out of a dense kind of light or a cool fire. I reached out and ran my fingers along the arm of the woman next to me. Her skin was smooth and cool but made my fingers feel hot. She brushed her arm unconsciously. She had felt my touch.

As they talked in their singsong voices I could feel their intelligence in my own brain as sharp lines of awareness that almost hurt. Their minds were intensely focused and electric. Sitting so close to them I began picking up on their emotions. Between the sharp waves of thought there were sudden deep valleys of longing or sadness, sudden peaks of ecstatic delight or a momentarily, deeply depressing sinking feeling that was immediately replaced by the sharp thought lines. Their emotions changed very quickly. They were explosively intense and yet so self-controlled!

There were four women seated at a table a couple tables away from me who had been laughing and hooting loudly. They were waving their arms around dramatically as they talked - or warbled. They were having a lot of fun. Their laughter calmed me from the intense emotions of the conversation near me. The three arm-linked girls stalked back into the marketplace with their tops now in place and proud, defiant and smug smiles on their faces.

One of the women at the table I was watching hollered out 'karoolia!' at the girls who screamed the word back with defiance. The other women also hooted. One of these women transfixed my attention. She was tall and had glowing bronze skin and long auburn hair fixed in a loose braid down her back that seemed to writhe with its own life force. Her mannerisms were very dignified, formal and yet feminine and wise and when she laughed aloud at what the other women were saying her laugh was low and personal. When she smiled her electric green eyes gleamed with such deep pleasure and awareness that I felt lit up inside by it. Even among the exotic beauty of these strange women she stood out for me. I was very attracted to her and as I was feeling this attraction, she turned suddenly and looked right at me so that I wondered if she could see me. A little sphere of glowing blue light bloomed between us, a blue like the ocean of waves and then one of the women spoke to her and she turned away. The sphere of blue light slowly faded in the air as I watched.

Suddenly a hush came over the sing song hum of chatter of people at the tables and one word was being repeated from table to table like a warning;

'Skandrr!' 'Skandrr!'

The voices became subdued and all attention was turned towards a group of five or six men walking slowly towards the street cafe along the grassy path. They were dressed in a kind of uniform so that I assumed they were police.

They had long, shiny black boots and wore light gray, waist length capes with black borders and cuffs. These were open at the chest to reveal shiny metallic objects strapped across their chests. Their vibration was also very different than those of the people at the tables. There was a closed density and menace about them. They slowed their pace as they came up to the tables, their boots clicking sharply on the flagstones. They looked around at the people with contempt and made comments among themselves and laughed mockingly.

One of the men, whose cape had bold designs on the lapels different than the other men, perhaps an insignia of rank, walked rapidly right through the seated crowd. As he passed the woman with the bronze skin he quickly leaned down, slid his hand down along her front and kissed her on the cheek. She screamed and kicked him in the leg and he instantly slapped her in the face. A man at another table leaped to his feet, drew a sword and slammed his palm into the officer's chest who then used a judo like move that threw the man to the ground. As the officer turned my way I noticed his high, narrow white forehead and the contrasting sharp black widow's peak of his hair.

The fallen man lurched to his feet to again confront the soldier. Immediately the five other men in capes rushed up. One of them pulled out the silver object on his chest and shot the man who had fallen to the ground with an electric bolt that cut through the air like lightning. A woman screamed. The man collapsed, hunched over around his wound with his clothes smoldering.

Then one of the group in the gray capes tossed the cape aside to reveal herself as a pale woman dressed in a belted, tight nylon-like body suit that revealed everything. She was clearly of another species. She had very large, unblinking black eyes and pronounced, exaggerated facial features, breasts and hips. Her skin tight suit was completely out of place in this public garden. She was wearing a black leather collar which I now saw was attached to a leash held by one of the men. She was a very strange, wild looking woman but very beautiful. Waves of black light pulsed out of her eyes. Looking at her eyes I had the sense that she didn't have a mind at all but only had emotions.

On seeing who or what she was, the people at the tables began hissing the word 'Siel' 'Siel' and a vibration of intense disgust filled the air. They feared and hated the men in gray but they were revolted by the strange woman.

The black eyed woman, sensing the hostility of the crowd laughed melodically and made an obscene gesture and replaced her cape. The soldiers with her burst into loud laughter and then turned and walked her away.

The man who had been shot was lifted up and seated in a chair. Someone patted his shirt front down with a wet napkin. He was groggy and stunned but didn't seem seriously hurt. The woman with the braid who had such a magnetic effect on me had gone over to the group around the fallen man. She spoke to him, probably thanking him for his heroism. Her friends picked up their shopping bags and were leaving along with everyone else at the restaurant. The woman with the braid joined the group walking with the shot man as he was being walked away by his friends.

What a shock! What had been a jolly and exotic experience became depressing and ugly. I continued to sit at one of the tables watching the woman with the braid as she boarded a bus and disappeared into the night.

When I looked back at the empty restaurant I noticed a man sitting alone. His aura looked different than the Ovvalans. A dark border surrounded him in heavy, sagging contrast to their bright energy. His face was waxy and pale. He was looking straight at me. He was in his fifties or so, had heavy pouches under his eyes which seemed watery and bloodshot. He looked very tired. As I continued to look at him I clearly heard his voice in my head;

'Hello!' he said without moving his lips. He continued to look at me calmly. I thought 'He can see me.'

'Of course I can see you. I've been watching you since you sat down. You're not a remote are you? You look different - your vibe is different.'

'A remote?' I formed the question in my mind more than in response to him.

'How did you get here anyway?' he asked me, clearly speaking telepathically. I felt his energy was penetrating mine and it felt uncomfortable, too familiar and close. But I was compelled to respond to him.

'I read a book by Robert Monroe and...'

'Oh! Monroe! And what? ...you just went down the rabbit hole and popped up here?' he asked.

His voice was whiny and somehow sticky. I didn't like him. He was very pushy, intrusive and aggressive. He felt dirty.

'How did get you here?' I asked, guarded now.

'I'm doing a remote. My ass is lying on a slab in Langley slathered with belladonna.' He stared at me puzzled. 'You don't know what the hell I'm talking about do you?' I could only stare at him wondering who or what he was.

'I'm with the BATS. Belladonna Attention Transference Syndrome Battalion. I'm a remote viewer. We're usually under guidance - we check out hostage situations or gather info on a target too risky to approach in the physical. The control then asks questions about locale, number of personnel, weapons systems, security levels stuff like that. But on my days off I sometimes do this alone. See - I invented a system - I rub on the belladonna, lie down on my bed at home and start a tape recording I made to guide myself to a location and then back home.

'I like to come to Ovvala and see what's happening. But the real hot stuff is the Siels - did you see that one with the Skandrr soldiers?' He sensed that I didn't understand him. 'You're green as grass aren't you ass wipe? You don't know where the hell you are or what's going on do you? You're probably astral projecting in a dream. You won't even remember talking to me.' He walked over and sat next to me.

'The Siel are Skandrr slaves from the Qlipoth. They're like demons - succubae in the Big Black Book. Here in Ovvala they can actually materialize physically. They're wild!'

'Where is Ovvala,' I asked him, my skin crawled at the creepy feel of his energy.

'Uh - it's a waste of energy talking to you. You won't remember a thing,' he stared at me. 'Ovvala is the parallel dimension to Earth,' he said impatiently, looking around for something of more interest than me. 'It's more etheric.' I looked at him blankly. The Knights Templars? Ha! You're a Dumbo for sure. But it sure is weird meeting a human here. I've never had a conversation with a human here. I'm always here alone floating around like Casper the Friendly Ghost. Unless the Adrrik spot me then I've got to go back pronto!'

'What's the Adrrik?'

'The Skandrr psychic police. They could see us just like we can see each other. But they'd try and trap you with an electrical net so watch your ass bud. Then there's the Siddhe - they're these revolutionaries who are fighting the Skandrr - some of them can see us too. They'll follow you back to your body and spy on you.' He leaned towards me, his eyes like a sick bloodhound's.

'Is Ovvala a real place or is it a dream...' I asked him.

'Is it real or is it a dream?' He mocked me making his voice nasal and preppy. 'Are we we're talking or are we dreaming we're talking? Ha! Gotcha!' He looked bored and exasperated again. 'It's just a different frequency of energy. It's the matter anti matter thing. Earth is matter this is anti-matter,' he spoke like he was bored to death. 'Sometimes you'll see entities from the next level above this pass through the sky. That's like the etheric plane to this place as this is the etheric to Earth...'

'I saw a fish or something fly through the air over at the market...' I felt exposed and odd like I couldn't stop telling the truth as though I were a little child with a demanding adult.

'Yeah. Like that. That's another world. Like the underworld where the Siel come from is another world. We can't go to those places - our energy structure won't let us. Imagine going where the Siel women live! Wowzers! But then you'd have to deal with the males - the Voluan. They fight dirty. Don't mess with them!'

'So - what'd you say your name was?' he asked me.

'Joe,' I said.

'And where did you say you live?' I knew I hadn't said either my name or where I lived and felt him trying to get behind me now. 'Istanbul,' I said sarcastically.

'Oh Istanbul huh? I've never been there.' Incredibly he believed me.

'Oh oh, he groaned and bent over and gagged. His aura got dark brown. 'I think I'm gonna be sick...' Then he vanished.

I sat at the table for a little while wondering what that had all been about. The guy left me with a very creepy feeling. Some Ovvalans were walking along the path through the gardens between the buildings. Their energy sparkled with a light green shimmer which seemed to bounce back to them from the plants in the boxes. I got up and walked closer to them. A beautiful bunch of flowers in a planter pulled my attention and I drifted over there. They were not Earthly flowers. Their beauty erased the presence of the BATS character from my energy field. The flowers had broad, wrinkled petals with violet veins in a crimson background; the droopy green leaves pulsed with radio waves of biological vitality. My attention became hazy and I began drifting upwards along the dark gold windows of an office and woke up.

Chapter Five

Dec/4/04 2:14 A.M.

I returned almost an hour ago now. I've been lying in the dark trying to absorb what just happened.

I just had sex - no - made real love - with a woman from Ovvala. Llueve. That's her name. It was the woman I saw at the market; the woman who looked at me.

I can barely breathe. My chest is burning. I feel like I'm expanding – stretching...Is this enlightenment? She is so exotic! I close my eyes and I can see her face, sea green eyes looking back at me as though she is right there inside my forehead. It is her cottage by the big boulder. I'm running it all together. I should start at the beginning...

I went out the back of my neck, across the dark space, through the ocean of blue waves and through the oval door. A small ball - a pearl - of that same blue remained in my field of vision and I followed it over the grove of evergreens to the cottages and came to the cottage by the boulder with the hump of quartz in it.

I felt pulled towards the house and drifted through a door - still following the promptings of the blue pearl. I found myself in a bedroom. Someone was sleeping in the wide, low bed. It was very still, dark and quiet. There were embroidered curtains on the windows and a shiny, black-lacquered bureau and a table with a lamp by the bed. I was standing on a wooden floor. I could smell a clean pleasant smell - it was feminine - like a mix of milk and clean laundry and something else - a flower smell. As I stood watching, wondering why I was there, the energy body of a woman rose up out of the sleeping form and stood up on the bed. She was completely naked and half asleep. The uniqueness of her body, of her motions as she steadied herself on the bed, were so different than human that I was hypnotized and just stood there, forgetting to breathe and watched her.

She sensed me standing at the foot of the bed and we locked eyes. Neither of us was prepared at that moment for an encounter with someone and our senses were wide open. One of her feet was going through her own sleeping body on the bed but she was oblivious to this. She became more aware and her arm lifted in self-protection. She was wearing only a gauzy robe that concealed about as much of her as would a wet Kleenex.

I hadn't yet looked at an Ovvalan, of any kind up close - much less a naked woman. The curve of her hips was slightly different than a human woman's. Her waist seemed higher. Her hair had a life of its own. It writhed slowly and seemed to pulse with its own heartbeat. The long slope of her waist leading to her oval breasts was surrealistic and out of time. Like an old album cover. I felt overwhelmed. The piercing intelligence in her eyes and the alien vitality of her naked, vulnerable body had me locked in wonder. She couldn't have been more unique if she had had the head and paws of a cheetah.

There was a distinct telepathy between us. It was eerie. The beginning of every thought of either of us was immediately neutralized by a responsive thought in the other. We stared at each other for the longest time, unable to take our eyes away, stop the telepathy or cause the communication to add up to something.

As I looked, a blue pearl of light on her forehead winked out and I realized it had been there all along coming through the Loosh. I realized that this is where it had been leading. I felt my own forehead glow with warmth. The vanishing of the blue pearl made me realize she was the woman I had seen at the market cafe. Her face and movements had crossed my mind a number of times since the incident. (Did I somehow magnetize this encounter through my subconscious? Does she exist outside my subconscious? Is this all dream-invention?)

We stared at each other knowing we were alien life forms to one another. I saw her features up close and clearly. The soft plane of her cheek, the mould of her chin, the curve of her forehead, the elf like, oval of her face, her glowing green eyes. One tapered ear stuck up through her glowing hair.

Present at the same time as one another's alien-ness was sex. An intense magnetism between us kept the alien-ness of our forms and vibes from becoming frightening. Our being sexy to each other was our one point of familiarity, a common language.

Her eyes curved delicately in a slant expressing the deep, volatile emotions I remembered feeling from other Ovvalans at the cafe, a kind of latent hysteria. Involuntarily I stepped nearer, controlled by the magnetism of her presence. Her hair, up close and in the dark, had a snaky, living luster. It writhed in slow motion as she'd risen out of her body and sensually slid off her shoulders as she stood shakily on the bed.

As I continued to stare at her, an opaque, creamy light covered her nakedness like a milky light. Desire took me over like a compass pointing in one direction. But it was desire laced with a kind of suspended fear. Also, I felt like I was having a spiritual vision and didn't know if feeling such desire was completely appropriate. In a dream-like way, I was fully conscious of what was going on even though I was overwhelmed by the strangeness.

'Who are you?' She said. Her voice was low and came out of her belly like a growl. She was speaking mentally, intensely excited. Her 'voice' vibrated and hummed, transmitted through an electric current straight into my brain.

'I...am ...Joe...' I said.

'Jwo?' She hugged herself protectively. Even in this mental communication she heard my foreign accent and it disturbed her even more than she already was. She looked around the room to see if there were others like me. She became more awake and her robes became more opaque. An unleashed electric current continued shooting between us. With long animal strides, she stepped off the bed and circled the room.

'You are not Ovvalan!' She said accusingly. I could feel all her skin become electrified - almost horror stricken. All the hair on my own body stood up in response. I felt my face molting and changing.

'I'm from Santa Fe!' I said this to try and calm her and with some resentment because I'm actually from Jaconita, to the north. But nobody knows where Jaconita is. This immediately felt like a stupid thing to have said.

'San-Fe!?' she sneered as though to say 'who would ever want to be from there!'

'New Mexico?'

'What is that?' She slitted her eyes and stood up straighter; the gauzy robe became thick as the curtains of a Holiday Inn. We were talking as though in a dream - the words didn't make sense but the act of talking while we looked at one another conveyed worlds.

'I'm Human!' I said with pride and some force but this seemed meaningless to her.

'Who are *you*?' I asked with an undertone of suspicion as though to say I'm not the only abnormal one in this room sugar lips. There was this powerful sexual competition going on that was making me think and talk like a teenager.

'I am Llueve.' I swear, when she said her name, a violet bloom of perfumed mist wafted out from her lips at me and made my knees quiver. She tossed her hair and took a deep breath that made all her parts move around inside her robe.

'Gieaow!' She screeched, letting out involuntary sounds as she tried to turn her head away from our staring and found she couldn't.

Erotic delirium was fighting with raw fear as my body took another involuntary step towards her. My hand reached out to touch her all by itself. Touching the skin of her arm was like petting a mild animal - I couldn't tell what she would do but I couldn't resist. As I watched, her hand involuntarily reached out to touch my face, lifting her breasts as her irises dilated and became deep purple in the darkness. The mental strangeness I felt was replaced by the safety and familiarity of pure sexual longing as we both began caressing one another. It was all like dreaming. We kissed, embraced and as we did so we began to float above the bed in slow motion. Without doing anything about it we became naked and sexually unified our faces so close that I could count her eyelashes. I wrapped my arms around her waist. For the longest time we barely moved and then in a slow, prolonged, recurring pulsation, we climaxed together, floating and turning slowly in the darkness of her room.

When we climaxed - how can I describe it? I felt myself expanding until I thought I would burst, except that, as I expanded I became more and more peaceful. I had the distinct image of being half of the entire solar system and of her being the other half. Our knowing each other contained this vast but specific amount of space.

We floated in the room like fish in an aquarium, embracing and drifting slowly in drunken warmth as the telepathy of alien intelligence vibrated between us. Her cat had been watching us from the edges of the room all along. As we floated along her hallway in our embrace, the cat stood beneath us looking up.

'Meow! Meow!' It said.

We turned our dream drenched minds to the cat and Llueve looked in my eyes and said softly -

'Meow!' And by God I said it back.

I felt the silky air around my body was somehow full of protons or ions. Spirals of electrical current passed around my skin like the smooth coils of a higher intelligence. At a certain point I knew I was fading. I'd used up a huge amount of energy and knew I was going to fall asleep and that this would make me to go back into my body. I also knew I had to find her again and needed some way of identifying this place so I could return. I don't think she knew this was actually happening. To her it really was a dream.

We had drifted onto the sofa in her living room. On a table under an unlit lamp there was a finely carved, little white stone figure. I fixed my attention on it. It had a moon-glow like alabaster in the dim light coming from a large bay window. It looked like the medieval sculpture of a robed Irish saint with exaggerated eyes. I memorized it with all my strength with the intent to return to it. It was the last thing I saw before I opened my eyes. Llueve.

12/7/04 1:17 A.M.

I followed the same procedure as before - got the buzzing bees feeling and went out the back of my head. I passed through darkness then the sea of blue vapor waves while all the time visualizing the carved alabaster figure in my mind. Sure enough I drifted down over the cottage and landed in Llueve's living room. Immediately, the sense of breathing an etheric hallucinogen began. The room began to pulse. She was sleeping, her face turned to the side, her hair spread over the pillow. I stood there looking around the room and noticed how the ceiling curved to meet the walls; I looked at the curves where the walls met the ceiling. I noticed the lozenge shaped bed. Everything was oval.

I stood there for a while, completely motionless. Suddenly she rose up out of her body. She recognized me right away and an intense glow of happiness came over her. It manifested as a luminous bloom of rose light in her chest and flared suddenly to a passionate ruby red jewel then began to vanish. As this happened a dense, dull white robe around her body. It diluted into a gauzy veil, and I saw her alien beauty again. This gauzy robe changed to hide her nakedness as the glow in her chest became a dusty rose light and in her eyes an intelligence turned on like a light. We embraced and a little shock of energy passed through us. The feeling at that moment wasn't really sexual. It was a direct energy meeting between us. We both laughed and became focused and still.

'It's you!' she said with wonder and a big smile.

'I've thought about you constantly since the other night!' I gushed shamelessly with the spontaneous honesty that seemed to rule my emotions when out of body.

'Yes! Me too! It was so beautiful! I remembered you when I awoke... You disappeared...' Chains of sparkling energy streamed through her mind with thoughts she wanted to say as she searched my eyes.'

'I had to go back.'

'Go back... where?'

'Home.'

'Where is your home?'

'In uh, Santa Fe,' I almost said Jaconita.

'Oh. You told me before,' she said vaguely so that I could tell she thought she was dreaming.

'Do you know you are out of your body?' As soon as a thought came into my mind it communicated itself.

She looked down at herself and a question-vibration came out of her. I directed her awareness towards her sleeping figure on the bed. She looked but didn't register anything out of the ordinary. I drifted over to her body and looked closely at her physical face so that she would look at her face. She leaned over and suddenly jumped back and gasped. Seeing her body scared her.

'It's all right. Don't be scared.' I said and touched her shoulder.

'What is this?' She looked between me and her sleeping body.

'You are in your dream body like me. We are outside our bodies.'

'I'm dreaming!'

'No you aren't dreaming. This is really happening.'

'You are outside your body? We are dreaming together?' she asked, baffled.

'I'm outside my body but I'm not dreaming. I chose to come here tonight. To see you.' Her body on the bed writhed and moaned. Her energy body sort of flickered. I reached out and touched her arm. I didn't want her to go.

'What do you do?' I was groping for some way to start a conversation with her. 'What do you eat?'

'I work at an architectural firm,' she was looking around her bedroom in amazement. 'I'm an architect,' she said distractedly. This answer surprised me.

'I'm not dreaming?' She said.

We were both getting that it didn't really matter what was said- only that we relate to one another - second by second. We sort of solidified on the floor and walked into the next room. Her robe, which had been momentarily transparent, became opaque. I noticed that I was dressed similarly - in a vaguely whitish robe that went to my ankles. I realized that these weren't clothes but shields of awareness.

There was a short hall that branched into different rooms. We walked into a large room with a couch and an oval coffee table. There were papers on the table and floor with the Cyrillic letters I had seen on the laptop keyboards at the cafe.

'What is this?' I nodded at the papers.

'It is letters to people about the depleted food.' I could tell that she too was being transparently honest.

'You're writing about food?'

'Yes. The food makes people sick because of the chemicals.' She plunged suddenly into a depth of despairing emotion. My heart lurched inside my chest in response to this sudden shift. It was almost like she was suddenly dying right before my eyes. Her energy had become heavy and sad. With a great effort she continued, her voice so soft I could barely hear her; 'And the river water is causing birth deformities to babies... I belong to a group,' she said, now carefully measuring her words 'It is called the Suura. We are trying to educate people about the Faal – the suicide sickness...' She turned her eyes to me, intense, bright lines of thought pierced through the gloom that had overtaken her mind and sliced like razor blades into my own mind.

'Are you an angel?' she said looking straight into my eyes. 'Can you stop the Faal?' Her eyes lit up wildly as she stared at me. I just kept watching her - she seemed very unstable and I was afraid something terrible was about to happen.

'We are fighting the Skandrr government that produces deformed food. This weakens people. They can't renew their vitality and want to go to the stars. And something has entered the drinking water - some substance that no one can identify. It causes the deformities in babies - everyone is so sad about these things ...the suicides.' She began talking very fast. Intense lines of mental energy were fighting the heavy sucking weight of her emotions. A brown, glob of energy appeared in her middle out of which a maroon ink began to spill down her chest.

'Maybe you are an angel?!' She reached for me suddenly, desperately, tears streaming down her face - her mental lines were shooting such intense, sharp trajectories that they hurt. She desperately wanted me to be an angel and I was afraid that to disappoint her would actually hurt her.

'I'm a human,' I said slowly and reached out to touch her. She was desperately afraid of her own emotions and was trying to get away from them in her mind as though they were deadly microbes.

'Hoomaan? Like Hunamunan?' I didn't know what she meant.

'I'm Human - from the Earth...' I stroked the curve of her waist. Her feverish eyes contracted with astonishment- her energy shifted, her mind cut through the emotional suck of her sadness and she looked at me with renewed self-possession. Her robes began to vaporize...

'A hunamunan! From Aurth? You are Terran?' She became electrified.

'What is that?'

The currents of energy that had already passed between us had created a deep sense of trust. We felt one another's alien-ness but now as a benevolent force and we sought the comfort and up-liftment we knew this contained. We embraced, our nakedness distracted her from the depressing emotions. We made love against the pain of her sadness and against my own loneliness. We became possessive and soul-hungry. When we climaxed it was like an emotional orgasm that made me sob uncontrollably. I began to black out. When I knew I was going to fade I said -

'Don't let us get separated!' She hugged me fiercely.

'I am here!' she said, her cheek against mine. We clutched at each other. I wanted to take her home with me and as soon as that thought went through my mind, we began to float up and out of her house. In a flash we passed through the timeless place of the blue waves and then we were in my bedroom, standing at the foot of my bed. We were still hugging, still naked, still crying.

'What is this?' She wiped at her tears with her fingers and looked around my room. She stared at the green, bubbling fish tank in horror, becoming really nervous at this change of place. She pulled away from me to look around and her 'robe' became thick. The different feel of the human dimension startled her and she almost vanished right there. I touched her arm gently. I looked at her in all her strangeness as she turned away, taking in my room. The lines of her long, curving hips were so lovely I felt compelled to stroke them. I started to run my hands down along her hips when she whipped around and slapped me in the face so hard that my neck popped.

'Oh! Sorry!' she said and laughed. 'I thought you were someone else!' She leaned out and stroked the cheek she'd slapped and smiled so sweetly I almost forgot what had just happened.

She was feeling the basic atomic difference of this dimension and felt disoriented, I explained to myself. She felt different to herself and this explained something to me about how I felt like a different me over there.

'This is my house. In Jaconita.' I said as I watched this exotic entity from another dimension standing at the foot of my bed while I was in my dream body. I was near the ceiling of my ability to process the experience and was taking fast shallow breaths like I've seen Yvonne do to calm her anger. I was trying to act calm so that the dream woman wouldn't get scared and split. The paned window looked out on the back yard. Neutron was sleeping half out of his old dog house. It's too small for him. I built another one but he won't use it.

'Gala-Bala!' Llueve said on seeing Neutron. She turned smiling at me and said aloud; ' Fisc gueldaa!' or something like that. I think it meant 'Holy Moly you have a dog!'

We walked through the kitchen, the living room, the extra bedroom beyond it that I use as a workshop. 'That's my radio,' I said. 'That's a model of a Spitfire. That's a dremmel. That's a glue gun...that's my guitar, that's my grandfather's violin' I said pointing to tools and the instruments hanging on the wall trying to keep things chatty.

'Ixtielda!' she said, reaching out and touching the violin. 'I play too!' She said proudly. I was about to ask what she meant when she turned and asked;

'Where is the rock that you said is like the one at my house?'

'Oh that's at my friends' house,' I said. I suddenly wanted her to see the rock, for her to know this link between us. I took her hands, clicked my heels - no - actually I visualized Lena's garden and zoom we were there under the towering boulder with the knob of quartz on it.

'That's it! That's my rock!' Llueve said and looked around at Spencer and Lena's house, the alien juniper and pinon trees growing up the slope of the hill, the different kind of soil.

'Oh! I'm getting dizzy!' she said. 'I need to go back to sleep! I have to go back!' Suddenly she was afraid. Her energy dipped. 'I need to go home now!' She gave me a dark look as though I could be dangerous, so I thought it best to let her go.

I started to explain how I went out the back of my head and then through the hole into the blue energy field. But seeing her flickering form and sensing her growing fear, I realized it was too complicated. I remembered Monroe saying that all you had to do to return from the astral was move any part of your physical body consciously.

'Just move your fingers,' I said. She stared at me uncomprehending. 'Try and move your fingers,' I said softly. She was staring at me one moment and the next she had vanished.

Two or three times I've gone out the back of my head and found Llueve's house but conditions weren't right for an encounter. Once she was still up, walking around the house in her normal body, doing the dishes, feeding her cat and couldn't see me. This was very frustrating.

I was more and more gaining the ability to be rational while knowing I was in a dream state. So that, as I hovered there outside her window like a peeping Tom from another planet, watching this beauty, wearing loose knitted pants and a sort of jersey with floppy lapels, moving around her kitchen doing completely mundane practical things, I was looking at the experience objectively and wondering at this shift of consciousness continuing to happen to me.

Twice she wasn't there. The bed was empty. I did wonder jealously if she had someone else because of the slapping incident.

Other times I couldn't get out of body when I tried. Twice I've gone out the back of my head and just ended up under the bed. Once I flew to Yvonne's house and tried to pinch her to see if she would remember it but Yvonne sleeps like a log.

And there were dreams. One night I dreamt of very tall people in white robes walking around me. They were very powerful, wise beings from another place. We walked on a path of blue flag stones - it was like walking under water - the path began to tilt up and then we were walking on thin air, up and away from a little round planet and towards another little round planet that was very close.

12/13/04 12:25 A.M.

When I got to Llueve's house she was already out of her body and floating in the living room.

'I did it!' She said. I telepathically knew she meant she had got out of body by herself. 'This is the third time!' So now she knew that this wasn't a dream. And she knew I wasn't a dream. An intense suspense I've been living with concerning the 'reality' of my encounters with her was eased by her coming to this realization. OBE experiences are just as much a new thing to her as to me. She really is my friend in this place out of time. If I'm crazy I at least have a friend in my delusion!

She told me she had been flying around her neighborhood and projected pictures of her travels to me. As we stared into each other's eyes I changed somehow. Being out of body became more real to me, she became more real to me. Popping and squirting sensations started in my brain and then... what can I say - her gauzy robes began to evaporate...

How can I ever show this to Yvonne?

I'm reading Monroe's 2nd book 'Far Journey'. He knew about everything I'm experiencing!

Met with Llueve. We 'equalized' energies by embracing and feeling the electrical shock of contact. We then 'exchanged rotes' - this is a term of Monroe's. He invented a language to describe the experiences that happen in the astral. Especially the speed at which things happen there

A 'rote' is a unit of information transferred directly from mind to mind. This can be directly transmitted in pictures and words by focusing and intending it. Monroe calls this 'scrolling'. I flashed this technique to Llueve and she used it to transmit some hard information.

I learned that Llueve lives in the city of Saala in the region of Daag in the country of Aran-Skaala, which is one of the great populations and cultural centers of Ovvala. It's like Paris by the Seine in France or like Greenwich Village in New York in America.

I learned that in Ovvala there is a royal lineage called the Skandrr that has global control of agriculture and industry and is centered in Ostrad and Vologa across an ocean from Aran-Skaala, her country. The Skandrr royalty slowly came to power over the last thousand years as it took over power from the more ancient lineage of the Siddhe who are remembered in Aran-Skaala as a highly artistic and benevolent royal lineage who were in power before the Skandrr. The Skandrr lineage is intermarried with most of the families that own most of the land. It sounds like how the royal houses of Europe at the turn of the last century were all intermarried.

Llueve went into more detail about something called the Faal. This is an epidemic of suicidal depression that is rampant all over the planet. It's caused by a collective energy leak among Ovvalans in general. Llueve couldn't explain it. She seems nervous even talking about it very much. She had an older brother she was very close to named Duraam who committed suicide because of this condition. Recalling his death made Llueve very sad and heavy hearted. When I've felt her emotions sag like this it's a little scary.

The Faal disease began fairly recently - like in the last half century or so. It grew into an epidemic as the biological decay of the land got worse. Over the last century the Skandrr government introduced mechanized agriculture. This is an artificial process that Llueve's activism group, the Suura, thinks is part of what causes the Faal. But the Faal is also a kind of spiritual depression - giving up hope - loosing interest in life.

There is a global media network owned by the Skandrr that, with its allies around the planet, broadcasts the same news. It seems to amount to an industrial hierarchy broadcasting propaganda. Skandrr mass communications don't discuss the daily suicides that happen in office buildings, on construction sites, on college campuses or in private homes so that the greater mass of society is in the dark about the extent of the problem. When a suicide happens in public, the media attributes it to drug overdoses or assassinations by terrorists.

Meeting me has registered in a serious way with Llueve. She doesn't understand it any more than I do. But she has lived with the fear of contracting the Faal just like her brother. Meeting me has given her hope.

There is an issue that makes Llueve physically sick to discuss. It's about deformed babies and has something to do with the river Uul that runs through Daag. Most of the deformities seem to be happening in connection with this water. This is something the Skandrr owned media also won't report on. Only recently - in the last few decades has there been electric power. This power appeared along with the food processing factories. The birth deformities began occurring at about the same time this power became available so the Suura believe there is a connection.

The Suura are doing mass mailings to encourage people to grow their own food, purify their water and not listen to the misinformation. The Suura is one of hundreds of such groups in Aran-Skaala that is doing such work. They are also encouraging people to form Suura collectives so as to try and separate news from propaganda.

There is an underground group that calls itself the Siddhe in memory of the kings and queens of Ovvala's golden era. It broadcasts information clips from secret locations that the Skandrr can't always block. The most recent of these broadcasts was about how the Suura is collecting water from various rivers to try and track where the poison is coming from. They also discuss the Faal and encourage people to grow home gardens to supplement their daily food. They tell people that the Skandrr need to be resisted to protect the vitality of life.

The idea of the ancient Siddhe plays a big part in the mythology of Daag culture. Llueve makes a lot of references to this. This original Siddhe included the existence of the Hunamunan. Llueve thought I was one of these the first time we encountered. In Daag mythology, Hunamunans were magical beings from another world but over time and through Skanddr influence they became evil trolls and the doors closed.

The existence of this ancient mythical world is honored in Daag culture by spelling words with double letters to represent a double world, a practice that the Skandrr rulers denounce as superstitious sentimentality.

Llueve showed me a world map of Ovvala and I was astounded to see that the continents are exactly like those on Earth!

The vast majority of the countries on the continents of Ovvala live agrarian lifestyles - something that is held in very high esteem by Daag culture as well as other Ovvalan cultures around the planet. Growing and eating food is the basis of a kind of cosmic religion to Ovvalans.

When I communicated to Llueve how I felt her become so deeply sad at times she told me that this isn't peculiar to her but is common to all Ovvalans. Happiness and friendliness are the only things that give living any value to Ovvalans. Ovvalans aren't materialistic and have a need to feel etheric radiance constantly in order to feel happy. They hunger for the same radiance that makes plants thrive; something called Aan that is believed to exist in the air and enter plants. Being deprived of Aan, she believes, causes the Faal.

When someone goes beyond a certain point of sadness they can't get back to vitality again and they want to stop living. The expression is that 'they want to go to the sky'. Hundreds of thousands of Ovvalans - maybe millions - have the Faal sickness. She thinks a thousand people commit suicide a month. I think Llueve fears having it herself which is why she devotes so much of her time to the work of the Suura.

The government issues drugs that are supposed to counteract the Faal but nothing really seems to work. Seeing drugged semi catatonic zombies walking around just depresses other Ovvalans and causes the Faal to start in them.

The flying disks are called Skaalin. They look just like standard pictures of UFO's and are regular cars on Ovvala. They have existed for hundreds of years. The particular atmospheric magnetism of Ovvala seems to make them possible. They run on anti-magnetics produced by a crystal generated force called Kavra. She took me out to her driveway and we sat in hers. She was frustrated that she couldn't start it and take me for a ride. It comes as a perk with her job!

Daag-Ovvalans prefer to watch large community video screens rather than sit at home and watch television alone so that there are group viewing rooms in most neighborhoods where people go to watch together. Even in cities, people watch broadcasts in theaters. Now, with the new phenomenon of laptops and an internet, which only appeared about a decade ago, more people are watching non-governmental broadcasts. Only the people who accept the Skandrr version of events still go to the public viewings.

When I've gone looking for Llueve and not found her I've flown around in her neighborhood or gone into some homes and watched the people interact. I went into Saala and walked around on the sidewalks with the night time crowds or strolled through factories and watched people caning vegetables. Except for the difference in the general look of things – the oval desks, light fixtures, doorways – and people's physical movements and the pointed ears – Ovvalans are no different than humans walking and working.

Yet, the physicality of Ovvalans is different from ours. I can't compare them to anything I can think of. Their logic is different. And they are very emotional. I'm getting this partly from Llueve telling me things, partly from the feelings I get from being with her and the feel of people when she takes me to different places. We visited her parents in their home outside Saala. Her father's name is Barntold and her mother's is Mier. He was sitting in an armchair reading and she was talking on a phone. He is a large man, getting portly, black hair, long Ovvalan face with jowls. He looks kind of like a big version of Elvis Costello - with pointy ears. The mother has light hair and is pretty. Still has a nice figure. She reminded me of a movie star from the fifties - June Allison? with pointy ears. I felt like we were intruding and didn't want to stay too long. Llueve thought the experience was hilarious. She tried to pinch her dad to get his attention but he just kept right on reading.

I get flash impressions of how Ovvalans are different than humans. There is a ray of hope that extends out of the Ovvalan heart towards some universal center. I can sometimes see this green ray extend out of people's chests. It is like a blind trust in goodness. They are like children in this way. This is a kind of emotional need that compulsively and constantly seeks confirmation from others and from the universe in general. Is everything O.K.? Is everything O.K.? their energy seems to ask. When this resonance is not felt their heart crumples. Ovvalans are emotionally transparent. You see all this just looking at them.

But what is Ovvala? Is it a physical place? An energy place? Llueve and I are meeting out of body so that's an energy place. But where is her 'physical' body? The BATS character I talked to at the market in Saala said this is a world in another frequency. What does this mean?

A fundamental Daag value - at least in Saala where Llueve comes from - is that food is cosmic energy. There are two parts to food – the physical nourishment and the spirit force called Aa. This cosmic energy exists in food, in air and in water and can't be owned. There is a special kind of money to provide for births, for medical care, for education, for burials. The costs of the spiritual passages in life are shared by society. This is thought to elevate all of society. People get paid a different kind of money or credit for working. Accumulating vouchers for everyday needs is a depressing absurdity in the anti-Skandrr Daag psyche. Most Daag Ovvalans are anti Skandrr. The main pro-Skandrr areas are called Vologa and Ostrad.

The Skandrr create laws and regulations attached to the transmission of the Aan vitality, something that is considered a hateful practice by Daags. Llueve and her friends in the Suura believe the Skandrr are trying to control the actual enthusiasm of life.

The Balatek is a ministry of the Skandrr royalty which controls education and information but which everyone knows is the basis of the manipulation of society. The many people belonging to the Suura feel that the educational system encourages unconsciousness and servitude.

We went flying in our astral bodies over Saala. Llueve showed me the building where she works. She showed me her office and sat at her drawing board laughing that she was in her astral body. We were on the eleventh floor. UFO's were flying by regularly right outside the windows! She didn't look up once.

'On Earth those ships are a great mystery.' I told Llueve. 'Many people have seen them but many more have not. Most people think the beings inside the UFO's are from outer space - from some other solar system.' We both found this very interesting wondering what it could mean. 'Belief in the reality of the disks has become a kind of psychological boundary between Humans.' I told her. I tried to relay to her the idea that at one time some Humans thought the earth was flat and others thought it was round as a kind of measure of how human consciousness once leaped and how UFO's represent this same kind of shift today.

'Urth is round?' She was amazed.

'Well, yeah! Isn't Ovvala round?'

'No! It's oval!' she said and laughed. I didn't get it.

We drifted out into the suburbs of Saala and came to an orchard where the trees were all planted in rows. We landed there and walked between the rows of leafless, dormant trees. Frozen pears lay on the ground so that I knew it was a pear orchard.

'Pears!' I said looking at the browned pears lying among the leaves.

'Oondas? You say pares?'

'Yes. Pears,' I said.

Suddenly we were both jolted by a wave of intense energy. It was like having an orgasm for no reason at all. We both laughed out loud and were magnetized up into the air and back to her house. We 'landed' in her front yard by the boulder. We stood there stunned for a moment and then out of the blue Llueve said;

'Let's each plant an Oonda tree right here,' Llueve stomped her foot down about ten feet in front of the boulder, right in front of the crystal. I'll plant a tree here in my yard and you plant one at your friend's house in the exact same place on Urth! Would your friends let you plant a tree on their land?'

'I'm sure they would,' As I said it I woke up.

Chapter Six

December, 22, 2004

This morning I watched a fading dream of a Crop Circle etched in a field of golden wheat as my eyes opened. I hadn't thought about Crop Circles for a long time. I'd heard that a couple of men in England had claimed making all of them and I lost interest. Then I watched a video with Spencer and Lena that convinced me Crop Circles couldn't be made by humans. They were too elaborate and exact for two men to make. And the video estimated there were a thousand crop circles a year made in England alone. An impossible number for two men to make. As I thought about the mystery of them, I wondered if they could have any significance to Ovvala. Had Llueve heard of Crop Circles? When I went to pick up Spencer this morning I went on line while he got ready. I Googled up a site that has current photos of Crop Circles and there was a bulletin; a large Crop Circle had appeared yesterday next to Stonehenge. And this was similar to the Crop Circle in my dream!

I looked over some of the more unique Crop Circles on the site and 'photographed' them in my mind - how the grain spiraled down flat or overlapped as it is in one of the pictures - hoping that I could transmit some of this to Llueve.

It is almost effortless for me to get out of body and go to Ovvala now. I can't wait for the day to be over and my other life to begin. The thought makes me work hard so as to be fully tired by the time I go to bed. It was about eleven thirty when I slid into the dreamy state and buzzed out the back of my head. We encountered and after we'd equalized energies, I projected the pictures of Crop Circles to her.

'Siddhe Circles!' She called them. 'People associate these designs with the ancient Siddhe and the Druiddas!'

'I know a place where we can see one of these,' I told Llueve. 'Let's go there now. Tonight!' Her eyes shined with curiosity.

I made an image of England across the ocean and passed her this as a rote.

Sitting on her living room floor, we got very still and focused on the journey. Then we took off. A blur of images and sensations passed - the energy opening between Earth and Ovvala passed, a quick blur of blue waves and then a whirlwind of energy surrounded us. When it cleared we saw Stonehenge below us. I was excited since it had dawned on me that it was Winter Solstice.

From the air above we could clearly see a large field of grain across the road from Stonehenge and the Crop Circle I'd seen on the Internet.

'That is a Siddhe design!' Llueve almost screamed, staring at the Crop Circle. Three spirals converging at the center were fixed in the grain glowing golden in the darkness.

The magnetism of both Stonehenge and the crop circle pulsed in waves of crystal light. From our perspective in the astral, it seemed like we were looking through a haze into light pulsing in a rhythm we could almost understand. It was like a complex Morse code or music made of digital transmissions.

The light constructs pulsing out of the Crop Circle came in spirals that quickened and then shot up and curved over towards Stonehenge before they vaporized. This light first sped around the outer rim of the Crop Circle and then pulsed through the spirals into the center. It did this a few times and then, from the axle of the Crop Circle, an electric green lightning arced up and then across the road into the center of Stonehenge. As the arc was formed, a white light shot out of Stonehenge into the Crop Circle.

This was awe inspiring and intense. We landed in the crop circle among the shimmering pulsations of crystal waves of light and walked around looking at the intricate organization with which the straw had been bent and shaped. Each time there was an arc of light, an electric jolt of energy shot up my spine causing my head to jerk up and look at the sky. This stream of pulsations began to lift us across the road to the Stonehenge Circle. As we were being transported another intense wave of white light shot out of Stonehenge and into us and left us gasping. This was all very unexpected and intense. I'd pictured just walking around in a field of rye holding hands.

We landed in the middle of the Stonehenge circle as a stream of light-magnetics between the Crop Circle and Stonehenge pulsed back and forth. The pulsations intensified and quickened into a rhythmic hum. An image of a woman's contractions in birth came to me. I felt this in my gut and saw Llueve spasm and bend over clutching her stomach. Our light bodies synchronized to the light-pulsations and we felt ourselves pulled by a magnetic energy towards the Western portal. Time changed. We were beyond the physical in a realm of pure energy.

The light pulsations from the Crop Circle became focused in the western portal where they accumulated in an intense blue white light. An iridescent shimmer began inside the portal and a thrilling tonal vibration began to resonate.

We became possessed of this quivering - ululating sound-light. The male-female energy between us became painfully magnetic, pressing our bodies together in the portal. An irresistible feeling of love and magnetism and sex rose between us and as it did, the light and sound interpenetrated our bodies and radiated out into space like water rings in a pool. As bizarre as this symphony of light and sound was, the sexual magnetism between us was even more intense. I felt an inspired intelligence descend through the top of my head. It was like forces greater than ourselves were making love to one another through our bodies.

This whole event was blindingly intense - we were driven by forces beyond our control - it was as though we were giving expression through our beings to the root forces of the cosmos - like salmon insanely trying to scale river rapids or eagles flying into arctic winds. How and why things were happening was beyond my ability to track but the sense of the purposefulness in the experience was undeniable. As we looked into each other's eyes I felt our hearts pulsing in a shared rhythm. At one point I hallucinated that we weren't in our astral bodies anymore - we had become physical!

It was overwhelming, so much going on at the same time. Llueve's skin was smooth as water. A light silky blue tint illumined her skin from the rhythmic flashings of the arcing energy. Her hair was like the windblown embers of a fire and sparkled with electric flickerings as it streamed in this otherworldly wind. The density of her lips on mine was different than before - her lips were a living tissue communicating information straight from her body into mine. Where our bodies joined was like a slow and deep running river of electric water surging through us.

We began to climax and lost what remaining control we had. Beginning at her vaginal lips her skin began to ripple in waves that traveled down her thighs and up her belly and across her breasts. These waves traveled down my legs and across my abdomen until the skin of both our bodies was undulating, possessed by what seemed an angelic rhythm of orgasmic love. We went into a catatonic state of pure experience as a diamond shaped sapphire jewel of thrilling energy descended majestically into us from above. The humming sound intensified. The low vibration in the ground, the singing vibration of the stones, the burning, penetrating emotion being transmitted through our bodies intensified until a shock of light cracked open and we convulsed involuntarily clutching at each other to keep from either falling down or being torn apart. This was followed by a huge boom at which point the wall of light began pulling away in two directions from the plane at the western portal and drew away back into the ground and sky. It was at this point I remember us drifting up slowly into a waterfall of moonlight washing down around us.

It was as we were floating some fifty feet above Stonehenge, clothed now in robes of blue moonlight that the UFO went by.

It was different than the UFO's I'd seen in Ovvala, not as streamlined. I could see rivets in the hull and lines of sheet metal plate out of which it was constructed. There were round windows and a dull yellow light coming from within the ship. It was very close to us - twenty or thirty feet away. We could see the silhouettes of heads in the windows. I felt Llueve stiffen in sudden excitement. She associates the disk-ships with the Skandrr military police. I thought she was afraid they'd spotted us.

'They can't see us,' I whispered which was stupid because they couldn't hear us either.

'That's Elsinaad!' Llueve said.

'What?' I said.

'Elsinaad! I know that woman!' I looked and saw an Ovvalan woman's face in one of the portholes. She had a chubby Ovvalan face yellowed from light inside the disk. She had a prominent forehead and the pointed Ovvalan ears and looked to be in early middle age. She had red hair, which is common among Daag-Ovvalans. Her gaze pierced us as she looked out into the night. It was almost as though she could see us. The ship passed on slowly and then vanished in the darkness.

Llueve and I were in an extreme state of over stimulation and this communicated itself between us. Rote images from each of us were storming into the other in senseless, disconnected pictures. We were both loosing our grip of self-control and were starting to flicker. I knew we had to get back to our bodies and sleep. We turned to look at each other acknowledging the power of what was happening to us, full of an unreasonable confidence that we would see each other later. As I looked in her eyes, she slowly faded and I woke up seeing that look of love and wonder in her eyes and hearing the fish tank bubbling in the corner of the room.

1/04/05

It's over three weeks since I've left my body. There haven't even been any dreams. The day after Stonehenge I could barely function. I stayed home the next day only going out for some groceries. I felt really strange. Weird popping and squirting sensations kept happening throughout my brain and body. We stopped work on the lawyer's wall over Christmas and New Year's and only started up again with just Spencer and me a couple of days ago. The bulk of the job is done.

Once, in a sound sleep, I heard Llueve calling my name from a great distance and then saw her gauzy white clad form floating towards me down a long dark hall. When she was near enough so I could see her face and eyes, I discovered I had floated up out of my body in my bed in my room and that she was standing at the foot of my bed in her astral body.

The first thing I noticed was that she was much more defined in her energy than before. There was a crisp, clear electric clarity to her body and her presence. It was really like she was there physically. Her robe now had specks of luminous colors twinkling in it - blues, greens, reds, yellows and some of those colors I only see in Ovvala that are like a green-violet and golden-blue. Her face looked very composed and self-assured. She'd put her hair in a braid. She smiled lovingly at me but there was a serious air about her.

We synchronized energies and the events of that last time we'd been together came back in their emotion and feverish intensity.

'You'll never guess what has happened now,' She smiled and tilted her head at me. I couldn't guess.

'I'm pregnant!'

'What!?' I said, shocked. 'How could you be pregnant?!' I was flabbergasted. 'Are you joking?' I asked her.

'No Jwo I'm jwoking!' she said (that's what it sounded like). 'I have not been with a man for a year! I took the test! I'm pregnant! I don't know how but that night, somehow, we really did it!'

The adoring look in her eyes intensified and she floated up off the ground and into my arms. We hugged, floating over my bed, slowly twirling and laughing.

'My God!' I didn't know what to think.

'It's so Lanaal,' she said tenderly. I got the image of spilling silver. Llueve uses the expression a lot. At times it's like how people from Colorado use 'awesome' every other sentence. Sometimes as a sentence.

After a while we calmed down. There was the sense of her having a lot of new information.

'That woman I saw, Elsinaad, she comes sometimes to the Suura Meetings. She is like a leader. She brings money and supplies.

'I got her alone and told her I had a dream in which she flew by a circle of stones in one of the old fashioned Skaalin and that I saw her face in the window. She was amazed at this. She asked me about what was on the land and when I described Stonehenge and the Siddhe Circle, her face looked shocked. She said we needed to talk and that she would call me at home.

'For the next few nights I had dreams where Elsinaad and others appeared and asked me questions in which I told them about you and some of our doings. I was taken to a cavern deep underground. They could have been dreams or I could have actually gone there out body I don't know!

'Then, about three days ago Elsinaad came to my house with a woman named Avaala. They are very good women. I liked them a lot. These are powerful people from within the Suura group. So I felt I could really trust them. I told them about you and what has been happening and they understood! They know about traveling in astral bodies! They weren't surprised at all! But they want to meet you and to take us to some kind of headquarters and meet people even higher up in the organization. They told me we will meet a woman named Isult!' She said this last name with real goosebumps making awe and her eyes went a little out of focus.

Psychically, I took a deep breath. Her astounding news that she was pregnant. From a dream? In a dream? With an extra-terrestrial? Would I have to get up at 3 AM to change astral diapers? Swab astral baby cheese? Would I need to send Llueve money? How? Would I need to meet her Mom and Dad in an astral living room? How could I tell all this to Yvonne?

My ceiling of reality was lifting up up and away at a rate that no drug or experience I ever had had, had prepared me for. More was coming and I could only stand still and take it in because of this love I feel for her.

'Isult, Matarpha, Kisolie, Antare - Is - the country of Ier, the mountains of Garam - these are all people and places that Daag people learn in mythical stories as children. These names are metaphors in everyday language for heroes and demons, paradise and hell. When we were children we believed they were real but as adults we came to understand that they are only stories!'

Looking at Llueve, her eyes gleaming with wonder and love, her body emanating brilliant expanding spheres of intense colors, knife-sharp, head on blasts of vibrational intensity, I could only absorb her transformations and try and keep up.

'I have known since I was a teenager that what the world promotes as reality and backs up with real laws and religious ideas is fake. People have been bent with fear and fantasy and so need to bend the young with fear and fantasy to defend themselves. But I never imagined that Isult and Matarpha and Ier could be real! But Elsinaad looked me right in the eyes and in perfect seriousness told me we were going to meet Isult. What can this mean? Isult is mentioned in history books from nine hundred years ago!'

Llueve looked at me in a way I had not yet experienced. The strangeness of her Ovvalan femininity had begun to be a recognizable quantity to me. But now, her eyes were open so completely that I could see into her Ovvalan soul and I began to see its strange spiritual depths.

'Jwo, they are waiting now for us at my house right now. I want you to meet them!' She took my hands, placed her forehead against mine and relayed a series of directions and intentions that I could tell she had been given by the women. We held hands and lifted up through the ceiling of my house and translated back to her house in Saala.

Chapter Seven

January 5, 2005

We entered into Llueve's house through the front door. Three women in their astral bodies were standing in Llueve's living room. Unlike Llueve and I who were in our white robes, these women, who were also in their astral bodies, were dressed in colorful Ovvalan clothes - I should say Saalan clothes - very stylish.

We all stood nervously in front of one another as the introductions took place. First was Elsinaad who Llueve has known for some time. She is in her forties I would guess. She was extremely cautious when I first entered the room, narrowing her eyes and bending at the waist in a concentration of looking at me. She had her hand tucked inside her clothes in an odd way. Later I wondered if she had a weapon.

There were two other women in the room. Kaelaa and Avaala. The three women stared at me hard, almost with hostility but mostly with caution. I felt like I was being x-rayed. The moment of guarded encounter passed and the three women sat down close together on Llueve's couch. Llueve and I sat together in her big chair. Llueve sensed my nervousness and was staying right next to me for reassurance. A glow of love and wonder radiated from Llueve as she held my arm. I felt the current of it surge through me and make my heart feel strong. I think the women sensed this. Slowly they seem to become less guarded.

Avaala was the eldest, in her fifties maybe. She had long dark hair with graying streaks and seemed shy and hesitant but had a diamond sparkle of craftiness in her eyes. She wore a simple dark dress with curlicues of odd embroidery on it. Kaelaa is a teenager with a brilliant aura. Wild pulses of mental electricity came out of her unexpectedly and her eyes darted around the room searchingly. She was tall and dressed in pants and a long shirt with pockets in it like a Russian peasant shirt. She had a large silver shield on a light chain around her neck.

It seemed to me that they were calculating how potentially dangerous I might be until Elsinaad finally stood up and smiling at me and indicated for me to do the same.

'Jwo I am pleased to welcome you!'

She stepped forward and embraced me firmly and we equalized energies just as Llueve and I do. When we touched there was a short intense jolt of energy that made us both laugh and feel a little embarrassed. After that I felt really at ease with her. The other Ovvalan women then stood and embraced me and we laughed as we electrocuted each other.

Llueve did this same thing with each woman and then we all sat down.

Elsinaad told us that we were about to travel to a secret place where others were waiting for us. She passed pictures of the journey to each of us and then led us up through the roof of Llueve's house and into the sky above Saala and off to the East. I took the chance to study the landscape and saw what could easily be the Sangre De Cristos Mountains where Santa Fe is, below us. If Saala is the counterpart to Santa Fe, it is much bigger. And in Ovvala it's not desert like at all. I saw lush fields and forests and a wide running river. Where the sage is on the plains around Santa Fe there are endless tall grasses and trees. There was a three quarter moon and passing through its light I felt as though I was moving through light, cool water.

We passed over country villages and cobbled roads and more thatched cottages asleep in the moonlight. Lights winked here and there in the dark hollows of the hills as we passed over. I could hear the wind in my ears. We gained altitude and flew faster and faster until we came to a great open plain that turned into a dense and dark forest which went on and on until the forest gave way to a shoreline and then we were over the ocean and came to a land of grassy, rolling hills.

We descended into a valley with mounds of earth and shelves of cracked rock. There were pastures with stone fences in countryside of hills with small groves of pines or spruce. We landed on a hillside next to some huge old evergreen trees that Llueve whispered to me were called Fiellistra. They are like a narrower and shorter form of spruce. These trees were very magnetic. If I passed my arm along one, the hair on my arm would lift. Well, not the hair...something. The ground was spongy with decaying needles. The moon illuminated the valley clearly. Dormant, leafless oaks grew in the valley where we landed.

We stood for a long time without anything happening. Pinhead lights of white and blue flickered around my head, which I figured were some peculiarity of having just traveled so far but later I thought they could have been astral guards watching our approach. We stood by a large rounded wall of stone that led into a huge, mounded hill in a clearing between the oaks where a little stream flowed. We stood silently beneath the ridge cutting across the stars above us in a long misty valley filled with moonlight.

Suddenly a man stepped quickly out of the tree next to us and stood in front of me. He was dressed in a reflective silver suit with what I was sure was a weapon strapped across his chest and which he was touching with his fingers. His eyes were piercing right through my mind. I felt paralyzed. A woman followed him more slowly coming out of a different tree. Llueve's eyes were big as saucers as she watched these people appear. I had almost pissed in my pants it was so weird for them to appear like that. Except I wasn't wearing pants but the gauzy, white robe. One minute there were five of us in the silent woods and the next moment there were seven of us. It was mind bending.

Elsinaad and the two other women burst into hysterical laughter, slapping each other's arms and nearly falling over. Llueve and I looked at each other uncertainly. This was the first time we had ever been in the astral with others and we both felt different, insecure. As the Ovvalan man came more into focus for me I saw that he was in his fifties and was powerful and serious. He smiled formally at me as he looked me over.

The woman had piercing coal black eyes, radiant white skin and long black glistening hair in a thick braid down her back. She was dressed elegantly in an ankle length dark red robe with flared sleeves with ornamented cuffs of embroidered hieroglyphics. She too was very serious and authoritative. The man was chunky and athletic, a little under six feet. He had a menacing presence during the initial first few moments of encounter but then became detached and unobtrusive. His long Ovvalan face and creased jaws, the coal black hair and Oriental, slanted, black oval eyes gave him a professional level of menace. The silver body suit he wore had an odd geometrical emblem on the shoulder that glowed like it was alive. Even though he was present and fully aware, part of his attention seemed to be separate, checking the spaces beyond us. I could tell that if there was a cause this guy would use that weapon in a heartbeat.

'This is Commander Silvaan of the Siddhe Guard,' the woman said with authority. Commander Silvaan and I nodded at one another. Llueve said hello. The woman inclined her head at me saying; 'and I am Oorden,' and then turned to smile at Llueve.

A well of intelligence throbbed electrically behind her luminous eyes. She turned to Llueve, Elsinaad, Kaelaa and Avaala who had hooked their arms through Llueve's in sisterly way. They giggled softly as though all the seriousness was just too much. They were just like elves I thought. But not Santa type elves. These were tricky, dangerous elves that you had to keep an eye on. I saw that Ovvalan women, when they are together, radiate a childlike love that is without any sympathy, as though they can turn their emotions on and off like a faucet. Oorden turned around and looked at me intensely for the longest time without saying a word. I felt her attention poking like fingers around inside of me. She was measuring me in some way. Then I realized that Silvaan was doing the same thing in a more subtle way. 'This is the most amazing thing I ever saw!' Oorden said, looking me over. She shook her head in real awe.

'They are ready for us now,' Silvaan said to the Ovvalan women with quiet force. Oorden spoke in rapid Ovvalan. Then turning to me she said -

'We are going to a high - um - security zone and I need you to give me your permission to lead you there in a blackout.' I looked at Llueve to see what she thought of this. She stepped to my side, looked in my eyes and held my hand. She trusted them and I trusted her.

'O.K. Yes,' I said nervously. A darkness like a curtain swallowed the trees, the moonlight and stars. Llueve and I continued to hold hands. We began to move, carried along by what felt like a wind tunnel. We went faster and faster until we came to a standstill and the black curtain rose.

We were in a high domed cavern of solid rock. It was lit by flaming torch sconces on the walls. The floor was covered by thick, ornate Persian carpets. A man dressed in the silver suit of the Siddhe Guard nodded briskly and respectfully at Silvaan ignoring the rest of us and led us down a long carpeted passageway. We passed something like a gymnasium where some fifty men and women dressed in colorful clothes practiced archery. They very politely all stood still but didn't stare at us as we passed. After passing many decorated empty rooms we came to a luxuriously decorated hall.

Burning torches set into the walls of stone lit up a sumptuously decorated room. Ornamental tapestries were fixed to the walls. These carpets depicted historical scenes and had writing on them that looked like a combination of geometric Crop Circles and Arabic script. I saw St. George spearing what looked like a velociraptor. There was another of naked men and women covered with blue tattoos fighting what looked like tall, standing insects and in another there was a sky full of black pterodactyl birds descending over a sea cliff where naked women with tattoos slashed at them with swords. Why did this seem familiar?

As we walked down the long room I heard music and looked up to see a man dressed in an ornate multicolored robe playing a full sized harp on a little candle lit wooden stage in a far corner while a woman played an instrument like a didgeridoo but which made sighing breath sounds - like wind. A woodsy, cedar-like incense was in the air.

A vortex of magnetic force drew my attention to a woman with pale white skin and red hair sitting erect and still as a statue on majestic throne carved out of the solid trunk of a huge oak which sat atop a thick, flat slab of bluish granite. In a semi-circle around the throne were standing a number of powerful looking people. Each stood in front of tall, ornately ornamented, wooden chairs set in a semi-circle. They were luxuriously dressed, each radiating a calm self-possession. They stood formally with their arms at their sides as for a meeting of state.

Llueve and I were led inside this semi-circle and in front of the throne where two vacant chairs in the center were placed. Each face there stared at us with great curiosity, even fascination. We were both speechless at all this. Llueve looked astounded, very nervous and excited. I felt intimidated by the intense energy I felt coming out of these people. My spine became erect, my skin turned to goose bumps and sensations like high quality ecstasy squirted in my brain.

A man dressed in a dark robe of a color I had never seen before - like a pewter-mauve - was softly swinging an ornate copper censer that gave off aromatic fumes. Later I realized that these smoking herbs allowed the people in the physical to see those of us who were in the astral. The astral and the physical were only slightly different here. Though I'm still not sure what was really going on.

The most arresting person in the group was the red headed woman seated on the throne. Her light green, almost white eyes, blazed with an intensity that actually felt hot when her eyes looked at me and seemed to see from yet another dimension and looked into places inside me I wasn't even aware existed. Her face, white as china plate glowed from within like moonlight and seemed ageless as a statue, framed by two curtains of shining, dark red hair. She had the long Ovvalan facial features and the peaked ears. Her skin was so eerily white that she seemed to belong to yet some other category. She wasn't smiling, she wasn't scowling. The expression on her face was undecipherable. She hardly blinked. A Sphinx.

She was dressed in an emerald green velvet robe with narrow black lapels and flared oriental sleeves embroidered with gold thread and was sitting sideways on the throne, her legs crossed and her foot flicking impatiently as her eyes took in everything. This, I thought to myself as I looked at her, is the meaning of supernatural. In her eerily white hands with their fine long white fingers she held a glowing cobalt blue, egg-shaped stone. She passed the stone from hand to hand, continuously caressing it. As she did this, waves of dark purple light radiated out of it in faint flowing waves. She calmly surveyed Llueve and I. The rest of the People present - about ten of them - were intense presences in their own right, especially a tall, older man in a charcoal gray robe who radiated a pregnant silence. But the red headed woman on the throne was so intense it was difficult to look away from her long enough to assess the rest.

'We welcome you to Logaana, the Inner Chamber of the Siddhe,' Oorden in her long blood red robes said, gently waving her hands around at the company.

'Counsuelaar Isult,' Avaala said, inclining her chin at the woman on the throne who cocked her head impatiently. Without attempting to say anything more about her Oorden went on. 'And this is Counsuelaar Djagda,' Oorden indicated the tall, silent man standing next to Silvaan. He was Human and had a beak like nose, long lined cheeks and piercing silver eyes. I can't describe how ancient he looked. His skin, like Isult's and like most of the persons around the room, was smooth, hard and reflective like finely polished leather. They all looked and felt ancient and yet were not old in the sense of looking wrinkled or worn or tired because the energy they all radiated together practically hummed. Djagda nodded with an elegant menace at me. Visible waves of energy pulsed out of him as he did this.

There was something untouchable about this Djagda. He was dressed in the glistening charcoal-silver robe with curling, spiral bands of feint silver down the sleeves and on the upturned cuffs. He had a reflective silver shield hung around his neck with hieroglyphics on it. The intense quiet that radiated out of him made him seem to be not wholly there and yet when I looked into the shadow of his eyes I was startled to encounter what felt like the razor's edge of a consciousness that then subtly withdrew.

'Welcome Joseph,' he said, nodding at me. His voice was low, soft and penetrating. 'Welcome Llueve Anaalia,' he said turning to Llueve and bowing his head towards her. This was the first time I had heard Llueve's last name. Llueve nodded, her head visibly quivering on her neck, her eyes staring in disbelief.

The man next to Djagda was black like a Hindu, tall and athletically and calmly aware, he wore a tan and black stripped robe with ivory cuffs on the flared sleeves, he had a long necklace of many stranded, glinting black seed pods around his neck.

'Counsuelaar Ideema,' Oorden said and a deep, slow smile revealing pearly white teeth opened on the ancient face. I felt series of loving electrical pulses radiate out of him towards us.

Oorden then nodded across to the other side of the semi-circle to the radiant young woman dressed in a fringed white deerskin dress that hung to her ankles.

'Counsuelaar Tantaala White Buffalo,' Oorden said.

A tall, strikingly beautiful and young - perhaps a teenage American Native woman with bronze like skin similar to Llueve's own coloring, smiled softly at us and inclined her head. Lights like vanishing lightning flashed out of her black eyes. A quail or pheasant feather stuck out of her black hair and necklaces of colored seeds glimmered across her breast.

Next to her was a huge, muscular woman, with a springy mane of curly, ant red hair and huge, naked, meaty, stick out tits. A thick white leather shoulder strap holding a silver sword crossed her chest. Her nipples were so large that her shoulder band was snagged on one.

'Bodiccea,' Oorden said forcefully. This woman had eyes like an angry pig and had engraved, bronze shields on her shins and a thick, triangular piece of engraved bronze over the crotch of her leather skirt. She stood with an impatient defiance, sneering at everyone and bounced on her heels, making her tits catapult as she stared at us.

'Yech!' she yelled. Her smile was more like a sneer and seemed to hurt her face.

There was an extremely Black woman I am encoded to not otherwise describe.

'Asaalen.' Oorden said next, indicating the man in the silver uniform who had greeted Silvaan earlier. He was younger than Silvaan and also wore the silver weapon. He nodded formally like a salute. Oorden then introduced the rest of the group whom I have also been encoded to not describe.

For some time we all stood in silence. The soft tones of the harp and wind-tube played nearly inaudible music and the man with the incense burner worked the smoke. The aromatic and transparent fumes didn't rise but sank to the floor and collected upwards in bands as the torch fires flickered and snapped.

Suddenly, in rapid-fire bursts of carefully articulated words that mixed Ovvalan and English seamlessly, Isult, the eerie woman on the throne spoke. Her accent sounded Irish or French to me.

'It is apparent to us that a powerful vortex of energy has come through in the meeting of the two of you. We see the hand of one of our circle who has been away for a long time in your coming together.' She looked with deep love and tenderness at Llueve, which made Llueve take deep, slow gasping breaths.

' Ea milicheen seraavria kin tel neah veer skaol.' Isult spoke in Ovvalan to the room at large but particularly to the tall Djagda who slowly nodded his head. Then Isult went on. Her voice, like her eyes, made me feel painfully awake. Her voice started a sense of motion like the wind gathering force before a storm.

'It is necessary for you to understand something of the energy construct you are in before we can begin to communicate to you who and what we are and what is going on here. There is much you cannot know about us.

'This is a 'Talking Stone'. Her words had a soft shattering effect as she indicated the egg shaped, blue stone cradled in her palm.

'Among other things the history of Mahaala is written in this stone. We will listen to its transmission together. Please be seated.' Everyone sat down. An emotion I cannot describe began to fill the room. It was like a religious ceremony had begun.

Isult cupped the Blue Stone in both her hands and became again as still as when we had first entered the room, hardly seeming to breathe. The waves of purple-blue energy streaming off the stone intensified and carried information straight into the center of my brain. I heard a strong, very articulate, low, woman's voice begin to speak. It spoke patiently and impersonally as you might hear an announcement at an airport. Everyone in the room was riveted to this voice and seemed to go into a similar trance as Isult. Taking steady deep breaths, I soon did myself.

Chapter Eight

The Blue Stone Transmission

'It is given that the solar system of Mahaala is an integration of the etheric and physical dimensions. This polarity is integrated by the connective tissue of Universal Soul Current called Loosh in Ovvala and known in Terra as Shakti. This interactive, dimensional ecology, is actuated by the Creative Intelligence of Love, called Suudilve, which is composed of All-Souls.

'The third planet in the solar system of Mahaala is called Illuva and is known as Terra in the Human realm and Aouvwhuaalla in the etheric. Aouvwhuaalla (Ovvala) means Etheric Fire. Terra means Firmament. Illuva, Terra and Ovvala are the one planet.

'Each planet in the Mahaalan solar system is also polarized and has conscious beings inhabiting it.

'Mahaala is simultaneously the name of the Solar System and the name of the Tribe of Souls that is creating this solar system and inhabiting it. Each of these planets and the entirety of Mahaala is generated and sustained by the process of co-creation called Ixtellar.

These are the fundamental structural components involved in the Great Work, called Ixtaal - meaning Ascension.

'The regenerative biological ecology unique to Illuva - the duality of Earth/Ovvala - is called the Biosoul Dynamic. This is the Seasonal transformation and renewal of Nature and is a Creator Technology for the evolving of Souls. The Biosoul Dynamic is a fluid, rhythmic, interactive sensory system constructed of and responding to the interface between Collective Soul and Suudilve.

'Souls in Ovvala and Terra exist as biopod, auric, fetal cells inter-connected by strings of Ixtellar Loosh. This cellular interconnection of souls, causes the cumulative expansion of consciousness to be generated between the individual soul and the collective whole of Mahaala. The Ixtellar language technology parallels the interconnective strings of Loosh, and is simultaneously the contextual design intelligence of the whole. Language both describes and constructs consciousness. The Ixtellar Continuum is an interface between the whole and its parts and as such is called Co-Creation.

'Let the above be understood before the history of Illuva is presented. Do I repeat the above?

'Go on,' Djagda said quietly.

'Biological development began on Illuva with the single celled plankton floating on the surface of the oceans during the paleophytic era when free oxygen was released. Biological development became accelerated during the Devonian period when trees were realized. Trees provided the first physical forms for the incarnation of Mahaalan souls rising out of the underworld called the Qlipoth.

'The refinement of Human and biological consciousness continued into the next major evolutionary stage which was the Triassic period, when dinosaur life began, and the Jurassic period, when dinosaur life matured. This period is given as 160 millions of years.

'From the beginning of the planet Illuva - by which is meant the Ovvala/Terra conjunction - there had been two Moons - the present moon and Iduuna - a smaller moon no longer existing.

'Planetary biology was accelerated during this time because of the effects on gravity by the two moons. Grasses and trees grew eight times faster and to twenty times the biomass of present biology. They also had short life spans and re-generated rapidly. This allowed for the evolution of the massive bodies of the dinosaurs. The purpose of the Triassic/Jurassic time had one goal; the development of the brain-stem in the dinosaur that would later evolve into the Human/Ovvalan brain.

'The initial incarnation of souls as trees, allowed souls to stabilize into physical form from out of the etheric. This period lasted approximately one hundred million years. To move into mammalian existence, these souls needed the brain that could respond to the Ixtellar webs. These are intelligent conduits of energy that interconnect the Universe. However, these virgin souls could not withstand the predatory violence necessary to produce the biological brain stem and so - Mahaala - the collective soul - contracted a race of beings from the Qlipothic underworld to do this work. This Qlipothic race, which became the dinosaurs, was contracted to exist in a state of unregulated predation for one hundred sixty million years in exchange for producing the Human/Ovvalan brain stem. Then, when the brain stem had been realized, they were to expire and go on to cosmic evolution. The breaking of this contract is at the core of the existing conflict.

'As had been designed, when the brain stem had been realized by the dinosaurs, Iduuna the smaller of the two moons, was captured by the gravity of Illuva and fell in the ocean at Sea of Aetlan - the Caribbean Circle. The explosion resulted in a global cloud that obscured the sun ending the Jurassic Era.

'The dinosaur culture had entered into existence knowing this was to take place. In exchange for experiencing full spectrum predatory satiation and the extreme corporeal experience of living in the massive and vital bodies of the dinosaurs for an extreme extension of time, they were to complete their task and then evolve. This lapse of time was expected to rid the dinosaur of the desire to be mere Reptilians and allow them to travel on into higher realms of consciousness.

'Over this vast passage of time the most intelligent of the Tyrannosaurus Rex created a reincarnation vortex in the Qlipothic Underworld from which they had originated. This is a small astral planetoid where they went at death and before rebirth as another Tyrannosaurus Rex during their fifty million year existence. This dimension they named Krrual and currently exists as an astral construct. When the Iduuna moon fell to earth, all the now dead Tyrannosaurus Rex and their servant subspecies - the Velociraptor, the Pterodactyl and the Pachycephalosauri - gathered as spirits in Krrual and came to the decision to break their contract with Mahaala.

'During the Jurassic Era, the constantly dying and regenerating plant and animal life had accumulated in the bowels of the Earth as biological putrefaction and had begun to transubstantiate into petroleum. This biologic essence of the Jurassic, and particularly the blood of the Tyrannosaurus Rex that had physically spilled into the ground, held so powerful an emotional pull on the Tyrannosaurs that they couldn't separate from it. Their collective, emotional body's devotion to the blood of their ancestral corpses became the dark soul force they named Draco.

'The sudden end of Jurassic biology was felt as a terrible injustice and betrayal to the Dracos. Despite their contract with Mahaala, which is recorded and signed in the Akashik Records for all to see, Tyrannosaurs were and remain convinced that they were betrayed - that it was all somehow a trick by Mahaalans to fool them into producing Homo/Ova/Sapiens whom they now hate like poison. They felt they had been cheated and were psycho-emotionally torn between leaving the Jurassic experience behind and entering Astro-evolution. It was thought the opportunity to attack smaller species, tear them to pieces and climb to the top of the heap of blood soaked corpses for 50 million years would be enough to make predation monotonous and repetitive to them but no. The Draco considered this as simply an introduction to the experience.

'The Draco felt that, not only was the Earth containing the blood of their ancestors and turning slowly into petroleum theirs, but that Human/Ovvalan beings themselves belonged to them, because the Draco had produced the brain stem that made this new species possible.

'Thus began their plot to re-enter life.

'As Human/Ovvalan beings appeared out of evolutionary time, the Dracos found they could enter their minds through the reptilian brain stem and seduce them with images of power and lust, madness and enlightenment.

'The first attempt by the Dracos to take over Illuva was in Atlantis. This progressed too fast - involved Human/animal cloning and the creation of synthetic and unstable power crystals.

The Core Mahaalan judgment was reached that the Draco contamination of Atlantis was going to deform the Ixtellar design for Humans and Ovvalans so that Atlantis itself needed to be destroyed. At this time, one of the Core Mahaalan designers of Mahaala, the Counsuelaar Ea, known as The Preceptor, was incarnate at Atlantis in the form of Iemanja, the Sea Priestess.

'To execute the judgment to cleanse Atlantis, Ea stole some of the massive crystals which the Draco Hierarchy used for power generation and turned them against the Dracos, sinking the island and destroying everything created there. Before this destruction, Ea and the entire Order of Sea Priestesses escaped to the then fertile Nile River Valley. This became the Egyptian culture in which Ea transmutated into Isis. Through these former Atlanteans, Ovvalan/Human life was purified and re-established at Sumeria where Human civilization then began.

'It was at this time that the OverSoul of Mahaala - called The Soul Traveler - which is the advanced energy Being from the Universal Core, transmitted the Ixtellarium which contained the systems of Astrology, Qabalah, sacred geometry, alchemy and Physics to the incarnate 33 most evolved Humans and Ovvalans of that time. These techniques were to be the basis of a cosmic literacy for Illuvans to evolve into Astral Free Souls and join the Galactic Co-creative Evolution of Suudilve.

'The ancient Dracos Lizards saw and understood the significance of this cosmic transmission. The Creator High Technology of Ixtellar Magik would ultimately allow Humans and Ovvalans to block the Dracos from entering the Human mind.

'In response, the Draco entered the minds of all 33 of the chosen adepts who had received the

Ixtellar Transmission and offered them an alternate existence. Whichever of the 33 accepted a relationship with the Dracos would receive acceptance into Krrual, the Draco homeland in Qlipoth. Once established in Krrual each magician who accepted Draconian beliefs - called the Ouroboros - could reincarnate as themselves, outside the laws of birth and death. Such an existence would allow these adepts to reincarnate with an undying single identity for eternity. In this way, they could refine their magikal powers to undreamed of perfection - not possible if they were to reincarnate serially and according to universal law.

'Entry to this realm of Krrual and into the Draco Council of Skarror, required submission to Draco Will and acceptance of psychical bonding with a Draco Entity. This involved mentally hosting a Tyranosaurian Lord. Acceptance of Auroboros meant rejection of the Ixtellar Technology. Fourteen of the thirty three adepts accepted.

'These came to be called the Andrr-Ka - meaning Those Who Go Passionately Into Darkness. These call themselves The Corporation, meaning 'of one body'. On Terra they distinguished themselves as the Assembly of the Only True God and in Ovvala as the Skandrr Royalty. These are nine Humans - six males and three females; and five Ovvalans - four males and one female who became, in essence, Draco. Their original Illuvan names have been removed from the records of Mahaala as their Humanity ended when they became Draco.

'In exchange for separation from evolutionary process, the Dracos required the Andrr-Ka magicians to promote a grand design; to manipulate Human/Ovvalan evolution toward the establishment of an industrial, theocratic hierarchy that would dig up the petroleum/blood of their Tyranosaurian ancestors, the Draco, and use it to create a global, industrial-state controlled by Draco.

It was envisioned that this would return the Dracos to absolute power at the top of the food chain. This was the Draco Master Plan. To achieve it, all Humans and Ovvalans needed to be implanted with a psychology that would make them willing servants of the Draco will. This is the purpose of the Ouroboros Language Technology, which is the reversal of the Ixtellar Linguistic.

'Be it understood that the individual Andrr-Ka members and their offspring were OvaSapien persons within whom High Draco Lords now lived and reincarnated. Being biological, each traitorous Andrr-Ka magician naturally died. At death, this identity remained in the astral Krrual for a time and then was born again within an ongoing blood lineage. Thusly, Draco spirits and Andrr-Ka bodies maintained their fixed identities through time.

'A Draco Lord was one who had lived as a Tyrannosaur for over a million years. Such a Lord could be reborn at will in the lineage of each of the Fourteen AndrrKa who had gone into the darkness. There are believed to be 17 Draco Lords who vie with one another for the opportunity to incarnate into only fourteen physical bodies of Ovvalan/Humans. The internal politics of which Lord gets to incarnate into which AndrrKa Magi is rife with controversy.'

The Blue Stone Transmission Part Two

The Implementation of Ouroboros

'The Ixtellar Technology is designed to guide Human and Ovvalan Souls through Crisis

Experience of physical incarnation and into cosmic spiritual freedom. Ixtellar means The Integrated Word. What is meant here by integrated refers to space and time.

'In the biology of Illuva, Trees are the extension of souls and Words are the extension of trees. Both are extensions of Ixtellar. Functioning in and speaking the Ixtellar language causes the individual to add individual adaptations to the collective whole. At the same time the whole is activated by individual intent.

'This interactive process of Ixtellar is of three main categories; Creative Speech, Time/Space Technology and Plant Resonance.

'These are the three modes of the Ixtellar Magik Technology of Co-Creation. Suudilve Creating and being Re-Created by Creation.

'In contrast, the Ouroboros Technology is the opposite and seeks to fight and kill to prevent change. It follows the Tyranosaurian mentality of the Collective Shock Attack after which dismemberment can be implemented at leisure. The Ouroboros is a direct reversal of the Democratic Co-Creation of Ixtellar. Where Ixtellar serves the whole of Creation, the Ouroboros isself serving and sends information and energy hierarchically up to a central Master to whom all others are subservient.

'Once the Dracos began entering the minds of Ovvalans and Humans, their first major act was to separate the two dimensions of Illuva from one another.

'This separation of the parallel races was simplified by the fact that at that time, the two dimensions only connected during the Equinoxes. It was only necessary to block these two days in the passage of a year to begin separating Ovvala and Terra.

'Draco possessed Humans and Ovvalans stole one another's babies, perpetrated murder and mutilated cattle to create supernatural fear of their dimensional opposite. Thusly Dracos demonized Ovvalans and Terrans in one another's eyes. Each Race stopped interacting with the other and the dimensions began to separate. Ovvalans came to be called 'the Fiery Beings' by Humans. The Humans came to be called 'Boogie' men, meaning 'thick-ones' by Ovvalans.

The dark AndrrKa magicians fully understood the effect this dimensional separation would have because they themselves were Ovvalan and Human. It would leave Ovvalans and Humans bereft and crazed as a mother having lost her baby. A sense of incompleteness and self-doubt would become the basis of a spiritual bereavement for both Ovvalans and Humans. This grief could then be manipulated.

'Draco centered their attention on Western Civilization on Terra as the mentality best suited to their Master Plan because here they found minds that worked with a machine-like precision, responsive to central authority.

'After the separation of Ovvalans and Humans, the Draco next major shock-attack was on the very monotheism seeded into Humanity by the Spiritual Traveler. This was done by introducing an impossible concept of God - presenting the drama of Abraham's willingness to murder his own son and calling this a good thing. Fear of God institutionalized as a response to Devine Love created a fundamental core of divine self-doubt in Humans. In such a state of mental fragmentation, the Ouroboros Technology of hierarchical service to a Master was introduced as a substitute for an individual interface with God.

'Creative Human energy was thus entrapped and used to grow the vengeful, jealous, psychic construct called God - an Entity who Loves Humankind and has Their salvation at Heart and simultaneously threatens them with Eternal Hell for independent thought.

'The implementation of Ouroboros on Ovvala has been different because of the etheric nature of the Ovvalan psyche. Being biologically semi-etheric, Ovvalans require fresh green foods daily. The Skandrr control of agriculture on Ovvala, promoting the synthetic cultivation of biological plant life, insures the disempowerment of Ovvalans by depriving them of the vital etheric energy they require for biological renewal. This causes Ovvalans to become docile through bio-sadness.

'On Terra, the Draco possessed AndrrKa migrated out of Sumeria in the four directions of Earth. Each was followed by a hoard of unseen Draco Souls from the Fourth dimension of Krrual who seeded themselves into the Human minds they encountered to advance the Ouroboros linguistic. These were the thousands of lesser Draco Tyrannosaurs; the Velociraptors, Pterodactyls, and Pachycephalosauri who are also a part of Draco.

'Breeding with the strongest genetic specimen of their time, the Dark Magi, established blood lineages. According to their abilities, some established Royal houses some Priesthoods.

'They organized armies and took over fertile river valleys. In these river valleys the AndrrKa introduced mass agriculture to replace the perpetual diversity on Earth that before Draco was called Eden.

'Mass Agriculture was a system of collective farming whose goal was to create a surplus of food and wealth which could be used for bribery. Thusly the Draco/AndrrKa bloodlines became wealthy and powerful Royal Houses and Priesthoods.

'Each new tribe of people that joined these Royal lineages and their system of agricultural overproduction accepted a contract of alliance with the Draco Ouroboros. This opened the reptilian brain stems in the Human bodies to Draco entities, which took up a subtle abode in that man or woman or child's mind.

'In the Draco vortex of Krrual exists a Tyranosaurian Lord too powerful to incarnate in a physical body. No Ovvalan or Human body seems able to withstand the power of this Lord. Something always happens that causes the physical host body to die within hours of this Lord entering it. This entity has never been witnessed. To receive instruction from this most powerful of the Tyranosaurian Dracos, The Master Tyrannosaur, it was necessary for the 'incarnated' Draco Lords to somehow commune with this Lord of Lords, as he was called, through Ouroboros Ritual Ceremonies. This is the religious mysticism of the Dracos. Thus contacted, the Master Tyrannosaur directs, generation by generation, the Dracos implementation of the Ouroboros Master Plan.

'Again, the Ouroboros Language is the Ixtellar Language reversed. Instead of advancing perpetuation, it advances exploitation. Armies raised for self-defense initiate war. Religions created to promote unity and preserve peace, become the basis for conflict. When a populace or nation grows too strong and begins to think indipendently, two or three of the AndrrKa Royal Lineages engage in conflict against other AndrrKa lineages in order to kill off the surplus peasants through war. In staged wars created by such conflicts, the populace of any rogue nation is decimated, impoverished and brought under control again.

'The Creative Intelligence of Love, was thus divided and scattered into past and future, Heaven and Hell and the heart of each Soul has thus become bereft with longing for the integrated experience that was the original design of Mahaala.

'Totalitarian agriculture, which allowed for the production of surplus grain and cattle, was given the People as a tangible replacement for the Biosoul integration of love. Prestige and status were granted from the Draco top, down through the AndrrKa hierarchies to replace the identity of belonging in the Ixtellar Continuum.

'Over time and by the Draco machinations injected into the Abrahamist Creed, secret factions among the three main religions of the West emerged, with the intent, that each should deny the sovereign value of the others. In each of these streams of Faith in the One God, a declension of Ouroboros double-think paralleled each True Faith, creating a basis for internecine conflict. In this way, the three-way split of Faiths insured that war could be invoked perpetually between the divisions of monotheism. Thusly, each could be maintained in instability and disintegration.

'This cultural identity of subservience to a higher power, the Promise of Heaven as a reward for self-sacrifice to a Master, and the ever increasing wealth and populations spread across the world. On Ovvala, the Skandrr royalty, which began in the olden tribes of Strereel, spread out into Skeelom, Wraiie, Tikool, Faarabehn, Aran-Skaala and Ultiaa. On Terra, from the Semitic deserts into Persia, the Mediterranean, Europe, Scandinavia, the Balkans and Russia and the New World.

'The kingdoms and religious organizations multiplied in both dimensions until they became the dominant power structures for Humans and Ovvalans.

'Spirituality to Ovvalans is not based in the belief in doctrines but in a need for psycho-electric experiences. It is normal for the Ovvalan to converse personally with astral Deities. Perceiving this, the Dracos, from their astral vantage point in the Krrual, began to synthesize astral deities. This is a holographic projection - called a psychogenetic construct - created to serve a similar function as the monotheistic conception of God among Humans. A psychogenetic construct is an inorganic being - an interactive, psychic projective screen - that feeds on individual soul energy and grows ever more magnetic and seductive. Ovvalans were encouraged to consciously interact with these astral constructs to anesthetize the grief of losing their congress with astral deities and Humans. Grieving for the loss of their dimensional counterparts – Ovvalans began to grow a soul sadness that is at the heart of the Faal suicide sickness. (Llueve choked back a cry.)

The Blue Stone Transmission

Part Three

The Siddhe

'Of the original 33 who received the original Ixtellar Transmission, 19 refused any involvement with the Dracos and vowed to resist the 14 Dark Magi of the AndrrKa. These 19 are called the Siddhe and are devoted to force Dracos to leave Mahaala or perish in so doing. The Humans of these are called Atlanteans of the Green Ray and the Ovvalans are called the Siddhe. To simplify things both groups are simply referred to as the Siddhe.

'The Siddhe then, established the underground fortresses here in Logaana, at Inxalrok, in Iemanja in Brazil, the Cucuru in Venezuela and other installations that are not to be voiced at this time. There are also meeting places in China, with the Hopi in Aridzona and in the Himalayas in India.

'The Restricted Information about Siddhe activities is here withheld as instructed.

'The Siddhe have also established evolving reincarnational lineages. Some of these were long ago interjected among the lineages of the Draco - AndrrKa. These lineages have existed in the form of minor nobilities and underground alchemical and Bohemian societies. Their intent was to lay the groundwork for a social system free of the Ouroboros Linguistic so as to one day surround and isolate the Dracos and prevent the execution of the Draconian Master Plan.

'At one point, the Siddhe gained control of a wormhole in France in the valley of Renne-le-Chateau among the Cathars in Terra. On the Ovvalan side, they held the corresponding wormhole at Ovaana. Ovvalan and Terran mating resumed during this time and led to the Inquisition.

'These caverns of Logaana in which you are now, have been one of three Siddhe Headquarters for 3600 years. Counsuelaar Isult took the throne when she was 81 years old in the year 1093. Counsuelaar Isult, Counsuelaar Tantaala, Counsuelaar Djagda and Counsuelaar Ideema are four reincarnates of the original Siddhe.' Isult bowed subtly. Ideema seemed lost in thought, Counsuelaar Tantaala seemed locked in a smoldering patience. Djagda merely nodded irritably.

'For six thousand years the dark AndrrKa magicians have been working to keep the dimensions of Illuva separate and to undermine the OvaSapien Races and for that same span of time, the Siddhe have been resisting them and building secret societies. The popular histories of both worlds are actually an esoteric code of the advances and retreats of Siddhe and Draco forces.

'The most adept of the Nineteen Siddhe is Ea who was a key designer of Mahaala at the formation of this Solar System. It was She who also implemented the destruction of Atlantis. Ea received the fullest Ixtellar Transmission from the Spiritual Traveler. She has had many names. Sildeva, Isis, Ooraan, Lilith, Quan Yin, Issa, Quinall, Facechial, Asaan, Babaji, Hercules, Ishtar, Morgana, Aphrodite, Magdalena, Vaara, Morgana, Indev, Mara, Joan of Arc, Guadalupe. She is the Maiden Consciousness of Mahaala - daughter of Uma – Universal Soul.

'There are extraterrestrial Races that are part of the Creator High Technology of Ixtellar Magik who are in League with the Siddhe to restore the Ixtellar continuum in Illuva. These are the Tankarugians, Andelmoths, Pleidians, Tau Cetians, Andromedans, Arcturians and the Vaddes who operate from the 5th, 6th and 7th dimensions. From their dimensions they are on a monthly basis currently cleansing tens of thousands of Ovvalans and Humans from the Ouroboros psychogenetic imprints. Some of these experiences are surfacing as abductions and various kinds of transdimensional experiences. These events are of great concern to the Dracos who cannot travel beyond the Fourth dimension to prevent these cleansings.

'Plutum is another concern. The AndrrKa have hidden communication passages through which they meet and import and export material. One of these materials is activated plutonium. The Terran AndrrKa produce enough activated plutonium to export to Ovvala to run the Skandrr power grids. This is seeping into the rivers in Daag in Ovvala causing birth deformities and poisoning arable lands.' (Llueve gasped) From this willful destruction of the ecosystems it is believed that the Draco Hosts do not plan to remain on this planet much longer.

'Technology on Ovvala has always been very advanced because of the Ovvalan mind perceives, in the Ixtellar webs the interconnectedness of all things. Skaalin disk ships have existed in modest forms on Ovvala for centuries. But only in the last century has Plutum been traded with the Skandrr by the One True God cartel on Terra. This has allowed for the recent building of very large and fast disk ships called the Aeron The Skandrr have recently imported lap-top technology and broadband Internet from Terra; technologies which were originally taken from the crashed Zeta craft at Roswell on Terra. .

'For some time now, Skandrr craft have intensified their flights over the remote country-side of Terra to terrorize Humans there. Simultaneously F-16 jets and Blackhawk helicopters are flying over similarly remote areas of Ovvala. It is not known just why this has begun. There is a new desperation in the AndrrKa activities that may be due to the intercession of the Extraterrestrials just spoken of, or because of the advent of Global Warming which is affecting both dimensions.

'The terrorization of this planet has been perceived by the Beings at the Universal Core and a wave of Creator Light has been generated in the Altandaar Star Streams that will cause Global Cosmosis at the Autumnal Equinox of 2013. This is a genetic remembering of the multidimensional structure of the Universe which will expose the AndrrKa manipulations.

'It is believed that the Draco don't know that Cosmosis is coming. But there is a heightened urgency in their activities that is not fully understood. It is expected that the final stages of the Draco Master Plan are about to be implemented.

This transmission is complete.'

The voice stopped speaking in my head and there was a profound silence and stillness in the chamber. Until this moment I hadn't noticed that I was sitting bolt upright, eyes closed and in a total trance of concentration. During the Transmission I had sensed that on another level of thought, specific information was entering my mind and being stored for later activation.

Slowly the people in the room returned to conscious presence. Then Isult leaned forward on the oak throne and spoke with an intensity that revoked my sense of present time to a greater immediacy. Making quick eye contact with all the other individuals in the Chamber, Isult turned to Llueve and me.

'What you are learning is that we are at war with the Dracos and the fallen AndrrKa adepts for possession of the evolutionary Biosoul of Illuva.' Her voice created a searing silence. Each syllable seemed isolated and hung in the air like a piercing musical note. She violently shook back the lustrous, dark red hair framing her paper white face.

'It is no doubt going to be a challenge to you to rewrite six thousand years of history in your minds and to comprehend the depth of deception that surrounds you in your lives.

'However, we feel you have the strength for what you are about to engage in or She would not have chosen you!' Changing her tone of voice she looked at Llueve tenderly.

'We know you are pregnant Llueve! And we know whom you are pregnant with!' Llueve could hardly have looked more startled and continued to stare at Isult on her throne like a deer caught in headlights of a thundering train. Oorden and Elsinaad had quietly moved to stand on either side of Llueve. They held her around the waist and stroked her hair and arms.

'Yes. It is Ea. You heard the Transmission describe the Counsuelaar who turned the Atlantean crystals against the Draco clone breeders and some of the incarnations she created. Isis. Vaara. Guadalupe. Ishtar.' Isult paused lovingly as though remembering each of these persons as friends.

'Mahaala - this solar system - was first conceived by Ea! It was she who undertook to organize the multitudes of disincarnate souls when we were still merged with the darkness of the Qlipoth. It is she who truly is our Queen. Me? I'm only sitting on this throne because the Counsuelaars are letting me!' At this everyone in the room burst into laughter and broke into applause. Djagda rolled his eyes. Isult smirked and continued;

'The Dracos and their AndrrKa slaves!'- she spit this word out – 'have suddenly grown very strong. They have contacted resources that we don't understand. The Aeron ships are a great threat to our communities in Ovvala and on Terra. But now you two appear out of the blue having made contact across the great divide! To us this is miraculous!' Everyone in the room made happy sounds of approval. 'It is just the sort of thing Ea would do! Come to us in our hour of need!

'It is very rare today for persons from each side of Illuva to encounter and procreate but not at all unique. At one time, in my youth, it used to happen all the time. At Ballytogue and Tara, at Logharne and Mayfair, Renne-le-Château, Ravenna and Koln - what sweet memories! But the passageways between Ovvala and Terra are war zones now. They are guarded and monitored by physical surveillance devices as well as psychic guards. Ea, in her genius, found a way to bring you two together in the astral so that she could return to us!' Isult paused and leaned forward resting her chin on her clasped hands.

'But we don't know just how it happened. We know, Llueve and Jwo that you were drawn to the Stonehenge Crop Circle on Solstice Night - but you were both in the astral! How did you make physical contact!?'

Isult looked at Llueve, embraced by the two Ovvalan women. Llueve tried to speak and began to cry. There was a long tender silence in the chamber before Llueve answered.

'In our childhoods we all learned your name Lady,' Llueve said through her tears. 'Of you, of the Siddhe and of the great deeds that have been done. By the time we grew up all of that had become only a myth that we used to remember as the beautiful stories of childhood. To see you here now in whatever this place or dimension is...' Llueve began sobbing openly as the Ovvalan women held her and tears glistened on their cheeks. 'It breaks my heart over again to think that you are real and that you know what is going on and are helping to stop it! I have felt so alone!' She sobbed violently and then shook herself and stood up straight, gently shook off Oorden and Ilsenaad and turned to me and smiled and said, 'it's his fault!'

Everyone burst out laughing - except me!

'I thought it was just a date to go see a Siddhe Circle!' Llueve continued, snuffling. The women laughed. Isult cackled with glee.

'Hey baby come up to my place and see my cave paintings!' Half naked Bodiccea shouted. 'Will we never learn! Same old lines!' I felt so embarrassed. Tall, mysterious Djagda had moved up next to me and whispered in my ear - 'Good work Lad!' Commander Silvaan leaned over and punched me hard in the arm and gave me a serious nod.

'But to answer your question,' Llueve turned to Isult. 'I don't know how it happened. Beams of light were shooting out of the field into the stones and we were just carried along by the force of it.'

'Beams of light you say?' Isult's eyes widened.

'Yes. Jwo? Isn't that how it happened?' Llueve turned to me. I felt a little nervous but there was an awful lot of love in the room so I just spoke my mind.

'We arrived at the Circle,' my voice sounded hollow in the cavern, 'and landed on the ground and then spirals of light began pulsing out of the ground and arcing over to the Stonehenge circle. The spirals of light floated us over there and then we were sort of got pulled into a portal and (I blushed) that's where it happened!'

'But how did you decide to go to Stonehenge on that particular night?' Oorden asked us both.

'I had a dream about a Crop Circle the night before,' I said and everyone murmured - 'Aah! A dream! Hmmm!' A meditative silence filled the room for a while.

'But not only do you bring us the Starry Lady, you two have very special powers!' Isult began again, the gentleness vanished and her white steely eyes were shooting laser beams as she looked from one to the other of us.

'The Draco interference never was anticipated. I know Ea feels it was her fault that they got a foot hold on evolution. This is her terrible burden and the source of her devotion to us.

'Now the Dracos – curse their name! - are planning something new that we can't see because our spies can't get within a league of them without their knowing. The Aeron ships they suddenly seem to have acquired are vastly more powerful than our old Skaalins so that we can't pursue them but they can pursue us! We need to penetrate their defenses before they attack like they did at Skevaal!' There was some murmuring among the others.

Isult had become very impassioned, sitting on the edge of her throne, her eyes blazing, she began waving her arms around. At one point she accidentally uncovered the Blue Stone and it started to speak...'...initially OvaSapiens incarnated into trees....' Isult screamed at it and clutched the stone which let out a strangled gargle. She yelled 'merde!' The stately and powerful Counsuelaar Djagda stepped forward into the crescent before the throne and spoke in a deep, soothing tone as he faced the assembly.

'The Dracos and the Fourteen AndrrKa are fully aware of the Siddhe in Ovvala and on Terra and track and pursue and sabotage us every chance they get - as we do them. But we have strongholds like here at Logaana, at Inxalrok and in psychic space that they cannot breach.' Isult threw up her arms and let out a yell of frustration. 'Ach!' But Djagda continued.

'The two of you meeting in such a manner as you have is a signal to us that seeds planted long ago are coming to fruit and that the Ixtellar integration of the parallel worlds has begun.' Djagda turned to look kindly at me and then at Llueve. 'You bring us a powerful new energy,' a soft, serious smile creased his face. He gave Isult a brief intense look and then said; 'Let us honor this great positive presence that has come and not harp on the negatives...' Isult tossed back her beautiful long hair and with irritated defiance interrupted Djagda;

'Bon, Bon, Bon!' She said. Ilsenaad and Kaelaa had moved to either side of the throne and began to soothe Isult by combing her hair and touching her shoulders. This seemed to calm Isult. She became regal and stately again.

'But you don't know the half of it,' she said, gently now, dismissing the two young women with impatient waves of her hands. 'Your love for each other integrates the two ends of the polarity of Illuva which has the effect of making you invisible to the Dracos!' Everyone there stared at us knowingly.

With a great flourish of robes Isult stood up, elegantly flipped back the lapels of her green robes to reveal a black dress and a firm, paper white cleavage in what looked like a green Wonder Bra just like the one Yvonne has. Her cleavage glowed in the flickering flames of the sconce torches on the walls. I mentally shook myself to concentrate.

'Ack!,' Djagda made a low, irritated noise in his throat, watching Isult out of the corner of his eye.

'Yes. Yes! Ea is very powerful and noble and all that...' Isult continued, turning her head so that her hair cascaded across her breasts. 'The underground movement she spawned among the witches certainly kept Napoleon and then Hitler out of the Holy Isles but nevertheless she can be so petulant and prissy...' Djagda forcefully interrupted her again and faced us.

'Your pregnancy, Llueve and Joseph, creates an integration of the dimensions of Mahaala so that to the Dracos - and by this we mean all Draco/AndrrKan influenced agents - you are perceived as empty space - as mere air! In the astral you are invisible!' Isult suddenly lunged forward on the throne.

'At about the seventh month of the Llueve's pregnancy, the vibrations of Ea will become apparent to the Draco Lords,' she said thoughtfully, glancing briefly at Djagda. 'Once the Dracos know She is coming, you, Llueve Anaalia and Joseph Soloski will be pursued on Ovvala, on Terra, in astral space, in your dreams - on the Moon... in every conceivable place and way so that when you reach that stage of the pregnancy, we will have to hide Llueve until Ea is born, and then protect Her until she develops a bit...' Isult shook back her hair and dramatically sat back on the throne and nodded mournfully at Djagda who cleared his throat and spoke.

'The Draco Council will soon meet in the trans-world wormhole of theirs,' Djagda began as Oorden and Kaelaa stroked Isult's flawless skin and arranged her hair and smoothed her robes. 'You could penetrate their chamber and be our eyes and ears and tell us what they plan. Why they are flying disk ships over Terra and helicopters over Ovvala - what they are preparing to do! It is of the utmost importance that we know this,' he paused. 'For we have reached a deadly crossroads,' he said looking at Silvaan who looked murderous and at Bodiccea who was quivering with fighting lust.

'But this is not without danger,' he continued, 'and you are of course free to decline.' Isult snapped, breaking away from the comforting women. You are under no power or force to do this! We don't like to put you at risk Llueve, or the pregnancy... or you either Joe!' She added as an afterthought.

'But we have no other means of gaining this intelligence right now...' Djagda said.

Counsuelaar Ideema had his hands clasped before him like a monk and seemed to be praying. White Buffalo had narrowed her eyes with intense curiosity.

Isult, who had leaned back in the throne now jumped up again. 'Dracos are capable of...' but Djagda interrupted her.

'The Draco psychic police are very adept...' he said in what seemed a forced calm. 'They are always inventing new means of spying out our activities and they continually destroy or capture our spies. When spotted in the astral, our agents are followed back to their physical bodies and tortured to reveal our secrets... Then we are forced to fight them so that they will not discover our physical locations. Your invisibility would allow us to take giant steps in knowing the Draco plans!'

'We know they have been mutilating cattle in New Mexico and in Uzbekistan.' Isult almost shouted, glaring at Djagda. 'They are kidnapping Terrans from Ivy League universities. They are taking risks they have never taken before! We must know why! But,' she paused, 'we are a democratic fellowship here and operate from free will and you are free to decline...there is *some* danger, 'Isult said, an odd grimace crossing her face.

'Some danger! HA!' Bodiccea yelled.

'Yes a little danger and yet...' Djagda spoke. '...Three Black helicopters flew down the length of the Instaal River in the Calaan Valley only last week,' Djagda said viciously. 'What could they want there? We believe it's a warning that if we try and approach the upcoming Draco Council, they will make hostages of innocent people. So there is naturally some danger in this but it may be minimal...'

'We will go!' Llueve leaped to her feet and shouted out the words, her voice ringing in the cavern. 'There is no *question*! We will give ourselves body and soul to reverse the killing of the planet! What choice is there!? Right Jwo?' she added, glaring ferociously at me. Everyone in the room had turned their heads and was staring at us. At me. Wanting my response.

'Yeah. Uh, Sure. You betcha!' I got that much out. I wasn't sure just what we were agreeing to but Llueve's eyes were on fire and I couldn't desert her in the clutch with everyone staring at us.

A deep rumbling murmur arose out of all present - an intense excitement vibrated through the chamber.

'Hekas ta!' Isult yelled out and everyone in unison yelled;

'Ta!'

'She volunteered of her own free will Isult,' I heard Djagd Djagda a say under his breath facing the throne.

'Yes, you fox!' Isult replied with a fiery look in her eyes.

Everyone in the hall was standing. Some began leaving the Chamber with a business like urgency. Each of the members of the assembly filed past us shaking our hands and embracing us each. The men patted me on the back, expressions of deep sympathy on their faces which I didn't fully understand. Isult signaled Kaelaa, Elsinaad, Llueve and I to step forward. Isult stepped off the blue granite throne onto the carpeted floor and stood with a tragic, regal authoritative silence until everyone had left the chambers.

'At last I can take off these stupid robes!' she burst out, cackling wildly in a high pitched liquid stream of laugh-notes and tossed her hair behind her shoulders. She unclasped the long emerald robe and flung it recklessly at the throne. Underneath she was wearing a tight black silk mini dress that showed her to have the figure of a twenty five year old babe. I couldn't believe my eyes. She also wore transparent charcoal hose and shiny, black patent leather, high heel pumps with golden, square buckles that reminded me of the shoes the Pilgrims wore. She shimmied for Llueve and said - incredibly -

'Let's cruise bebbe!' and cackled wildly.

She then turned to me and, smoothing her skirt down along her hips and said with a deadly serious face - 'Not bad for an older woman eh?' then cackled wildly again and pulled up on her tights and the women all started laughing too. Llueve's eyes were like plates, so full of joy, she seemed transformed. I had never seen her like this.

From behind the wall tapestry Isult brought out an old fashioned cottager's broom and straddled it with emphasis. She floated up in mid air, twisting in a curlicue of flight causing the incense smoke to swirl and began to drift upwards towards the ceiling of the cavern. She had been in the astral all along! I think.

Elsinaad, Kaelaa, Llueve and I all began to float upwards pulled by her intense magnetism. We passed through the cavern ceiling and up into the dark Ovvalan night where the full moon was shining on glowing pastures enclosed by stone walls. We passed over moon reflecting ponds with trees growing on their shores.

As we accelerated up into the starry night, Isult threw back her head and let out a really blood curdling scream as she banked on her broom and looked back at us with her eyes blazing with a fire of defiance and passion.

'Kaarrrooooooolliiaaaaaaa!' She screamed out a sound that contained within it all the pain, horror and longing that had built up in me as I had listened to this history of Ovvala and Earth - this history of the multi-dimensional realm that is my world. I thought that Isult herself was probably the source of the Halloween image of the night-witch in the Western world.

That scream made my skin crawl. And it made a deep emotional pain and anger surface out of me for all the pain and misunderstanding I had never had explanations for so that a similar screaming cry came out of me as though it had been waiting for release all my life. Llueve, Kaelaa and Elsinaad all screamed at the same time I did. With total abandon and unearthly courage, a blood curdling stream of horror and defiance bellowed out of our mouths as the wind whipped at our hair and clothes. The sound bounced off the rolling hills below and echoed across the valleys.

Deep memories flickered in the depths of my mind. I am not just Joe - let me put it that way. I'm not sure where all this is leading but a sense of identity is growing in me that I have known all this stuff before and have been with these people before.

I looked at Llueve who was on fire with love for Isult and with the revelations we had each just absorbed. She was flying through the night in her dream body with the witch heroine of every teenage girl's dreams. I watched her lips draw back in a sneering, feral smile of rage and love and lust as the scream came out of her lungs. I saw that she had psychically constructed a broom on which she rode imitating Isult and that she had changed her outfit to match Isult's except that Llueve's skirt was green and pleated with a pink leotard on top, black stockings and blue patent leather stiletto heels hooked to the back of her broom. She rolled her eyes at me in a way that gave me the wildest ideas about her. The other women were also on brooms and had altered their clothes. Kaelaa and Elsinaad were in matching blue and yellow go-go girl-like outfits with gleaming red shoes. As the scream cut across the night, I started laughing hysterically when the image came to me that I was night riding across sky of another planet with the Shirells.

I flew along like superman, hands outstretched - still in my flapping white cassock. Seeming to read my thoughts, Isult turned to me and looked me up and down with disapproval, her red hair whipping in the wind as we sped along, the dark bands of her stockings showing beneath the hem of her strained, fluttering skirt. She sent me an image of black linen pants, a very dark green, tailored shirt and sleek calf skin boots which, when I thought '...yeah, O.K.' I was then wearing.

Isult snapped her bra straps, adjusted a cute pointed black hat with a bent tip and said - 'Yahup! I am the cat's pajamas daddy.' and winked at me.

I vaguely remember Isult releasing me from her spell as the women flew off by themselves towards the Moon. I drifted in a daze through the ocean of blue waves and back to my body and sleep. I didn't wake up until the phone rang in the morning. It was Yvonne inviting me to dinner.

'Sweet dreams?' she asked over the phone in her murmuring, intimate tone.

'Yahup,' I heard myself say in a choked and stupefied voice as those dreams shimmered in my mind.

Chapter Nine

January/10/05

I let myself in to Yvonne's place with the key on top of the fire extinguisher box in the hall of her second floor condo. I knew the key would still be there. Yvonne is very methodical. There is a mail slot for the mail. A parking space for the car. And this is the 'hiding place' for the key. That it's the most obvious place in the hall to put a key doesn't matter a bit.

I got there early thinking I'd start dinner and surprise her; I mean, we had a date. Right now she was meeting with a late client at her office, which was in the same building as a large Santa Fe spa, where I sometimes went to use the stationary bikes and then the steam bath. Which is how I met her.

Yvonne has done well in the last few years. She has her own business, shared, with two partners. She has her condo nearly paid off. She's shopping around for a newer model car. I'm proud of her - I mean that she's been my girlfriend and is so together. That she used to read tarot cards through an internet site, where she had a four star reputation as a psychic rubbed me the wrong way but I'd learned to keep my mouth shut about her New Age assumptions. What is this thing about women all needing to be healers and wise priestesses? Isn't being women enough? I'll see a photo of a pretty, cheerful woman in her mid-twenties on a poster advertising Akashik counseling and life enhancement, when the woman hasn't had her first broken heart!

I used to hear Yvonne blathering away on the phone, telling some poor girl whose ex, was two timing her, that the guy would be back sometime between Thanksgiving and Christmas but that if the guy didn't leave the new flame before Groundhog day, it meant that a new love was on the horizon for the poor, heartbroken, bleeding woman.

I'd tried to reason with Yvonne about this, saying that someone left in the lurch or living with the aftermath of confusion and pain that is common when most relationships end, will clutch at straws to avoid the heart ache. To offer them hope is cruel and inhuman punishment. Someone heartbroken enough to pay good money to a complete stranger, to find out when love will come again, would cling to any crumb of hope to postpone romantic death. But, this was treason to Yvonne. She believed herself to be a visionary healer with karmic connections to a Russian witch.

I put a pot of water on to boil, slit two bags of frozen mussels, shrimp and clams and chopped up squid and octopus. I poured this into a colander to thaw and lit a burner and put on another pot of water for white, basmati rice and then popped open a liter of medium expensive , red, red wine. I unpacked a large red onion and a bunch of garlic, some chives and cilantro and laid these on a cutting board. This would really impress her with how aware of food plants I had become. I pulled out a double fist full of asparagus stalks and laid them aside. I pulled a good sharp knife out of her knife stand and began dicing.

Yvonne's living room windows face west on to the sage and chamisa covered prairie that rolls away for ten miles to the Jemez Mountains. There were patches of snow among the sage and tall, tringy chamisa bushes. It looked cold and lonely out there, and there wasn't anything to eat either. So I felt pretty good in Yvonne's warm, brightly lit kitchen. I wandered over to the stack of black, rectangular technological devices sitting on top of Yvonne's huge TV, and considered putting on a CD. I read the titles; 'Utopian Mind Massage', 'Ancient Mayan Yoga Workout' and 'Cloud Ten!' and wandered back to my cooking.

I was concentrating on chopping up the onion and garlic when Yvonne walked in to find steaming pots on the stove and the smell of wine and seafood wafting through her living room.

She looked clean and radiant in silky turquoise, bib overalls and a short sleeved white blouse. Her hair was shiny mahogany, still damp from a shower. She was carrying a couple of clipboards, some books and a small bag of groceries. She smiled uncertainly at seeing me cooking in her kitchen as I used to do back when.

'Chopped up octopus on a bed of basmati, salad and vino! How's that sound?' I smiled cheerily at her.

'Here,' she frowned and handed me her clipboards. 'The rice is turning into glue! It's boiling too fast!' She stalked across her kitchen, grabbed a sponge out of the sink and wiped the cutting board and completely took possession of the kitchen. She turned down the burner saying; 'and you have to sauté the onions and garlic <u>before</u> you cook the octopus...she needlessly dumped the pan of seafood in a bowl and started chopping up the onion and garlic herself. I could see she was nervous at having me there. Maybe it hadn't been such a good idea to come over early and have her find me in her space. I set the clipboard and books down on a chair and took a deep breath. I'd pictured a long slow kiss as she walked into the kitchen.

'Long day eh?' I asked her.

'Oh no. Not really,' she said airily, taking advantage of the opportunity to contradict. 'I often have people who want treatments after work and it's extra money. What'd you quit early just to get over here and thaw the squid?'

'Yeah.' My spirits sagged a bit.

'I stopped by Inner Visions to get some hand lotion and picked up this video called 'Bringers of the Dawn' I've been hearing about. She pulled a cassette out of the paper bag, and smiled her sweet and sour smile. She was starting over. 'You want to watch it?' She asked trying out a real smile.

'Sure,' I said and grinned. I reached out and stroked her hair. She leaned into my touch, murmuring . . . 'the rice needs water'. I circled her waist and pulled her to me - she let me and said ' uh,' as in no, so I kissed her and she pecked me back flicking a look at the rice and then stared at me aghast that we were doing this again.

I looked into her dark green eyes, so familiar and known, and the two years of our alienation seemed to dissolve away for me. I could see all her mixed feelings moving around inside her - wanting the intimacy back, fearing the alienations; wanting the reliable warmth, fearing giving up the independence. She let me really kiss her and then started really kissing me back. We took some long, breathy, deep looks at each other.

Yvonne put on the video and we ate off the coffee table. She looked farm girl cute in the shiny, turquoise overalls. Her new look, with the short hair and defined clothing brought a quickness and a lightness to her that I had only seen in passing before. The long elegant lines of her forehead and cheeks, her long smooth arms...it was all so familiar but also now, new. We ate the oceanic flesh which filled the air with a salty weather watching the video and moved closer and closer until we were all tangled up and sighing all over each other. This happened before second glasses of wine. I never got what the video was about. It was difficult for me to pay attention. By the time they were bringing in the dawn, Yvonne had taken off my shirt and was pressing her lavender bra against my chest. Red hair, turquoise pants, lavender bra, pink lips, green eyes. I was drowning in technicolor.

We moved to her bedroom where she punched on a CD called Chants from the Pleidian Code - which sounded pleasantly like angels humming in a tile bathroom. Listening was supposed to synchronize the two halves of your brain and access your supermind. All I know is that making love with Yvonne accessed my supermind. She says that because she's a Scorpio and I'm a Capricorn we connect to Spirit through sensual emotion. I don't even know what that means since I was taught that sensual emotion is illegal and frowned on by Spirit but I do know that for me, heaven has to be similar to making out on Yvonne's couch or I'm not going. I was floating on a purple cloud, my body humming with the angels when I heard Yvonne's voice as if in the distance...

'Get lower and move up a little - no, not like that - over to the side - there that's it - no, to the left - hold me here - it takes a while, but after it gets going it's fine. . . .' and it all came back to me. Yvonne's problem with having an orgasm. Or more specifically, the orgasm Yvonne thinks she deserves! I did what she wanted to avoid an argument because I knew that after a while, I could just follow my feelings and she'd be happy.

Yvonne only really had a real orgasm once in a while. But when she did, it was really historical, and she lived craving that one experience. When IT happened, her body convulsed in spine jarring snaps and breath expelled from her lungs in helpless rushes, while helpless, bewildered screams jumped out of her like little animals running off into the night. It was amazing. But between these experiences, she sometimes couldn't come in any but a superficial way and became frustrated and very demanding.

This wasn't one of the orgasmic nights. The night she had spent at my house, a few weeks before, had really been one of her orgasmic nights. That's probably what led to our taking another step. Eventually she quivered a little and was still. We were all tangled up. One of her breasts was cupped in my armpit, and I could taste the chlorophyl of her natural shampoo. The intimate love feeling was threatening to unravel between us by her failure or my failure - as she probably thought it - for her to reach orgasm. She eventually sighed and turned over to sleep.

'I have to leave early in the morning sweetie and its trash day,' she said in her deep, genital voice. 'Could you roll my bin out front?' She added a sweet, little grace note at the end. 'Hm?'

'Uhn-hu,' I heard my voice say. The orgasmic opiate that comes over me when I make it with Yvonne was flooding my veins and I could barely understand English.

'And on Thursday ,Jill - you know, my partner - is showing her art at the office and I told her I would help hang the pictures. I don't want to go alone so could you come with me?'

'Uhn-huh,'

'You're just such a doll!' she murmured into my neck. 'I love the feel of you in my bed! she added, turned over, extended her full, warm, rounded body against my side and clasped her kitten around my leg. She had me purring and making deals in my sleep. I remember a woman once telling me that she was going to tell me a secret about women; a secret, she said, she shouldn't tell me because it would be a betrayal of the secret code of women. The secret was that young girls first experience of males was as boy dolls who did everything the girl told them to do, so that when a grown up woman had a man's confidence in a love situation, she began telling the man who, how and what he was supposed to be. This memory was vaguely sparked by Yvonne's saying 'you're such a doll'. But before I could really grok it, you see; I was asleep.

I didn't fully realize I was out of body until I was going down through the roof of Llueve's house and into her bedroom. I was still feeling the warmth of Yvonne's body against my side as I became aware of Llueve sitting up in bed in a lotus posture, fully awake and eyes fully open, staring at me. I settled into a seated posture in front of her as though this were a prearranged agreement.

The now familiar sight of Llueve's almond eyes with their golden lights, her peculiarly pursed, smiling lips, the intelligence of her face and an enveloping love that made me feel really wanted, brought me back in a rush to this other world. This other me. The fine etheric electricity that is Llueve and I in Ovvala, and the focused, purposeful identity it brings out in me came back as our breathing synchronized. I was a finer me with Llueve in Ovvala, more interested and determined to accomplish something, more aware of being an extension of the living Universe. A fleeting sense of offering Yvonne a piece of my heart and it's being ignored was contrasted by the thrilling sense of Llueve accepting and actively reaching out for that same offering.

Llueve's Ovvalan face, like a classic profile carved on the wooden prow of some ancient Peloponnesian ship moved me into this other identity as though a different set of senses, a second attention, were suddenly awakened in me. We looked into each other's eyes and resumed the communication we had last had as though it hadn't been interrupted, and the different identity she invoked in me awoke. Though my body was curled up around Yvonne's in Yvonne's bed at that moment, the stream of consciousness that resumed with Llueve was total - it took all my attention and interest. I was totally there.

'You are right on time,' Llueve said softly in a low musical voice and smiled at me sadly. 'I was sending you a signal to meet me.' Something was different in her presence and I slowly became aware of it. She was very serious. Sharp lines of intention vibrated in her aura. An awareness of the problems in Ovvala relayed themselves through her emotions into mine. The babies deformed from the plutonium in the water, the Faal suicide sickness, the Nazi like Falkarr who roamed the cities at will snatching people up into their disks, the obscene display at the café with the viscious officer of the Skandrr that had man handled Llueves right tit and the Siel demon-woman on a leash; the deformities of children because of the plutonium in the rivers, all these images converged into a strange and intense sadness and anger, fear and horror in her eyes. I became very sober looking at her and felt the depths of her emotion all included in her love for me. A shadow crossed my mind and I realized at that moment that she was vulnerable to the Faal sickness. Our happiness wasn't guaranteed. It was as though love itself was being threatened in her awareness by dark, insidious forces and I was forced to consider that she could change, give up and begin to float off into the stars - loose her will to live. She sensed my awareness of these feelings in her and we silently measured the possibilities as she hooked into my will to live, in the desire I felt for her connected to the drive to fly that she inspired in me.

Since the encounter with the Siddhe and Isult, I realized that she had been thinking deeply about things. She had been empowered and altered to a radical degree by being forced to realize that the myths of her childhood weren't fiction but reality. Only this reality was in a different dimension, just as it was for me. Simultaneously, she had become saddened at learning the depth of the problem. She had to act or die. For the first time the thought crossed my mind that I could lose her.

'We must go to the Draco Council,' she said, when she realized I could sense her, understand her state of mind. We sat in silence for a while. The information that had been relayed to us by the Siddhe hit me with renewed force. I remembered the severe cautioning Isult and Djagda had given us. They had said that our going near the Dracos could be dangerous. Isult and Djagda believed that our combined energies would make us invisible to the Draco guards. But this had yet to be proved. I remembered my terror when the weird amoebas from the bar had stuck to me and followed me home. It was possible. We could secretly be followed back to our homes by the Adrrik, who sounded a bit more cunning than amoebas. It was not impossible that we could be captured somehow in the astral and made to reveal information about the Siddhe underground. I wondered - if my astral body were imprisoned would I become a vegetable in my sleep and stay that way for thirty years, lying in a bed in a hospital, no one able to explain why I was in a coma? As I write this I realize that I didn't take any of those warnings seriously. I just thought it was all a dream. I still believed that all reason for fear would evaporate with waking up.

But for me, in her presence, the ungraspable miracle of Llueve's pregnancy created such a bond of love and intimacy that I just wanted to bask in the glow of that feeling. The astounding fact of the existence of Ovvala - of Llueve herself! Whether dream or hallucination, was now becoming threatened. If the Ovvalans and the Siddhe were a dream, were the forces which threatened them a dream as well? Could one dream annihilate another? Would my love for Llueve lead me into the nightmare of losing it? These were the kinds of confused thoughts going through my mind.

Apparently, the Draco Council met only rarely when new plans were introduced. The Siddhe felt that knowing what those plans were could both help protect the Siddhe Underground and possibly prevent whatever the Dracos were about to do. The miracle of our love and the existence of the Siddhe all added up to a duty to go to the Draco Council. It wasn't really necessary for Llueve to voice these conclusions for me to get it. Before signaling me to meet her, Llueve had been in communication with the Siddhe and their part of the plan had been activated. There was already forward motion.

We held hands and gazed deeply into one another's eyes in preparation for our journey. We activated the instructions relayed to us during the Council and became very quiet and focused. Streams of information relayed during the Blue Stone Transmission coursed through my mind. I became aware of astral techniques for creating cloaks of invisibility, escape strategies, how to cut travel time between a point of origin and a destination, how to instantly get back to my physical body. Lines of energy led to the Draco Chamber in a living, vibratory vortex of personally, critically purposeful challenge.

I also recalled instructions about the astral nature of the Draco forces, the Adrrik - the Draco psychic police - and the BATS, their counterpart on Earth. These were hostile persons who were adept at functioning in their astral bodies and who wanted to hurt us. Our greatest weapon was supposed to be the Human/Ovvalan harmonic created by the baby growing in Llueve and by our love for one another. This harmonic love was somehow beyond the ability of the Dracos to either perceive or track because it fused with the universal intelligence and couldn't be reversed by . . .

anything.

The Dracos are an illegal energy form in the universe - their time of existence as tyranosaurs - 50 million years! is long past, and their responsibility to evolve in new and creative and adaptive ways is overdue. This rogue band of spirits that made up the Dracos were psychic pirates out to devour Ovvalan/Human energy - even though the Draco were only astral memories of existence, they were re-existing through the possessed bodies of Ovvalans and Humans working through religious belief, corporate power and propaganda. They've become poltergeists that refuse to believe they are dead and, like craven junkies, hunger for nearness to the Solar Blood, the warmth of life, that to them is in the approximate physical nearness to the ancient pools of their ancestral blood - the petroleum - under the ground of our planet.

With one last look of love and suspense, Llueve stuck her tits out, pouted menacingly and, tossing back her hair, smiled at me and softly sang 'karoolia!' and shivered - her entire will surrounding the baby within her, and her love for Ovvala, as well as our extraterrestrial love and our new Noble allies in the Siddhe. Her looking into my eyes activated my love of the Earth, of trees, of rock and roll , and my allegiance to Democracy and my hopes for a Humanity free of liars and cowards and pricks. We were each very self-contained and focused when we floated up through the ceiling of her house.

Chapter Ten

The only danger I had encountered in the astral so far had been the amoebas from the bar that had followed me home that night. They had clung to me because they sensed my fear and lack of control and I think simply because I didn't have a clue as to how to shield myself from them. I didn't know at that time that I could have made a reflective silver aura and would have been made me invisible to such parasites. Or I could have visualized a hot branding iron in the shape of a pentagram and stabbed them with it or visualized a mega powered cattle prod and poked them with it and they would have skedaddled away.

Where we were now going required a serious level of focus because we would encounter real predators. Psychic Reptilian beings surrounded by intelligent, armed psychic guards actively searching for intruders.

The Adrrik psychic police are disincarnate Pachycephalosauri and Velociraptors able to travel between the Draco fourth dimension of Krrual and both Ovvalan and Earth's astral zones. Besides the Adrrik to contend with, there would be the Human BATS. These were the Human covert operatives hidden within the various intelligence agencies of the shadow governments of Earth run by Reptilian possessed Humans. I had encountered one already. The BATS used drugs to go into a trance from where they did 'remote psychic viewing' of things happening in both physical realms and astral space. Most important political leaders, industrial executives and media CEO's on Earth had BATS guards monitoring the space around them - particularly in sleep. This was the kind of information the Blue Stone transmission had catalogued in my mind.

In his first book, Monroe had written about an experience he had with a Remote Viewer. Monroe was a successful businessman who traveled a lot in the course of promoting his radio stations. On one such trip he had flown into Nantucket and, tired from the flight, had taken a nap in his hotel. As often happened to him when he was sleeping, he spontaneously left is body. This time he found himself walking on a lawn in the sunshine around a Nantucket house. Suddenly, a physical man appeared pointing a gun at him. This so frightened Monroe that he was jolted back to his body in the hotel room and woke up. Sitting up and thinking about it, he realized that then President Kennedy was expected to fly into Nantucket for the start of a vacation. This, he figured, was the house where Kennedy was staying and it had an armed psychic guard patrolling the grounds. The implications of this were staggering.

Silvaan had conveyed to me, in a short intense communication-relay, the vicious nature of the Draco soul and the endlessly deceptive nature of the AndrrKa sorcerers. No lie or misrepresentation was too extreme or silly for them to use - in either physical reality or astral space. He impressed on me one main idea - the intensity with which the Adrrik pursued someone outside their own kind. It was beyond an inexperienced mind to grasp, he'd told me. It wasn't that they hated us, or saw us as their enemy, he'd said. To them we were prey. We were like rebellious cattle that have broken through the fence. We are their steaks. After scaring me half to death with this warning he then emphasized this; 'especially don't generate fear or you will attract them.' Right.

At the end of this exchange, Silvaan had gripped my forearm and I his in the Siddhe expression of brotherhood. I was moved to feel we were genuinely allies.

How can I describe my feelings at this point? When I'm in the OBE state, there is a timeless sense as though this has always been happening and is completely normal. It's like when you're dreaming and the most fantastical things are happening to you - you drive a bus up a brick wall and find yourself holding a gold fish while lying in a baby carriage and it's all in the flow. But now I was feeling an increasing sense of rationalism in the OBE state and a sense of firmness in the images as people and places appeared again and again so that the experience has become both an abstract dream and a heart stoppingly intense reality at the same time. Now was added the sense of malevolence. And danger.

Isult and Llueve had a brief but intense exchange during the Blue Stone Transmission in which a similar urgency and evasion techniques were relayed to her.

All these thoughts ran through our minds as Llueve and I followed energy lines over the night landscape. Under clear skies pulsing with stars, we passed over a desert like land with rolling hills and weather beaten cliffs. With specific directions to follow this valley then that line of mountains, we came to a deep canyon that we were to descended to a river, and then follow this upstream. At a certain rock formation we were to ascend vertically and head south a few hundred yards.

Djagda, Isult, Silvaan, Oorden and a few others of the high ranking Siddhe were following us protectively, cloaked and at a distance. At various locations we were to stop and send out awareness signals to see if anyone sensed alien watchers. This was a kind of mental sonar; a blip of awareness you sent out and then 'listened' to see if it bounced off anything in any peculiar way. Going along like this we came to the entry point.

This was simply a flat desert plain near the edge of the canyon we had followed. There were small trees, widely spaced, with sandy soil between them. There was nothing there out of the ordinary.

As instructed, Llueve and I embraced, and focused on on our child to be - this mysterious Ea. I concentrated on clearing all extraneous thought from my mind as we let ourselves love. We placed shields of opaque, deflective silver light around ourselves and hovered very still and then, very slowly, descended into the ground.

We passed through sand and then sand stone and then suddenly into a huge, rounded, vault. A luminous glow that seemed to come out of the sandstone walls lit up the cavern. Concentrating on not projecting our presence, we glided slowly towards where the ceiling and wall met. This was to be our lookout.

The murmur of hundreds of voices rose from the floor of a cavern about the size of a large auditorium. Men and women - both Human and Ovvalan - were speaking urgently to one another in groups. A growling undertone of aggression vibrated throughout the vault.

Though the cut of their clothes was uniquely tailored to each person, all wore oversized robes of either red or black. Some of the robes had high peaked collars reaching above the head. Others had wide lapels. All had flared, flowing Oriental sleeves.

Enclosing the center of the chamber floor was a ten foot wide band, fifty feet in circumference, made of white crisscrosses. Inside this band was a second inner band of glistening red. Inside this was a third band made of glittering crystal grains, about a yard wide. In the very center of these concentric bands, there was a sparkling, golden triangle. On the ground around the triangle of gold dust there were strange, unearthly symbols drawn in gold and brilliant red. Every few yards around the outer perimeter were what looked like water troughs or planters.

The mass of people stood at arm's length from one another in groups a little distance out from the perimeter. Their keeping a distance from the edge of the circle showed a definite respect for the powers at play because these people were themselves radiating a tremendous dark, churning force.

The feeling was one of suppressed and imminent menace. They were speaking to one another in a businesslike way but all the while a tremendous impatience was in the air controlled only by severe discipline. As the moments passed the set of circles began vibrating with a pulsing suction and I knew that magikal forces were coming alive.

Llueve and I held hands and beamed waves of urgency and information to one another where we hovered, motionless and tight against the angle of the ceiling. 'Maintain the reflective cover' she would beam at me. 'Stay close' I would beam back. We had been instructed to do this.

We looked at the assembly below - registering what Isult had told us - that this was most of the AndrrKa hierarchy - Humans possessed by Draco entities in Human and Ovvalan bodies - entities who had once been living Tyrannosaurs and Pachycephalosauri now possessing the minds and bodies of Humans and Ovvalans, from ancient, carefully bred lineages of power. There were aids to these Draco chiefs numbering in the hundreds of thousands but these were most of the operating chieftains now on earth. These beings were in willful opposition to cosmic order and dedicated to the control of Human and Ovvalan evolution and possession of the planet. Rogue souls. I was starting to feel sick with the horror and wonder of it.

These were the CEO's - overt and covert, of government agencies and vast corporate enterprises. They controlled economic systems, communication systems, industrial, manufacturing and transportation systems. They operated commercial slave systems, international drug operations, gambling conglomerates, weapons factories. Some were the heads of state of countries. They ran and owned sports complexes, universities, real estate and investment operations. They controlled massive industrial farming operations, pharmaceutical conglomerates and global retail chains. They operated secret intelligence systems and covert military groups. These were the powers behind the powers. The great majority were from old AndrrKa royal families and had been raised learning Ouroboros sorcery skills and been linked from birth through private social clubs and universities to other AndrrKa families. The one code of conduct they shared in common was a predatory competition with one another for the subjugation of Humanity and Ovvalans. Their only allegiance was to the blood of their ancestors buried in the Earth and to the Draco Master Plan of Full Spectrum Dominance and access to a power known as Vrryl - Predatory Creativity. And all of this was skillfully camouflaged from the people of the world by the perfected use of the Ouroboros linguistic by which they said one thing and meant another.

Astrally, this environment was radiating dark pulses of electricity where the atoms were at some distance from one another - a rough, elemental electrical discharge that purposefully resisted the finer points of intelligence in favor of an aggressive elemental force.

In contrast to this, Llueve and I amplified the presence of the warmth and love-filled mysterious life growing inside of us, the wonder of our meeting, our alliance with Universal forces and our awareness of the extraordinary Siddhe leaders out there monitoring us in the night. These Things below us, these possessed people, were the current incarnation of the leaders who had fought with the Siddhe for seven thousand years. They were the core powers that create senseless wars and ethnic conflicts, depressions and heating oil shortages. To these beings our baby was just a Cheerio. In the most ghoulish way imaginable, I was completely fascinated.

The intelligence within these beings was not for life. Life - the Solar-Blood - as Djagda had called it - was missing here. There was no glow to any of them. They were like black holes pulling light inwards.

We had been instructed above all to be prepared to zero in on our physical bodies should we be challenged or even witnessed. We couldn't allow the strange forces we were experiencing to distract us from the fact that right now the Adrrik and the BATS were invisibly and continuously scanning every inch of the area looking for foreign radiations. An Ovvalan or Human astral spy would have been sensed in seconds. But our unique energy construct seemed to be, so far, beyond their perceptions because nothing was coming near us. We were just air in the room.

I looked at some of the individuals - resisting the impulse to get magnetized by their power by tightening my hold around Llueve's hips. There were Ovvalans and Humans of every Race and color down there. I looked at a tall Oriental man dressed in a floor length black robe of some fine, rich, flowing material that shimmered opalescent in the glowing cavern light. His face was chiseled, intelligent and commanding. A tension of focused will and dangerously intense passion reverberated in his energy field. As I looked at him, he blinked once, then twice and then quickly turned his head scanning the room - to left – to right - sensing my intrusion and ready to bite somebody. I looked away.

I looked at another man, this one a black Ovvalan - dressed in blood red robes and saw his cheek twitch in awareness of something touching him. I quickly looked away. These people were hyper aware.

The Oriental Ovvalan in black appeared to be using a tremendous amount of raw will power to hold a state of passionate violence towards the other people directly around him, under control. I watched him out of the corner of my eye. There was distinctly one arm's length of space between each person. I realized that a lot of mental energy was going into making sure no one got any closer. It was as though each person here could barely stand the presence of the others. They tolerated each other for the sake of the common purpose in their meeting but they didn't like each other. They were allies for what they could make possible for one another and that only.

Taking quick glimpses and then looking away, I studied the Ovvalan black man. His cheeks were lean, his face long, his ears peaked, his forehead high, and eyes bright with awareness and glittering curiosity. His robes concealed a body loaded with athletic strength and skill. As I watched him, his gaze shifted within himself and I could feel him begin to scan from within what it was that had made him watchful. I quickly shifted my gaze away and as instructed, placed a silver star-shield between him and me inscribed with a certain banishing design I had been shown. A snap visualization. I then caressed the curve of Llueve's waist beneath her robe to shift my focus. Her still taut, flat belly radiated feline animal strength that soothed me. I squeezed myself against her. There was a warm security in our touch. We made up a dream bubble from within which we watched these strange, menacing creatures.

A very beautiful blond Human woman dressed in red and with a wide lapelled collar that rose into a point behind her back, had the same cold, glittering, reptilian eyes as those around her and the intensely contained will - her face was a frozen mask of beauty and cold, detached refinement - ageless, proud and impatient for the proceedings to begin, she squirmed in place. There was one man, dressed in red, in his mid forties to whom people deferred. He seemed to have two bodyguards. A quick glance showed me something odd about him. He was deathly calm. His eyes were wide open, his stance relaxed and his skin, though healthy seemed waxed and fixed in place. I wanted to look at him more but Llueve zapped me with a caution - 'stay focused' 'maintain the visualizations' so I stopped looking at him and concentrated on our job.

Quickly scanning from face to face, I saw in each person an extraordinary individuality and definition and in each face a power and will, an intelligence and refinement like I had never seen before. These were men and women who thought very highly of themselves and brooked no interference even from persons just like themselves. These were superior people itching to fight for the next mark of distinction.

I saw a number of Human faces I actually recognized (names omitted as per publishing contract) - a senator, a famous real estate magnate, a famous aging lawyer, a television newscaster, a computer mogul, an aging male movie star next to a famous model who was young and beautiful and hungry.

A murmur of voices arose as very tall men, giants, dressed in elegant, dark, tailored suits entered bearing silver trays loaded with tall fluted wine glasses. Lusty laughter rose as these waiters entered the throng of people and the tension momentarily lifted as people removed glasses from the trays. I thought naturally it was wine. But then I watched a woman carefully as she drank from her glass.

Her lips seemed to writhe around the rim of the glass as she swallowed the whole of the contents in one breathless gulp. Immediately her energy field quivered, shook and expanded with intense vitality. Her skin began to glow with health, vitality and beauty. A clear, circular globe of bright garnet light expanded around her. She turned towards the center of the circled triangle and became intensely still. One after another of the people drank down in one gulp what I realized was fresh blood and became entranced. The entire mass of people became positioned around the edge of the circle and turned towards the center. Complete silence fell. The intensity of focused will I had seen in each of these individuals was as nothing compared to what took place after they had drunk their cups of blood. Their auras joined together into one focused ray of luminous dark will fixed on the golden triangle.

The giants returned in sets of twos - each set carrying large canvas sacks suspended between polished brass poles. As they circulated through the crowd everyone carelessly threw their glasses into the bags where they smashed faintly. The giants disappeared through a doorway and shortly after that, six of the giants returned surrounding four even larger, muscular giants who carried a golden cage atop a platform by thick brass carrying poles balanced on their shoulders.

In the cage, seated in an ornate golden chair was a Human woman with long blond hair. She was dressed in a reflecting gold, hooded, floor length robe with violet piping around the hem and along the arms.

Her energy field was completely different from everyone else's in the room. She radiated organic Human warmth and vulnerability and as the cage was carried through the crowd, I could see a warm, honey hued force around her that physically drew the Dracos towards her. Golden honey ripples of vibrating mammalian warmth radiated outwards from her like sunbeams. Under the black and red robes, the Draco possessed forms jerked and heaved spasmodically as the cage passed near them. One man actually reached between the bars to pet the woman at which point one of the giants turned with lightning speed and struck him with the silver rod he carried. A blue-white electrical charge arced against his arm setting his robe on fire. With equal speed, the man ripped off the sleeve and threw it to the ground and stomped the flame out, grunted once and then resumed his silent trance. There was no reaction at all from the people surrounding him.

A rumbling groan arose out of the assembly as the procession with the cage crossed the red and white bands and lowered the platform to the ground. The silence became denser then took over the assembly. The woman climbed out of the golden cage, I heard the hinges squeal distantly as she pushed open the door and stepped down onto the triangle of gold dust

The woman was tall and full bodied. Her golden robe covered all her skin from her ankles to her ears - she even wore golden sandals. She quickly stepped inside the golden triangle with an obvious urgency. She stood alone looking upwards to avoid looking into the eyes of any of the silent assembly, clasped her hands in front of herself and waited.

At that point, her escort of giants took positions around the perimeter, their silver cattle prods held erect. There were a few moments of silence and then the other giants in black suits came rushing out of the door in the wall carrying what looked like red five-gallon gasoline jugs. They poured the contents of the jugs into the troughs inside the crisscross bands. This was a red viscous liquid that I realized with growing horror was fresh blood in glass containers. A thrilling, jewel like energy expanded inwards and upwards from the blood. The entire assembly shuddered and moaned.

The deathly still man now crossed from the outside of the bands to stand next to the woman. He was holding a long black wand and in a voice far more powerful than I expected to hear from his pale form, he intoned;

'Hekas Hekas Eberstray Bliblioyes!'

An invisible presence entered the chamber that felt like a compressed and mounting pressure.

Llueve squeezed my hand with three rapid motions - 'hold the constructs – 'don't get spaced out' – 'stay close.' The thought forms followed the hand-squeezes. I looked at Llueve and saw she was enclosed in her white psychic robes, a high collar tight around her throat, the material thick and protective. I saw that I was dressed similarly but in an electric blue material. The energy in the room was becoming frighteningly dark and magnetic. She wrapped her arms around my waist and squeezed her belly against me.

The sorcerer waved his wand through the honeyed aura of the woman dressed in gold and drew projected geometrical figures on the top of the cavern from their combined energy. This took on the shape of a portal. He surrounded this portal with letters and geometrical shapes that turned blood red and hung suspended, fading in brilliance but remaining visible. Once this drawing had been placed on the ceiling of the chamber, the man with the wand abruptly walked back into the crowd. It came to me that he was one of the original 14 magicians who had allowed a Tyranosaurian Lord to take over his mind. 7000 years ago.

The priestess raised her arms and let her robes fall away so that except for a gold bikini she stood naked. Her figure was robustly perfect with a flat belly and wide hips. She had very large, stick out breasts, from which clouds of a milky vapor wafted out and upwards.

Golden energy pulsed from between the woman's legs and breasts and spiraled up inside the golden triangle to the ceiling of the vault without leaving the boundaries of the triangle beneath her feet. Vertical planes of energy coming off her flesh carried the golden energy to the ceiling and glowed in a triangular column of honey light. A silent sigh came out of the assembly at the sight of the golden energy as of something precious and adored. It was very beautiful.

In contrast to the fertile, living energy of the Priestess, the collective energy of the assembly looked like a shredded black sailcloth blowing in a winter wind. A craven, sucking hunger lusted for the energy inside the golden triangle. Serrated energies emanated from the assembly and compressed into a vacuum. Hunger and lust from the assembly began pulling, pulling against the vertical golden triangle, pulling down at whatever was beyond the top of the brilliant column of standing sunlight in the pressure filled, darkly lit chamber.

Weird black serrated energy lines lurched aggressively downwards towards the woman but stopped at the vertical plane around the golden triangle, leaving her untouched. A growling hum grew out of the assembly as the black jagged lines and the golden energy seemed to battle one another.

The Priestess now started invocations that were repeated by the assembly.

A kind of life sucking thunder was contained in this groaning, moaning chant coming from the group. It was the sound of pure, undiluted lust and greed. The priestess was transfixed, looking directly upwards as the golden warm energy surrounding her began to pulse, her mind seemed to become vacant as the energy rose up and met thunderous serrated waves of dark energy ripping into the astral portal. The two opposing energies grew in intensity until suddenly from the center of the ceiling vault, an energy crack appeared and a black and red mixed ectoplasm oozed down along the outside of the golden triangle - it was thick and flowing like red oil or black blood - it began filling the entire vault with a dark pungent odor - a thrilling, violent, anti-energy - it was like nothing I can compare it to - it was like a hunger for destruction and lust and rage finely balanced inside a piercing intelligence of lust - thrilling, terrifying, possessing. This was the Draco Vrryl anti-energy I had been warned to expect. The assembly began to growl and masticate and thrash their heads spasmodically from side to side as the energy descended. Their bodies swelled and filled their robes and snouts began to protrude from their faces, as their skin became leather like and green.

Llueve squeezed me tighter and I squeezed her back just as tightly. I seriously wondered at that point if we shouldn't get the hell out of there as it felt like all control - by everybody - was about to be lost – 'f-o-c-u-s!' Llueve hissed through clenched teeth, in a strange mix of rage and sadness, love and determination - ' I heard a high-pitched tone ring in my ears and felt a fevered awareness but still remembered to scan the air around us for Adrrik or Bats but could see nothing.

The Vrryl energy spilled down the outside edge of the golden triangle then down onto the floor like blood laced molasses as dark green scaled reptilian legs appeared dropping down from the energy crack at the ceiling. Huge, tight bands of muscle quivering with life and power descended - muscles, scales, claws. Then a torso of rippling muscles, incredibly alive, powerful, different than any physical flesh I have ever seen - like a huge snake with each of its muscles quivering independently. Thick muscular arms, with little delicate paws and long clawed fingers solidified out of the ectoplasmic smoke. Sharper and sharper this came into defined reality through the waves of energy rising up from the troughs of blood and the golden glow from the naked woman. The reptilian skin, shining, dense, snake-rippling. Then the head appeared - part Human, part

Ovvalan - all Reptilian - jaws of protruding bone and muscle - ears like horns - huge eyes with luminous, pale green reptilian irises and blacker than black, vertically slit incandescent pupils out of which came the final evil black light - all the energies in the room had been leading to this culmination - a crisis of energy - in the waves of dark intelligence coming from those eyes. Right then and there I had no doubt where the ideas of satanic evil had come from. It was this Thing!

Three stories tall, weighing tons, its weight settled athletically down on its haunches. Then with shocking finality the long, spined, muscular tail dropped down out of the heights, slowly sliding down the wall of vertical golden light. With a sickening, wet thwack, like a massive, evil afterbirth, it slammed onto the floor and slowly writhed.

The reptile towered twenty feet above the heads of the assembly. The massive head turned with quick reptilian jerks and looked over the people. Its huge unblinking, green, eyes with their slit pupils of black-light scanned the crowd as it slowly turned in a full circle. The assembly, their heads tilted up, looked back with abandoned adoration. The thing's jaw muscles bunched and protruded as it masticated slowly with dense, electrically rippling muscles - brilliant white pointed teeth showed behind the leathery lips as the head quivered with restrained violence.

Tyrannosaurus Rex - with the intelligent face of a man. It looked around the room - unblinking – with unquenchable defiance, lust, rage and mastery. I had never seen something so powerful and in control. I felt pulled towards it, my thoughts reversing themselves inside my mind. I couldn't help feeling an intense admiration and awe.

'REXXON!' A deep, gravelly voice yelled passionately and then everyone in the assembly began screaming the name over and over –'REXXON! REXXON! REXXON! REXXON!'

A cold thundering voice exploded out of the massive Reptilian.

'THEY ARE BURNING THE BLOOD OF OUR ANCESTORS IN THEIR CARS!!!'

Rexxon's voice effortlessly filled the cavern with a subsonic thunder and drowned out all the other combined voices. The clarity of its pronunciation, with a slight, upper crust English accent was thrilling and terrifying at the same time.

'SIXTY MILLION YEARS WE HAVE WAITED FOR THIS DAY!!!' It said.

More screams of "REXXON REXXON REXXON!!!'

'WE CAN NOT FAIL NOW!'

Delirious shouts of enthusiasm echoed in the cavern. Figures advanced from outside the circle of the group carrying some kind of cylinders but my attention was fixed on the being.

'THE ARCTIC! ARABIA! VENEZUELA! THE OCEAN FLOOR!!! WE WILL POSSESS THAT BLOOD OF OUR ANCESTRAL SOUL!' Silence grew among the raging throng.

'WE MUST INCREASE GLOBAL INDUSTRIAL CONSUMPTION TO TWENTY FIVE TIMES WHAT IT IS TODAY! IN INDIA, CHINA, UZBEKISTAN, AFGHANISTAN, SOUTH AMERICA, AFRICA AND ALL THE REST OF THE UNTOUCHED MARKETS AWAITING ACTIVATION. WE WILL BUILD AUTO PLANTS, ATOMIC ENERGY PLANTS, SUPER MALLS IN THE CONGO, SIBERIA, MACHU PICHU - NO MARKET MUST GO UNEXPLOITED! WE WILL HAVE NOT MERE FIELDS OF GENETICALLY IMPROVED SOY AND CORN BUT ENTIRE PLAINS! - AND THESE NEW HYBRID GRAINS WILL BE THE SIZE OF GORILLA TESTICLES! THEY WILL BE HARVESTED WITH FIFTY WHEEL COMBINES THAT WILL HOUSE A THOUSAND LIVE IN

WORKERS AND CONVEY BOXED, CANNED PRODUCT DIRECTLY INTO MOVING SEMIS INSTANTLY EN ROUTE TO FEED THE POOR HUDDLED HUNGRY MASSES! WHO WILL PAY FOR IT WITH CASH MONEY!!!' Hysterical laughter catapulted out of the assembly. Snapping his rows of pointed teeth for silence, Rexxon continued. As his talking grew more intense, thick, gleaming, pearly slime began dribbling from his jaws and down his chest onto the floor.

'THE UNIFIED GLOBAL ECONOMY MUST SUBVERT THE GROWING ENVIRONMENTAL REGULATIONS THAT ARE LIMITING OUR USES OF FREE MARKET INDUSTRIAL PROCESSES! THESE PROCESSES WERE CREATED WITH OUR BLOOD! WE ARE OIL! OIL IS US! GAK GAK GAK!' The Reptilian let out a low, menacing laugh. The people screamed approval.

'WE MUST CREATE THE ATMOSPHERE FOR A FASTER CONSUMERISM. WE MUST TEACH THEIR YOUNG OUR VALUE SYSTEM! OUROBOROS! EAT OR BE EATEN!! THEY NEED TO THINK OF THEMSELVES AS BIGGER AND BADDER! BIGGER HOUSES! BIGGER CARS! BIGGER BANK ACCOUNTS! BIGGER APPETITES! THERE IS AN ECONOMIC CRISIS?! WHY?! BECAUSE OF THE SO CALLED MINIMUM WAGE! THE MINIMUM WAGE IS RUINING VENTURE CAPITAL AND MUST BE ABOLISHED! WE WILL INTRODUCE THE MICRO WAGE!' Enraptured screams. Shouts of delirious approval. 'THE PISSANT WAGE! ONLY A LOOSER WOULD ACCEPT SUCH WAGES TO BEGIN WITH! AND ENVIRONMENTALISTS! ENVIRONMENTALISTS MUST BE UNDERSTOOD AS THE ENEMIES OF PROGRESS! PEOPLE THE WORLD OVER MUST SEE THEM AS THE DEVILS THEY ARE - PREVENTING A MOTHER FROM FEEDING HER BABIES! - A REAL MAN FROM BUYING HIS WIFE WHAT SHE DESIRES! A TEENAGER MUST SEE ENVIRONMENTALISTS AS INFERIOR AND IMPOVERISHED AND SEXLESS LOSERS! IT IS THIS DAMNED ENVIRONMENTAL CAUTION THAT IS HOLDING US UP WITH THEIR GIRLIE ECONOMICS!'

'WE MUST MAKE THE POPULATIONS OF EARTH AND OVVALA MORE RECEPTIVE TO OUR NEW WORLD ORDER. THEY NEED TO FEEL THE URGENCY WE OURSELVES FEEL. IN ARAN SKAALA AND IN THE UNITED STATES THE NATIONAL DEBT IS ALMOST BEYOND CONTROL. BUT NOT QUITE! WE STILL HAVE TIME! WE STILL HAVE CREDIT!!' Screams of lustful joy.

The tenor of the voice changed to a low, methodical drone and ground like a diesel truck above intensifying silence. The thundering voice boomed off the walls of the chamber to rapt attention.

'TODAY I WILL REVEAL TO YOU TWO IMPORTANT THINGS!'

'THE FIRST IS THIS.

'THE AMOUNT OF OIL LEFT IN THE GROUND OF THE PLANET HAS, AS WE SUSPECTED, PASSED THE 'PEAK OIL' STAGE. FROM NOW ON THE EXTRACTION AND PROCESSING OF OIL WILL BECOME MORE AND MORE EXPENSIVE. THE OIL BURNED IN SHIPS AND TRUCKS TO TRANSPORT OIL WILL ITSELF BE MORE AND MORE EXPENSIVE. THE OIL BURNED BY INDUSTRY TO MAKE STEEL, PLASTIC, CLOTHES, COMPUTERS WILL BE MORE EXPENSIVE. THE OIL TO HEAT THE HOMES OF THE TAX PAYING CATTLE WILL BE MORE EXPENSIVE AS THERE IS LESS AND CRUDER OIL. WE ARE IN THE BOTTOM HALF OF THE BARREL NOW AND PROFIT WILL AMORTIZE AGAINST US! AS PROFITS GROW LESS WE MUST CUT EXCESS SPENDING TO THE BONE!' The crowd gasped. 'A deep, uncertain hiss passed through the crowd. SOCIAL SECURITY, RETIREMENT ACCOUNTS, SAVINGS ACCOUNTS, LONG TERM STOCKS AND CREDIT DEFAULT SWAP EXTENSIONS, MORTGAGE HOLDING COMPANIES - ALL THAT PASSIVE CAPITAL NEEDS TO BE RETURNED TO

CIRCULATION TO GENERATE MORE CASH! YOU WILL HAVE TO REDUCE PROFITS AND SALARIES AT THE BOTTOM! AND AT THE TOP!!'

Hisses and bared teeth ,sucking noises came out of some of the assembly.

'I KNOW!! I KNOW! I'VE ALWAYS SAID MORE IS BETTER. AND IT IS!! BUT NOW IS THE TIME TO FULLY SHIFT THE GLOBAL ECONOMY INTO OUR POSSESSION. YOUR TAKING LESS IS ONLY TEMPORARY! AND WILL STIMULATE THE PROFIT MARGIN AS THE VALUE OF OIL GOES DOWN AND STABILIZE THE ECONOMY SO THAT WE CAN LURE THE NEW CASH ECONOMIES IN INDIA AND CHINA INTO CREDIT DEPENDENCE. THEN, WE EXPAND UNILATERALLY TO ITS SUBSIDIARIES ON EVERY CONTINENT, ISLAND AND ISTHMUS ON TERRA AND ILLUVA.' The crowd seemed to mutter hopefully. There was a cheer. The assembly swayed dreamily on its feet, stunned to silence. 'WHEN THE NEW, EXTENDED GLOBAL INFRASTRUCTURE IS IN PLACE THEN BAAM! RAISE PRICES! Shouts of approval. YES! BUT THIS IS NOTHING TO WHAT I AM ABOUT TO TELL YOU.'

'GLOBAL WARMING, INDUSTRIAL POLLUTION OF THE SKIES, WATER AND LAND. ONE THIRD OF INDUSTRIAL SOCIETY ON ANTI DEPRESSANTS. ALL OF THIS POINTS TO ONE THING. THIS PLANET IS EXHAUSTED! IT CANNOT PRODUCE A TWENTY OR EVEN A FIFTEEN PER CENT PROFIT FOR US FOR EVEN ANOTHER DECADE! Startled cries of protest began. Cries of real pain arose. SEVEN TO TWELVE PERCENT. THAT'S IT. IT'S AS MUCH AS YOU WE CAN EXPECT- AND THAT'S WITH THE TAXFREE OFFSHORE ACCOUNTS.

SO WHAT WOULD YOU SAY IF I GAVE YOU...silence

A NEW...The group drew in its breath...

PLANET!?

Rexxon's voice boomed off the cavern walls actually making the robes of the people in front of him flap. An intensifying hiss, sounding like the ocean gathering into a large wave, began a long, deep sucking sound that more and more filled the chamber as the wheels in the minds of the predators computed the levels of profit possible from an entire - new - planet. When the sucking sound was complete, the assembly looked up at Rexxon with the shinning eyes of choir boys and girls facing the heavenly host. A perfect silence held as the towering Reptilian turned slowly in place, a little grin lifting the corners of its mouth. Rexxon's long muscular tail quivered happily behind him as he minced in tightly controlled steps inside the perimeter of the magikal bands. His massive weight heaved elastically from foot to foot, his head lowered and thrust forward, the jaws and muscles working slowly under the green scales, the eyes flashing their black luminosity into the eyes of each and every individual there. People's mouths were literally hanging open in wonder.

Unconsciously I had separated from Llueve. Only faintly aware that she was desperately calling me back, I hovered over to the center of the chamber and stood in midair at eye level with Rexxon looking at the beautiful green gold scales arranged in fascinating geometrical designs around his eyes and along his snout.

*

'FOR SIXTY YEARS NOW THE HIGH DRACO COUNCIL OF OVERLORDS HAS BEEN IN PARTNERSHIP WITH THE JANOSIAN ARMADA. IN FACT WE MET WITH THE JANOS THE SAME WEEK WE MET WITH EISENHOWER. THE JANOSIANS ARE ANCIENT AND HOMELESS NOMADS ON NIBIRU NOW BUT ORIGINALLY FROM THE UDRAN SECTOR OF

THE UNIVERSE. THEY EXHAUSTED THEIR BIOSPHERE AND THEIR PLANET DIED. BOO-HOO! NINE THOUSAND YEARS AGO, THEY BEGAN LIVING IN LIFE SUPPORT SYSTEMS AND HAVE BEEN TRAVELING IN AN ARMADA OF SPACE CRAFT THROUGH DEEP SPACE LOOKING FOR A TENABLE BIOSPHERE THAT THEY COULD COLONIZE. THEY WANT TO STOP NOW. THEY WANT EARTH! BUT WHAT WILL THEY PAY FOR IT? Quizzical sounds came out of the crowd.

JANOSIANS ARE SUPREME MASTERS OF CLONE ENGINEERING AS DEMONSTRATED BY THEIR CREATION OF THE GRAYS - THEIR HIGHLY INTELLIGENT AND TECHNOLOGICALLY PROFICIENT REPLICATIONS.

'FOR FORTY YEARS THE ABDUCTION SQUADS HAVE BEEN GATHERING GENETIC MATERIAL IN SAALA AND CHEVY CHASE, ULAARAN AND BEL AIR, MOSCOW, TOKYO, (OTHER CITIES) AND ALL THE OTHER HOT SHOT CITIES.

'WE HAVE ACCUMULATED QUITE A LIBRARY OF GENETIC MATERIAL FROM THE BEST HUMAN AND OVVALAN BLOODLINES! FROM THE AGGRESSORS!'

'IN EXCHANGE FOR THIS PLANET JANOSIANS WILL GROW CLONES WITH THAT GENETIC MATERIAL FOR US TO INHABIT. HENCEFORTH THERE WILL BE NO NEED TO DISPLACE SOME HUMAN SOUL WITH SLOPPY HABITS. FOR THESE BODIES ARE VIRGINS! NO ONE EVER LIVED IN THEM! GAK! GAK! GAK! A gasp of disbelief hissed through the chamber as people absorbed this new line.

Thrilled, staccato screeches came from a few individuals who seemed to intuit what REXXON was about to reveal.

WE HAVE BLOOD DRIVES IN PALM BEACH, ELBAEL, OCCOTA, BERLIN, PARIS AND BEIJING, SANTA BARBARA, DUBAI, SAU PAULO, OCELLO, AND BANG COCK GOING NOW! WE WILL HAVE A WAREHOUSE OF BODIES TO POSSESS, PLAY WITH, EAT AND THEN JUST JUMP IN ANOTHER BODY! A CONTINUOUS SUPPLY OF YOUNG BLOOD!' The crowd hummed in wonder.

'UNDER OUR INSTRUCTIONS, THE JANOSIANS HAVE PLACED THEIR LABORATORY MOTHERSHIP IN DEEP SPACE ORBIT BEHIND THE MOON TO AVOID HUMAN AND OVVALAN OBSERVATION. THERE WILL BE NO NEED TO CAPTURE LIVING PEOPLE AND KEEP THEM ALIVE UNTIL WE NEED HOSTS AS WE HAVE TO NOW. THIS WILL SAVE TREMENDOUSLY ON OVERHEAD EXPENSES. AND BE ASSURED THAT I GET THE TWENTY PERCENT TRANSACTION FEE FOR SELLING THE PLANET SO DON'T DICK ME AROUND!'

'AND WE WILL HAPPILY LET THE JANOSIANS HAVE THE EARTH BECAUSE WE ... at this point I was so caught up in the suspense that I pissed in my robe.

'ARE GOING...the silence was deafening.

'TO MARS!'

After a moment's stunned silence the assembly began screaming wildly, uncontrollably, Rexxon threw back his enormous jawed head and laughed

'GAK GAK GAK' - and I too laughed at what seemed the incredible genius of his plan as the reptilian possessed bodies below me howled and slapped each other on their arms and backs.

'BUT LISTEN! WE MUST HURRY!' REXXON roared and silence fell.

'ALREADY THE ARTIC ICE IS MELTING FASTER THAN WE ANTICIPATED. 'WITHIN TEN YEARS IT WILL BE ENTIRELY LIQUIFIED! THE MARTIAN PROBES SENT UP 17 YEARS AGO HAVE LANDED INTACT AND ARE LAYING THE FOUNDATIONS FOR THE HUTS WHERE THE FIRST COLONISTS WILL LIVE AND WORK. AND THE PRESIDENT...' '...YES, - ARRAGONLOCON! HAS BEEN RE-ELECTED AND PRINCE KABAKADAKABA - MY OWN BROTHER! - WHO NOW STANDS THIS CLOSE TO THE THRONE OF POWER,' Rexxon held two curved and glistening claws together which elicited cheers. 'HAS ANNOUNCED THE GOAL OF REVIVING THE SPACE PROGRAM AS A MAJOR GLOBAL PRIORITY! THIS DREAM MUST BE SOLD WITH THE GREATEST AGGRESSION WE CAN GENERATE BECAUSE IT WILL TAKE ONE QUADRILLION DOLLARS U.S. TO ESTABLISH THE MARTIAN COLONIES! WE WILL BUILD SHIPS AND LOAD THEM WITH THOUSANDS OF HUMANS AND OVVALANS WHO WILL BELIEVE THEY ARE GOING TO COLONIZE THE NEW PLANET. BUT OF COURSE THEY WILL BE OUR MEAT, OUR DRINK, OUR SPORT, OUR CADDIES AND ULTIMATELY THE COMPOST THAT WILL FERTILIZE THE SOIL OF OUR NEW HOME JUST AS OUR ANCESTORS FERTILIZED THE SOIL OF THIS PLANET BY CRASHING XILICA ON TOP OF US. AND WE WILL NEED FERTILE SOIL ON MARS.

BECAUSE THE JANOSIANS HAVE A SECOND CLONING ASSIGNMENT FROM US! THE FINAL PAYMENT FOR THE JANNIES WILL BE TO REVIVE THE ECO-SYSTEM OF OUR ANCESTORS! WE WILL BRING TO LIFE - WAIT FOR IT -

THE JURASSIC!

I couldn't even breathe.

YES! OUR JURASSIC HOMELAND IN ITS ENTIRETY WILL BE REVIVED AGAIN - ALL THE PLANTS - ALL THE MINOR EDIBLE SPECIES THAT WERE OUR LIVING FOOD! WE WILL WALK LIKE KINGS ONCE MORE! THIS ISN'T JURASSIC PARK! - THIS IS JURA-LISCIOUS PARADISE!!! GAK! GAK! GAK! The assembly was delirious with love now; swaying, hugging and arm waving was going on everywhere.

'SILENCE!'

'A QUADRILLION BUCKS ISN'T JUST GOING TO FALL IN OUR LAPS! WE WILL STILL HAVE TO WORK FOR IT. HUMANS AND OVVALANS ONLY RISE TO REAL PRODUCTIVITY WHEN THERE IS WAR. UNTIL NOW WE HAVE BEEN CONTENT TO PIT NATION AGAINST NATION TO DIRECT SUCH PRODUCTIVITY. BUT THIS ENTAILS TOO MUCH LOSS OF INFRASTRUCTURE.

'WHAT WE NEED IS AN ENEMY COMMON TO ALL HUMANS AND OVVALANS. AN EXTRATERRESTRIAL ENEMY!

'THE JANOSIANS HAVE THEIR OWN LIBRARY OF INTERGALACTIC GENETIC CLONING MATERIAL FROM ABDUCTIONS AND RECOMBINATION EXPERIMENTS. IN EXCHANGE FOR OUR ALLOWING THEM TO ABDUCT A QUOTA OF HUMANS AND TO HARVEST WATER FROM THE OCEAN, THEY ARE GROWING THESE EXTRATERRESTRIAL CLONES FOR US TO SHOW TO HUMANS AND OVVALANS. AND LET ME TELL YOU, THEY'RE REALLY UGLY CUSTOMERS. EVEN I WOULDN'T EAT ONE! GAK GAK GAK! THESE CLONES WILL BE DISCOVERED IN OVVALA IN CRASHED HELICOPTERS AND ON EARTH IN DISPOSABLE ANTI GRAVITY DISKS TO CREATE THE IMPRESSION OF AN EXTRATERRESTRIAL INVASION.

'WE NEED TO MOVE VERY FAST FROM THIS POINT OR THIS WILL ALL REMAIN BUT A

DREAM! YOU ARE TO DRIVE HUMANS AND OVVALANS TO THE NECESSARY LEVEL OF PRODUCTIVITY WITH THE NEWS OF AN EXTRATERRESTRIAL INVASION IMMEDIATELY! FLY-OVERS MUST BEGIN YESTERDAY! EVEN THOUGH THE CLONES WON'T BE READY FOR A FEW MONTHS, WE WILL SOON BROADCAST FROM EVERY SATELLITE THAT THE INVASION IS BASED ON THE RED PLANET AND THAT WE MUST SET UP A MILITARY POSITION ON THE MOON FROM WHICH TO DEFEND EARTH! IT WILL BE REVEALED THAT MARS IS THE DEAD SEA SCROLL SECRET CODE NAME FOR HEAVEN! WHEN PEOPLE LEARN THAT IT IS BEING TAKEN OVER BY EVIL EXTRATERRESTRIALS THEY WILL SEE WE HAVE NO CHOICE BUT TO BOMB HEAVEN TO GET IT BACK!! WE WILL RAISE PEOPLE TO A LEVEL OF TERROR THEY HAVE NEVER IMAGINED AND HARNESS THAT ENERGY FOR A PRODUCTIVITY AND CONSUMERISM NEVER CONCEIVED IN THE HISTORY OF THE MILKY WAY!!!'

'REXXON! REXXON! REXXON!' Glassy eyed, the mob of Reptilians chanted as one voice.

In my trance I saw the sense of this. Human evolution was taking too long. The teeming masses of the uneducated and unmotivated poor all over the world were just a massive burden holding back the accomplishment of a true excellence and realization of the only real democracy possible - a democracy of owners - of masters. I myself could play a part in this. Images of prefabricated gazebos and garages, fencing and ornamental tool sheds of my design, manufactured cheaply in China and Brazil for sale in Super WalMarts and all around the world through the Internet flashed across my mind. I could have a Georgian mansion in Georgia and a castle in Spain. I could drive up to sky scrapers in Thailand, travel between airports in a limo with Victoria's Angels dressed in confetti and gossamer tripping over themselves to press their curving bodies against me. I could also go to Mars and landscape the new developments - Sun City Mars! – I could help colonize space for the true kings of Earth and be among these elect of the Human-Ovvalan elite... REXXON'S voice woke me up from this dream.

'ACROSS THE ENTIRE SURFACE OF MARS, IN THE CLEARINGS BETWEEN FORESTS OF JURASSIC GREENERY, WHERE OUR PREY WILL BE REPRODUCING, THERE WILL BE FAIRWAYS AND GREENS, METEOR HOLE SAND TRAPS AND MESAS FOR TEEING OFF. YOU CAN JOIN ME IN THE DARNDEST GAME OF GOLF YOU EVER SAW! WE CAN PLAY OUR WAY FROM CONTINENT TO CONTINENT, EATING OUR CADDIES...

FOOOUUUUURRRRRRR!!!!!

Rexxon screamed this last word and the entire assembly echoed it like angels singing from another world as everyone, myself included, gazed adoringly at REXXON! - Lizard Number One.

Tall men in robes had advanced through the group carrying more shiny, red jugs which they now poured into the vats standing around the periphery of the circle. When the giants kicked over the vats I saw they were full of raw petroleum and that what they had added was congealing blood. Oil... Oil and Blood! - That's what it was - Oil and Blood! The Tyrannosaur began roaring, his reptilian snout snapping his teeth. He threw himself on the ground and flung himself around wildly, licking the oil and blood off his little, childlike arms. He licked the ground. One of the giants was too slow stepping away from the perimeter and REXXON's lightning jaws lunged out and crunched down around him. The head and a leg fell off and slid into the crowd. He tossed the remaining carcass into the mass of shouting, cheering Reptilians, knocking over about twenty of them who began licking the dead giant's blood off their clothes.

The Priestess had frozen in a trance inside the gold triangle, she stared vertically up, white eyed with terror, naked and drained of energy. She slumped, quivering, trying to not make eye contact with the maddened Reptilians.

Four giants dressed in red surrounded her. One of them threw her golden robe around her and roughly stuffed her into the golden cage. Locking her in, the giants advanced through the crowd with their shock-wands extended. They carried the cage through the hundreds of screaming Draco vampires, moving as quickly as they could, as the Priestess drunkenly clutched the golden bars in an exhausted stupor.

'REXXON! REXXON! REXXON!' The crowd screamed in a frenzy of renewed lust and greed. 'FFOOOOOOUUUUURRRRRRR!!!' others yelled.

Both females and males, with Homosauran faces leaped at the golden cage as it passed them, held high on the shoulders of the giants. Their faces distorted, with fanatical, haunted eyes, they licked the bars of the cage with incredibly long tongues and were electrocuted by the weapons of the guards and just laughed at their seared arms and legs and burning robes.

'Jwo! Jwo!' I faintly and uncomprehendingly heard Llueve's cries behind me.

At this point the vibrations were overwhelming. Suddenly, Rexxon stood on his massive haunches, oil and blood dripping off his magnificent body, blood, saliva and oil dripping out of his opened jaws. He stood to his full height, vibrating with vitality and power. Thrusting his snout forwards, he screamed a long, howling Tyrannosaur scream as he looked right into my eyes.

'Jwo! Turn around! Turn around Jwo!' Llueve's voice was cracking with the effort of getting my attention.

Quicker than thought, the monster leaned forward and raked my chest with its claws, slicing my robe open and throwing me back against the wall. Rexxon squatted down on his haunches and with an ear splitting roar, leaped up and vanished beyond the top of the golden triangle in a bone jarring clap of thunder.

I was pierced to the heart and immobilized, suspended against the ceiling in midair over the hundreds of wild, screaming Homosaurs who were looking up to see what had happened. Their exstatic celebration had been interrupted and rabid rage was spreading between them.

I dimly felt Llueve jerk my arm and pull me up through the layers of sandstone into the silent desert night as she pleaded with me to respond.

'Home Jwo! Home!' Djagda and Isult, Silvaan and Oorden emerged out of cloaked hiding and sped at me, grabbing my arms and legs and pulling me down into the massive, darkened canyon as Adrrik and BATS operatives closed in pursuit.

Desperately I tried to clear my head. As if from a long distance I saw the faces of Djagda, Silvaan and Oorden reaching out to me, calling me, surrounding me as we sped through the air. Dark silhouettes emerged from the space beyond. Spider like tentacles whipped out and tried to snare my astral body. I saw Silvaan shoot white light out of his palm at one of these tentacled shadows and then Djagda and Oorden were shooting razor sharp planes of light outwards at shadow beings as we flew up a narrow side canyon, trying to hide behind mesa-like stone formations. I couldn't track everything that was happening. We accelerated up into the night sky.

We continued jetting up and away in an arc, dematerializing until we were in a realm of atomic particles, which began to blur for me as we traveled at inconceivable speeds at which point I blacked out.

When I came out of it I was in Llueve's arms, on the floor of a hallway in the caverns of Logaana. Blue ink like fluid was spilling out of my chest. It was all over Llueve's clothes. Her face was swollen with crying. I was paralyzed and freezing. All my heat had been sucked out by the slash across my chest. The psychic robes around Llueve were so thick I could barely feel her body. We lay in a clutching embrace on the rug where we had landed on coming out of deep space. Wounded Siddhe warriors with gashes on their bodies were gasping for air and were being attended to on either side of me. Down the hall I saw Djagda and Isult with their heads close together looking at me sadly.

A rosy love coming out of Llueve slowly penetrated me and the other miracle - us - our encounter - our love - the life growing within her- took over and from deep within the core of me, a glowing, vibrant radiance began to expand outwards, pushing back the cold and dark presence. Kaelaa, Elsinaad and Avaala came up and knelt beside Llueve around me and placed their hands on my body. The glowing rose light began to pulse inside all of us as they huddled over me on the carpet and I felt the fearful shard of darkness pulled out of the gash in my chest by a tremendous love intelligence that hovered above us. Then life and love radiated into my heart from these warrior soul friends and I sobbed helplessly.

'It's her,' Llueve said. I looked at her through my streaming tears, puzzled by what she meant. 'It's Ea.' Tears of love spilled down her cheeks and mingled with my own as I began to understand. A serene purity of love was vibrating in intense waves out of Llueve's belly into my heart even as I felt the blood pumping out of my chest in great liquid spurts.

When I awoke in Yvonne's bed it was to an early winter sunset. I'd slept all day. A phosphorescent rosy glow illumined the apartment. I looked out the bedroom window and saw the Sangre de Cristos Mountains bathed in the forgiving rosy sweetness of that otherworldly light. I lay in bed alone in the silence of the apartment. The pillow was wet with the tears that were still in my eyes.

I was overwhelmed by the images still streaming through my mind - love, terror, and the black light in the heart of the Draco Beast. REXXON!

I felt totally strange being in Yvonne's house. My heart felt like it was crushed. I wanted to be home as quickly as possible. I stumbled into my clothes. As I walked out the front door I saw the yellow Stick-Its with Yvonne's writing about taking out the trash, asking me to be sure and make the bed, put the dishes in the machine and asking me to take the video back and to not forget about going to the office party on Tuesday. I was in a fog, I couldn't relate to any of it as I lurched down the stairs to my truck. Once outside the building, the rosy sunset glow surrounded me and I felt the moon waves of love radiating again out of Llueve's belly and the healing hands of the Siddhe women touching my chest. As I walked across the parking lot, Rexxon's head suddenly flashed alive in front of me, completely real. He turned towards me, the jaws snapping together in front of my face, the huge vertically slit reptilian eyes, full of hate and power looked straight into mine knocking me against my truck. My heart convulsed. Pain seared across my chest where the claws had raked me making me double over. I couldn't handle any more horror, my mind shut down. I drove like a zombie.

Chapter Eleven

1/14/05

When I got home from Yvonne's I lay down on the couch in my clothes and went right to sleep. I woke up near dawn to take a leak, changed into running pants and a sweatshirt and slept until afternoon when Spencer came by with Lena to check on me because I hadn't shown up at the job or answered the phone. I knew I should have got up but just couldn't focus. I kept sliding off into this trance and felt really depressed.

When they asked me what the matter was, I said I thought I had the flu. What could I say? That I'd been slashed by a Tyrannosaurus Rex in a dream and been rescued by the mother of my child-to-be and a bunch of flying elves? I just stared at them feeling paranoid, my mind a blank, my chest on fire and the depressing sense of having betrayed Llueve. Spencer reassured me that everything at the job was under control. Lena, a nurse, knew it was no flu. She gave me a kiss and they left with questions in their eyes.

Getting slashed by Rexxon has made me feel like I failed Llueve and the Siddhe in the worst way. There she was, putting her life on the line to prevent children from being deformed and to keep her people from committing suicide and I joined the enemy! I feel disgusted with myself. The burning pain in my chest is part of a nausea that won't go away.

I re-read parts of the Monroe book where he describes how he dealt with the fear produced by the clinging, sucking, psychic parasites and the cat spirits that had attached themselves to his back. I'm trying to understand the dark side of this. I can't produce the buzzing feeling I need to induce the OBE state. I need a different technique or a deeper level of inspiration. Monroe describes experimenting with different methods of getting out but I can't get them to work for me. I found another book about OBE's called 'Out of Body Experiences' by a guy named Robert Peterson. He seems to spend a lot of the book dangling half in and half out of his body while his mother is making breakfast downstairs, but at least he gets halfway there.

I lie awake at night seeing Llueve's swollen tear stained face and her pupils dilated with fear as she bent over me in the underground chambers. I remember the horror of seeing Rexxon lurch up and stare straight into my eyes after I had floated away from Llueve. I remember seeing Isult and Djagda, their faces looking fearful and worried as they whispered to each other, looking at me as I lay on the floor dripping ink. I think about Llueve and feel sick at the thought that she saw me submit to Rexxon's power. It was she who saved me, endangering herself, the Siddhe, the baby! I nearly ruined everything. Could she still love me after that?

How could I have become so unconscious of what was at stake?! This is the really shocking thing to me. It reveals something about me that frightens me. I was attracted to that cold power. I was fascinated with Rexxon and the energy that he and the Dracos radiated. They had no restraint.

They were completely free in their minds about what to do with themselves. Lust and greed is what is at the core of their identities and there's no wishy-washy mediocrity or troublesome internal inhibition going on within them about right and wrong, good and bad. There's just power and they want it and are reaching out with everything they can to possess it. This is so unlike any state of consciousness I've ever had. For me, there is always doubt, restraint, inhibition, right and wrong. Rexxon is the ultimate embodiment of total, self-serving forward motion and to his followers he is a god. What sickens me is that something in me responded to his power. Am I like them? Could I actually be seduced into becoming one of them? With all the horrors taking place because of their manipulations, what must the Siddhe think of me losing my will in their presence? And Llueve...

There's a dark red and purple welt across my chest. It looks like scar tissue. When I touch it is so tender it feels like I'm touching the raw tissue of my heart. It really hurts. I feel stupefied and exposed. I don't want to be at the job - out in the sun - hearing the damn nail gun pounding. God am I grateful for Llueve's holding me right afterwards, I felt like my insides were gushing out. That's a kind of proof that at least she didn't just cut me right off in disgust.

Lying in my bed with the curtains drawn, with everything so familiar and still, the quiet bubbling of the fish tank, the spitfire model turning slowly on its string, Neutron's nose in the crack between the curtains looking in the window – everything being so normal now seems like a nightmare.

There is no immediate danger. Everything is as it always is. And yet it feels like there should be guns going off and people running down the streets. The massive, mind numbing lie of this war, Wall Street tricking Americans with cheap bait and switch mortgages, paper tricks to suck money out of thin air, CIA torture, child molesting priests, major corporations stealing their own employees retirement funds - and yet the traffic whooshes calmly down my street, there are no sirens, no explosions, no storm troopers pounding on the door with rifle butts - just silence, calm. The Siddhe and Llueve are fully aware of the evil and danger in their midst and are acting on it. Here there is a semblance of complete normality. The news streams by with horror stories spoken by such intelligent people in such perfectly normal tones of voice that it's hypnotic. It acts like a drug on everyone. And now I'm the casualty of a life threatening dream - that has left a painful welt across my chest - what does it all mean?

Lena came by late the next morning and made me some scrambled eggs and turkey sausages and gave me a cold beer. What the hell, the day was shot. She sat on the edge of the bed while I ate and her sympathetic presence and our old friendship eventually made me open up. I just had to talk. I finally told her about Ovvala and the Siddhe and the Reptilians.

'When I'm in a room with these people Lena, they're just as real as you sitting on the bed,' I told her.

'Well, that's what's so weird about dreams though isn't it?' she said. 'You really feel like you're going to drown in a bathtub or die when you fall off your front steps.'

'Yeah, I know. But this is different. There are long extended conversations - Ovvala has a long history and people have names that aren't Human names.'

'Like what,' she asked sympathetically.

'Djagda, Silvaan, Isult, Elsinaad, Llueve...' I said as she looked at me with the Nurse Look that said - the drug wore off sonny - time to come back down.

Listening to myself I saw myself through her eyes and it made me doubt the 'reality' I was trying to convince her of.

She smiled and held my hand in a kindly, patient way. As I talked about the Draco Council and Rexxon the talking Tyrannosaurus, I began to sound really deranged to myself. Lena's normal, practical down to earth presence and the humorous sparkle in her eyes made me start to laugh at myself and I started to reconsider the whole deal. She asked me if I wanted to see Yvonne but I said not yet. I needed to think. She thought I could have got a concussion when I fell off the ladder and that from her medical experience, a concussion could have subtle prolonged effects. Nightmares were a common reaction and that the best thing to do was rest. Spencer came by to pick her up. He said that he could run things at the job while I had the 'flu'. This was his polite way of avoiding saying 'coo-coo'.

1/19/05

It's Wednesday. Lena's take on my 'dreams' being hallucinations caused by the concussion is so plausible and this on-going opera of fairies so far-out that it's got me wondering... could it be just dreams?

I wanted Yvonne's view even if it risked one of her smurffy, New Age interpretations. I've never talked about Llueve to Yvonne - it just felt too private.

I called her last night at about seven and she came over. I got a button down shirt out of the closet so as to not look too casual and put on fresh jeans. I felt she was doing me a big favor and I didn't want to look like I'd been just lying around moping - which I guess I have been. We sat on my couch with cups of tea and I decided to just say it all and see what the feedback would be.

'We sat in these big gothic chairs in a cavern with torches,' I told her. 'The soldiers had silver suits on and the chiefs wore long robes,' She was wearing jeans and a shapeless, puffy, long sleeved yellow blouse. I guess she didn't want to excite the patient. She was very considerate and sweet as she listened to me ramble on.

'A soldier and I were sent to spy on a council of lizard possessed people who are the executives of various industries on Earth and on Ovvala. The chief lizard - a Tyrannosaurus Rex actually - slid down a triangle of golden light and flopped down on the floor - this stuff that was like mucus was dripping off him.' Yvonne smiled sweetly. Her eyes were so sympathetic. 'So then I drifted away from my friend,' (I kept my friend kind of vague), 'and the reptilian being slashed me across the chest.' I went to show her the welt across my chest but it had faded since I'd last looked at it. I insisted there had been a purple welt there the day before.

'Could you have slept with the sheet bunched up Joe?' she asked me, with a sweet smile. I hadn't thought of that.

'When did you first start dreaming about this place?' she asked. I'd given her the first few entries of my 'diary' but then we'd sort of cooled it and I hadn't shown her what I'd been writing. So I told Yvonne about the city of Saala and the market place and the UFO's flying overhead and the eighteenth century farms. Yvonne took my hand and petted it.

When I'd finished she silently held my hand and thought for a while and then looked me straight in the eye;

'Joe, I think you've created a valiant troop of Robin Hood type warriors to battle the evil kingdom because you find the the challenges of a competitive economy too bureaucratic and laborious.

'You have a childlike view of adult society and reject its complexities because they challenge your defiant childhood ego.

'You're still hoping for the Ideal mom and dad - a heroic king and queen - and the happy home life you never had.

'You have a Peter Pan syndrome and tend to demonize people with real power in the world because they expose your immature view of reality.

'You have a fear of success which prevents you from succeeding in a competitive economy that demands you learn to play ball with the big boys. That you're even beginning to take such dreams seriously should reveal to you just how desperate you are to avoid adult responsibility!'

I swallowed my pride and listened to the end. It hurt to hear her say such conventional things but I had to admit to myself it was a reasonable interpretation of my mental state, by a loving friend, giving a responsible response to someone who could actually be losing it. And how else could an intelligent person interpret such ideas?

We kissed a little and I refrained from recon even though she gave me plenty of time to do so. Then Yvonne gave me her sweet, compassionate, fake, smile and left. I poured the herbal tea in the sink and got a beer out of the fridge and thought about it all.

I'm having to admit that things are getting too far out. I'm beginning to think that the concussion actually did make me go crazy! Thank God it was only played out in my dreams! I did have a serious whack on the head and a professional nurse has told me this can cause mental instability. It's dangerous to believe that things I've dreamed could be real. It's got to be a series of dreams showing me things about my subconscious. But Llueve!

Bumping into Yvonne at Spencer's that night must have stirred up old emotions and listening drunkenly to Spencer and Yvonne talk about elves and goblins when I was so depressed about the election and freaked about global warming started some psychological process in me - I do feel I'm an outsider to my world; I don't believe in the 'competitive economy' and I do fear for the life of the planet. The inhumanity - the lack of environmental awareness of the people in power, scares me. I do want to belong to a more sane society - I have been very lonely, and do fantasize about the perfect girlfriend - so I could have created these things. Maybe Spencer and Yvonne's conversation about the man from Earth and the buxom chick from another dimension cavorting among the wildflowers planted an image in my mind - so a blood clot in my brain blocked off the lobe of reason and my hurting ego found release by fantasying free from responsibility for a little while. Thusly I subconsciously created a fantasy world?

I called Lena after Yvonne left and discussed my new thoughts with her. Lena thinks I'm getting on the right track. She said;

'It's a normal thing to want to stop destructive things from going on. And to not have any power while the killing goes on plus drug gangs and droughts and hurricanes all happening is making us all a little crazy.' True. O.K. So I'm not alone. She thought getting slashed by a large lizard was symbolic of my feeling personally injured by destructive forces I can't stop and that does sound accurate.

Wow. What a letdown. I feel ridiculous.

When I was there, Ovvala seemed so real. But then, when I'm 'here', it's so easy to doubt it all. Where's the proof? I just looked at my chest in the mirror and the 'scar tissue' has completely vanished. Was that all about bunched up sheets?

1/25/05

Night after night I lie awake in bed, unable to go into the trance that leads to the buzzing feeling and leaving my body. I watch my mind flip between believing Ovvala is real and believing it's all hallucination. I think about Isult and Djagda, Silvaan and all the Ovvalans I met. About the city of Saala, the huge underground chambers of Logaana, the unique look of Ovvala – the trees - the sky - so unique to Ovvala and so different from here. How could a fantasy be so consistent and repetitive? It's gone on for 2 months! I think of the light in the eyes of the Siddhe warriors and the power of their consciousness, the motivation they have to fight against the Dracos and that I've shared so completely when I'm with them. The picture of Llueve's face, her pale silky skin, her noble cheek bones, the tender, loving look in her eyes, the unique sexiness of her body, her house, her cat, her UFO. And the sex! Such sex! It isn't as though I've only seen these things once or twice because I've seen them over and over and they have always been exactly the same.

This growing cynicism I have felt about what is happening in the world really is powerful enough to bring about such hallucinations in me. Sometimes when I'm working, my mind is just paralyzed with disbelief at what is happening in the world around me. Multinational society thinks global warming is just a wrinkle in their plans. Mass starvation, AIDS and smallpox in Africa. Depression and poverty everywhere. Right after Katrina, the oil corporations bragged that they'd made more during that fiscal quarter than had ever been made before. This was while a major American city was underwater, tens of thousands of homes had been destroyed and gas was above four dollars a gallon. While corporations make billions each quarter from stealing the resources that people around the world need to survive, they pay their workers the least they can get away with and then brag about their profits? Don't these high powered executives realize that their own kids are going to inherit this world – and inherit us with it?

I'm realizing just how bitter I'm becoming. I've come to feel that the world is saturated with evil. Lying politicians, corrupt industries, preachers quoting all the noble Biblical clichés to justify sending other people's children off to fight an industrial war on the other side of the world. How do their minds justify this? For the longest time I really thought America, despite having crooks and liars in government and industry really was the keeper of the flame of freedom. But more and more I feel like we aren't the solution but just another problem.

And what has made all this possible is the naive and credulous breadbasket of Bible belt America trained to fear and obey authority and that now can't grasp that in the name of their ethics and their God, murder and genocide are acted out under the guise of Christian Democracy. Under the sacred Idea of freedom of religion murder is being committed. Why does clear language about factual events not cause a more sane response? Why are the very people undermined by these things so incapable of demanding the crooks be made responsible?

At what point does stretching the truth create a lie? At what point does a lie become something more than opportunism? At what point does greed become evil? Evil.

The educated and refined classes think of good people as having nice manners and wearing nice clothes. Evil people would be coarse, stupid and ugly and have a constant four O'clock shadow. They would speak bad English and wave their hands around a lot like Italians. Evil women would be slutty and have shifty hips, fallen bra straps and always speak in double meanings. Well groomed dentists and investment brokers, trade analysts and history professors couldn't be evil - they're educated! People who live in two story houses on tree lined streets and who give their kids piano lessons and drive them to the pool in winter couldn't be evil - they love their kids!

Yet it's the well educated and supposedly moral classes in America who are most blind to what is going on. They just don't want to know. Just like the middle classes in Nazi Germany didn't want to know. They don't want to know just how American corporations get sugar and rubber and oil from foreign countries or what life on the minimum wage circuit is like for tens of millions of people. Six dollars and fifty cents an hour with gas at three dollars a gallon!? They don't want to know that rich people are rich because poor people are poor. The reasons why some people suffer has to be unfathomably complex and metaphysically glamorous.

Being condemned to a life of peanut butter and spaghetti is not glamorous. This Land is Your Land? Good moral people don't want to know that their tax dollars buy the weapons that assassinate other good moral people in East Timor and Guatemala, in Gaza and Tibet. No. They're bright, hard working, cheerful and successful members of the most modern of democracies. They're positive thinkers!

It's the education itself that shapes the minds of the educated to blindness. People are being educated into insensitivity.

If I could only get out of body again. Just to prove to myself Ovvala is real. In all my doubts about my sanity, Ovvala, and the Dracos, the love feeling with Llueve is what keeps pulling me back to hope it's real. I think I'd better go have a serious talk with Spencer. At least he won't feed me good natured bullshit.

2/02/05

I bought a ten gallon pear tree and planted it in Lena's yard under the boulder. The ground was pretty frozen for about a foot down but then it got softer. The dormant tree is eight feet tall, and has a few branches coming off its trunk. I can start to train it in the spring. It's my farewell gift to Llueve - my dream lover. I promised a dream girl a tree - at least I can keep that promise. Goodbye Llueve.

Chapter Twelve

February/5/05

I drove over to Spencer's through a moonless, really cold night. It was fifteen below. There were more stars than I ever remembered seeing, which is really saying something after seven, eight years in the high desert. I had a six of light and six of dark of a pricey German beer and some Chinese takeout I'd picked up in town.

We were meeting in The Cavern. This is what Spencer calls the back half of the school bus parked next to his house. It's The Cavern in honor of The Beatles. Though I think of Spencer's den as the Clan of the Cave Bear and of Spencer, with his protruding forehead bone and sunken Norse eye sockets as that cave bear.

The bus is divided in half by a framed wall with a door in it. In the front there's the wood stove which was dully roaring away. There's a worktable on one side, where I dropped my jacket, with shelves of tools on the other wall. The back half is fixed up like the library in the type of home from the Forties where Alfred Hitcock murder films were made.

There's a dark blue rug with light blue and lipstick red, art deco tulips embroidered in it, an old, faded, purple, velvet couch with chipped wooden claw feet and a sun bleached emerald green arm chair with big rounded arm rests. There's an old fashioned, heavy stand up lamp with a big faded white cloth shade and a fancy little coffee table with the legs cut down - all salvaged from street corners during the city's free autumn hauls to the dump.

Mahogany stained bookshelves cover most of the walls and frame the rear window through which I could see my pear tree through the overhanging branches of the walnut tree that grows next to the bus. I could just see the rounded belly of the big boulder with the stars above it in a sky black as murder.

Were the roots of our pear trees holding fingers? Aww.

Spencer knew something serious was going on with me by my staying away from a job that's nearly finished. Especially this job, which he knows I badly want to finish so we can say goodbye to the wicked witch of the Southwest. Spencer really is a good friend. If ever I need a father confessor, he's it.

Spencer was sitting in the old, worn sofa chair with a little black lacquered tray on his lap, separating seeds from some pungent smelling bud. He was wearing one of his painfully bright Hawaiian shirts. His nearly white blond hair parted more or less in the middle framed his moon face and bulldog jowls. His blue-white physicist eyes glanced at me and he mumbled 'hi-how-ya-doin' as I set the sixes and Chinese food down on the table and sat down on the purple couch.

In that glance he saw how deflated I was. Maybe in his acid days he had experienced what it means to hallucinate something and then have to accept that it's a complete fantasy. We both sort of rambled on for a while about trivial things as we tackled the immediate questions; light or dark? Rice or noodles? garlic beef or chicken Schezhuan? By the time we were passing the pipe back and forth I was remembering.

'I feel like my mind is split in two,' I said. 'Those dreams were so real, so consistent that it's hard for me to believe that they weren't actual events!' I'd wake up with real feelings for these people - the Siddhe, the warriors, were so distinctly different than the evil Dracos...'

Spencer cross-examined me until we came to the last dream - when I got slashed by Rexxon.

'...there was this chamber was a huge room in the middle of a long tunnel carved out of solid sandstone. There were hundreds of people surrounding the painted circles where the priestess with big knockers stood and invoked the Tyrannosaurus Rex. I saw a dozen famous people I recognized from TV. There was (CENSORED) and (CENSORED)' I wanted him to see it like I had. 'Then the big Tyrannosaurus sort of hypnotized the crowd with his plan to colonize Mars and I became - like - a believer - started drifting away from - my...friend... and then the Tyrannosaur saw me and slashed me across the chest and that was the end of it.' why did this sound so infantile when I put it into words? Spencer absorbed my thoughts and then said;

'Didn't we talk about Mars on Halloween night?' he stared into the void of the noodle carton.

'Oh Yeah!' I said. I'd forgotten all about that.

'And you were making smart remarks about the Fairy's and people crossing the dimensional warp in pre Christian Europe....'

'Yeah?' I could see he still had an attitude about that.

'Lena said that crack on your head was pretty serious...that it could have really shaken your brains up - especially with all the hollow space you have in there!'

'Ha!' I said straight faced. 'Just dreams?' I was asking myself over and over. Just dreams? I told him Yvonne's conclusions that I was basically not taking responsibility for being a modern adult.

'Being grown up is Yvonne's new placebo,' he said. 'It's her new cure all - be patient with her. It wasn't that long ago that she was gonna make a career out of being a spiritual adviser to self-absorbed trust fund babies.

'But her idea that you created fantasy images to give expression to a sense of impotence with the problems of the world, does seem pretty reasonable you know,' he said. 'And it's not so far-fetched considering what's going on. The world has *never* been so messed up. There really is a kind of collective mass-insanity happening below the surface. At least in America it's below the surface. It's not that far below the surface in Europe or South America!' He'd finished off the noodles and the beef and was eyeing the chicken carton but popped a light instead. After a while he said;

'A million people demonstrated against America invading Iraq in Italy! Half a million in London. They're freaked about Islam because they're closer to it all than we are. They don't see the sense in kicking the ant hill when the problem is a transient band of terrorists.

'With the blockade in place since Kuwait, lack of hospital supplies and food has caused hundreds of thousands of Iraqi deaths, a lot of them children. This only serves the fanatics by helping them recruit more suicide bombers and psychos to their cause.' I reached out as he spoke and felt the intense cold radiating from the panes of glass.

'Islamic expansionism is a reality you know. It's been going on since Mohammed. By the late sixteen hundreds, Moslems had overrun half of Europe. But so is the corporate greed of the West a reality. Modern Islamic rage against the West didn't just come out of the blue. Ever since oil became a central part of the global economy, the West has been promoting divide and conquer in the Middle East to get their oil. Witness the puppet government of the Shah of Iran. This was the manipulation of another nation, not for the national interests of Western democracies but for the benefit of the economic aristocracy. This has been going on since the 50's. So now the minority of Islamic Fundamentalists is capitalizing on the injustices of the corporate minority in the West.

'Those demonstrations aren't just against Western imperialism! They're a mass reaction to all the old style power politics and ways of thinking that has again divided society into rich and poor. Let me tell you, those European demonstrations signal a new global consciousness. The Earth can no longer support this new royalty.' He took a few deep breaths.

'There's a growing awareness that we may have mortally injured the planet,' he lit the pipe and became momentarily speechless. 'This is a level of insecurity humans have never known before,' he squeaked and then blew his smoke out. 'It may the one thing that could override even the human compulsion for prestige. The end of biology would mean the annihilation of everything.

'I remember when 'Silent Spring' was published in the early Sixties. At the time most people thought the book was an over dramatization. Nobody really thought we could *make nature sick*! The big thing then was the cold war and fear of nuclear missiles. Atomic bomb drills in grade schools - diving under the desk...sheesh. The Idea that the 'environment', meaning 'the planet', could be endangered by a few little chemicals, a few open pit mines, and a bit of logging, seemed absurd. The planet, we thought, is like huge - gargantuan. What could possibly affect The Planet? But we didn't know everything that was going on. We weren't aware how big the bulldozers had got or what the word 'deforestation' really meant. We were coming out of the Fifties and were sort of like Hansel and Gretel go to college,' he laughed at his own joke and gulped half a beer.

'We heard Eisenhower say the words 'military industrial complex' but we thought he meant in like fifty years - not as in Viet Nam. We were so naive! We were unable to conceive that the CIA was setting up Pinochet, Noriega, Marcos, the Shah of Iran, the Kemer Rouge so as to get cheap bananas, heroin, cocaine and tungsten right then and there.'

'Didn't people wonder where all the inexpensive houses and cars and washing machines - all the stuff - was coming from?' I popped another dark and hit the pipe.

'No. People didn't ask those kinds of questions then. Americans were stunned from the vacuum created by the killing of two hundred million people in the Second World War. And the fear of communism and atomic bombs was getting worked hard then. It was because of that climate that McCarthy got so far.

'After the 2nd World War some kind of resource network took over American industry. At the end of the War, we were in half the countries the world. They had untapped resources they didn't even know about and no knowledge of how to get at them or transport them. So this network set up ports and started bringing it all back home!'

'Like taking candy from a baby.' I propped my feet up on the couch.

'Yeah. I was just reading D.H. Lawrence's 'Lady Chatterley's Lover' which was written before the

First World War. What a prophetic book! He saw the coming dehumanization of the West in the emerging industrial machine. He'd been born at a time and in a place - the late 1800's in rural England - when the agricultural cycle was still a real part of an individual's identity. Just think - from the mid-1800's back to the time of Sumer in what? 5000 B.C.? everybody did something with the land or their activities were related to the land every day of their lives. Milk, eggs, wheat, cattle, corn, fish, were either abundant or scarce according to the seasons. You didn't travel when the roads were pits of mud. You 'made hay while the sun shined' and hibernated in winter. Every day people went to the well to get water and looked up at the sky and wondered if the cattle would be fat or skinny which meant money or no money at the spring fair. People shit in outhouses and used the composted crap to grow their daily bread. They knew the personality of their cows and horses, their geese and hunting dogs. People were part of the land and this had been true for forty thousand years! There's this scene in Lady Chatterley's Lover where one of the first motor cars is speeding through these farm towns in England, the engine roaring along, passing all the pastoral scenes - a guy walking behind a herd of sheep, women hoeing a garden, a horse-cart hauling barrels of beer - are all left behind in a cloud of exhaust fumes and D.H. imagines the towering metal monsters to come. It's all come true.'

'It's hard now to believe all that ever existed. Mrs. Maggilicuddy talking to her geese and all. ' I sucked on a hole in my index finger left from a sliver I'd got the day before.

'When people lived liked that, they all had something in common and it came out in the way they used language. Talking about the weather was a way of talking about the mysteries of life. When people said the word 'work', it meant the weight of logs or how long it took to mow down twenty acres of wheat by hand or drive the nails to build a barn. Words had weight. An individual's identity included the group identity of being part of nature as a powerful and mysterious force. The seasonal cycles of the land were the central, living experience everyone shared, and language expressed that. Life and language were a unit. In Germany and France they were selectively cutting firewood to preserve the forests five hundred years ago! That was a cultural agreement that honored the generations to come. They couldn't help caring for life and made decisions that honored the continuity of life.' Spencer bent over his own bulk to get another beer. I noticed he was staying with light.'

'The Japanese are sinking hollow ship hulls full of Canadian Spruce to use later when there's no more trees,' I said and chugged a dark.

'The problems of today go back to what is fundamentally a language problem. Language is not working! And it hasn't been working for so long that people don't even remember that this is not how it used to be.

'The really big shift was the Inquisition,' Oh good, I thought, Spencer was going to make a speech and I could just look out the window. 'After the Inquisition people became rabid. They were pounded with the idea that they were weak and immoral, separate and lost and by God they became that!

'The Inquisition removed the pagan elements from the life of Europe. And it was the pagans who were steeped in the art of husbanding the land and cultivating the human community. The pagans were the European Indians. As the pagans were removed, the industrial mind came alive.'

'So, global warming happened because of the Inquisition?,' I just have this sarcastic streak which is probably why I liked Yvonne. He hit the pipe.

'As the relationship with the land changed, so did the meanings of language change, and this then, changed human relationships. Language was a living breathing being for thousands of years. Now it's a set of function to accommodate commercial processes. Words used to be a bridge between people. The life of the land and of the weather were living things that people traded with metaphors and similies. There was a sense of ethics, of good and bad behavior stemming from husbanding the land that was exchanged in jokes and quotes and old sayings. Now words invoke legal precedents and Biblical clichés. With a few dramatic flourishes, Spencer said in a helium voice as he tried to hold his smoke, 'Christ and Christianity are fundamentally the same concept as paganism - redemption is just a fancy word for the renewal of spring and the dawn of a new day. It's not that sunrise and spring are like redemption - they <u>are</u> redemption, rebirth, and renewal. The Sun isn't just a metaphor for God, the Sun is the life giver and the light of life. Nature's sustainability is the mind of God in nature. All life philosophies and religions get their authority from reflecting the life forces released by nature. Nature was the first Bible, the first Koran, and the first Talmud. There were commonly understood boundaries - limits to things...if you cut down all the trees at once there wouldn't be any next winter when you needed them...if you farmed a piece of land without letting it rest the crops would get weak. These weren't opinions. These were real things that everyone agreed on because they experienced them all their lives.'

I could see the Big Dipper pointing to the North Star out the window behind the nerve-like, leafless branches of the walnut tree.

'The great innovation introduced by Western religion was the idea of one abstract God who secretly and mysteriously controlled everything. The word God became a way of representing the essence of the Sun - and then controlling that meaning - saying no it doesn't mean this it means that. If you talk about the sun it's obvious to anyone when it's light and when it's dark. But anything said about God is just an opinion. In the Middle Ages, what GOd was or wasn't was written into law. If you're viewpoint didn't agree with what The Church had made law, you could be ostracized and branded an apostate, one of those special words the Church invented to make you feel God had made it up. Like the word recuse which the judiciary invoked in the 90's to obviate their collusion with the elites and neutralize their own knowledge of the actual facts regarding the criminality of selling out.

'What God was or wasn't, is or isn't, has been manipulated into keeping the have not's under the haves by the rearrangement of the contextual parameters that link the elite chains of authority. The poor got the grace of God. The Kings got the money!

'The self-evident boundaries of nature that were the basis for agrarian cultures, and that were reinforced with language, were re-interpreted through religious laws into commercial opportunism for mankind to turn nature into wealth until there were no boundaries, no limits. 'After the Inquisition, the Church and the royal families began engineering both civil and religious laws so as to maximize profits for the few. The life of the community, of people, of folk culture became incidental. The priests and their endless re-interpretations of the Bible made heaven more important than life! The Holy Book replaced nature! The Royals made property laws that benefited the Lords and their children and managment and cut out everyone else. What they were doing was taking possession of the meanings in language. Words became contracts that bound men to casts. Words came to be owned by the have's.

'Now with this denatured language we've inherited from two thousand years of religious abstraction and royal control, the meanings of language are up to a higher court to decide. And the higher court is made up of the have's.

'Pagan culture was a folk culture that had developed over the span of time it took Homo sapiens to evolve out of animals. Pagan, from the Italian pagani means people from the country - meaning people of the land. Heathen means people from the heather - country people! Paganism was human identity based on the experience of living with the land and the animals. It was a million years old! The word pagan only has meaning in relation to the religions that wiped it out! Time itself is pagan. Language is a pagan tradition.'

'Sounds good Spence,' I said. 'But didn't the pagans have slavery?'

'Uh excuse me? American sneaker companies flying South Sea child labor into encampments on U.S. protectorates? Forcing GMO's on consumers and chemtrails on everyone...amortized credit card debt with sandtraps... billions invested in maintaining a minimum wage while the corporations don't pay taxes...'

'O.K. O.K. O.K....' I said. Christ these damn know it alls!

'I'm not talking about Utopia. The weird thing about the history of institutions like the monarchies and The Church is that there are always two things going on. It's like there is a visible, staged history that's written down and accepted as legitimate, while there is a second history of manipulation that's actually documented but glossed over and delegitimized, camflauged with alternative information. Politically correct New Agers are the worst at this. If it's not sweet, positive, includes all races and religions it's not spiritual! The sun shines on everyone, they say. but they won't share the money! They've played right into the hands of the elites who don't want anyone lifting up the rock they're hiding under! I mean, after Bay of Tonkin, Watergate, Contragate, you have to ask yourself if King and Ghandi's non-violence strategies weren't actually advanced by the elites! At the Republican Convention in New York, Giulianni roped off a back street, far from the television cameras, for demonstrators to demonstrate to their hearts content! He even provided a blackboard for people to write graffiti diatribes on! The elites are masters at evasion tactics and at injecting Draconian laws and executive orders on to the backs of liberal legislature. Non-violence couldn't suit the Illuminati better! We have to grasp that the Cabal of the Have's uses impenetrably correct language to advance their greed while branding progressive humanitarian programs as socialism. By 1955 the Roman Catholic Church was the third wealthiest NATION on earth! That didn't happen by accident.' A little breeze was shaking the tree branches outdoors.

'There was a group of people that got caught trying to set bombs off in Israel at the millennium to make the Rapture come true! What makes people want that instead of real things like land restoration and a living wage? If earthly life were happier, salvation wouldn't mean anything! To most people, salvation means being dead and not having to talk to your relatives anymore!' Spencer was glowering at the half filled Chicken Szechuan box.

'Now, global warming is threatening life itself and still the religious people and their politicians go on spewing these clichés of sin and salvation while physical reality is disintegrating - even when their own children's lives are threatened by this willful violation of nature's needs, preachers go on spouting about Ezekiel this and Deuturonomy that.'

Spencer was getting inspired to wrath. I quickly reloaded the pipe to keep him going while he went for a dark. I was feeling much better.

'Yvonne thinks it's Pleidians,' I said just to stir the soup.

'No, no, no! You've got it all wrong,' he took me seriously! 'Pleidians are the good guys!' He popped the beer and tossed the cap towards a dented, Victorian trash can in the corner and hit the lamp. 'Religions have filled us with these presets - like the Church pushed love and forgiveness and turn the other cheek while priests sold tickets to heaven, molested children, sided with oppressive regimes and paid standing armies. Their flocks were then to either love them or forgive them as they had been taught. Those were the options. Here you see the premeditated manipulation of language taking place - the meanings in language fixed to create a specialized context. Designed consent.

A woman in a dream had planted a tree right under that boulder out there. In a dream!

'Before the Inquisition, when agriculture was a religion in itself, the word was used in the context of nature - of sustainability - words and nature were like a mother and child. The words sustained nature. After the Inquisition, the word was used in the context of the Church's welfare and words sustained the Church. And the Church sided with Royalty that treated people like penned cattle. The mother was taken out of the picture and was replaced by old bald priests in dresses. I don't know maybe it was pussy envy.' Spencer laughed maliciously and burped profoundly.

'St. Patrick ended Human slavery in Ireland,' I said. At least I knew that much.

'And Pope John told South America it's a sin to use contraception so that people have a duty to produce children they can't feed. Christianity is whatever the regime in power wants it to be. It controls Human values to its own benefit. And besides - about St. Patrick - you can't trust events that aren't on video.'

'You trust video?'

'The Guttenberg Bible was the first book ever mass produced and distributed,' Spencer glared at me as though it was my fault. 'Literacy and religious indoctrination were basically the same thing. The Bible stories were the first stories that became standardized. Before this, in little villages in the Balkans, the Hebrides, the French countryside, people repeated the fables and folk stories of their great great grandparents. And in the telling, they twisted the personalities and plots to illustrate current events and people. This was creative language at work. This was the poetry of nature in human mouths.

'Between the Inquisition and the Guttenberg, the folk history of hundreds of generation' experience of the land was replaced with the sterile drama of you know who and the twelve elves with an inconclusive ending; He died or didn't die. It helped or it didn't help. Ten million people have now read 'The DaVinci Code' and 'Holy Blood Holy Grail' which are about Jesus having married Mary Magdalene and having children whose children supposedly survive to this day. How did a religion supposedly based on truth and love leave this little detail out?'

'That wasn't the only detail that got left out,' I said. It was a relief to hear Spencer on the attack. I had been feeling too depressed to even care. I'd been dreaming the battle plan for Armageddon! I'd been in another world! I'd loved someone in another world! Now I was back on earth where we were forced to discuss the Bible even to get free of it. But to prove I had an open mind I went for a light. 'George Carlin points out that if God is All Powerful, how come he needs our money?' Spencer ignored my incisive observation and thundered on.

'We know now from books like Pagel's 'The Gnostic Gospels' that there were twenty or more apostles and that Mary Magdalene was the main apostle!' He sat up straighter and glared at me. 'The number twelve was picked because it coincided with the twelve signs of the Zodiac,

Astrology and the Tarot. These things were the folk language of the people back then. The units on early clocks were two hours long because that's how long it took for a zodiac sign to pass over the horizon. Astrology and magick were so much a part of daily life that time itself was determined by them. So, they gave Jesus credit for the winter solstice and made it twelve apostles and turned La Magdalena into a whore. They were manipulating the facts from the start! Now - in whose interest was Mary made a whore? Who benefits from twisting history like this?'

'Pleidian pimps?' I asked. Spencer snorted.

'A very savvy intelligence was twisting the meanings of language towards a desired end! First there was the colorful story of the Zodiac where the Ram and the Cow become the man and woman and then transubstantiate through the cauldron of experience into cosmic eagles. Then there were people guilty even before they were born and who only saved from ETERNAL HELL by submitting to the priests who collected a stipend from kings for locking up the people's minds! You could say that Kings paid rent to the Priests for keeping the People distracted with Holy Fire.

'From the Zodiac symbolizing divisions of the seasons of growth, we were given the story of a god who lets himself get tacked up and by doing so wins divinity for the meek to endure poverty and servility. This was Abraham all over again. The message became - let yourself loose and you win! The beginning of New-Speak. And the learned moguls at the Vatican knew that the divine birth/death/resurrection story had occurred DOZENS of times ...Horus, Mithras, Ahura Mazda...it was an archetypal symbol for the rebirth of the sun at solstice...they knew this and lied! And they still know it and they're still lying!

Spencer was in full rant, waving his arms around wildly like a dethroned Pope in a back street tavern. The stars out the window were like diamonds scattered on a velvet tablecloth.

'The extension of the Bible today is TV. It's manipulated by the descendants of kings and popes - the owners of the weapons and pharmaceutical companies. They expose us to conflicts that resolve in the justification of our buying their products, their politics and their wars. And they're doing all of this through talk - with words - words that don't mean what they say and that you can't pin down to lying. Denatured language that has led to denatured food and a denatured ecosystem.

'The root that makes the word flower is nature - nature - the reliable, sustainable, *heterosexual*, nature that makes trees bloom and each spring produces Bambi. It's the context of nature that gives words the meanings the words were invented to convey. Nature itself created the alphabet.'

'Oh come on!' I thought he was going outside the lines here. 'How could nature create the *alphabet*?'

'No. Really. 'The White Goddess' Robert Graves, this English professor of mythology; He shows how the alphabets of the Celts, the Hebrews, the Norse and the Sanskrit Hindus evolved from sounds attributed to the major trees in the forest.

'How could trees turn into alphabets?' I asked fairly reasonably I thought putting the box of Schezhuan chicken on the little coffee table so it wouldn't fall off the arm of the couch. I swam out for another dark.

'Trees are the oldest most sophisticated life forms on earth! They existed way before the dinosaurs and existed way after. Once trees evolved from simple grasses and became forests and groves, they really determined the course of evolution. So trees helped produce Humans. Each genus of tree is a complex history of adaption and creativity and memory and it is to each adaptive complexity that a letter was assigned - or deciphered.

'Trees...' I looked at my skinny little pear tree shivering out there under the freezing stars. Spencer's great passion was Permaculture. He believed that most people could grow their own food and that if they did it would completely disempower the politicians and weapons manufacturers.

'In dry areas trees created shade and retained moisture in the soil. In the jungles they provided food and safety from predators. The earliest ancestors to Humanity are believed to have climbed down from trees to begin human evolution. Animals climbed up into trees and humans climbed down from them. This is an anthropological echo of the Norse myth of Odin hanging from the Tree of Life for three days and nights to receive the vision of language. In the great northern forests, trees provided a home and food for most animal life as well as fire for Humans as the earth came out of the ice age.

'Earth's atmosphere was created by the ancestors of trees - the photo-plankton - and trees developed and sustained the atmosphere to provide oxygen and insulate the earth from the frozen universe. In a way, trees are all that stand between life and that cold cold darkness out there. Trees have been intimately linked to human existence.'

'So uh, what's your point Bud?'

'That the God of the Establishment is a manipulative abstraction, separate from biological processes. That life is exalted by engagement with the Earth, not diminished by it. That it is immoral to separate language from ecology. That the laws that protect the rich are based in thin air and that people allow such laws because of a long program of systematized mind control. That cops and soldiers should be paid a living wage by the consensus of society not by political interest so that they will protect the people and not the idle rich. That we the people stop tolerating fancy talk that violates the spirit of real democracy!

'Global warming is going to put an end to all the gobbledygook about prophesy Joe. When it sinks in that the biosphere is sick with carbon emissions, Jehovah making nature an enemy to be dominated by man isn't gonna to sell anymore. Global Warming is a logical outcome to environmental abuses by the driving forces of 'faiths', which have promoted exploitation. There is no pie in the sky. The pie is nature and it's being divided up between psychotics...

'The deeply imprinted prohibition of criticizing someone's 'faith' prevents people with common sense from openly exposing the humanitarian violations of those faiths! If a weapons manufacturer, through his publicist, claims he's defending The True Faith, there is no point of leverage for a humanitarian argument without saying such Faith is a mental illness! And you can't say faith is an illness in a Democracy that separates Church and State.

'There are a lot of people who would feed the hungry, house the homeless and give medical treatment to the sick just because it's the right thing to do. So - what's it going to be - blindly honoring prepackaged 'faith' or adjusting Human behavior to global conditions?'

Spencer's talk about language evolving out of trees had tickled something in the back of my mind. I remembered Djagda and Isult talking about the Ixtellar language - saying language was a cosmic technology. The Ixtellar was somehow the use of language on a level above poetry or prayer. Language was a living tissue. A knowledgeable use of Language was an act of creation. The Ixtellar allowed a person to become a direct energetic link in the cosmos. It wasn't 'faith in', but 'participation with' divinity.

As Spencer rattled on about language and nature, I'd been looking out the window at the silhouettes of the leafless branches sticking up into the stars and connections were clicking in my mind. I actually felt channels of energy shifting in the back of my neck and puffs of awareness blooming in my brain. At one point, my mind became intensely clear and calm and vaguely - was it the grass? - I began to see waves of the blue loosh pulsing in the room. The frightening sense I'd been carrying that my mind had split in two - one half seeing a dull physical entrapment, the other half seeing this vast cosmic interconnectedness - suddenly snapped into an integrated whole where everyday reality extended out into cosmic meanings. That tree I'd planted for Llueve was a living link between the two of us. It activated a current between the earth and sky. Between reality and dreams.

If the sounds of letters came from trees, were words a connective tissue linking biology and humanity? Nature itself, the bodies of plants and animals and humans were the nerve endings of God. I got the image of ancient trees growing on a planet with no animals or people. Just trees standing up and pointing into outer space and receiving star transmissions like antennas and rooting these energies into the planet.

Then come humans speaking the sounds prompted by trees. So that language was trees themselves talking through human voices - the Ixtellar was the stars talking through the sounds of trees in human voices - and this tree-speech linked the stars, galaxies and planet energies between human hearts. Physical sound grounded the stars to earth like an encrypted download from the Universal Hard Drive to the lap top brains of individuals.

Language captured real energies in the mind and heart like flowers collected the pollen of distant plants and captured their adaptations. Maybe the geometrical forms of stars I could see outside the bus window weren't just dots of light but geometrical mansions, captured by trees and flowers and then relayed to human experience through sounds, words and flavors and scents. The night sky was like a fluid screen of shifting geometrical forms that had real meanings. As you imagined them to be, so they became. Isn't that what physics had come to? I was seeing an integrated dual-energy system that linked Ovvala and Earth! If such an understanding were the basis of politics, a spoken truth would matter. Speaking words integrated to nature would affect things.

'Wow,' I said unconsciously.

'What?' Spencer said darkly. I'd interrupted his rant.

For a moment a spark had shot up in me and I'd felt that Ovvala was a real place. I saw that imagination was a bottomless well of potential possibilities. All it needed was to be engaged by a person - by me - to become reality. Ovvala and Llueve might be pure imaginary constructs I was experiencing in dreams, but they were still a *real* imaginary experience! A wild hope quivered in me that I could bring it all back.

I was grasping at straws to support a hallucination. It was all too dangerous. I didn't want an impossible longing for Llueve and Ovvala to begin again. It would be too painful to have to cut it off.

The whole point has become to let it all go and it's so hard. It's like being in love with someone who doesn't know you exist. Spencer felt me sag. He said,

'I'm sorry man - I got kind of caught up in sub-history. Here you are having some kind of brain fever and I'm getting cosmic on you.'

'No Spence. It's O.K. I was starting to think I was insane but listening to you I realized what crazy really is!' I said, our lips genuflected sarcastically at one another. 'I just need to get out of this fantasy I've fallen into and think about something else.'

'So the uh, people in the dreams...what were they called?' Here comes the patronizing I thought.

'Ovvalans,' I said deadpan.

'And the uh, evil dinosaurs?'

'Dracos,' I said feeling stupid.

'That's pretty uhm, amazing. How many dreams would you say you had?'

'About twenty, thirty maybe.' Now I really didn't want to talk about it.

'That is a lot of dreams about one thing.'

In self defense I told him how I had read the Monroe books and how Monroe had experienced something similar so that it wasn't like I'd just made it all up.

'It sounds to me like you're grieving for things you can't understand. That none of us can understand.'

'There's a consolation,' I said and asked him; 'Is there something I could do to get involved with your Internet group and the rain forest and all that? I need to focus on something other than my own thoughts - get involved in something.'

'Hell, it's a war out there! There's no end of things to get involved in. At the Plantation up in Sunshine Valley the BLM is threatening to blow up the artesian well that's been flowing for a century because it's got some cat hairs in it or something. The whole neighborhood is up in arms. They've entered a stay of execution at the county court house but they're afraid someone's gonna bomb the spring in the middle of the night. Then there's the take-back-the-land-movement in Brazil. You know, it's time you got your own computer and joined the real world.' I did what little emailing I did on Spencer and Lena's machine. 'You could help us co-ordinate the website.' He said. 'I don't know. I'll think of something.'

I drove home beneath thundering stars and went to bed.

MondayFebruary 7/05

It's a sunny morning. I can see the sun shining on the pallet of adobe bricks. Neutron is staring at me and flaring his nostrils. I'm going over to attach the wrought iron gates to The Wall and wire in the sconce lanterns. I need to get out of the house.

Chapter Thirteen

2/10/05

I bought an HP lap top and paid some dues to the server Spencer uses. Spencer set it all up for me. It does everything but cook dinner. I'm so clumsy that I wanted a lap top that could withstand being dropped a few times and HP sounds tough. I've been using other people's computers or going to cyber cafes for years to do casual emails. Now I've got my own machine! I've been spending hours checking out these web sites Spencer and Lena are in touch with. I've even begun keeping the journal on the laptop.

2/14/05

When I lay down to sleep and close my eyes, the impulse to have an OBE is irresistible, even though I feel I'm almost doing something illegal, now that I've admitted it's all a fantasy. To even consider trying to go there again feels schizoid.

But I'll remember things the Siddhe showed Llueve and me about making astral constructs - spheres of protective light and images of integration, and I automatically start doing these things. I've been building an imaginative, protective cocoon in mid air above my bed that I can enter if I ever do succeed in leaving my body. This cocoon is a Spitfire made out of astral energy. I imagine that I can see out of it, but an outsider looking in, would be blinded by the ultra reflective, silver shield on the outside. Embedded in its walls are protective symbols I saw in Logaana that the Siddhe use for deflection - pentagrams, hexagrams, and Ovvalan sigils that look like elf script. They have an alien beauty and look powerful. When Llueve and I were in Logaana and she was talking with Isult, I asked Silvaan what those symbols meant and he told me the images came from a place called Sahasra-Dal-Kanwal. This was a mysterious astral city that has existed for millions of years. Silvaan told me that no one knows who built it.

I know the Spitfire so well by now, having built five from models. When I close my eyes, I can easily imagine the dashboard with its altitude, gas and speed gauges. I have to tap the gas gauge to get it to read correctly. The leather on the seat in the cockpit is shiny and ripped with use and the ivory Bakelite joy stick has a blackened crack in it. The fuselage has even got Shark's teeth and flames - what the hell.

In case my body could be invaded and stolen or something when I'm out of it, I've built shields around my bed for protection - like a barbed wire fence and walls of electrified chrome plasma that surround the house. They run on cosmic electricity stored in ultra high tech batteries so that if an'entity' tried to pass through the plasma to get in my body - EEEERRRKKRRGHL!!! Cosmic electrocution! Zap fucker!

At times I can see myself in a mental institution sitting on the edge of the bed and a psych intern writing all this down on a yellow legal pad. He gives me my pill and I stick it between my gums. When he's gone I add it to my stash hidden under the linoleum...I'm not crazy! I'm not crazy!

I'm spending a lot of time at my kitchen table on the laptop. Hooking into these activist chat groups and watching YouTube clips has made me realize how intense things are in the world. So many dictatorships and oppressive regimes. People are dying of hunger and from lack of medical supplies. Thousand year old glaciers on mountaintops are melting in some places and droughts in others. And then so many videos of UFO's! The usual blurry photos. Is this stuff just made up?

I'm working steady. The Wall at the lawyers is basically done. I just need to wire some more lights and attach the quadra surround speakers. I think I'll take a break once this job's done - maybe finish my patio. Nothing much to report really. Yvonne is still mad at me for not taking out the trash or returning the video that day. She's incommunicado. But then I also haven't been calling her. I also forgot about the party at her office. We've kind of cooled it.

If Llueve is a dream, and I see her again, will her pregnancy be where it was at when I last saw her or will it have grown?

2/17/05

Went with Spencer and Lena to a presentation about the Brazilian farming collectives they track on the web. Two brothers resisting deforestation were murdered. There was a speaker named Caitano Veloso who played guitar and sang some songs he called 'Tropicalistas'. He then spoke about the awakening of South America to the rape of resources by the multinationals and the growing awareness of Global Warming and how dealing with it is becoming a passionate movement in South America as, apparently, it is all over the world. This news just doesn't get on the mainstream media.

Veloso talked about a new South American attitude towards poverty. The people don't see it as poverty at all but as economic marginalization, almost a type of warfare. He talked about how farmers and construction workers and workers generally have been marginalized by the economic hierarchy for the very reason that their work is the foundation of the economy. Manipulating the value of money against workers forces them to go into debt, and prevents them from organizing by the old divide and conquer.

He said that in South America there is a growing reaction to rhetorical promises of a better life through sacrifice. People there know that the stock brokers and wheeler dealers in the cities are making fortunes while the people who do the actually work on the ground are getting peanuts. They don't want to hear any more about a better tomorrow, he said. They want their share of the money. They see the models in American magazine adds for cars and clothes as industrial prostitutes. They see Hollywood movies and advertising as a kind of pornography. He showed mocked up photos of smiling, scantily clad sex goddesses smiling and holding up toothpaste tubes as they walk through fields of white crosses of mass graves in Normandy.

He said that all across South America people want unpolluted food and safe housing - period. They don't want American status and wealth they just want to stop being hungry, sad, sick and in need. When I got home I used glass cleaner on the dusty picture of Zapata on my kitchen wall. I liked the spirit at this thing tonight.

3/3/05

Took a long drive up into the Jemez mountains with Neutron.

Saw a report of new UFO sightings on YouTube. One in China the other in Russia. Who is distributing these things?

Yvonne is visiting her sister in Flagstaff.

3/7/05

Spencer and I went to a bar we go to sometimes after work. We were sitting at the bar and the TV was on. There was a panel discussion between Democratic and Republican senators. One of the Senators at the table was a face I saw at the Draco Council! I felt a kind of terror remembering this which also invoked the presence of Rexxon. Spencer had been talking to me and I completely zoned out. He finally butted me with his elbow to get my attention. When I turned to look at him, I could tell by his reaction that my eyes were full of my love for Llueve and of the Siddhe. He didn't say anything but I think he knew I was wandering my maze.

3/12/05

I got out!

I focused on Llueve and Ea and prepared to die! and - zoom - I was out.

The whole time I was drifting into the trance, I focused on the Spitfire as I always do, so that as I rose up out of my body I automatically entered the Spitfire, gripped the steering wheel and pivoted around in the room looking for enemies. There wasn't anything. I 'flew' the Spitfire slowly around the house looking for evil presences but there was nothing. Then I flew around the house and scanned the horizons. I went back and lay on my bed and flew out the back of my head. I flew through the waves blue loosh and slid through the opening into Ovvala without incident.

I drifted in low over the Daag countryside - and there they were - the familiar farm houses, groves of trees, Skaalin disk ships in lanes going the speed limit over Saala and the M&M's in the driveways. I came to Llueve's road and flew in low over her garden and saw the boulder with the quartz on it.

I dropped down to the lawn in front of the house and looked through the window. I could see Llueve moving around in her kitchen doing the dishes. The reality of Ovvala and Llueve came alive again with a huge emotional rush, and all the resolutions I've been building up about it all being a dream and a projection of my unconscious were just stripped away. It made me cry out loud to be there again.

I drifted into the house and stood next to Llueve just to be near her, sure she wouldn't be aware of me. She was wearing dark blue pants and a white blouse that made her look completely human. She turned slowly from the sink, aware of something behind her. As she turned, her astral body came out of her physical body and faced me wearing the white robe.

'Jwo!' She flung her arms around me and we kissed passionately and both started sobbing. Her robes turned to gauze in my hands and we began to float up into the middle of her kitchen. Her physical body slumped and became very still with its hands sunk in the soapy dishwater.

We cried and laughed. She was safe and unharmed. She was fatter. The baby was perfectly safe inside her. Warmth and strength returned to me. I felt myself glowing with happiness. I felt I was back to what has become the other half of my whole existence. Not just to be with Llueve - but to be back in Ovvala and know this greater reality.

'I was so afraid that lizard had killed you!' She said, tears of happiness pouring down her beautiful cheeks. Where have you been!?' she asked me.

'Oh, I was sick.' I said. 'I began doubting everything. I was convinced that all this was just a dream!' I said looking at the familiar things I recognized. 'No matter how I tried I couldn't get out of my body! I didn't even have dreams about anything. It was like the door just closed.'

We calmed down and exchanged rotes. She has become deeply involved with the Siddhe. Isult has given her certain responsibilities and she frequently goes to Logaana. She has also been to a place called Inxalrok. Because of her pregnancy she is taken care of by the Siddhe and frequently finds psychic guards hovering around her in both waking and dreaming life.

She said she demanded to continue to live in Saala and work at her architectural firm and live in her house in case I came looking for her. Also to keep track of her parents, afraid the Skandrr will try and harm them because of her involvement with the Suura. But so far no one has approached them.

Elsinaad and Kaelaa have become close friends and she often visits them or they come over to her house. They told her not to worry about me. They told her the Siddhe guard was keeping track of me and that I wasn't dead but just recovering from the injury and would eventually either return in the astral or they would come and actually take me to Ovvala in a disk. Llueve wondered if they were just appeasing her. I seem to have gained a certain status because of Llueve's pregnancy. If I could only see one of the Siddhe in a disk ship in Santa Fe it would free me of all this wondering about my sanity.

At the same moment, we both became aware of her body at the kitchen sink. Her torso was slumping over and her hair was hanging in the dishwater. Her nose was almost touching the suds.

'Just a minute,' she said. 'I better put the baby to bed!' She laughed as she slipped into her physical body and in it, walked to her bedroom with me following her. Her physical body lay down on the bed and fell into a deep sleep and let out a grinding snore and then was quiet. She then lifted up out of her physical and stood next to me.

'Let's fly!' she said looking down at her white robes. 'Yu-uk!' she said grinning a tarty little grin and transformed her clothes into a long, billowing black skirt with tiny multicolored flowers and a shimmering violet blouse under a short, electric blue jacket. I felt like an immigrant from a century ago in my white cassock and transformed my clothing to - jeans and a green T-shirt. Well, it's comfortable! She laughed at my attitude. We shot up through the roof of her house and flew through the night sky over the countryside. As we were flying I stroked her swollen belly. She smiled from the depths of her being and looked straight into my heart and crooned 'Meaaoowwwwww!'

I got a huge lump in my throat.

Chapter Fourteen

3/17/05

I was fast asleep and not dreaming of anything when a force pulled me out of my body and directed me with great authority to cross the bridge of Loosh to Ovvala. It wasn't an evil force, I knew that right away. But it had such a tremendous authority I couldn't even consider resisting. In mid flight to Llueve's, I was intercepted by Asaalen, one of the Siddhe Guard. He gave me a rote direct from the Siddhe Central Council. It was a complex message from Isult. An emergency was occurring among the Siddhe and I was needed at a certain meeting. I was to proceed to an off world location in a certain astral region of space. I was to proceed there immediately.

Asaalen led me to a streamlined astral pod with semi transparent walls shaped like a mini submarine. It had aerodynamic lines of dark gold with silver-green fins and crystal windows, all made of pure energy. As soon as I was seated, the Lambourginni-like hatch closed and the ship began to hum electrically. I could see nothing outside the windows but pulses of light. When the vibrations slowed down, I saw shimmering lights come into focus below me. In the distance there was a massive three or four tiered waterfall shimmering in the ultraviolet light of a purple dwarf star. The waterfalls cascaded over high cliffs with roaring oceanic falls as clouds of vapor rose into the air above it making rainbow sundogs within which swallows were swooping catching insects. These waterfalls were indescribably huge. Dense forests of ancient, old, deciduous trees led away up mountain foothills. A violet crescent moon, reflecting the dwarf star, rose over the horizon.

The colors of light and the density of the air were all different than anything I'd yet experienced. There was a diamond like clarity to the air and I could see stars through the dark blue sky.

Below the falls and on a wide shelf was the city. Sahasrah dal Kanwal. It was made of interspersed towers of crystalline glass joined by elevated walkways and plazas. There was a great, rounded crystal dome. It was supported by towering arches of crystal inlaid with flying buttresses and arches of contiguous crystal. The flight pod I was in directed itself to the wide, white marble landing at the top of a curving stairway leading into the main entry to the dome. There were some fifteen of the Siddhe guard standing areound talking in groups where I got out of the pod. I recognized Brodd, Toraag, Bodiccea and Elaak from various encounters at Logaana. They nodded towards me with serious faces as I walked into the towering Crystal Dome.

There were hundreds of people and many strange beings gathered in groups across the wide crystal clear floor. I recognized the Ovvalans and Humans right away. For the first time I saw real extraterrestrials. First off there were three Solarians who shifted between being particles and waves, like sequential, still shots, of lightning. There were almost a dozen Venutians who were small people, about five feet tall. They were slender and very graceful with exotically beautiful features and dressed in fantastic colors. They had faces not so different from humans but their eyes were huge and liquid-like. In the astral, it was apparent that their physicality - what they were when not in the astral - was of a different flesh than either Ovvalans or Humans. They sang or warbled to each other in flute-like tones gesticulating gracefully. There were also Lunarians - these were etherics for whom the astral was their normal state. They were like silhouettes of pearly tinted moonlight; they subtly and continually changed shapes like smoke. They were extremely emotional. There were Neptunians who were tall but also by nature etheric but of a dense, blue liquid-like mist. They stood behind the Lunarians protectively.

And at last I got to see the fabled Andromedans. They were incredibly tall - about twelve feet - and clothed in long flowing gowns. They had basically Human shapes in that they had arms and legs but they moved like a fluid, static electricity - or like lightning moving in continuous snap-shots. They had long mask-like, ancient faces and deep dark eyes. Patterns of magnetic vibrations streamed from their bodies. They were tremendously respected and loved by everyone there. They were considered very ancient and very wise. They were looked on as a guiding cosmic race. Too look at them for very long was to go into a dream. Then there were Saturnians, tall, slender, stern, monk-like beings who were gathered with actual Martians who were human in every respect; serious and tense and all of them were blond and muscular, even the females. They looked like a grouping of all athe phys ed teachers and camp counselors you ever had.

There were Uranians who were really weird, electric, and not completely in control of themselves. Flashes of electrical discharge pulsed randomly out of their heads seeming to continually surprise their own selves. Small, slight Mercurians were interspersed among them with severe, clever faces and quick electric eyes. They all looked like Bob Dylan dwarfs. They kept peeling one liners off at each other and snickering. I took all this in just walking in the door but didn't have time to really mingle.

There were also Pliedians present. They also looked completely human in every sense except that they were visibly more energetically evolved and some were as tall as eight feet. Sparkling lights twinkled out of their eyes. Geometrical forms radiated faintly out of their minds and then faded into the air around them with a jolly playfulness. They were very happy beings. There were other beings I couldn't intuitively place and had no time to consider. Like the Verdants, Endelmoths and the Tartajulans who radiated the color Vjian which is impossible to go into.

This was a meeting completely in the astral. There were no physical beings here. The entire city was astral. It had been designed millions of years ago by an unknown race that had left no records, no phone number, no forwarding address. Just this beautiful city. I remembered Silvaan telling me of its existence.

I noticed how elegantly and purposefully dressed everyone was. Rather than Star Trek uniform similarity, each person was dressed in a highly individuated way - stylish and even sexy. Cleverly woven blouses and jackets, flared trousers in reds and blues and turquoise like French courtesans. Shirts and blouses of elegant cuts with jewel like buttons. Boots that reached up to the thigh or sandals with spiraled toes or fringes or flaps. Hats and caps of bright cloth or simulated leather or metal and even astral substances I couldn't identify. Fantastic glimmering jewelry of unfamiliar stones and metals that radiated magnetic patterns and even scents.

All these strange wondrous beings were standing around in groups on the polished crystal floor under the high crystal dome with violet sunlight pouring through the walls and the enormous crescent moon rising above the multi tiered waterfalls. There was a great spirit of loving-kindness within a profound, religious like seriousness.

Seeing so much style and color I suddenly remembered that I was dressed in jeans and a T-shirt. I felt like a hick. Feeling a certain pride to make a good showing as a representative of Terra, I gave myself knee high boots with the tops folded over and coarse, baggy brown linen trousers like a buccaneer. I added a billowing, dark green silk shirt like in Pirates of the Caribbean and a fancy if hastily conceived leather jacket with steep lapels and cuffed sleeves. I didn't want to mess with a hat. I was tempted to add a dagger in a sheath but thought that might be uncivilized. Was I wrong! In the higher densities, tools of self-protection are taken for granted. Al Capone's famous quote; 'an armed society is a polite society', was here demonstrated in an elevated manner. I learned right there that heightened consciousness is intrinsically dangerous; the consequence of inattention towards a High Being was self disintegration. Compassion is present like the awareness of a martial artist towards a merely muscular man. And this sense of self protection in high consciousness is not mono-toned but is individualized; each to their kind.

When I spotted the Ovvalans, I walked across the crystal floor towards them. There were waiters passing by with trays of what looked like sea-weed grapes and blue pearls of Shakti on crackers of live, wiggling, kelp. There were turquoise and coral colored drinks. It was like a fancy high ball. A Lunarian woman writhed in front of me as I crossed the floor wearing an opaque dress of which parts became momentarily and selectively transparent. She tilted her huge cat-like eyes up at me and rotated subtly inside her gown as her eyes swallowed my gaze. When I just kept walking she let out a cry of frustration and stomped back to her group with tears stinging her eyes. Just then I spotted Llueve next to Djagda and Isult. Silvaan, Oorden, Elsinaad, Kaelaa, two commanders I've seen talking with Silvaan, some Siddhe Guards new to me and Seshena and Avaala. They were all in a group next to some Arcturians. There was a serious tone to their conversation.

Llueve was dressed in a silky carmine dress that made her dark, bronze skin radiant like old gold. She had pearl earrings and a necklace of polished sea shells. Her hair was up in a kind of beehive with strands coursing down the back of her neck. She wasn't showing through the loose material. I felt a stab of jealousy toward an Arcturian who towered over her and seemed to be bathing her with little crop circles of admiration. Cosmic elder or whatever – I didn't like it! With the Vogue style dress, Llueve wore brown combat boots with overflowing Kelly green socks. Strands of her luminous, writhing, auburn hair framed her face. She looked so feminine and beautiful. I couldn't believe what I was seeing. The moment she saw me, her eyes lit up and she advanced across the floor and kissed me unselfconsciously in front of everyone. I felt indescribably proud of her. She sent me a cautioning rote as if saying brace yourself! It was understood that we would talk later. Silvaan had noticed me, given Llueve and I a moment to touch base and then walked up to me purposefully. We grasped forearms Siddhe warrior style. He acknowledged me in a serious manner looking hard into my eyes to measure my awareness. He then passed me a rote of what had happened:

There had been an attack on the Inxalrok valley where nearly two dozen of the Siddhe community had been killed by a Skandrr attack. Some of the big Aeron disk ships as well as Blackhawk helicopters and some F-16 fighter jets had attacked at dawn. A lot of the valley farms were fire bombed. Inxalrok and all the Siddhe on Ovvala and Earth were on high alert. This conference was to consolidate collective intent in case all out war with the Dracos had begun.

One good thing that had happened; when an Aeron disk tried to enter one of the big cave shelters at Inxalrok, it was captured by Asaalen and a band of the Siddhe who blew up the entrance and trapped it, boarded it and captured the pilots.

The sense of tragedy and urgency this attack had caused, was visible in the faces of all the Siddhe, and I sobered up to it. I began to see that the energy dazzle of this meeting was also a strange mix of emotions. There was a general sense of exaltation in the transdimensional encounter. Emotions of happiness and sorrow, wisdom and war were all intermixed. There was grief for the families killed and for the land and crops and houses bombed. But in the representation of such far flung cosmic races, there was a thrilling awareness of the far boundaries of the intelligence populating the Universe. This made the dark Qlipothic power of the Dracos present by default. And though it was not something to be underestimated, it was a minor power in relation to the bigger picture created by the multiversal integration of the Races present.

As soon as I had been informed of the Skandrr attack, the Counsuelaars and Commanders of the Siddhe intensified their focus on the issues at hand and called the meeting to order. They had been tracking me psychically and knew about when I would arrive. I could hardly believe my role was that important.

Everyone arranged themselves in a wide circle around the center of the floor. The crystal dome became opaque and the room darkened. My sense of belonging to the Siddhe, of there being a continuity to my identity with them became intensified. Wherever Sahasra-dal Kanwal was located in space, I felt we were meeting at the very center of Mahaala itself.

I had just passed nearly a month trapped in my body - in Joe's body as I think of it when I am 'there'. Now I was not only back with Llueve but at this interstellar oasis with an intelligence council of interplanetarians and Exalted Beings from star systems light years from Earth, planning defensive measures against a demon hoard of phantom wraiths strangling the Soul of Illuva. The part of me that is invested in Joe was in speechless awe. But the older, deeper me was acclimating to having been here before - many times. A deep sense of familiarity and belonging was vibrating to the surface in me. I could see this was true for Llueve as well. We are incarnations that normally, I think, never would have been in the company of these leaders at Sahasra-Dal-Kanwal. But we had been chosen by Ea to further her purposes at a moment when there was great urgency, because the Draco plans were so advanced. Llueve and I looked into each other's eyes as layers of time shifted within both of us.

The doubts I had been feeling about the reality of OBE's now seemed absurd. It had been like being trapped in the brain of a hamster. I was vaguely beginning to understand that this entrapment in a limited imagination was the very problem itself. There were cultural imprints that caused me to forget this big view. Reinforcing this memory loss is the ultimate weapon of the Dracos. The shrunken scope of the imagination that 'Joe Soloski' was locked in for most of my life, illustrates the underlying effects of the Ouroboros. We are so vulnerable to suggestion, so trusting of authority. I was typical of an indoctrinated Human mind. I had inherited generations of belief limitations that my forebears had been imprinted with. We were working class Irish and Polish Catholics who had been locked into a mindset for centuries. We believed what we had been told to believe. If I hadn't fallen off the ladder I'd never have woken up in this lifetime. The New Age ideas of Yvonne's had been completely alien to me when she and I were together. But, now, with just a shift of the imagination, a universe opened up. My mind was ordinarily all tangled up in rationalizations and contradictions, justifications of meaningless information that consumed my confidence in my own identity. I took a detour around all that when I fell off the ladder and regained the part of my mind that is part of the central cosmic dream.

These thoughts circled in me as open rotes passed between various people in the Council Circle and expanded the scope of my understanding of the conflict with the Dracos and their infiltration of Earth's evolution. Seeing the Venutians, Mercurians and Lunarians, Neptunians, Saturnians,

Martians and Plutonians (who were all little, intense people, dressed in black and purple with eyes like black holes), the Andromedans and Pleidians there, I realized how ancient and widespread this conflict was. For these Beings, the conflict with the Dracos was on the level of a battle with the primal dark forces of the Universal underworld. And this underworld, I was beginning to realize, manifested in all the worlds of all these Beings, and was part and parcel of the spiritual ecology. Where there is freedom of choice in consciousness, there is an opening to the corrupting influences of the Underworld. Darkness itself is not evil but is a necessary ingredient in consciousness. But evil Beings can use it to attach themselves to Consciousness and feed from it. And this happens in endless permutations during the act of Self Creation; so that finding the creative good is as much a personal responsibility as finding the alien in the shadows.

Standing next to Djagda and Isult were three Human and Ovvalan elders – Ideema and Tantaala and another older Asian woman who was introduced as KwanYin and by whose vibes I recognized another Counsuelaar, as ancient and deep as Djagda and Isult. With them were seven young men and women of various Ovvalan and Human origins who were so much younger, that at first I thought them aides of some kind. But I realized, by the intensity of their vibes, that they were actually Counsuelaars themselves - members of the original 19 Siddhe, but in fresh incarnations. Though most of the doings of the actual Counsuelaars are highly secret, it is commonly known that there are currently 11 who are incarnate. Five are in between incarnations, two have gone on to Aaltare and then there is Ea. I have been cautioned about revealing very many details about the Counsuelaars. Though I will say that the men seemed to favor clothes from the Middle Ages with flared sleeves and trousers. The gowns on the women were timeless, maybe Grecian, except for Isult who seemed to like cheap, Cosmo Girl fashions. They are fascinating beings, the Counsuelaars. You can see the solar system turning in their minds. But now was not the time to look into this as a convergence of thought was being engineered. I needed all my energy and attention to track it.

There were more Siddhe commanders together around the circle than I had seen before. The names I remember are Sleardon, Monua, Illiesis, Donbrol, Aaen, Tavlia, Mimieglim, Alavaom, Edda, Assiemdlt, Idedidedom, Aeia, Eisr, Oliaonm. Luthien, besides Brodd, Toraag, Bodiccea and Elaak whom I had seen at the entry and of course Oorden, Silvaan and Asaalen.

The mood became serious. Actually it was deadly. A tornado full of razor blades? Incredible what the minds of Ovvalan warriors feel like when they're angry and preparing for battle.

Standing next to Llueve and with Silvaan on my other side, I was tuning into the frequencies of thought transference and picking up on various streams of information.

A river of information was openly flowing through the collective group-mind.

The following is a brief review of the rotes passing through the collective mind at Sahasrah. This constitutes the collective relationship between the Galactic Federation and Mahaala;

The Dracos are phantasms existing as intelligent and disciplined ghosts in the Qlipothic underworld – a place that is itself like a parallel universe – vast and fathomless. Dracos themselves have no physical existence. It is only through the 14 Ovvalan and Human AndarrAka that they have entry into physicality on Illuva. So that conflict with them could not take place in the physical – it needed to take place in the astral. If they were to make all out physical war on the Siddhe, it would kill too many physical Ovvalans and Humans, destroying the infrastructures the Dracos need to maintain control and profit.

From the Draco side, there are too few Reptilian hosts to risk open warfare. Less than fifty thousand Reptilians are in control of eight billion Humans and perhaps two billion Ovvalans. And while most Humans are mentally entrapped by the Ouroboros linguistic, there are tens of millions of Humans who are not and who could be brought into physical battle with the Draco forces if it came down to dog eat dog.

For Humans to believe they are under attack by extraterrestrial UFO's, would cause mental paralysis and psychological breakdown for hundreds of millions, probably billions. In a state of great panic, small minded leaders might order the detonation of hydrogen bombs and begin a nuclear winter. In Ovvala, there are Draco psychogenetic thought-constructs, manifesting as auditory hallucinations that can be manipulated to heighten the Faal syndrome causing mass suicides. It was very possible that Reptilian forces could cause an uncontrollable Faal epidemic.

It was generally agreed that until at least thirty five percent of each of the populations of Ovvala and Earth was liberated from their fixed, mono-dimensional mindset in the Ouroboros, that the reality of the dual dimensional world could not be openly revealed. To do so would only cause mental paralysis. If the Siddhe, for instance, began making contact with Iranian and Chinese farmers or Italian or Brazilian environmentalists, the Dracos could too easily brand such pointy eared Ovvalans as demons from hell. Then religious fanatics could be unleashed to wipe them out. This is what, I learned, had set off the Inquisition.

So, the fight that would take place between the Siddhe and the Dracos would have to be in the astral, with astral weapons and not in the physical with physical weapons. The astral precedes the physical in the energy-realm, so that to neutralize an astral being, automatically neutralized its physical counterpart. By keeping the confrontation, if only at first, in the astral, no bodies would be maimed or hearts torn open with bombs or farmland poisoned with radioactivity or factories destroyed.

The battle would be one of vibrations, cosmic intent and astral skill. To approach it this way was also the basic ethic of transdimensional democracy. Though this could change if things became desperate.

The key to everything was to pierce the Ouroboros lies about the nature of the multiverse, thus allowing the Ixtellar webs to be freed in the imaginative mind extension of entrapped Humans and Ovvalans. Then, highly adept visualizers - the Druiddaa Kalkaavae and the Wixxalia, could access the Altaraan, the higher-octave energy webs, and collect all available consciousness to sever Reptilian power from feeding on the Earth. This would unleash a force field of Lexl-light that neither the Dracos nor the AndrrKa wizards could withstand. But this last was a drastic measure as such a heightened vibratory state would kill many Humans and Ovvalans.

The contest was one of purposefulness. Whosoever's purpose was stronger and more relevant to the evolution of Mahaala, could produce the more powerful mind constructs. The weapons of the Federation would be made of intelligence and the cohesive thought-forms of love intent. The collective Ixtellar Integration produced by this Council, now, at this meeting, was the thought weapon that would serve as a rudder to dismantle the Draco Master Plan. This was to be a work of High Art and Consciousness War.

The Circle formed. The little Venutians and Lunarians stood together in front of the taller Neptunians in one part of the cirlce. The Mercurians and Martians, Uranians and Saturnians stood apart while Solarians and Jupiterians stood together on the other side with the Andromedans and Arcturians and the various exotic transdimensionals. Humans and Ovvalans stood together within the inner circle since it was our fight.

Everyone became very still. A ritual of collective thought was conducted. The Siddhe Counsuelaars directed the proceedings. The Counsuelaars projected a mental sphere of light above the center of the circle and everyone began adding parts to it. This central sphere became a set of colored, geometrically precise concentric spheres, one within the other, connected by snaking spiral energy lines of intense, living colors. Each and any part could be focused on to receive its rote of information - like touching an icon on a computer with the mind.

The spheres began to re-arrange themselves within one another which created a discontinuation with normal parameters. Silvaan explained to me in a silent rote that this was a security measure as it made it very difficult for intruders of any kind to energetically penetrate the place and astrally spy on the proceedings. Sahasra-dal Kanwal is already protected by the level of its vibratory frequency but this was an extra measure.

When the thought spheres were in place, everyone let out a long, undulating tone which was an Ixtellar invocation to Suudilve - the Creative Intelligence of Love. This was to create universal continuity with the Ixtellar strings in our solar system. Tall waves of cobalt blue loosh began to wash through the dome, the giant waves crashing in hissing whispers, bathing the collective thought sphere.

A thrilling vibration entered my mind and I internalized a directive from one of the Pleidians. Llueve was getting the same thing. We were being asked to relay a direct transmission of our experience at the Draco Council and add it to the mandala.

We walked into the center of the circle and stood, our sides pressed together. We took ourselves back to what had happened in the Draco Council Chamber. Holographic images of the Draco Chamber, generated by our memories, appeared in the sphere overhead - the sandstone vault, the Red circle inside the white jagged lines - the golden triangle inside the white circle - the tall naked Priestess with her protective gold anklets and bracelets – the wax-like AndrrKa sorcerer, the malevolent Homosauran CEO's in their black and Red robes quaffing glasses of fresh blood and then Rexxon's green scaled muscles dropping down onto the floor and the black sucking light of his reptilian eyes taking in the assembly and speaking about the intent to terrorize Ovvalans and Humans to a state of hyper consumerism; the plan to colonize Mars and the existence of the Janosian clone mothership. Then Rexxon slashing me across the chest, screaming, and leaping out of the chamber. These things were witnessed by everyone, and I felt a renewed humiliation. Llueve squeezed my hand reassuringly. Silvaan's eyes bored into mine with a warrior like intention that said 'be in the present, don't let a memory steal your energy'. That bucked me up. When it was done and Llueve and I returned to our place in the perimeter.

For some time nothing happened as everyone absorbed the information we had presented.

Then, as one collective mind, the company began plotting a course and a battle plan formed. The strength and resources of various factions of the Siddhe were reported on. The Venutians and Lunarians, who have alliances with trees, herbs, flowers and with grain were gauging the karmic rights of Homosaurs to receive love, sex and even food. Apparently, the nutritional content of food could be blocked. The Pleidians had undergone a similar confrontation in their evolution with a different rogue group of Qlipoths. Knowledge of this was imparted to the group.

The greatest mistake in dealing with the Dark Force was to fight it blow for blow. This caused entanglement with its depleting and parasitic nature so that Darkness knowingly used such engagement as a way to infect Galactic Federation integration with Suudilve which depleted the entire Federation front.

When all the constructs were in place and the mandala of current energies operating in the Mahaala had been inserted, the picture looked like a mix between a Navajo Sand painting and a 3-D hologram. A profound meditative stillness came over us as each individual internalized the picture and its meaning.

After Rexxon had offered his followers Mars in the holographic presentation, Isult walked into the center of the Circle. The geometrical lines of the thought construct shimmered and turned above her as she spoke;

'Mars you see! So! They plan to terrorize Illuva with Aeron Disks and hiquelopters to simulate an invasion from outer space! They are already colonizing Mars and tried to take over the moon but were kicked out by Federation allies. This staged invasion should distract everyone for a while from their wars for oil and from global warming and the so called recession! They could use this to bomb and attack Ovvalan and Terran population centers, to kill off elected leaders and blame it on fictitious extraterrestrials!' Isult reached up to her lapels to adjust her robe when Djagda quickly stepped forward and raised his voice to fill the hall.

'They must know there is enough underground water on Mars to re-create a living atmosphere to sustain their Janosian clones. Shifting global attention to an extraterrestrial invasion from Mars would create a huge disruption in the upcoming elections of the European Union. It would also distract the populations of every major industrial nation from the over extended credit gap between the East and the West. An invasion from Mars would make the global economic downturn seem insignificant by comparison. And what are the AIDS epidemic in Africa, the threat of Bird Flu or HAARP guided hurricanes to that!?' Barely letting him finish, Isult tossed her mane of lustrous red hair back and again took the floor. Her lilting French accent seemed stronger to me than when I'd heard her speak at Logaana. She walked slowly and elegantly across the center of the Circle, her hard boots clicking ostentatiously on the crystal floor.

'Mars as Heaven would also allow the Dracos to minimize concerns about climate change by promoting the belief that the Rapture has begun and that Mars colonists have actually gone to Heaven! What does atmospheric chaos on Terra matter to those in Heaven? So, first they tell their followers that Mars is the Heaven of the ancient prophesies, then they announce that only those who help raise funds for the spaceships will get seats! This way they can get astronomical sums for tickets to the Rapture! Whoever fails to buy a seat can go to hell!' Isult reached up to her lapels again to adjust her robe when Djagda harrumphed and himself strode directly in front of her and across the center of the circle. In his understated dignified way, he held out his arms in an appeal;

'The Dracos are masters at twisting public opinion. They can create video clips of weird, deformed extraterrestrials bombing Heaven from shining Aeron ships! Then show noble, executive Homosaurs in Armani and Gucci on Fleet Street and Wall Street waving their crocodile briefcases yelling – 'We will fight them on the cloud tops! We will fight them at St. Peter's gate! We will fight them at the throne of God! We will never surrender!' Djagda slammed his great staff down on the floor of the dome hall and the sound echoed with his rage and determination.

'Incredible that even the AndrrKa Magi believe Draco lies!' he raged. 'Knowing the Homosaurs feed on Ovvalan and Human blood! People are betrayed by overt treachery century after century and then the Reptilians generate even bigger lies to justify the former ones. But that is the anti-logic of the Ouroboros linguistic. It bypasses the rational mind and dives straight for the reptilian brain that is ruled by lust, fear, and greed!'

Two Lunarians burst into tears and started to float up into the air in complete exasperation. A tall Neptunian pulled them back by their trailing robes. The Venutians threw some kind of sparkle dust on them and they calmed down. Meanwhile, the Thought Sphere Hologram continued to rearrange itself as each new bit of information was relayed to it. Everyone continued to study it carefully.

'We must somehow prevent the building of these ships!' Isult shouted out, tossing back her emerald green cape to reveal a shimmering, tight, sage green dress that set off her hair beautifully and within which her ivory cleavage quivered like hard vanilla pudding when she slapped her thighs for emphasis. I thought again; Wonderbra? Djagda groaned aloud as she continued. 'Once the first Martian ships are built and begin flying up into space, the AndrrKa will intensify the illusion of an extraterrestrial invasion. They will manufacture war films showing rubber extraterrestrials hovering above the cities in unmarked black UFO's, shooting down jets and helicopters with ray guns. Teen age soldiers will be sent to fight them and be killed - then the Skandrr and the One God Cartel will tell people that we must honor those fallen lives so that they will not have died in vain. These are the tried and true tactitcs of fascism; capture the people's sense of horror and injustice and move the military and welath out of the coutnry and then re-assign it. The people are told they can't waste the billions of tax payer dollars of destroyed aircraft and tanks, so that more jets and tanks must be built to recoup the losses and more young people sent to their deaths. These are the same tactics they used in the World Wars and the Napoleonic wars before that!' Isult leaned forwards and glared at the assembly with her hands on her hips.

'Once large segments of the population believe the extraterrestrial attacks are real, it will be easy for the New World Order Cabal to suspend the Constitution and civil rights.' Djagda waved the wide sleeves of his robe in front of Isult as he spoke, his steely green eyes looking accusingly at her and then passing searchingly over the Assembly. 'Special wartime laws will be implemented to limit civil liberties and in the general chaos, these laws will be impossible to oppose. By the time the citizenry see these laws were tricks to usurp power from the people, it will be too late! The mind set of obedience to authority will have been established!'

'We must consider introducing Ovvalans and humans to one another in small numbers - in friendship - and start a people's judiciary to judge and sentence the criminal leaders *before* the Dracos set us at each others throats! There are, after all, hundreds of millions of people who are on the very edge of 5D as we speak!' Isult shouted and then glared at everyone with her arms extended, her robe parting to reveal a hard, flat stomach and impressive cleavage.

'We need to see what is aboard this Mothership first!' She screeched, striding across the center of the room and away from Djagda extended arms, her outer robe flapping elegantly. 'These clones! What are they capable of? Could we create our own replications and program such clones with a different intent?'

'And these Janosians!' Djagda said, his voice quivering with baritone passion. 'Who are they? Are they evil? Are they really strong? Has any interstellar contact taken place with them or do they only deal with the Dracos? And can the Dracos control them? Or will they become a menace once they've entered our planetary space?'

There was a long silence as the Counsuelaars and Commanders, Jupiterians, Saturnians, Martians and Mercurians, Pleidians and Arcturians and Andromedans, Tankarugians and Andelmoths considered the implications of the Janosians skills and powers. The colors and geometry within the collective thought-sphere turned and vibrated as everyone watched attentively. Then one of the Arcturians stepped forward and spoke in a multi-voice;

'Without knowing what is in the Janosian Mothership or how the Dracos plan to use what tools or weapons the Janosians bring with them, grave errors of judgment could undermine Siddhe organization and cause irreparable harm. It is our judgment that the Janosians ship must be boarded before anything else takes place!'

'With what is known about the AndrrKan psychic police units and their use of remote viewers, it would be impossible to approach the Mothership in physical craft closely enough to board the ship. One thing only that you now possess can bypass their sensory system and this is the invisibility of the couple Joe Soloski and Llueve Anaalia.' I was amazed the Pleidian pronounced my name correctly.

'No!' Isult leaped forward, hands on hips, fearlessly confronting the tall Pleidian. 'You know who Llueve is pregnant with! We cannot risk the capture of Ea or any shock that could affect the birth! With Ea back among the living, we would at last have a real weapon against the Reptilians! We can't risk loosing that or of endangering Llueve!'

'They went in and out of the Draco Council unseen!' Silvaan said in a very forceful tone from where he stood with Elsinaad in the circle. He might have as great a respect for Isult as any but didn't seem phased about speaking his mind. 'If they could be invisible there - with the most intense surveillance there is among the Dracos - their very Council Chambers! – then there is a good chance that, with Joe's greater experience now, they could remain under cover among these Janosians' Thankfully, Silvaan didn't dwell on the reason why we had been spotted - my almost volunteering to join the Reptilians!

'I acknowledge the probability of this,' Djagda said. 'If not for Joe and Llueve penetrating the Draco Council we wouldn't have learned about the Janosians or Mars or the planned invasion. We would be in the dark. What we can gain from seeing what is on this Mothership is too great to pass up or delay. The question we should ask is how can we provide protection for Joseph and Llueve while they are in this ship?'

Isult turned to the cluster of Siddhe Commanders and challenged them; 'Can the Aeron ship we've just captured reach deep space?' As she spoke, Isult thrust her chest forward and then stuck her chin out at Dagaan defiantly. Isult's cleavage was so robust I wondered if she was wearing falsies. Which apparently Llueve picked up on because she slapped my leg indicating with her eyes the hologram where I saw a picture of a swollen Wonderbra dissolving from my segment of the mandala. I was brought back to the seriousness of the assembly by Isult's nearly hysterical shout.

'Are this ship's weapons strong enough to sabotage the Annanokian Mothership if there is a fight? And can the Federation be present in the astral to monitor Jwo and Llueve and come to their aid in an emergency? Can the Aeron disk even get to the other side of the moon or is it going to run out of gas?' Isult asked scornfully looking contemptuously at Silvaan and Djagda and the tall gangly Arcturian who had spoken.

'The disk-ship can easily travel to the other side of the Moon!' Silvaan said defiantly. 'We have been tracking these ships for a year. They can reach Mars. The moon is nothing. Their plasma canons can slice through twenty inches of hardened steel and their prodigy bombs can sneak up from behind a target. The fuel system runs on enriched hydrogen in a fusion state. It uses three and half tablespoons for each million and half miles. It has a range of eight hundred million miles! There is an EM overdrive much like the Toyota Prius that can bolster the thrust with solar wind so that it could conceivably travel for 16 light years in a few weeks time.' Isult let her arms drop, shifted her weight to one hip and with furrowed brow, looked sarcastically sceptical and not entirely convinced.

'And what is there at 16 light years from our solar system!?" She demanded, pivoting suddenly, hands on hips, and stomped her foot, her cleavage quivering angrily in a very French way.

'Nothing. Just empty space.' Silvaan said, looking baffled. Isult threw up her arms as though having made her point and yelled 'Ahh! Empty space!' Djagda rolled his eyes.

'A party of seasoned warriors could go up in the disk,' Elsinaad spoke up, coming to Silvaan's aid. 'Another battalion could travel with Jwo and Llueve in the astral and wait near the ship. At the slightest danger, these all could be sent for or we would call the whole thing off and return to base.' Isult glared at her as though she were a traitor.

'We could do this! If we can get a jump on them with some vital information, we may be able to trip them up so that if nothing else they become greatly delayed,' Bodiccea looked straight at Isult with squinting, piggy eyes. She threw up her massive head of ant red hair and bouncing hard on her heels for emphasis, stood perfectly still while her great meaty breasts kept moving up and down. Isult actually looked intimidated for a second.

'We will do anything we can in the service of the Siddhe! Right Jwo?' Llueve said turning to me. he eyes like slits. I nodded, determined to prove I was made of better stuff than I had shown at the Draco Council.

'Thank you merehalla ke-aeldea - and Jwo - brother in arms - we are honored by your courage and generosity,' Isult said, whipping her robe back around herself chastely and giving us and those pushing for the mission her grudging support. 'Ea would want this. I'll shut up!' She said in a thick Parisian accent and the whole Circle laughed appreciatively at Isult's political incorrectness.

Everyone beamed at us as I was thinking, oh my God, where is this leading?

Llueve and I were again asked to manifest our presence in the center. We looked at one another and concentrated on creating a blue, oval egg of light containing our love for our planet and of our willingness to fight for it. When you get good at this sort of visualizing, it's possible to embroider your creations with embellishments. As our thoughts were registering in the sphere above, Llueve added a curlicue of little red hearts joined by white valentine like filigree lacing up through the geometry. In the same spirit, I made a Spitfire fly around and do circling dives with a little trail of smoke. People laughed as they saw us doing this and began adding their own embellishments. Isult's broomstick with her witch's hat on it appeared. Silvaan added an early, clumsy looking Nazi Foo Fighter UFO disk that pursued my Spitfire. I thought this was pretty funny and laughed aloud. Elsinaad added a rainbow of stars while Bodiccea added a huge naked man with curly red hair that hid nothing and everyone laughed wildly, even the Arcturians who sounded like foghorns.

These images vanished as a sobering silence came over the group and serious lines of battle and defense were placed in the aural egg. Presets for evasion and escape were constructed. Communications lines and shields were all encapsulated shared awareness.

When this was complete the Assembly was over. The company stood and bowed to one another, then turned again to face the center of the circle. A stillness came over everyone as a ray of evanescent light formed at the core of the construct and began pulsating. A diamond like gem of a light I had not yet seen in the astral took shape before our eyes. The shape was a two pointed diamond standing vertically. It had endless facets and faces that both generated this quivering light and reflected everyone's thoughts. I knew at once that this was the Source Energy - Suudilve - the core Universal Ixtellar Vibration. This Diamond Light made me feel such a wonder and a sense of honor. I felt energized in a way that made it clear as day to me that dying in its service was the point of everything. To dedicate one's existence and effort to this intelligence was the very meaning of having purpose. As I watched, I saw that beneath the outer layer of faces and facets on the diamond were more layers leading deeper and deeper into the interior of the gem from where a conscious light shimmered. It knew us. It knew me. I felt exalted in its presence as it subtly winked out making the mental sound of 'Tah!'

'Tah!' The entire Assembly shouted in response. Immediately the Siddhe Guard moved to the positions laid out in the plan to board the Annanokian ship. The Lunarians, Venutians, and the other Planetaries, the Pleidians and Arcturians and we Ovvalans and Terrans said our goodbyes. Llueve and I walked across the crystal floor and out between the columns of the Dome's front landing.

I saw that the astral pod I had arrived in was still there. Llueve got in and I followed her. I looked at the strange little dashboard but had no idea what to do to make it fly. The sense of expanded awareness I'd just experienced had begun dissolving and the practical me as Joe came back trying to figure out how to operate this thing. I saw a button that looked like first gear and thought of pressing it. Llueve laughed at the expression on my face and quickly touched a series of geometrical shapes on a screen and we lifted up and out over the the huge waterfalls and down into a forest above the falls. We flew in silence, absorbing what had just happened and landed softly on the forest floor.

'How do you feel?' I asked Llueve and placed my hand on her belly looking into those eyes that at one point I had feared I would never see again.

'I feel strong! There is no choice anyhow! We have to go - we're the only one's who can! It's what we are alive for Jwo! How do *you* feel?' She asked me. I think the memory of Suudilve was still shinning in my eyes when I smiled at her. The radiance of her own smile told me there was nothing more to say.

'Look!' she said. A transparent white deer was walking calmly through the forest where the sunlight fell in bands of violet-gold. A purple light radiated softly out of the deer's eyes as it looked calmly at us each in turn. All the really beautiful places I have seen streamed through my mind – the redwood forests on the California coast, the still waters on a summer's night in Key West reflecting the moon and stars, desert mesas in New Mexico. I thought of all the defenseless animals, the trees and flowers of earth now in danger of extinction. The Reptilians saw in all of this only the opportunity for profit and ownership. I felt a deep sense of my duty to protect these things and how this feeling of respect for such beauty was the presence of Suudilve within me. It was my love for these things that made me a cosmic man. I held Llueve's hands and prepared for battle.

'If we get separated - or we die Jwo - it's O.K. We know that we don't die forever. Somewhere, somehow, we'll find a new way of living - find a way of forgiving them.' Llueve looked off towards the great domed hall below us. 'You know,' she said, 'a love like ours, will never die,' and she turned to me and put her arms around my neck, 'as long as I have you near me!' Two small, binary moons had risen above the horizon with green and black rings around them. Stars were shinning through the violet sunlight. Her words made tears well in my eyes. We looked out past the moons and stars and she said; 'Some where - beyond that sea - you'll be there watching for me and I'll be watching for you too and then we'll just continue eh?' She sniffed. 'Fucking Dracos!' She made the sound of an angry cat 'fffffffft!' and we laughed through our tears. It was time to go.

We stood face to face touching each other's fingertips. Llueve looked down at her carmine dress and concentrated, pursing her lips for a moment. Her clothing changed to a shimmering midnight blue body suit with a thick utility belt holding mace, a knife, a GPS, a canteen and a flashlight. I changed my clothing to jeans and a really dark green T-shirt with the picture of a smoking biplane zeroing in for the kill. Die with your boots on!

We ascended shifting dimensions back to Earth/space where we could see our own moon above China in the star filled sky and flew up towards it. Faster and faster we flew as the moon grew larger and larger. When we were almost at the Moon, we orbited around to the dark side and began searching space for this ship that was supposed to be out there somewhere. We passed the cloaked Aeron disk in which we knew Ilsenaad and Djagda were watching over us and received a burst of encouraging parallelograms. Then we saw a vague cloudy mist and received a telepathic rote from Djagda that Isult; Silvaan and a company of Siddhe Guard were all near, cloaked as planned. There were no spies sighted yet.

We continued advancing into the darkness. I couldn't see or sense anything at first. Then we saw it...

Still distant, the ship was a massive black doughnut with a few faintly twinkling lights in it. The nearer we got the bigger it got until we saw that it was an epic, Manhattan sized craft with four central spokes radiating from its hub. I would guess that the radius of the doughnut was a half mile across. There were thousands of windows in four tiers glistening across the face of the tube, reflecting the brilliance of the stars in space. Only a quarter of the windows were lit from within. Sections of the doughnut had structural webbing without an outer skin so that you could look right through parts of it, making the thing look deserted or wrecked. We approached cautiously as we had been instructed, trying to sense either satellite probes or psychic guards between the ship and us.

We were both in a heightened state, and continuously looked to the sides and behind ourselves for a sneak attack. We glided along outside the riveted black plates - looking in the windows and searching for a clue as to what this was all about.

In one of the lighted windows we saw a large, lighted chamber. The walls and floor looked basically like the Enterprise, as you would expect. Except that the floor was covered by rows and rows of clear glass boxes with glistening curved domes set in mathematically precise rows. There were a few groups of little gray aliens moving between the boxes - the ones with the big black, watery, slanted eyes you see on T-shirts. They had long skinny arms and long insect like fingers. They walked in a waddling, rocking back-and-forth way - a lot like teddy-bears actually, as they passed between the rows of glass boxes in groups of three and four, carrying what looked like large transparent watering cans. From this they poured some kind of glistening viscous liquid into the opened boxes while another Gray poured in a colored powder from a little carton. A third Gray then stirred the liquid and powder together with a big plastic spoon. They then closed the lid of the coffin like box and moved on to the next one. We decided to enter through the wall and see what was going on.

We picked an area where there were no aliens and glided through the wall, crouching down behind a broad computer sort of device with a lot of blinking, colored LED's on it. This was connected to a rack of suspended test tubes in a large glass case. We stayed perfectly still for a while to see if any alarms went off or if anyone noticed us. We had been told that the Annanokian Grays are extremely sensitive and capable of feeling even Llueve and my combined presence, but nothing happened. So we stood in a half crouch and inspected the coffins.

I froze in shock! Lying before me, naked and floating in pink Jello was Ronald Reagan! He was only as old as he was when first in office in seemed perfect health and physical fitness. And he was breathing! I could see bubbles rising through the gelatinous substance he was immersed in, which was quivering with the throbbing of his heart. A faint vapor from his breath clouded the lid. In the next box was a duplicate Reagan and in the next another Reagan! Then another. And another. I counted fifteen Ronald Reagan's just in my row, some in pink plasma, some in blue, one or two in two tone lime green and cherry red. His appendectomy scar was vivid and stretched. When I ran out of Ronald Regan's I saw some Kim Kardassians and then some XXXX. (Deleted)

Llueve beamed me an info rote that she was finding human's in the boxes but recognized no one. I was about to go over to her when I saw a Hillary Clinton lying in orange plasma, another in the next box and then another and another and another Hillary Clinton. I counted 11 Clintons in orange plasma. There could have been more in parallel rows. I was moving along in a straight line. Looking at the rows running along side the one I was in, I saw a few Ben Bernankes, some Hanna Montanas and then a row of Obamas. (Arizona Senator etc. *) Standing on tip toe I could see an entire row of Bin Ladens and beyond that some Christie Turlingtons. I was about to go over there to get a better view when I felt Llueve vibrating me intense waves of awareness. Suddenly the lights in the room became brilliant and a honking alarm began to sound. Large steel doors slammed open and dozens of little extraterrestrial Grays in riot gear came running through. They looked adorable, like friendly teddy bears with backpacks except that they were all holding silver cattle prod-like rods and were about to try and kill us. They moved really oddly - kind of like adolescent girls on a soccer team - their knees knocked as they ran and they made high, squeaky noises. They all held the clear plastic batons and spread around the glass boxes waving these in the air. Then I got it! They were sweeping the room with sensors.

I leaped over next to Llueve. 'Can they see us?'

'Maybe not,' she said. 'But what are those things they're carrying?' A group of them was getting closer and as they did, their wands began to glow first yellow then orange and finally red as rays of infra-red plasmic light extended out towards where we stood.

Llueve stepped forward to get past one of these rays and screamed. The rays were electric. The Gray holding the wand that had zapped Llueve started squealing in long high pitched sounds and other Grays began squealing and moving in her direction. The rest of the group answered with more squeals and turned towards us.

Suddenly I understood - they were surrounding us and pushing us towards an open area against a wall at one end of the room - they circled us and began moving forwards. As we retreated - I was trying to think of what to do. Llueve yelled 'through the floor!' Just then, a thin meshed screen dropped from the ceiling surrounding us and the floor lit up in an electric mesh design and began throwing sparks - we were caged in an electrically charged screen, enclosed on all four sides so that we were forced to float in the center.

A hush came over the E.T.'s. at the sound of rattling glass, they turned as one towards the opened steel doors where they had come through. A weird looking life form was advancing in a gleaming very high tech, self powered chrome wheel chair. Sticking out the side and aimed towards us was what could only be a ray gun. An IV bottle was suspended from a steel rod on the chair and it was rattling against its support. A plastic IV tube from the bottle hung down and was inserted in the neck of the Thing driving the wheelchair.

All the Grays made a clearing as the wheelchair advanced and the Thing came up to the electrical enclosure where we were. In the hand of one of the Grays I noticed a little, empty box of rasberry Jell-O.

The wheelchair advanced to the edge of the mesh screen net and the Thing squinted its eyes looking for us as though it had bad eyesight. Its desiccated head wobbled spastically on top of a skinny little cabled neck as it looked in the cage at us through huge, bloodshot eyes. The Thing's arms and legs were strapped to the wheel chair. Its face was a blob of pink flabby folds of flesh, gelatinous and transparent through which blue veins were clearly visible. This transparent, flaccid, skin hung in folds from its face and arms even though it was very skinny. A shiny steel band around the forehead held the head erect against the steel post sticking up from the back of the chair. The I.V. bottle, full of what looked like pure alcohol was clamped to the post and gurgled down the tube hanging from it and into the thing's neck. The veins pulsed through its skin as the alcohol-like liquid was sucked into its blue veins. A Blue Blood I thought. Except for the long, transparent twitching fingers, the body seemed completely paralyzed. But the eyes were alive and huge, nearly completely white, they whipped around, lightning fast inside the sockets, taking in everything. Somehow I just knew this was an Annanokian.

The forearms and hands of the thing were tightly strapped to the arms of the chair and the fingers were moving rapidly over buttons on the ends of the chair arms. The walls of the electric grid began to close in around us. He was going to box us in and shoot us!

'Dematerialize!' I shouted in a choked voice to Llueve. It was one of the escape techniques posted in the hologram at the Dome. This involved becoming so tiny that you could slip through the atoms of solid material. But even as I said it, arcs of intense electric voltage cracked out of the ray gun on the chair, shooting across the mesh cage from wall to wall stunning me. I tried to turn and see how Llueve was doing when another set of electric arcs electrocuted the space and froze me in place. Llueve too was stunned, paralized. She couldn't speak or move. I began to feel heavy and slow. I couldn't think. All around us, dozens of the beady eyed Grays watched us and right in front of us the large, lanky, pink skinned Annanokian stared at us with its wrinkled freak face.

'Hmmphmgrnmssm', it said. And then 'ooohwah!' it's blobby lips moving gelatinously and glistening with spit. It jabbed at one of the buttons on the arms of its wheelchair. A field of violent electrical arcs traversed the cage - side to side and top to bottom until we were encased in a graph paper of electrical charges. Where the pulsating electrical charges stopped, silhouettes of our forms were revealed. A thin, coiled, chrome tube began extending out from under the wheelchair base - it looked like an electrical syringe.

Just then a wild wailing scream filled the chamber and all the extraterrestrials clapped their three fingered hands over their pointy ears - many of them falling to the ground and writhing wildly in pain. A piercing, warbling sound was echoing off the metal walls of the chamber. Then I saw Silvaan, dressed in a plaid kilt, standing on a little flying flight-seat that looked like a seat taken off a tractor. He was blowing a set of Ovvalan bagpipes. Isult in the tight, green dress, her red hair streaming behind her and riding on her broomstick - was speeding right at our Annanokian as the syringe extended through the electrical mesh towards Llueve. At the last minute she banked left and the end of her broom slammed into the back of the wheel chair which toppled over, crashing against some of the incubation chambers, which smashed to the floor. Gelatinous colored fluids spilled out in a mix. The little grays were writhing crazily, splashing in the gelatinous fluid, holding their hands to their ears, kicking their feet and making stress noises as Silvaan continued to play the pipes.

The cross hatching of electrical lines stopped arcing and I began coming out of the state of shock. Suddenly I could think and move. I reached out for Llueve. She was looking around wildly for a way to escape. But neither of us had enough mental clarity to act.

The clones in the incubation chambers that had shattered sat up and started climbing out of the boxes, dripping fruit colored plasma. Two naked Ronald Regan's gave each other beaming smiles and said to one another - 'There you go again, he he he.'

Isult and Silvaan flew low over rows of the boxes flipping the lids open as they passed. Dozens of famous naked people, Prince Andrew and Kate, (*) climbed out of the colored ooze, stood up and began wandering around aimlessly, tripping over the E.T.s who were quivering and writhing on the floor holding their ears.

Three Arnold Swarzneggers, dripping red and blue plasma, began flexing their muscles for each other and saying lines from the movies - 'Hasta luego hombre' and 'I'll be back! - I'll be back!' and 'YOU are terminated!' and laughing. 'Nice latisimus dorsi governor!' one said to another and the other replied; 'Nice legs Mr. President!' laughing hoarsely.

Three Hannah Montanas were chasing a little Gray calling out 'Daddy! Daddy!' A sea of battle Grays, dressed in armor and carrying ray guns came through the portals at the end of the chamber with a number of Annanokian Things in wheelchairs following them, rolling right over grays writhing on the ground. Ray guns extending from the wheelchairs started shooting deadly plasma bolts across the room. Naked clones were wandering around casually, laughing and muttering while the Grays squealed trying to plug their ears.

Isult flew up to us and beamed a very intense rote; 'Dematerialize into oxygen!' She held the thought construct with great intensity until we both latched on to it. Llueve and I looked at each other and concentrated on oxygen.

Outside the Mothership, the stolen Aeron disk had docked, extended an atmospheric suction pod over a window and then blasted the window open. Djagda, Elsinaad, Bodiccea and Asaalen entered. Dressed in his usual Druid's robe, Djagda was thrashing Janosian out of his way with his staff while Bodiccea tossed Grays around with judo moves.

As I defragmented, I saw Djagda moving swiftly towards the tall, glass case, where hundreds of test tubes in different colors were arranged in rows. He smashed the glass covering with his staff and started stuffing test tubes into a square shoulder bag. He walked quickly back towards the broken window he'd entered calling to Elsinaad and the others to follow. Silvaan was wailing away on the pipes while Isult continued her fly-overs, knocking down wheel chairs and plasma coffins. Janosian wheel chairs were tangled in a heap, Janosians were desperately trying to stick the IV's back in their necks while the terrified little Grays were squirming all around them. Plasmic rays from the ray guns were bouncing around off the walls.

Llueve and I both fully defragmented and began to hum in the concentrated way we had been shown. We became smaller and smaller until we were atoms in a field of atoms. Then we shot up and out into space. I thought we were alone and free when I saw what looked like a cloud of mist pursuing us and sensed from its vibrations that it was the astral body of a Janosian in pursuit.

We were in a world of atoms shooting through orbiting particles with the gray cloud of the Janosian astral body following us. I could see the atom traveling beside me had Llueve's face.

'It's catching up!' I yelled.

'Don't get separated!' she cried out.

We were flying through energy fields - their colors and shapes, their boundaries and frequencies were things we knew how to deal with instantly as though we had been here - a lot - before.

The Annanokian was very familiar with this domain and knew what to do. Free of its useless body, it was very adept at flying through the atoms. While we were atomic spheres in the environment of atomic spheres, it was a formless, gaseous cloud with abilities beyond ours. It knew how to manipulate itself very well and traveled like a speeding serpent, streaming through the particles. It was gaining fast. I realized it had more power in this realm than it appeared to have in its withered physical shape and was about to do something we couldn't anticipate.

A misty tentacle advanced and circled around Llueve's spinning particles and synchronized to her spinning and began to introduce a new particle and I realized intuitively that it was going to alter her atomic structure capturing her in a different atomic frequency where I wouldn't be able to follow.

In the highest emergency, I was to beam a certain signal to Isult that she had privately given me that was her personal signature vibration. I did that, concentrating to the point where I let go of my concern for Llueve because that is how much it required of me to focus to create this distress signal.

I felt an electrical shock in the center of me and out of it came Isult and Silvaan and three other of the Siddhe. They were hydrogen particles and even as they materialized - they scanned the danger to Llueve and shot, as particles into Llueve and the Annanokian. I felt myself dissolving into salt and hydrogen. They surrounded Llueve and isolated the Annanokian's energy. A violent shock jerked me to a stop and I woke up in bed quivering with rage.

I sat up in bed, tears of frustration streaming down my cheeks with my jaws clenched. The silence and calm familiarity of my room was, for a moment, a violent nightmare. My emotions were in a state of chaos - the sense of danger, emergency, fear for Llueve and our child, the aggression of the Annanokian and the burning heat of Isult and Silvaan face to face, atom to atom with the Annanokian were what my insides were still dealing with. But my outsides saw a fish tank bubbling quietly with soft green light and the Coral Angel Fish sleeping quietly among the bubbles. Moonlight came in through the window. It lit up the piles of adobe bricks in the yard that looked just the same as they had for the last year.

It was 1:17 in the morning. I got up and went to the fridge and got a beer. My hands were shaking and kept slipping on the damn tab. I stood at the window staring up at the moon where Llueve and the Siddhe were mano a mano with those Annanokian freaks. It looked like an ordinary night while my thoughts raced thinking - my God, what have we done to Llueve? And then thought - so, I've got my dream-world back! In spades!

Chapter Fifteen

3/17/05

After I'd written on the laptop for a while, I stood at the window in T-shirt and sweat pants with a gargantuan cold green can of Foster's in my hand looking out at the starry night. There had been a quarter moon earlier but it had now set. The image of Llueve's face, as we were pursued by the desiccated Annanokian, somewhere out there, below the horizon, wouldn't leave my mind. The fear in her eyes and the depth of familiarity that has grown so deeply between us, was branded inside my eyelids. What if they captured her astral body? I felt cold with a sick fear. There was nothing I could do but pray for her. I looked at my magnet of Guadalupe on the fridge. I looked deeply into her kindly, slightly crossed eyes and pleaded with her to protect Llueve.

I couldn't possibly sleep. I had to talk to someone about Llueve. But I'd convinced Yvonne, Spencer and Lena that I'd stopped believing Ovvala and the astral beings existed!

I looked at the clock on the wall next to the picture of Zapata. It was 2:52 A.M. I dialed Yvonne's number anyway. After three or four rings she answered sounding sleepy and alarmed.

'Vonnie,' I said softly when she knew it was me. 'I've got a problem.'

'Joe?! Joe Soloski!? You've got a problem!? You are a fucking problem! It's goddamned - what - three O'clock in the blinking morning for Christmas sake! What? Ghwak! Ugh! Wait! Let me get the hair out of my mouth. O.K. What!?'

Yvonne's ability to go from asleep to pissed off is a genuine talent. Probably a Scorpio thing.

'I can't just tell you over the phone. Can I come over?' I heard her taking deep yoga breaths.

'This isn't about sex is it?' She said with dark feline menace. I reassured her it wasn't.

'O.K. You know where the key is,' she said darkly and hung up.

So I got dressed and drove over there. Half of me felt totally normal, driving calmly through the night, seeing the dusty trail of the Milky Way curving overhead, the cars parked in front of sleeping houses under the street lights. And half of me felt strangled in an emotional knot that needed to yell and scream, fight somebody, get punched in the face, to get the fear and anxiety for Llueve out of my body. I would have to tell Yvonne everything. I couldn't keep all this secret anymore. Could I feel love for Llueve and a kind of affection for Yvonne at the same time? Did their existing in different dimensions still make it two timing?

I let myself into the condo with the key in the hall. She was lying in bed with a candle and incense burning on her bedside table. She flung the covers aside for me to get in and smiled sourly. We'd never made up after I didn't show for her office party. But it's not often that I've ever asked Yvonne for help or consolation in the emotional area so she knew something serious was on my mind. I'd tossed my jacket at the living room couch. I took off my shoes and climbed into bed with her with my clothes on.

'What's going on Joe?' She said softly, reaching out to touch my arm. She was awake now and prepared to listen with a tolerant, politically correct compassion.

I told her I'd started astral traveling again and that I was sure it was all real. She sighed knowingly, visibly thinking: Nutsoid.

I talked about Llueve and the love and sex she and I had been sharing all along and that I'd been afraid to tell Yvonne about. I talked for an hour. I felt Yvonne was really listening and that she really cared. What a blessing to have a friend you can tell you innermost secrets to, I thought!

Yvonne got more awake with each minute. I geared down with the Mothership escapade and the Annanokian attacking Llueve in the atomic zone, the fear in her eyes and her beautiful long auburn hair flying atomically behind her with the black and green ice crevasses of the moon in the back ground as Isult and Silvaan speeded in to try and save her. I didn't realize how emotional my voice had become. I'd been talking like a little boy remembering his dog being run over by a car. When I finished, I felt all tear-jerky and so grateful to Yvonne for being my friend.

'Jesus!' she said. She was hugging me tight as I sobbed out all the tension and sense of alienation that had accumulated in me through the months I'd been keeping all this bottled up inside. Then we lay in silence as I pressed my face into her damp flannel nightgown. The warmth of her body, and the sympathy of our old friendship seeped deep into my heart, and I stopped feeling so isolated and crazy. After a long comforting silence, while she hugged me tenderly, she spoke in her sweetest, most intimate voice...

'Baby, what you're doing is projecting a love affair with a woman who only exists in outer space so that she can't call you on your shit. You've created a fantasy lover in your imagination because you can't be responsible for the emotional interplay with a real woman!' She said this ever so gently, patting the top of my head as she spoke. 'It's sort of an adolescent masturbation fantasy with a rubber dolly that smiles and does everything you want - she doesn't burp or fart, she only exists to please you and has no individuality or needs of her own.'

'Yvonne! You don't understand a thing!' I was stunned.

'What I understand is that you need professional help Joe! You're having deep emotional experiences about a complete fantasy! You never cried on my shoulder about me!

'But that's different! You're you! Look,' it was hopeless. 'It was you who told me to go ahead into the astral. You gave me the map to get to Ovvala for Christ sake!' Now I was getting angry. So much for revealing your true emotions to a New Age witch!

'I know baby, but it sounds like you're in over your head. Entities fighting in outer space? A nine hundred year old sex pot? Being in love with a woman with oval boobs who can't speak English? A woman who is safely in another world so she can't call you on the phone?

'The space ship with clones of famous people could be your judgmental unconscious seeing people like potentialities - like sleeping babies with no qualities...this whole other world thing could really be a repressed you that you are accessing through an altered imagery... the lizard people sound like a demonization of powerful people to compensate for your own shortcomings.'

I slumped on the pillow. The clarity of standing in the forest with Llueve and holding hands as the deer looked us in the eyes came back to me. That had happened less than an hour ago! I missed Llueve so intensely at that moment.

'O.K.' I said. 'So this could be an amazing continuity of dreams created by my sublimated subconscious or ... just give me a tiny bit of room...it could just possibly have been real events in another dimension! I mean, it's you who convinced me to think outside the box Yvonne!'

'Well, yeah. But I said 'the box' not 'outside the planet!' If only you could somehow prove the reality of being out of your body!'

'Oh I know. I tried to pinch you one night when you were doing the dishes.'

'You spied on me again Joseph Soloski!? How fucking dare you!'

'I wasn't *spying* on you! I was trying to prove the existence of the dimension you led me to by giving me the Monroe book!'

'Well...you should have asked my permission first!' She sniffed.

'But you don't even think it's real!'

'Still.'

'I've tried to think of some way to even give myself proof but I can't think of anything. God. This is so weird. Your New Age Ideas were too far out for me and now I'm too far out for you!' We lay in hostile intimacy. Her softness and warmth, despite the shards of glass sticking out of her, was still so comforting. It just missed the core of me. I had almost released the pent up sorrow but it had been eclipsed by her analytical anality. Yet, the milky feminine smell of her sleepy body took the edge off. She whispered in my ear -

'Your pants are scratchy.'

3/23/05

Last night Llueve came to me in a dream. She stood at the foot of my bed. She wore a ripped gown, her hair was matted and dirty and her face was without any color or expression. There was no recognition of me in her eyes or any sparkle at all from her mental vibrations. Her arms dangled at her sides and tears were running down her cheeks. She tried to open her mouth to speak and it looked like a bottomless black hole. She couldn't seem to stay focused and her eyes turned up inside her head. Then she vanished.

This visitation was so spooky. I woke up and felt a terrible sense of dread.

3/26/05

I got the buzzing bees sensation going effortlessly and went out of body without incident. At least that hasn't been affected. I tried to find Llueve but the lights in her house were dark. I went to Logaana and tried to contact Silvaan but something was going on and he and Djagda and Isult were gone. Asaalen, who I am familiar with now, was called. For once he wasn't wearing his silver suit but just plain tan pants and a long, thick red shirt. He led me down the cavern passages in silence to an area of Logaana I'd never been in before. He left me outside the entry to a room, nodded in a friendly way and left. I entered and found Oorden.

The room she was in was deeper into Logaana than I had yet been. This room had a very long table covered with black sand. On the table were all kinds of colored glass spheres, triangles, hexagrams and pentagrams made of copper and silver. With a long pole Oorden was carefully sliding these objects around a central bowl half full of some kind of pearly liquid which caused electromagnetic lines of force to rearrange themselves. It was a very interesting thing she was doing but I was too concerned about Llueve to get into it just then.

She greeted me in a formal but friendly way and led the way through a portal into an open air garden. Oorden is pretty high up in the scheme of things among the Siddhe. But then so apparently am I. She was wearing loose pants and a dark green, almost black blouse against which her hair, black as Spanish lace, melted away. An aide appeared and gave Oorden a small box and left. Oorden opened the box and took out a little vial and sniffed the scent it gave off.

'To see and hear you better!' she said and smiled in her slow formal way. She indicated that we should have the energy encounter. Instead of embracing she held out her palm and I mine and we pressed our palms together. Instead of the usual embarrassed delight, there was a shared sense of tender, sad familiarity.

I told her I was concerned that I couldn't find Llueve and she told me that Llueve had been injured in the battle with the Janosians and was resting at a place called Wixxal.

'Is it serious?' I asked.

'It may be. It's hard to say.'

'What happened?' Oorden projected a rote: the Janosian never managed to enter Llueve's construct before Isult and Silvaan killed it by tearing its atoms apart. But the violence and fear caused by the confrontation deeply affected Llueve.

'Jwo, you can not see Llueve for a little while.' Oorden watched me carefully. I had a sense of dread that was not going away and this didn't help.

'You must not be disheartened, whatever happens! You have made contact with the Siddhe and we are now your family. This fight goes on.' But I did feel disheartened.

'Before they killed the Janosian, Djagda extracted a rote of Janosian history,' Oorden relayed this rote to me.

"Janosians are ancient life forms whose planet died from industrial pollution. They created an artificial, technological support system in space ships and have been floating around the universe looking for a new home for 10 thousand years. They can no longer reproduce themselves. In trying to clone themselves they mastered the science of cloning other life forms. The Grays are the artificial life forms they created as living tools. They also altered the genetic makeup of Humans when their orbiting, dwarf solar system passed through our solar system 3600 years ago. Now they have returned and expect to do this again with more advanced techniques.

"The Janosians want to live on Earth because it is beautiful and temperate and has a lot of water – a rare element to find in quantity in the universe. They especially like Arizona and Arabia because all the Janosians have arthritis. They want to team up with the Dracos and share humanity between them. The Dracos will trade them humanity and the Earth for clones that the Dracos can inhabit and use to live on Mars. This would bypass the time consuming process for the Dracos of slowly taking over a human or Ovvalan incarnate, and training them to be an efficient host. There are about seventy thousand Janosians on the Mothership.

"The Rote revealed that the Janosians have amazingly advanced technologies. They believe they can reverse the global warming effect. They plan to build skyscraper sized vacuum cleaners to filter the carbon out of the air and reforest the deserts with heavy-breather trees to suck up even more carbon and produce oxygen and stabilize the weather patterns. They may have the technology to refreeze the poles and stabilize the planet's rotation.

"Not being able to reproduce, they can only live as long as they can maintain a kind of chemical suspension of death. This they have accomplished by saturating their blood streams with a chemical compound similar to vodka."

'They have lost all interest in any normal existence and have become these sort of cosmic voyeurs who crave looking in the windows of the living,' Oorden explained to me. 'If they had captured Llueve's astral form, they would have attempted to confiscate her body and probably have done experiments on her or traded her to the Dracos for human abductees. But in a combined move, Djagda and Isult separated the pursuer's astral atoms and charged these with repelling ionic magnetism so that its blueprint disintegrated like a bunch of marbles exploding into space.'

'What will happen to Llueve now?' I asked her.

'Llueve has been taken to a new home in a canyon along the Inxalrok valley called the Wixxal. She has her own cabin and a garden terraced into the hillside,' she told me.

It's from the Inxalrok Valley that the Siddhe broadcast over the Daag Internet through the same microwave relays that the Skandrr use to carry television signals. Inxalrok and all Siddhe communities are on high alert because of the recent Skandrr attack discussed at Sahasrah-dal-Kanwal. The Dracos have gone to full code purple, implementing the invasion.

The Skandrr disk-ship flyovers have been happening in South America and Asia. Jet fighters have begun flying over parts of Daag, Karaaleen and Aza-mazuul on Ovvala. Siddhe outposts on Earth and Ovvala are preparing for bombing raids. They think the only solution may be to import hundreds of Humans to Ovvala and send Ovvalans to Earth as suggested and just start explaining the reality of the Mahaalan dual dimension. But this may be too dangerous. An alternate plan is to distribute millions of DVD's all over Earth and Ovvala that explain the real history of Earth and Ovvala. Another plan is to create a broadband Internet satellite link between Earth and Ovvala and then broadcast Mahaalan history on Google Plus, YouTube and on the Yahoo dating service.

The Siddhe now have two of the high powered Aeron disk ships. They used the first to capture a second. These are capable of flying into deep space as Silvaan said.

Djagda managed to steal a number of vials of cloning material from the Annanokian lab during the battle. These are being processed in underground chambers in Inxalrok.

Oorden stopped telepathing and looked at me seriously. Then relayed this;

'Llueve has caught the Faal Jwo. She wants to 'take to the sky'. She has lost all interest in people, in the fight against the Dracos...in living.'

'But what about her pregnancy?' I asked, really rattled now.

'Jwo, she doesn't remember that she's pregnant. Her soul is too sad to live - that's the Faal to an Ovvalan.' The sadness causes a person to disassociate from reality and dream. Any demand to remember the struggles in life is too painful.'

Oorden wants me to meet Llueve in the Inxalrok Valley at a particular place and time when a ceremony called the Magaan-Da is to take place. This, they hope, will bring Llueve back to herself. The women think it would be good for me to be present because Ea chose me for a father and may have some use for me to help pull Llueve through. Oorden projected a kind of psychic hyper-link to cause me to be called to this ceremony and we parted.

3/28/05

Yvonne called and left a very correctly compassionate message about what she sees as my compensatory delusions. She sure knows how to say all the right things. I wonder if people were more human with each other before psychological buzzwords became all the rage. I feel sick with worry about Llueve.

4/2/05

The Berlin Wall is done and I got paid. It's over thank God. I tried starting a new model plane project I've had lying around but can't get into it. I don't like being alone in the house. Spencer and Lena are really busy with their Brazilian Internet project.

4/07/05

I've been to the Wixxal Ceremony.

I was asleep and viewing disconnected dream images; undecided whether I wanted to produce an OBE or just sleep when I felt an intense pull on my attention. Then I heard Oorden's disembodied voice.

'Come *now* Jwo,' she said. A current of consciousness flowed up and away from me. I easily produced the buzzing sensation and let the current pull me. I sped through the sea of Loosh and fro there zoomed quickly to the Inxalrok valley.

What a place! Fields and gardens were planted as far as the eye can see on both sides of a wide, brown river. A couple of bridges spanned the water and there were cottages and houses in the fields. Large caves were visible in the valley walls. This is a huge settlement.

I was guided along the wide, slow river until I came to a stream flowing out of a smaller, steep canyon and was then guided into this canyon by Oorden's vibes.

Here were smaller terraced gardens set out between the stream and the vertical canyon walls. The ground became a steeper and steeper grade as I followed the gurgling, white-water stream up the narrowing canyon which became boxed in at a vertical wall, swiss cheesed with cavern openings. The stream I'd been following flowed out of one of these caves.

A long, flat shelf at the mouth of the stream was the floor for a long low ceilinged cavern out of which the stream flowed. Around this opening a flat ceremonial ground opened out and was surrounded by lit torches where a hundred or more women were milling around or sitting on the ground. Fires crackled and threw shadows as sparks rose up into a moonless sky.

Oorden telepathically instructed me to stay on the edge of the ceremonial area. She indicated a low tree in whose branches I could climb, the better to see.

I saw most of the Siddhe women I had met so far either sitting with Isult or in other circles of women. Seshena, Shenella, Kaelaa, Matarpha, Bodiccea, Ilsenaad, Oorden, and Avaala and Isult were seated on blankets on a level, crescent landing, around the outside of the wide, low ceilinged cave, where the stream came out, silently stretching across the shelf like a sheet of black glass before it hit the first of many waterfalls leading down to the Ilaan river.

A rumbling sound came from somewhere. I couldn't identify it. It was a quivering in the air. This seemed connected to an intense excitement and feeling of expectancy in the women. The women were all dressed in long gowns or robes and talking quietly and intensely as this quivering sensation enveloped them. Their physical movements became more and more electric and spasmodic.

I finally saw Llueve. She was sitting in a group of older women who were kind of plump and slow. They were all dressed in similar black robes. They were, I think, anchorites or something like that. Llueve was enveloped in a thick blue blanket and was looking vaguely into the distance. She had no expression on her face. Her lips were smiling slightly and her eyes were wide open but she looked catatonic and empty.

I felt a growing anxiety. I was actually feeling kind of sick as the women seemed to become more and more possessed by a kind of hysteria as the quivering vibrations increased. Their eyes were strange, projecting an odd combination of very female silliness and withering cynicism. At one point Isult stood up and scanned the area until our eyes met. I felt a jolt, like a punch in the chest when she spotted me. As she stared at me, sparkling gold-green light began to flicker out of her breast and accumulate in a sphere around me in the astral. It was like insulation. I could see and hear perfectly but the hysteria and intense feminine electricity no longer touched me.

'Sorry Jwo,' I heard Isult telepath to me. 'I should have thought of doing this before. Maybe now the women's vibes won't kill you! Ha ha ha!' Her voice said this as her face remained impassive. She sat back down and seemed to forget all about me.

The women's heads began to turn this way and that and their bodies to spasm as the weird magnetism coming from somewhere - the ground? - grew stronger and stronger. All the women's attention seemed pulled by this magnetism.

A tall, thin, woman dressed in long, black robe appeared. She had thick black hair hanging to her waist and large, dark ,sad eyes, and a heavy emotional presence. Her movements were phantom like. I later learned her name was Aroona and that she is a Wixxal priestess. She radiated a deep tenderness and a strange, dark magnetism. Reaching into a large cloth bag, she took out what looked like intestines – glistening, bloody and wet. It turned out to be a long braid of hair, contributed by each woman there. It was soaked in menstrual blood, saliva, strips of bloody umbilical cords and coated with globs of placenta and totally gave me the heebie-jeebies. She placed this carefully and tenderly in a wide hole in the ground. Young women came and poured a thick, dark liquid on top of the other stuff in the hole and sprinkled the ground all around the shelf with this fluid. I didn't even want to know what it was.

The mounting intensity I hadn't been able to identify now began pulsing out of the ground and climbing up my body as all the women began murmuring and babbling. It was almost like they were all bitching about something and weren't even listening to each other. I began to feel terrible. I thought I was getting sick and wanted to throw up. Then I realized I was feeling this incredible sorrow. It began to overwhelm me. Images from my childhood rose before my eyes. Scenes of arguments and misunderstandings, betrayals and lies that I had been told and that I had told to others came to me. Things having to do with my father, my mother, my sister and brother, broken love affairs, all rose up inside of me, until my chest was heaving with pent up sadness. I started to gag and then started dry heaving.

At one point I looked up and saw that the women all around me were doing the same thing – weeping, gagging and crying in anguish. A woman would suddenly stand up and scream in vicious anger and then slump back down on the ground clutching her belly, tears and snot running down her face. The intensity of this gradually lessened until there was silence and stillness, each woman looking off in her own direction, absorbed in her own private interior world.

A band of women with string instruments and drums surrounded the circle of hair and body parts and began playing a really weird, disjointed music that became a chant, picked up by the rest of the women which, as it proceeded, divided into different parts as the women stood up and circled around the pit, singing softly and swaying. The music never actually became a rhythm or had a melody and the movements of the women weren't exactly dancing but a kind of chaotic gyrating. (It will seem extraordinary that I could remember the words to what they sang but memory is nine times stronger in the astral.)

Morgaana from the meadows of green fire
Where black oak branches twist up between the stars
Silver raindrops glisten on your leather armor
As you watch Venus rise up to lead Mars

She-fire daughter of the pure Black Mother
The priests of Eden have begun to loose their power
Open our eyes to trust the wisdom
Of the circle of the seasons that makes the flower

The underworld opens to free the raven
To eat the fears that holds the body back
From living in the full colors of this human heart
She enters now the council dress us black

Dress us in black to wipe out the false colors
Of smiling faces unconnected to their souls
We will chant again the sound of babies
And make our selves whole...

Morgana Wixxal warrior of the soul world

Lead us into the open day

We will chant again the sounds of babies

The natural heart will know the way

This chant went on and on with the weird dissonant music in the background, while the women stared into the fires.

In a trance, I watched as waves of Loosh separated from the air and formed into detailed etheric waves washing, bubbling and crashing above our heads. This went on for a long time until the women were overcome with an intensity of emotion. Again they grew quiet - swaying to the weird, chaotic music - until many in the group began to contort spasmodically from their bellies. They began to groan and yelp. I realized they were in a collective rhythm of birth contractions and remembered what had happened to me at Stonehenge. This transferred itself to me and I too - though in the astral - clutched the branch of the tree next to me and began to have contractions and my nipples throbbed as deep sensual vibrations traveled through my nipples into my heart. I saw that this was happening to Llueve too where she was sitting. The catatonic look had been replaced by one of fierceness, desperation and pain.

The group contractions lessened and all the women became still as they took deep breaths. Slowly and silently all attention turned to the cavern in the cliff face where some figures were emerging. Two of the black robed priestesses appeared at the mouth of the cave leading a very old, hunched over, woman draped in a brilliant white robe and leaning on a stick. They walked her slowly out of the cavern to two tall backed chairs at the center of the flat landing near the mouth of the cave.

She was incredibly old and wrinkled with a severely hooked nose and blind white eyes just like the other image of a witch we all grew up with. A sneering, smile through her thin, bloodless lips sliced her toothless, wrinkled face open at moments as though she could barely contain her contempt or pleasure or insanity. She was led to one of the chairs and sat down.

Oorden and Elsinaad stood on either side of Llueve, helped her to her feet, and led her to the other chair.

Llueve looked agitated, squinting painfully out of tear streaked eyes, her shoulders hunched. She stared at the old woman who looked back with a blind, pitiless raw faced look. A cold, impersonal light radiated from the old woman; a dispassionate naked truthfulness. No illusions. No glamour. No sentiment. No sex. The magnetism that had been swirling around the women now concentrated in the old woman and all the women present crowded in close to see better.

The old woman began taking deep, slow gasping breaths as she faced Llueve, smiling her insane smile. The priestesses started a slow, swooping chant and all the women joined in. Llueve began to clutch her belly. Her eyes dilated, she suddenly sat up very straight with sheer terror in her eyes. At one point the old woman let out a dry, strangled cry and Llueve lurched forwards, clutched her belly and vomited, heaving violently and then sat up again straight, still and glassy eyed.

The old woman became very still. Then she slowly reached out her hand to Llueve. Oorden placed Llueve's hand in the old woman's. At a certain point, first Llueve and then the old woman were jolted by an energy force and then let go their hands. The old woman closed her eyes, a quiver ran through her, and she became limp, folded over and began falling off her chair. The two priestesses caught her and gently lowered her to the ground where she curled into a fetal position and died.

The chanting stopped and all the women stood up and were still. No one moved to touch the old woman. Llueve was hunched over and shaking softly. Isult and Oorden helped Llueve to stand and began leading her down the path along the stream. The group split up with most of the women staying around the fallen old woman. They rolled her onto a blanket and carried her back into the cave.

I followed at a distance feeling sick and out of place.

At the first house the group with Llueve came to, there was a fire burning in a pit and the group around Llueve and Isult sat on blankets around the fire. A steaming drink was poured into goblets and passed around. I caught pieces of conversation.

'The sickness went right out of the girl,' one old woman said with a strange clipped accent.

'Yeah. She did want it gone.' There was silence as the women sipped their drinks.

'There were so few convulsions! Not like last month. One heave and it was out!' a woman said.

'It happened dreadful fast,' the first woman agreed.

'The girl was in a hurt but she did manage to throw it off,' another one said.

'The Old One was well ready.'

'So,' a woman's voice said quietly and with wonder 'Ea is new!' . There was a silence. And then all the women, in unison, said softly,

'Ea is new!' and stared silently into the flames for a long time.

A harsh vibration passed through the group. It was like cold love.

Chapter Sixteen

4/14/05

Last night Oorden came to me in a dream and smiled, holding out her hand, calling to me. I knew this dream meant that it was O.K. for me to see Llueve now. About an hour later I got out of body and zeroed in on Inxalrok.

I found Llueve at the cabin she has been living in since going to Inxalrok. It was a nicely made, wooden, yurt-like structure, with a conical roof covered in what looked like sun bleached cedar shingles, with a tin smokestack sticking up out of it. The interior walls of Llueve's cabin were tongue and groove, finished, Ovvalan pine planks. There was a semi enclosed kitchen area with a sink and a counter and cupboards. There was a cushioned sitting area by one of the two bay windows, and a desk placed under the other, with an open, blinking laptop on it. The windows looked down a slope, and across wide farm fields bordering the river where new green sprouts were coming up out of black earth and an orchard of budding dwarf fruit trees was laid out in rows. A number of very large oak trees spread their limbs majestically over pastures where the large turkey like saams birds grazed.

Llueve was sleeping in a huge bed under fluffy quilts. I stood at the foot of the bed for a while gazing at her and wondering what she had been through. In sleep she looked as I knew her but older. She stirred and slowly rose out of her body. She was covered in the white cassock and her luxurious hair was loose. She was pleased to see me but subdued. I could see that she had been through the fire. Her eyes looked naked. There was a thrill of familiarity when we embraced and equalized energies but something had changed. There was a formality and an overt purposefulness in her that seemed to absorb her. She felt distant and it made my heart ache to think the sweetness we had shared could be ending. In her eyes I saw an urgency that matched the look I've seen in the eyes of some of the Siddhe. The ones totally devoted to the cause of saving Ovvala from the Reptilians. It is an identity that never forgets the Big Picture and the possibility of failure. Siddhe warriors are rarely casual. Was this happening to Llueve?

Llueve led me into the next room where there was a couch facing the farm fields and beyond them the shinning, silver river Ilaan. We sat down close to one another and held hands in silence.

'I want to relay to you an encounter I had with Isult,' she said. 'It will help you understand how things are with me. There is very important information you must know. I need to know that you know it. I think it will be useful to us and what lies ahead.' I did as she wanted. She sounded so formal it made me feel like a stranger. We sat very still and touched palms. Llueve passed me this rote. I closed my eyes and became receptive. Pictures formed in my mind.

Llueve and Isult were sitting in the sunshine at the mouth of a cave in the mountains above

Inxalrok, beyond the end of the Wixxal canyon, deep in forested mountains. The cave looked out over misty, wooded, mountain tops; the white granite bones of the mountains sticking out at the peaks and ridges. A crisp wind gusted, swaying the treetops below. A well worn path led up to the cavern and a few little stone huts could be seen hidden among the rocks. The cave where they sat was a shrine where women came to deliver their devotions or stay in retreats built into the crags and crannies of the mountains. Llueve and Isult were dressed in thick wool robes, with deep hoods and long sleeves. Llueve's was a dark rusty red and Isult's was a green so dark it was nearly black. The wind whipped at their sleeves and cowls. They were talking and laughing softly as they hugged themselves against the cold, their cheeks flared with frost.

They were speaking in hushed tones. A flickering oil lamp with a huge wick and a glass reservoir that must have held five gallons of oil burned brightly against one wall of the room. The room had a bare floor that was evidently swept clean regularly. All around the walls were weavings and tapestries that had been collected from other holy sites.

In the center of the room and against the cavern wall, raised on a platform of ancient, blackened oak beams, a cowelled female statue, her skin and face jet black, sat in an ornate chair, still and silent. The robes draped over her were made of many layers of very fine white cotton, silk and wool. She wore a necklace of large black pearls around her neck and in her hands, clasped in her lap, was an oval sphere of obsidian. Her face was carefully hand painted to look very lifelike though completely black. In a calm, serious face, the eyes looked directly at you and sent a shiver up the back of your neck in the knowingness of the expression.

This was a shrine to Uma, the Ovvalan High Priestess of Universal Mercy. She is an ancient spiritual figure that exists still as a living deity in Daag culture, but also in many other parts of Ovvalan civilization.

Being a once upon a time Catholic, I immediately associated this figure with Our Lady of Czestochowa, the Polish Black Madonna. My father had told me something about her. Apparently there are only two or three sites dedicated to the Black Madonna in Europe one of these being in Poland. He showed me an article from an old National Geographic with photos of the annual pilgrimage that Poles take to honor her day. She is a very mysterious being whose shrines are built on pre Christian sites. One myth is that she is a remembrance of Isis.

As Llueve gazed reverently at the sight of the figure, Isult explained to her;

'Uma is the Deity of the Universal Dark who exists beneath the Qlipothic Underworld. She is the Mercy of the Cosmic Mother who accepts all souls as her children. Even the Qlipothic monsters!

'The Qlipoth exist just below the bottom of our world. They are attracted to the light they see here. But in the depths below the Qlipoth is a pure darkness that is innocent and unconscious and that is the domain of Uma.'

In the cavern there were also primitive icons of women warriors and holy women hanging on the walls or propped up on slabs of wood and raised on stones. There were shawls and vials of water and twigs from trees, dried flowers, veils and whole dresses and pieces of clothing. Isult explained to Llueve that she liked to come here sometimes when her heart was sore or she felt world weary.

Isult showed Llueve around the cave of relics and then they returned to sit in the sun at the opening of the cave. Isult was very calm and for once soft spoken. She was very tender to Llueve and seemed herself in need of comforting. What happened next was Isult relaying information to Llueve about the esoteric spiritual practices of the Wixxal.

The old woman Meggan-Da at the Wixxal ceremony absorbed the Faal sickness out of Llueve and let it kill her. In the process, Llueve absorbed the life prayer of the old woman whose name was Muurial though she was referred to as The Hekaate, which was a kind of title of veneration for her age and her knowledge. Muurial had been an old and very close friend to Isult who was now in mourning for her passing. And passing in such a purposeful way; giving her protection and healing to Llueve so that Ea, who is very dear to Isult as well as to Muurial, could live.

Isult looked different. For once she wasn't dressed in her brilliant, hip hugging dresses or revealing green gowns. She was covered head to foot in the dark woolen cloak and hood. Her red hair was pulled tightly back so that only the paper white skin of her face showed from within the shadow of her cowl. Llueve looked very young, like a scrub faced girl, she was deeply happy. Her hood was off her head and her rich auburn hair sparkled in the sunshine while her bronze skin glowed radiantly so that she looked molten. This all seemed to be a part of the healing process that Llueve had undergone. This is the part Llueve especially wanted me to know. Isult was speaking;

'You see, the stars emit an energy frequency. This is the creative force field, the Aa, which pulses the intelligence of creative love throughout the Universe. Each star and combination of stars creates a modulation of Aa. Combined frequencies create constructs of sacred geometry that are storage places of dimensional information and these are spiritual food.

'This vocabulary of astral processes is called the Aaltandaev and accesses the Altandaar. The Altandaar is an oceanic tide of Aa moving throughout galactic space carrying Suudilve - the Creative Intelligence of Love. The Altandaar distributes the different star frequencies, renewing creative consciousness and drawing souls progressively upwards. The Altandaar is a radiance from the yoga of God.

'There are astral rivers and weather systems in the Altandaar that carry energy and information to us here, to Mahaala. Wormholes are created, time is altered, alliances sustained. Energies are rejected. When an individual consciousness achieves the next level of their integration, they align with the harmonies appropriate to them and travel forwards through inner space and time.

'The SxtraJiel is the astral diamond of our being - a person is organized on the astral level around this diamond-like construct. This is like a formula activated into flesh and blood in incarnation. But the SxtraJiel itself continues to exist in astral time and interact in the Ixtellar - the web of continuity that connects everything.

'This Jewel is a sacred geometrical construct that resonates intelligently to star and planet frequencies and to trees and flowers – to nature. The SxtraJiel is a receptor and energy relay. It is harmonized to a code in the Ixtellar.; the Ixtellar being the living strings of potentiality in the universal body of Suudilve. The outcome of activating this resonance - this yoga – is fusing in the Altandaar.

'The current of Altandaar stimulates the SxtraJiel relays within us each and by hooking into this vibration it is possible to harvest energy and ride it to new frequencies. Altandaar means Star-Talking. The practice is like sailing a boat. The Aa is the wind. The ocean is Suudilve. The boat is the SxtraJiel diamond. When we activate our personal SxtraJiel - the jewel of ourselves - we interact with the Altandaar. The weather of Universal consciousness and of our higher selves kaleidoscopically reintegrates - this is SkaTaal - an orgasmic pooling of personal transdimensional identities - gathering dimensions of past and present, existences by which we enter into Aaltare – the Higher Octave. This is like letting a far future identity influence the identity that exists now.

The living wheels within that are activated become magnets to pull us forward and exert a dominant direction, creating a doorway into another existence. In a far future place, the Dracos have been removed from Illuva and everyone alive has achieved Aaltare. It is possible to draw on one's identity there to influence the world around us here. This is Ixtaal. Dimensional superimposition.'

As I absorbed Llueve's experience with Isult, I felt channels of energy in my own senses become unblocked and joined together into a tighter smoother flow. I imagine this is what a laptop would feel when it runs an antivirus program. I sensed memories out of time and space activating.

Isult and Llueve sat for a long time in silence at the mouth of the cave looking out over the mountain peaks. Llueve asked Isult;

'Isult, why are you not already in Aaltare?'

'I need to be here when the Cosmic Wave comes. It will be the wind beneath my wings!' Isult looked into the far distance and remained very still. Again the silence. Then Isult continued. 'Ea and I are indebted to one another and I need what Ea can give me – a part of myself I lost once. You see, we are linked to others through the strings of Ixtellar and need to travel to the ends of these strings of awareness - to free our circuits - complete them - activate them, in preparation for the crossing into Aaltare.'

'Like Meggan-Da opened my circuits?' Llueve asked. Isult turned to Llueve and nodded slowly, somberly.

'With her help, you let that identity in you that was infected with Faal die. She took that identity, and you moved forwards to that in your heart that is just being born - that is new. Your new love and your baby, the Siddhe and the war.

'Habitual identity blinds us to the nature of the Altandaar. Life and love are ever new. Our minds get fixed on definitions and we need the picture of an emerging identity to dissolve us out of the past. But then that too becomes a prison. To regain the flow, to re-enact SkaTaal, we have to volunteer to burn - to let go of useless identity and create a more current, relevant identity. This doesn't just happen by itself. You have to consciously burn off what becomes irrelevant to your emerging integration. You have to volunteer.

'Co-creation in Suudilve is an active thing. It is like dreaming but involves intending an identity as a direction. We commit to a new identification with love-as-action and this creates a self-birth and becomes the connection to Suudilve Itself, which then completes the creative process. But we have to start the creative process.

'The bridge between Ovvala and Terra for instance, is achieved by actively creating it. Astral strings of Ixtellar respond to this intent, and this creates a pathway of perception. Then, by actively focusing on the frequency of one's own identity as God, Suudilve comes forward and co-creation begins. When both these frequencies of the self are in contact, the incarnate and the eternal - a living dream is awakened and the energy strings of Ixtellar respond and cause manifestation. This is how life purposes are achieved."

'Did Jwo and I intend our meeting?'

'Of course!'

'But we didn't even know the other existed!'

'Ah - but you did! Because everything you can imagine already exists!' Isult pulled the hood of her robe tightly around her face. 'Both of you are very old souls. Your incarnations now are the result of a long process. And curiously, this process has always been integrated with the energy process of Ea. Her need for you two to come together and create a gate for her return, is part of the attraction you have for each other. That wasn't a cat that caused Jwo to fall off the ladder!' Isult laughed. Llueve gasped.

'Love, in its many forms, places stepping stones of transformation for us to continue our forward motion. But we have to step forward for these stepping stones to manifest. Tricky. We are dreaming our way into God and love is the mechanism that drives us forwards. We are imagining our way into God, and God is receiving our dreams and matching us up with other dreamers. At first this is an unconscious process. But then it becomes yoga, an intentional process, requiring sustained intent, and a dedicated resistance to seductive divergences. This Yoga of the imagination is what is being interfered with by the Draco Reptilians!

'The Dracos are astral beings. They have no actual physical existence. And they have no spiritual identity until they choose to make one. They are very powerful *memories* of themselves. It is their sentimentality for their lost Jurassic world that gives them authority. And it is their longing for the past that has created such a strong sentimental tendency among Humans. People idolize past times of history like Atlantis and Zion, Mecca, the Bohddi Tree, Greece, Jerusalem and Sumer as though these things were flawless times of uninterrupted ecstasy. But these times had their problems and limitations too. History exaggerates. I mean really, how much can you miss living in a land of stalking predators or wandering around in the desert with nothing to eat but manna for breakfast, lunch and dinner? The present is so much more alive than the memory of it. But the Dracos seduce pilgrims with this emotional longing for the dark blood of their mindless youth. And they have bred in us a sentimental longing for a place and time when we didn't have to burn off our own dross - where we didn't have to work! It's like those vacation photos that show the models lying happily on a white sandy beach in front of a turquoise sea. They don't show you the mosquitoes!

'A construct of consciousness in the context of this living world has a thrilling vitality. This is the vitality of truth. And it is a force of beauty. It is quite similar to the freshness of food. When an astral construct is new and immediately linked to a purpose in Suudilve - in co-creating with the intelligence of Love - fresh identity-constructs take precedence over other thought constructs. This is what burning achieves. It is the conscious creation of love and is its own reward.

'Illuva supersedes Draco in present time. Because of this, a fundamental drive for self preservation among Draco phantasms, has been to suppress the spiritual dreaming that reinforces present time. They live in holy terror of Humans and Ovvalans finding out that we can dissolve evil by simply looking it in the eye. And this is why they are taking over the production of denatured food. Natural food that is grown consciously and with care carries Lexl-light and Loosh and nourishes the strings of Ixtellar within us. Denatured food has no light. It is this that begins the Faal process of separating from Suudilve - which is a separation from joy.'

Isult gazed out across the mountains. Her face took on a childlike glow.

'Dividing the parallel worlds of Ovvala and Terra was a massive, almost a mortal wound to the imagination skills of our ancestors. It was stupefying. We have learned to cope with this by anesthetizing our minds. It is time to wake up! Release the sentimental romance of the past in exchange for living love in the present! To choose the Tree of Life over the Tree of Knowledge and

Memory.

'In deep space there are times when a tide of color and frequency moves through the Ixtellar and an entire galaxy takes on the same vibration. When this happens, the collective imaginations of hundreds of millions of persons in Illuva - whether in Terra or Ovvala or both! - are all moved to imagine a similar mood or attitude. This could be for love or for invention or discovery or rebellion - it becomes a fever of enthusiasm and it has devastating effects on the Draco webs. The Draco Ouroboros is a synthetic form of the Ixtellar. It mimics its structure and influence. This is a negative radio frequency, broadcast from Saturn and re-amplified by the Black Cube on the Moon to keep Humans locked in a process that feels like nature but is not natural.

Creative Love dissolves these discontinuities in collective dreaming. This happened in the French Revolution and in the 1960's in Terra when children left their homes en mass to celebrate life and music in the face of the fear of nuclear war. And it's about to happen in 2018 on level of intensity that will transform the race memory of all Illuva. All over the world, the inspiration for change and creativity will replace the sentimental longing for the past and reinvent life.

'Fifty thousand people with one sustained, focused and directed imaginative construct, sent forward in a collective construct are capable of creating a hole in Mahaala through which to push the Dracos with one united thrust and sever their hold on Illuva. We are laying plans to see this carried out. In Kalkaava - the Energy Garden of the Druidda - this construct is being grown in the Ixtellar webs in preparation for the day when it can be activated.'

Llueve, entranced, her own eyes like glimmering diamonds, her face shinning in happiness, looked out over the white and emerald mountains as she listened.

'The separation of Ovvala and Terra created an original wound in the aura of each individual through which the imagination drains away. The spiritual imagination is a subtle complex of hope and desire, fantasy and prayer, sexual wonder and thrilling vitality. It's an interface with the unbelievable. Creating a bridge across the non-existent - this was the purpose of the old magikal formulas and bardic songs. To be in the proximity of Suudilve and create together is true and pure love. It is what Human love hints at. And yet, most persons in Illuva feel they are unworthy of this and that such ideas are too fantastic to be true. The Faal was *planted* in our minds by the Dracos. We believe we aren't worthy of love. We fear our hopes dreams are meaningless and this is by design

'Happiness is co-created. You don't achieve it alone. Happiness is achieved together with Suudilve. This is an act of ensouling the Altandaar star streams and claiming the joy to resonate in the SkaTaal meditation. Irrationally choosing it! It is really like a different kind of breathing. Such happiness creates invulnerability to Draco because in such happiness nothing is desired or missing or hoped for. This is the total application of one's creative function and when it is activated, there is no energy or attention left to mourn or despair, no division within the self to become sublimated into shadow desires or perversions of love.

'To choose to generate pure happiness within the SkaTaal resonance is like injecting antibiotic stardust into the global bloodstream; the Draco and all their webs and diversions and parasitic black holes and pornographic projections all melt away helplessly in the face of the Joy of Co-Creating.

'Religions have taught people to pray for guidance, hope for relief, but these things are largely ineffectual. They are ineffectual when the seeker isn't investing himself in the outcome by generating intention in a specific direction. Personal energy has to be invested in an outcome and extended outwards to a goal. What is Godlike only responds to what is Godlike. Without this investment of personal energy, there is nothing for Suudilve to respond to! This is the essential core of the AltandaarYoga - assuming divinity.

'The Dracos have created a negative ceiling web to the Illuvan imagination because when that higher imagination is regained, the Dracos will loose power over our world. Our war is with phantasms that have kidnapped our imaginations! And it is only by reinstating imagination as a form of active thought and devotion to love that we can cut ourselves free from this parasite. It isn't simply about doing good works or feeling compassion. It's about breaking the social mold and irrationally, unreasonably, feeling joy.'

Isult pushed back the hood of her robe and pulled a golden chain over her head. She unfastened the chain and presented Llueve with a glinting emerald ring set in a pale oval of reddened gold.

'This is Ea's ring. You carry it now,' she said.

Llueve placed the ring on the middle finger of her left hand. A force field of power shivered through her. They both sat for a long time looking out over the mountain peaks.

This ended Llueve's rote. I briefly saw detailed wheels with balls of colors leaping from wheel to wheel when Llueve said to me;

'I know there is a lot there. You can think about it later. Because right now we have a job to do!' she said, unconsciously rubbing the emerald ring I that now saw was on her hand.

'You see Jwo, we have to have an unearthly courage to imagine a way to end this horror. You and I have this incredible gift to travel into the Draco world and spy on them. Going to the Draco Council and to the Annanokian Spacecraft has had huge benefits to what the Siddhe are doing.

'Now, the place where the Reptilians are most vulnerable is in their wormhole that allows the jets and helicopters to enter Ovvala and Skandrr disks to reach Terra. Silvaan wants to take one of the new Aeron Ships and try and bomb the wormhole closed but this may not be possible. For one thing, they don't know exactly where it is in physical space - which complicates how to get there and how to get away. Also it may be just too heavily guarded.

'Jwo - if we could go there and just see where it is, what is there, perhaps then Silvaan can find some way to close the wormhole!' I was stunned at what she had just done. She had shown me the most beautiful exchange of love and consciousness with Isult to soften me up and then dropped this bomb on me.

'Llueve!' I was horrified. She had just survived a mortal illness that had cost an old wise woman her life and now, she wanted to risk everything again. I tried to speak calmly and reasonably. 'You've been forbidden to put yourself in danger again! I am forbidden! It's too dangerous! You're nearly four months pregnant!' I feared the worst. 'Look what happened to you after you got chased by the Janosians! And you know now, everyone is saying the child is Ea. Ea is the Dracos greatest threat! And the Siddhe's greatest hope. If you were killed or captured - so would Ea be and this would be so discouraging to everyone. And what about me?! Have you any idea how sick at heart I've been to see you walking the edge? And the Dracos know now about you and me and our ability to be invisible to them - they'll be watching for us in ways we can't even imagine.'

'Jwo, I have been thinking about this a lot,' Llueve said exercising a tremendous control of her emotions. She placed her right hand on my arm and I felt a surge of cosmic radiations from the ring. 'I know we are forbidden. And I know the risks. But I also know the costs - the children, the Faal...so many people in despair...We could go in slowly and at the very first sign of being sensed, we could return to Inxalrok where the Skandrr can't follow!' She passionately searched in my eyes for the thoughts that would match her own.

'Llueve,' I tried to match her self control and pulled away from her grasp and the strange power of that ring. 'We said all this before going to the Draco Council and yet I completely forgot the instructions! And we said we'd leave the Janosian deal if there were the slightest hint of danger but we were in too deep before we knew how dangerous it was. You were within an inch of that Janosian freak getting at you. They may have devised some special force or ray to hurt Ea!' I had come to accept that what I had witnessed at Wixxal had really happened - a woman consciously died for Llueve and my daughter. But, having survived such despair, Llueve still wanted to run this deadly risk. I couldn't believe she would seriously think about doing this. I felt like I was seeing the edge of real craziness here and it scared me. I tried to reach her with my vibes.

'From what Isult and Djagda say, the Dracos are interested in Ea more than they are in you and me, even more than in the other Counsuelaars - Ea is their prime target. Killing you could be their number one priority on the entire planet!'

'Don't you think I too think about this? Jwo!' she shouted, 'we have a power you and me that nobody else has! It is a power that the Dracos never considered dealing with!' This was the first time Llueve had got really angry with me. 'Once they begin this war - this Terrorization - it could go on for the rest of our lives! - this baby would live the life of a refugee in a world filled with war her whole life! Sure, maybe the child is this great reincarnation and maybe she's just a baby. But we can't let her enter a world that is dying as she comes alive! Only you and I have this power that could make a huge difference. I know you find me to be different now. Living here in Inxalrok has changed me. The Wixxal have changed me. People at Inxalrok are truly cleansed of the Ouroboros fears and lies. I hope you will come and live here and see what they know. Please Jwo - we must do this! There really is no choice!'

'Absolutely not!' I said. 'I will not go and without me you will not be invisible! Do you have any idea how sick with worry I've been since I saw you shooting away with that Annanokian deformity almost touching you!? And seeing you at the Wixxal - so weak and sick!'

The vibrations of her anger and of my refusal to go against the directives of Isult and Djagda made us get so alienated that we couldn't hold the astral dimension. I snapped awake in bed and sat bolt upright shaking with hurt and anger.

4/20/0

I had a dream where Llueve was banging on my bedroom door, which was closed. I clearly heard the bangs after I awoke. The lawyer says The Wall is a foot short of what she contracted for and wants to get out of three thousand bucks of materials and labor. Somehow I knew this would come.

4/22/05

I flew to Llueve's cottage in Inxalrok. She had placed a shield around her house that wouldn't let me closer than the boulder outside her garden. She was inside talking with Shenella and Kaelaa. I stood out in the yard and called and called but they pretended not to hear me.

4/26/05

I flew to Llueve's house. Again she had the shield up. This time the shield was closer to the house. I stared through the living room window at her looking over some papers as she physically sat in her living room. After a while she left the room and when she came back she was in the astral and dressed in a rose hued, gauzy robe - the kind that stuck to her like a wet paper towel. She began doing the dishes - tidying up her living room and generally walking around in the transparent sheath while pointedly ignoring me. At one point she started cleaning the windows so that she was right in front of my nose but her shields prevented any communication vibrations from traveling across. As though in her own little world she was running a cloth across the window in wide arcs. Her breasts swayed from side to side as she cleaned the corners with fierce, quick little strokes. It was driving me crazy not being able to communicate with her.

Then she began manifesting these subtly different kinds of gauzy sheaths. My god! I could barely hold my astral! Suddenly I realized she was trying to seduce me so as to change my mind! I got so angry that when I wiggled the feet of my physical body in order to leave, I heard a sonic boom as I dematerialized or whatever the hell happens.

4/29/05

I got to Llueve's and she let me in. She was very civil and formal. Obviously still closed off.

'If you won't come with me to case the wormhole - I have decided - I'm going to try and get there with an Atlantean Human I met at Logaana!'

'But Llueve!' I said, feeling the fully intended flash of jealousy. (She wouldn't dare!) 'That's suicide! It's not just that I'm human that gives you and I invisibility - it's ...the...love...Llueve!' She stared out the window at the river. 'No,' I said. 'If it doesn't work - it's murder because you will kill Ea!' I said. 'Though probably they won't kill you but take you hostage and then they will have power over the Siddhe!'

'You are my mate now and you are supposed to help me!' She said with intense frustration, tears pricking her eyes.

'Well you are my mate now and have to listen to reason!' I said almost yelling at her. She stormed out of the room and slammed the door.

The forces contending within Llueve were scaring me. On the one hand she felt personally responsible for the deformed children and the Skandrr kidnappings and for all the people, especially her brother, dying of the Faal. On the other hand she had only just escaped the deadly influences of the Faal herself.

I tried to go through the door into her room but she had put up one of these new shields that I couldn't pierce. She had learned some interesting tricks from the Wixxal. I stood there a while and decided this was too serious to handle alone. I had to talk to Djagda. I don't know what to do.

5/01/05

It's Sunday morning. It's a beautiful sunny day. The buds are opening on all the trees.

I haven't been able to stop thinking about Llueve and her demand of me to go to the Draco wormhole. I'm not talking with anyone about all this - Yvonne, Spencer and Lena would have me committed if they knew how behind my calm demeanor I am obsessively thinking about the impending invasion. About killer UFO's flying over Santa Fe, of Llueve and Ea captured by the Draco Lords.

After my encounter with Rexxon, after her encounter with the Janosian leading to her wanting to commit suicide, I now see there is a real danger in the astral. My choices are to block it all out - come to a firm decision that it's all a sustained hallucination caused by my fall - or to take it all as real and make strategic choices within those dreams. I can't even imagine letting go of Llueve and the Siddhe now. So I have to make the dream world win! This will be my Secret Garden!

I need to see Djagda I need him to help her see that the risks are too great. Everything isn't up to her! And I need a crash course in how to fight in the astral.

With these thoughts giving me a new sense of gravity I regularized my breathing and reached for the buzzing bees feeling. Once out of body, I opened the Akasha astral memory banks for the instructions I had internalized on how to get to the entry of Logaana. This is like Googling the Universe. The Akasha is like a hardrive in astral space where all the memories in Mahaala are stored. I mentally invoked the formula and activated it.

I entered a whirlwind of vibrations. I saw tall rows of bookshelves stretching away into the distance. Endless streams of information, faces and scenes passed through my mind until I came to a map. The map went from being a little piece of paper in a folder taken from a shelf to becoming the life sized reality the map represented. A mist cleared and I found myself in the grove of oaks at the base of the bulging hill in the pasture land with its ancient lichen covered, heaped stone fences. This was the same entry where we had met Silvaan the first time we had gone to Logaana. I realized what country this is. It's ~~sensored~~.

As instructed I created a mental signal and placed it inside a golden geometrical pentagram contained within a flame-blue triangle and projected this into the depths of Logaana. This was a request to speak with Djagda. I sat on a rock in the moonlight waiting nervously.

At one point a shimmering column of light vibrated next to me and as I watched, Asaalen appeared in his silver suit. His Tsaat weapon was extended straight out from his body, ready to fire. When he recognized me he nodded once with a cautious seriousness and lowered his weapon. He scanned the general area around the entry and then vanished. After a little while Djagda arrived.

He was dressed in a woven shirt with colors that seemed to bleed into one another. He wore loose flowing brown pants, and had what looked like handmade moccasins on. At a glance, the belt around his overflowing shirt looked like liquid mercury faced with a band of feint iridescent colors on the reflective silver background. Very dressy. I wondered what he had been doing when he got the call to talk to me. Did he have a girlfriend? Was he beyond that sort of thing? Had he been studying some ancient magikal work? I wondered if I was really being a pain in the ass.

'Hello Joseph,' he said and held out his hand, palm facing me. I recognized this as the formal mode of astral encounter and placed my palm against his. The sting of electricity that snapped through us really woke me up and we laughed together at this. It was like a light slap in the face. No matter how prepared you think you are for this psychic encounter it always catches you by surprise.

His smile was reassuring. I always feel in speaking to Djagda that I am speaking to a superior, like a busy head of state and steel myself in anticipation of being rejected and sent off to some underling. But once we'd equalized energies I felt OK.

'Come, let's go to my chambers.' Effortlessly, he surrounded us with an energy band that caused us to transmute. We emerged in the stone hall of an elaborate cavern with various rooms leading off it. We entered a room which had tapestries on the walls, carpets on the floor, floor to ceiling bookshelves with some large leather bound books that looked like they were hundreds of years old. There were comfortable looking sofa chairs and bright electric lamps. Djagda seemed dissatisfied with the room. He rose and said; 'Come.'

We walked down a hall, past closed, thick oak doors and into a kitchen where there was, surprisingly, a perfectly modern, double door refrigerator of brushed stainless steel and a gas range with a convection oven on top. These however were the only new things in the room. There were ancient looking blackened pots and pans hanging from the ceiling rack and tall cupboards with stained, solid wood doors. A large stone sink and marble counter spaces lined half the room which opened on a passage carved in the stone wall that led to a larder with shelves crammed with jars and boxes of all kinds of food and spices. Here too there were electric lights of modern design.

In the kitchen there was a small, thick wooden kitchen table with an unpainted surface polished by use against a wall. Djagda indicated for me to sit in one of the three chairs around it. He then disappeared into the larder and came back with a decanter of cut glass half full of what looked like blue mist. Reaching into a cupboard he took out two white, ceramic saki cups with crackled glaze and ancient dark stains on them and placed these on the table. He then poured the blue mist into the goblets and holding his goblet up said -

'Slainte!' and we toasted.

I took a sip of the blue mist and felt a glow of clarity and well being surge in me. I looked at him inquisitively.

'Loosh!' he said. I was amazed to realize it really was fluid from that ocean I cross every time I go to Ovvala.

Djagda's face is hard to read. It's not so much his features. He is tall, well built in a whipcord fashion and moves with a certain athletic precision - like a razorblade sliding through water. He has long arms and long fingers and a hatchet face. He has two vertical creases under his eyes that aren't exactly laugh lines. His eyes are an opaque silver and seem to look through you, and make him appear blind. As you look in his eyes, his attention seems to move away slowly so that you find yourself searching for his focus only to suddenly find him looking right inside you with a piercing awareness. He has an intense aura of power but it's so hard to really see him that I'm never sure just what that is. There were so many questions I wanted to ask and didn't know where to begin.

'Counsuelaar Djagda...' I started but felt intimidated. The Counsuelaar is perhaps as old as Isult - maybe older for all I know! And in his own way he is just as intense but in a very different way.

His authority among the Siddhe and among the Siddhe Guard particularly is very strong. Djagda I think is the top General of the troops.

'My whole reality has changed...' I started. I had an urgent sense of mission. The thought of Llueve again becoming infected with the Faal and loosing that fighting fire in her eyes and just slumping passively like I had seen her doing the night of the Wixxal, was too sad to think of. I groped for the words to tell Djagda what I needed.

'I used to just be a man who went to work everyday to pay on a mortgage and then I came here, met Llueve and all of you and my whole sense of reality has flipped... I...'

I wanted to explain my fear of being seduced by Draco power again and putting Llueve in danger. And about my feeling ashamed of this and all the thoughts and realizations I'd been having since shooting through the atoms while escaping the Janosian. I felt powerless to protect myself and Llueve. I feared being really thought insane by my friends and particularly I needed him to forbid Llueve going to the Draco Chamber. My thoughts bottlenecked and I ran out of words.

Djagda put his hand on my arm.

'Joseph - you have been in the fire. I can see that exposure to our world -' by which I knew he meant all of it - the astral, Ovvala, Rexxon and Llueve's shenanigans - 'has begun to sink in. It is a lot. You cannot successfully communicate all this in a linear fashion. Concentrate your thoughts and feelings into a thought construct and pass it to me.'

I took a deep breath, got centered and dredged up all the doubts and fears I'd been considering and put them into a Rote. I tried to make it clear that I wasn't just whining but that I wanted to fight back and needed to know how. We sat silently in the room as I collected myself. When I had it together, I transferred this energy ball to him and he silently absorbed it. He then transmitted this rote that I want to write down in its entirety.

Chapter Seventeen

'Well...we were bound to come to this point.' Djagda said patiently, wrapping his large hands around the cup of Loosh. A violet mist wafted over the brim of his cup, cascading over his fingers.

'To fight the Draco, you will need to understand the illegal nature of their presence in life, for they are not alive and can't be dealt with physically. They only exist astrally and so need to be encountered astrally. This is a war of dreams.'

Djagda looked down into his cup and was silent for a long time. I realized he was really digging for the answers I needed from him. He was vibing me that he was going to really speak and I should really listen. Nevertheless he radiated a kindly patience that said there was all the time in world for this, and that my questions really mattered. I felt a real sense of his love for me. That and a powerful humane strength is the core of his force. He felt like the father a man wished he'd had.

'You will remember from the Blue Stone transmission that knowledge of the Ixtellar energy processes was introduced to the adept incarnates in the time of Ishtar by the Spiritual Traveler. I think you will understand the Ixtellaria better as the more familiar word - magik. Ixtellaria is magikal action.' As he spoke to me, Djagda was simultaneously seeding my mind with information that would surface later.

'Magik is achieved by creating resonant correspondences, and thusly raising energy, and then directing this energy with the higher will to a desired end. It is an act of co-creation with the Universe. It involves surfing a wave of newness. The Universe is conscious and alive. It is composed of tendrils of awareness that are collected into constructs by thought and identification. The solar system of Mahaala itself is a thought generated in transdimensional time by our own higher selves. Magik is the way God thinks!' Djagda looked at me carefully and then added; 'God is *newness*!'

'The food grown in Illun and that the Kalkaava eat is tended as part of their Ska-Taal meditation. Energy is harvested from the Aaltandar – the star streams – and invested in the plants. A fully healthy person has transdimensional DNA, that is, DNA that has parallel structures in the six dimensions. DNA restoration is at the heart of the work of the Kalkaava. This methodology is being taught to more and more groups of Ovvalans and Humans. The grain in the Arcturian crop circles stimulate this multidimensional DNA. This is part of the reason for them. This is an example of magik that plays into battling with the Reptilians.'

Images came to me of a garden in a valley where fantastic, astral plants made of radiant energy and pulsing colors were growing side by side with physical plants. From this place, through a deep, narrow cavern, it was possible to go to a similar garden in the crystal dome city of Sahasra-dal-Kanwal, where the Grand Council took place. Momentarily, I saw a broad sunny hillside in Sahasra where colors glowed in the air around plants and trees. In the brief vision I saw Ovvalans, Humans and other Races, in their astral bodies, working in the sun alongside beings made of rainbow colors from Aaltare – what I guess would be called angels. These beings were very defined, magnetic and vital. Djagda continued;

'The Earth is a dense physical place where souls incarnate to experience individualized form. Each incarnate individuality is independently purposeful, but it is also purposeful to a group-soul, of which it is a part. Most individuals are part of a group soul. Ultimately, each group soul is a building block in a bridge to Aaltare, for all Illuvan Souls.

'One aspect of magik is the renewal of spiritual and physical energy. And to a great extent this is automatic. The cycles of the Sun and Moon are continuously renewed in us by our simply cycling through their natural orbits. Sunrise, new moons, solstices, spring, are all cathartic points of the reintegration into newness of astrophysical energy. These are biosoul pulsations, renewing the individual and the whole of Mahaala.

'Each return of newness is a return to the creative effects of the intelligence of love – of Suddilve. Each return to newness is a birth of a new experience and the death of a former experience. Life is a practice of births and deaths. This conditions the soul towards Aaltare. This applies equally to Humans as to Ovvalans, as well as any other Lyran race...that is, humanoids like the Pleidians and Andromedans, Tau Cetans and ourselves.

'If a person did nothing but live and breathe and eat and sleep they would pass through the cycles of renewal and achieve a vehicle. However, when one begins to use the Ixtellar technology and the SkaTaal meditations, they begin to consciously form a route to Aaltare.

As Djagda spoke, his thought streams showed me how energy intention can be sustained and directed, by placing them within different geometrical constructs. A golden triangle could hold the construct - 'awareness of danger'. This became a psychic radio that read the Ixtellar energy webs for danger. The outcome of an event could be influenced by investing a pentagram with a color such as red for urgency, or blue or tranquility. This could apply to finding a place, or a lost tool, or creating an opportunity. Hexagrams could be created to protect an inspiration, or a realization, or to act as a shield. A sphere could be turned into a space pod directed to arrive at a destination. Many such images surface in my thoughts now when I close my eyes at night.

'The interface of individual identity with collective intent, serves the common purpose of empowering a magikal design. Suddilve is the shared intent for everything – for gods, people, demons and animals. There really is no need to name this shared fundamental intelligence. This is what is thinking. This is what the super-ego is and this is what the goal is. 'I am that, So-Ham, God is Love.

'In contrast to the expanding and ascending system of Ixtellar-Magik is the contracting, and self centered Qlipothic underworld. This is the region of unconsciousness teeming with spirits with no fixed identity. 'The Qlipothic underworld is a place of living monstrosities and deformities that lust for the existence they see happening in the world above them. Our world. And while all is Suddilve, the Qlipoths are like deformed fish looking up through murky water at persons standing on the shore in sunlight. They hunger to be those persons and live those events.

'They see people living lives with an identity, love, emotions, dreams, powers, and they want to leap into this experience, without entering through the front door, so to speak. To enter into the realms above the Qlipoth, the Qlipothic being needs to integrate their own light and dark. Energy integration is the vehicle for traveling here. Yet the act of integration for the Qlipoth, is death to their underworld identity.

'Identity for the Qlipoth is a dark exaggerated fantasy of great power and self importance. The Qlipoth is a predatory realm of incompletely formed beings, where there is endless psychic carnage going on. There are really no actual beings, only continuously transforming desires, vying for power and control over one another. Semi-formed beings are killed and consumed by other desire-beings, which is the only purpose for power, as they understand it, to overcome others.

'Because integration is death to Qlipothic lust, they are compelled to cheat their way into Human and Ovvalan consciousness, by entering our minds when we are weak, or distracted, or corrupt, or deluded. In the early civilizations of Earth, when the planets were seen as gods, and astrology was a poetic science of the soul, people knew of the underworld, and had means for dealing with it. But the priests of the new religions banned such knowledge because they wanted sole ownership of such powers. This weakened people to penetration by both priests and Qlipothic monsters.

'The Draco Reptilians are unique Qlipothic beings for us, because they are a part of our own biological evolution. They are, in a sense our ancestors, having been physical in our world, and having developed our brain stem. This gives them a unique ability to enter us that was never anticipated by the designers of Mahaala. They have fooled God!

'The Dracos have created an organized, collective complex system of penetration into our world, with the express goal of taking the entirety of us over. They are committed to enter and remain. They live in the conviction that we are the intruders into *their* domain, and have stolen physical existence from *them*. This is truly cosmic psychosis. Remember that they don't see us simply as enemies. They see us as *prey*. This predatory energy – the Vrryl energy – is very tiring to the mammalian mind. It saps the creativity with which to think through such contradictions.

'To understand what you want to know, how to protect yourself, Llueve and Ea from them, and how to fight back, you need to grasp that Ouroboros, their form of magik, is the mirror-opposite of the Ixtellar.

'The primitive Reptilian mind was a set of compartments connected to the brain stem. Each compartment indicated a function. Kill. Eat. Fight. Sleep. The structure for the Ouroboros language, by which to dominate humans, was taken directly from this compartmentalized mind.

'Draco society is organized around this compartmentalization. Hierarchically ascending compartmentalization of group functions are driven by a single alpha predator. These hunt. These guard the eggs. These capture and kill food. This one commands.

'It is this compartmentalized structure that Dracos are imposing on our race. This is Ouroboros.

'The Ixtellar, Suudilve and Aaltare are fluid, creative thought streams deeply integrated within the Universe. They are liquid, spontaneously adaptive states of imaginative energy. For Dracos to penetrate this stream, they had to violently interrupt it, and cause it to fragment into parts, because for them, it is like a herd of prey running in all directions simultaneously. To cause arrest and fragmentation, Dracos dipped into their arsenal of Tyrannosaurean tricks used to attack dinosaur prey. This is the full spectrum terrorization of shock and awe. Overkill. This sudden, dramatic shock attack has always been the Draco's opening move. Once prey is held in a state of shock and awe, a discontinuity with the familiar can be imposed.

'For Human and Ovvalan minds to reconcile with the alien Ouroboros mentality, the reptilians needed our faith to be stronger than our understanding. They needed us to feel grateful for being imprisoned! The Stockholm Syndrome. One form of faith, is a passive surrendering of creative thought. The image of a god who will do your creating for you, was carefully cultivated by the Draco through the Andrr-ka priests, using these basic Reptilian methods. First shock. Then the establishment of authority. Then compartmentalization. Your oppressor is your friend. In fact, your God!

'One shock was created by making taboo the passage between the parallel worlds. This was accomplished through religious warfare between tribal groups. Askalen, Troy, the Viking raids. The three hundred year war between Daag and Mannan. Thermopylae. The Inquisition. Over time Humans and Ovvalans were trained to an inability to see beyond their one, separated dimension. Transdimensionalism was outlawed in the imagination as dabbling with witchcraft.

'Separating Humans and Ovvalans was the original injury done to Illuvan minds. Ovvala and Terra are symbiotically connected, they make one ecology. Dividing us from one another created a psychic crack in consciousness, which the Draco then exploited.

'The next shock for Humans was accomplished with the idea of Abraham sacrificing his son to God, and presenting this as spiritual love, an impossible idea, that contradicts human instinct. There is a parallel event in Ovvala with Aalarrdan, when a deity commanded he kill himself to prove his love of God. Such shock tactics of forced belief, create separation between oneself and God-as- Self, making God separate from and superior to the Self. This is the vengeful merciless God of the Bible from whom the mind needed protection. As long as one could enter into the compartment and faith and servitude to this God, one was safe both from the God and from other believers in this God. This was the beginning of institutionalized compartmentalization of humanity. Divide and conquer – not just the people. But the mind!

'In Homosauran society, language and mind are compartmentalized hierarchically, to feed energy, prestige, and authority, from the bottom to the top. Separate and isolated groupings on the bottom capture and carry energy upwards. The very structure of the Ouroboros language is designed to do this. The little only has value by virtue of the top that rules it. In contrast, by Ixtellar logic, the little has the value of the whole it completes.

'In the Ouroboros mind, one compartment is the identity of pure service to a superior being of perfect idealized power. This is devolution to the leader, and is the compartment of faith by which a person believes they are benefited by their leader-God, and are worthy of his blessing. Blind obedience to this God is itself the price for being in the God's care. This first compartmentalization then allows for other compartments with different functions.

'The ever present sorrow in the Illuvan soul caused by splitting the dimensional ecology of Ovvala and Earth, is also the broken self esteem that results from a fragmented psyche. This sorrow longs for consolation and numbness, for which the Ouroboros thoelogy beat into the multitudes, offers the compartment of fantasy and projection. The missing half of the heart – of the Self - can be artificially constructed through such fantasy, just like beings in the Qlipoth do! Random fantasy has taken the place of directed imaginative constructs. This is the basis of glamour, by which the mind can be captured by a sexy carrot on an invisible stick. Like television and pop music.

'Psychological childhood injuries, alienations from a mother or a father, become fragmented selves; self pity, arrogance, abuse of others. Passive-aggressive or predatory attitudes, become identities played out in secret fantasies that can't be perceived by others – hidden behind the camouflage of the compartment of faith where one is good and holy, whole and happy and presents this face to the world as a shield. In the compartment of faith, each individual is also the group, and the group is confident and dominant. In this way, the Ouroboros emulates in appearance what the Ixtellar actually is.

'When a compartmentalized person steps forward into the compartment of faith, and under the guidance of a superior leader, their compartments of sorrow and guilt and fear and lust are hidden away. That repressed compartment becomes the back room, with the closed door where one is free to indulge in numbing distractions, for their unmet needs.

'This becomes an irresolvable division in the identity of an individual. It is a perpetual form of fragmentation. This state of fragmentation is a state of sustained insecurity that can only be numbed by more distraction. This is called a Negative Mystery – an irresolvable problem that is reinforced by its own discussion. Saurian Theology and the daily news are based in this Negative Mystery. An irresolvable conundrum that feeds on itself, and never gets resolved or nourished.

'Compartmentalization also provides an invisible front for aggression. In confrontation with non-believers, a group of compartmentalized beings can, in concert, assert a non-rational even a senseless, disconnected narrative - with which other compartmentalized minds fully agree. Not because of a real shared understanding, but simply because the compartment of faith is a collective compartment that has only one collective face.

'Persons who are thusly camouflaged, can enter into a collective action against people who are autonomous. Autonomous individuals are sensed as being alone and defenseless. The shield of collective faith and the drive to proselytize, is advanced against such isolated individuals as concern, disguising predation as compassion.

'In the structure of compartmentalization, there is an inner sanctum of holiness and reverence that is never to be entered or investigated. This prohibition is presented with deep seriousness to open minded children, by adult priests who extract a deep and terrorized promise from the child; Do Not Question This! Coming as it does from adults, this taboo becomes centrally imprinted in the child's budding mind. This place is the holy of holies that is not to be investigated, or even looked into. To doubt or desire to penetrate this area of taboo is imprinted as a sin, with terrible consequences. This place is understood to be the unquestioned abode, in the self, of the higher being who directs one's thoughts and actions. It is the abode of God in the self, whose understanding is greater than one's own, and which should be blindly obeyed. This is the area of self critical social inhibitions. One is good ,and a part of the group, as long as one has this inhibition to not penetrate this area. And this is where the Reptilian entity itself takes root inside the mind. From here, the Draco's collective plan is directed and the different groupings are coordinated from the central Draco vortex of Skarror – the capitol of Krrual.

'Each part of the Homosauran social hierarchy is compartmentally separated from the rest. Each group only understands their individual task. None see the overall Master Plan for which they are collectively working. Even the Andrr-Ka Magi don't understand that they are separated from each other by the Draco Lords; to be discarded when they are no longer useful. These deep and knowledgeable wizards are seduced by their own compartmentalized fantasies of dark glamour and power – the Dracos know this. The Andrr-Kz are like the the chicken that believes the nice lady who comes out every morning to feed them is their best friend until one morning she comes out with an ax! Ha ha ha.' Djagda flew out of character when he threw back his head and laughed out loud.

'So here you have the two thought forms that are in conflict for the soul of Mahaala, the Ixtellar Magik and the Ourboros linguistic of the lizards.' Djagda squinted his eyes and gave me a piercing look that I felt down to my belly button.

The Loosh we were drinking was delicious to my astral taste buds. It was like a liqueur of dark herbs and flowers – sweet and bitter like say Chartreuse. But its effect was more like a psychedelic mushrooms than alcohol. I felt my entire being had expanded with a sense of tremendous curiosity and enthusiasm. Djagda's words connected the different parts of me in one continuous tissue of confidence. And this confidence brought up a feeling of courage and love in me.

Pyramids of understanding interpenetrated to construct layered planes. I felt like a flaming genius as all my separate thoughts were joined into a stream of shifting geometry and color. Love became a continuum of intelligent, regulated, adaptive waves that sustained inspiration just as physical food sustained my body. This intelligence of love we were at heart discussing, was the parallel life of Eternity.

Djagda refilled our empty glasses as I looked around at the ancient polished walls of living stone, and the wrought iron frames and pedestals holding his kitchen appliances. I noticed the blacksmith's hammer strokes in his ancient iron and copper pots and skillets. The extreme age of these objects was impressive. The razor sharpness in Djagda's eyes helped me isolate each thought as it was presented ,and then organize each within the whole of what he was explaining.

'Now,' Djagda continued, watching me carefully, 'the Ixtellar is an alphabet of energy constructs that recreate Suudilve within the Universe. For the good of all the Universe. The conscious tendrils that make up the continuum of Suudilve can, and do connect the heart of one soul to the heart of another, across a Galaxy. Huge and ancient algorithmic constructs link Earth and Ovvala, the Pleiades, Arcturus, Vannay and Aldanvaar throughout our portion of the Galaxy, into one vast network of the Ixtellar Linguistic Continuum.'

String-theory, as physics had come to understand it, clearly became a universal substance, available to be organized into anything at all. The thoughts I'd had looking out the window of Spencer's bus flashed vividly across my mind. This was like an astral frequency that connected other frequencies, a code that linked energies as seemingly separate as trees and thoughts, speech and weather.

'By contrast, Krrual, the Draco dimension, is hermetically separated from the rest of the Universe. Likewise, Homosaurs are separate minorities in their societies, making up about a quarter of the population. But they are very aggressive, acting out their collective compartmentalization to serve their leader. To divide and conquer everyone outside their own society has been imprinted in them as their orthodoxy. Their mission is to enlighten the universe to their superior values.

'The other seventy five percent of those societies are humanitarian agnostics for whom religions are more of a social language than a belief system. Heaven and hell, enlightenment and sin, redemption and forgiveness, Ezekiel did this and Allah did that - these references provide a kind of shorthand by which most people refer to their births and deaths in the cycles of life. Myths and parables are the comic dimension boiled down to earthly experiences. 'You don't miss your water 'till your well runs dry' 'You reap what you sow', 'a bird in the hand is worth two in the bush' 'nail that sticks out gets bent'. These are sayings from experience, not faith, and are innocent ways of speaking from the pagan origins of culture, about the overriding dimension in which physicality is contained.

'Orthodox traditionalists demand everyone say and do and act in prescribed ways, because they fear their own imaginations; they fear a living interaction with God. They quote historical and scriptural passages to impose their sect's version of God on the nameless, fathomless, Universal God – the God that is Love and fluid creativity. Their compartmentalization demands of them that everyone be compartmentalized and subject to their language use – subject to their power.

'In modern times, language and culture are used – of necessity – largely as camouflage, to hide from the predators. Even good, loving people, not part of any hierarchy, use the vocabulary of compartmentalization to camouflage themselves as being like the compartmentalized people in their society. Whether the society is Moslem, or Jewish, or Christian, or Hindu, the agnostics within it use the language of the predator priests to evade the predators! This has been required behavior after Inquisitions and Jihads, ethnic cleansings and religious purges, through all of the Draco's manipulations, and has only really begun to change very recently – since democracy set a standard for freedom of speech.

'The insistent push by capitalism for a Free Market economy, is fundamentally a demand to not limit their predation.

'It's easy to associate fixated ways of thinking with cultural conservatives. But the Draco lust for control of humanity knows no party bounds. Liberalism can be just as servile to a liberal authority as conservatives can be to their authority. Liberalism has come to mean a kind of formless or spineless identity. Liberals give others permission to be whatever they fantasize. The supportive skeletal structure of an original nature with co-dependent ecological roles has been disolved. Genders are disolved. This frees a person to have no strong opinions, or conflicts, and cultivates the idea that un-attached, non-involvement, is close to enlightenment. This permissiveness plays right into the Reptilian hierarchies.

The vast majority of Humans and Ovvalans simply want justice. We share a Universal Commonwealth and everyone is entitled to enough of it to make ends meet *and* tie a bow. To have a peaceful life, a fair wage, the chance to raise a family in dignity without having to become pirates or assassins, is the fundamental cosmic right of a soul.

'Reptilian logic obsessively wants to do everything as it was done before. There is no idea of evolution to a higher intelligence. This is the missing part of the Reptilian psyche. They have never had evolution as a window of opportunity. By refusing to evolve they have contracted into a position of defensiveness, and feel that the whole Universe is against them – which it now is. The Reptilian mind is locked in a time and a place that no longer exists, but that, for the survival of their own significance, they need to assert. Overcoming Reptilian logic within *ourselves*, is now a key part of our own evolution.

By placing a greater value on our own emerging Higher Self, participating in a conscious global society, we deprive the Reptilian of any reflection of themselves in our eyes, so that they cease to exist! Not having a way to indulge their fragmented identity, by parasitically living through us, they will come to a place of cosmic irrelevance. Then, their choice will be between evolution and non-existence.

'In response to the global destruction wreaked by the Reptilians, the progressive world has become sentimental and compulsively sympathetic to fragility. There is the tendency to refuse to see darkness, to not brand evil, but to suspend judgment and play for time. This too plays right into the Reptilians game, and they know it!

'See no evil. Hear no evil. Speak no evil; this attitude towards evil needs to be reconsidered. This was the lesson of Bush; evil only triumphs because good people do nothing. Excessive liberalism, no less than excessive conservatism, is not real individualism. And lack of real individuality, of *self possession*, allows the Reptilians to enter and whisper sweet nothings in your ear. Each individual has a divine responsibility to be individually creative, and digest information from their personal Higher Self. This is the meaning of embodying enlightenment. In this world, the shadows and light shift - social values change - and you have to take sides to stay out of the shadows. Love means taking sides. You can't feel love for all values, and all the people that have those values. But you do love those that you must! And can feel charity for the rest.

'There will come a time, when the 75% of society that is agnostic about orthodoxies, will need to stand up to the fanatics in their own cultures. This is the zeitgeist, the spirit of our times. Whether Moslem or Christian or Jewish, Hindu, Buddhist or anything else, each society has a responsibility to question the fanatics inside their own culture, who would embroil the rest in servility and war with other nations. The reasonable majority in each tradition needs to say to the minority %25 - you *are* the problem! This homicidal demand that 'mine is the only true God' of 'the only workable solution' needs to be re-evaluated in terms of the welfare of the whole of Humankind. These archaic concepts of isolated tribal identity do not match the present world.

'What prophesy has ever come true? If there is no Armageddon, no Rapture, no End of the World in 2012 - so what? Is the miracle of existence less? Is the miracle of the imagination less? Is love less? Reality, like God and like the Self are adaptive; everything is fluid. This is why prophesies don't come true.

'The Draco's long work of manipulating humanity with artificial wars, and manufactured emergencies is now, itself, threatened by climate change. They are obsessively spraying the skies of the planet with a chemical haze to try and both keep the oil infrastructure and insulate the planet from the sun with no concern for what the consequences will be for biology or human life. Spraying aluminum and barium into the environment is suicidal! They don't understand that what is causing climate change - the electron cloud the galaxy has entered, is a natural event that we have not only survived before, but that we are built to benefit from! But the linear, material science of the reptilian elite, tells them everything is going to burn up, so they are maximizing overproduction, to glean the last possible profits from the system they have constructed, while building their underground bunkers and leaving the rest of us out to burn!

'Distrust of the industrial and religious forces that have led to ecological chaos, is creating a global drive to address real physical problems, without the confusion of superstition. Shifting from the carbon economy that benefits the few, to a solar economy that benefits all, is a mystical and alchemical act. The entire Human Race is on the threshold of claiming a higher consciousness. And this is making the Draco desperate! The Ouroboros Linguistic and the Master Plan to subjugate humankind only exists on Ovvala and Terra. This is a sub-reality that is parasitic on our world and, through our world, is parasitic on Suudilve! On Love! Immense counter measures are radiating throughout the Ixtellar webs. The forces deconstructing Ouroboros are majestic!

'The Draco and the Andrr-Ka wizards are fundamentally unbalanced. They are living in a dark fantasy of self-worth with which they are obsessed. They are continually running this dark fantasy of domination through their minds, in alteration with the faith compartment, where they feel they share in the mastery of their predatory God.'

The bubblings and poppings inside my head had reached a steady simmer. I was remembering another self. Images of other identities flashed through my mind to the degree that the point of origin I know as Joe, Connecticut where I grew up, my parents and sister and brother – these things were only one scenario among others, which began streaming faster and faster through my mind. I briefly saw myself as the pilot of a starship; a barefoot farmer in Sumer, an etheric life form floating in a mist; the change from a fixed identity to a Universal one happens so fast. What one minute seems incredible becomes normal in such a way that an entire lifetime lived in a fixed identity becomes a memory – in minutes. Djagda continue;

'An integrated being produces higher, quicker and more expanded vibrations than the contracted Homosauran identity. Integration penetrates the compartmentalization of the fragmented mind, causing it to become self-conscious. Such self-consciousness dissolves the walls separating artificial compartments, and the dark fantasies within. This is death to the compartmentalized identity.' Djagda's eyes were boring into my skull. The razor of light I'd seen in his gaze before, began cutting me to pieces. It was merciless the way he went on and on when I could barely keep up. I was starting to resent this intensely.

'Looking into the mirror of the self is terrifying for a compartmentalized being, because it creates a freedom they are unfamiliar with. Used to having a controller, they are suddenly in control and aren't equipped to deal with this.'

I tried to wiggle the feet of my body in bed at home to snap me back to Jaconita, but nothing happened. But taking that action caused what had been a single stream of thought to suddenly branch out into so many streams of images that I felt myself dissolving. Who was I? What was my own internal dialogue? Which stream of images was mine? I suddenly felt in danger from a burning mental intensity, and felt a desperate urge to run away. Where was I in this dream? Who were these Siddhe and Ovvalans? What after all is a demon but something that overwhelms you with strangeness. Were these demons? My Catholic upbringing suddenly kicked in and I saw Djagda as a devil – a potent entity that had penetrated my mind and which I couldn't remove – I felt possessed by a growing terror. I jumped up and looked around wildly for a way out and began hyperventilating when I saw there was none. Fear and hatred twisted around inside me like a short circuit of my own energy – my head started to shake spasmodically with an alternating current of indecision – black spots appeared in my sight and began to expand uncontrollably. I was terrified!

Djagda clapped his hands and an ear splitting thunder exploded in my mind. My thought bubbles burst and I stood looking at him, with my mouth open, completely stunned.

'You see?' Djagda said quietly. I had run into his greater integration of energy and had begun to hallucinate out of my own past imprints. My inability to match his level of integration had put me in reaction and defensiveness. This is what a Qlipothic entity, a Reptilian, would experience in the face of a sustained, projected integration of light and dark.

I did see. Sobs of laughter escaped me. I felt dizzy and grabbed the back of the chair for support.

'Here is the point of all this,' Djagda smiled and continued speaking softly.

'The Reptilians broke their contract with evolution and discovered a way to exist here illegally. This makes them vulnerable. Magik can be used to activate their re-integration to Suddilve. Just as people unconsciously aid the Reptilian Agenda with the Ouroboros Linguistic laced through their thoughts, it is now possible to cause the Higher Self in the Reptilians to sever their parasitism on our Race and move towards the light of evolution.

'For six thousand years the nerves of the human mind have been whipped by Reptilian paradoxes and made to respond to their authority. Our natural biological language has been seeded with Ouroboros promptings so that we have learned to imprison ourselves. People have been trained to yank each other's chain of servitude to Reptilian authority. This was their intention all along.

'Now, the weapons you see the Siddhe Guard wear are concentrators of thought. The Tsaat, the weapons, have two crystals inside them, which collide when triggered. These crystals are owned and cared for by a Guard. They hold mental constructs activated by SkaTaal meditation. The crystals store Aa, prana. A crystal is unique in that it is simultaneously physical and astral. When these crystals collide inside the Tsaat, a spark shoots out the Guard's own identity - their own integrated energy - into their challenger. When they draw the weapon, they are directing their higher integrated selves at some aspect of Qlipothic disintegration that is threatening them. The colliding crystals produce a ray of real electrical force that carries the integration-frequency of the shooter, and can knock someone out or actually kill them. When the Guard asserts this integration, he or she is also asserting the universal integration that is Suudilve. As you refine your Ska Taal meditation this projection will become stronger.'

I nodded in amazement at a technology of love used for spiritual combat. Now if he could only help me pull Llueve back from her madness.

'Llueve is demanding I go with her to do something that could endanger her and the baby,' I said. 'I can't reason with her. If I don't help her in some way, I believe she's going do it anyway and this could be worse! I've tried in every way I can think of to reason with her but she won't listen. I don't know what to do.'

I knew I was betraying Llueve here, by going up the chain of command, but the stakes were too high to come to a decision alone.

'I know about the Wixxal ceremony Llueve went through,' Djagda said. 'It's causing a deep transformation in her. Getting rid of the actual germ of sadness may only be the first step in a process of renewal for her. She may need to take action - start a new conduit of energy into Suudilve - put distance between herself and the identity in her that was infected with the Faal.

'If she is that insistent, it may be because she has no choice in the matter! She may need to act because she knows it's not over. That she and the baby are still vulnerable to the sickness.'

I hadn't considered this.

'Also,' Djagda went on, 'it might be Ea prompting her to do something none of us can see as a possibility. That is just the kind of thing Ea would risk!'

By this time an electric fever was burning inside me from this sustained transmission of such intense information. I had maxed out and needed to switch off. Djagda's energy was like acid eating deeper and deeper into me. I was beginning to vaporize.

I polished off the last of the Loosh in my cup and to keep it together, started the circle eight breathing Yvonne taught me and tried to hang on. Waves of Loosh appeared around me and the shush-shing sound of their waves enveloped me. Djagda stood up and I did too. He made a golden triangle around us and transported us to the middle of a grove of oaks outside an entry to Logaana. Waves of Loosh continued crashing down on me like a sparkling sapphire mist and my consciousness began to shift into a dream.

Djagda looked deep into my eyes and nodded, and then walked away between the trees. I drifted into the ocean of Loosh and became absorbed in watching the towering waves crashing in slow motion into an endless sea of tenderness.

Chapter Eighteen

5/8/05

We stood face to face in dead seriousness. Llueve was completely in her power. She had one hand on her outthrust hip and a no compromise attitude that was as human as any woman I ever saw.

'Jwo - I feel Ea speaking to me now and I think her guidance will help us succeed!' (How would she know if it was Ea speaking to her or not since she'd already decided what she was going to do?) 'We only need to locate the wormhole so Silvaan can take a ship there and close the entry. We don't need to encounter them in *any* way - we may even be able to see what is needed from a distance.' While her voice felt completely present and her features remained composed and calm, her eyes had a cool, otherworldly glimmer.

I thought for a while. There was no way out. I considered what Djagda had said - that forward motion for Llueve could mean the difference between life and death. I had to go with her. I feared that this could lead to disaster but there was no way I could let her go alone or risk her going with some other human yahoo she'd found. Yvonne's curly haired New Age salesman came to mind in a bad way. And if she went alone, and failed, it would haunt me forever. And, I felt almost *sure*, if she continued to beat herself up about the urgency of things, she would start the Faal all over in herself again. I, possibly, had power to prevent that.

We looked at each other with defiance. It's at this point, it seems to me. that a relationship really begins. When you nearly hate someone you love. We were suddenly new and different to each other. This combat of wills had both placed us farther apart, and made us more real to one another. We were familiars enough now to make demands on each other.

'O.K.' I said. 'But if we run into what looks *anything* like real danger - anything! - we get out *when I say so!*' I tried to stare her down and just as I was about to cave in she said...

'O. Whay!' Daag speakers can't say j's or k's very well. The damn cuteness of this made me grin. Whew. Close call.

We began the ritual of creating protection shields and energy constructs that could be activated in emergency situations. With one word, either of us would wake up immediately in our beds, or both of us would zoom to Inxalrok and find refuge with the Siddhe. Part of the deal was that we couldn't call on the Siddhe for protection and backup because they would tell Isult and Llueve was sure Isult would stop us going. I felt I had to go along with this.

We had both learned so much about creative visualization by now, that our shields were pretty elaborate.

When we were ready, we set off for the Kovrro Flight Base where the wormhole was thought to be located. The Skandrr Air Force keeps a mass of disk ships there. Siddhe spies have also seen helicopters and different fighter jets there so this was the obvious place to start. The base is in a remote desert area and has a very sinister reputation among the Siddhe.

In Ovvala, the equivalent to Earth's alien cattle mutilations, is the abduction of people from remote, and sometimes even suburban areas. Witnesses who have seen such abductions and escaped describe black whirling mechanical monsters that thud and hiss. They drop down suddenly on a street and people dressed in black jump out of these things and shoot tranquilizer darts at them and they are never seen again.

Because these things were nothing like Ovvalan Skaalin disks - which are silent - it is generally assumed by Ovvalans that these other craft are from outer space.

Some ten years ago, a pilot in the Skandrr Air Force defected to the Siddhe. This was Asaalen. He was interviewed on a rogue television broadcast from Inxalrok, and said he had personally seen such craft hidden in hangars at Kovrro. So this was where we were going.

The Siddhe had tried for years to approach this base astrally with no success because the Adrrik - the Skandrr psychic police - keep a twenty-four hour watch there. The Siddhe could not afford to be followed back to their own bases at Inxalrok or Logaana by these psychic operatives, and so had to stay away from Kovrro. Getting close physically was completely impossible. There are ground sensors and the Skandrr keep dozens of the fastest disk-craft on continual alert.

Once Llueve and I had internalized the constructs we had created, we established a basic plan of approach and took off. After a fairly long flight, we emerged in a desert area. As we beamed in on Kovrro we could see a wide dark shadow snake across the desert. This was a long, very deep canyon. We followed this west and at a certain point, where a ridge dropped away from the edge of the canyon we saw the Kovrro base.

Once we recognized it, we stopped and hovered, holding hands and enacted SkaTaal. This activates Lexl-light between us and amplifies the phenomenon of invisibility. We finally made a real peace as we did this and really smiled and kissed.

We looked around for signs of vigilance. As we had agreed, we stayed close together and allowed our hearts to resonate - this is what creates our invisibility. We were in a very serious headspace. I felt Llueve was gauging my whole being as a man and as an Earthling as well as my potential worth as the father of her child. Her Ovvalan mental lines were painfully sharp in my Human mind and against my denser Human will. My hyper caution and mammalian protectiveness, were a powerful challenge to her quick, Ovvalan instincts to be etherially spontaneous.

We came to a heavily patrolled area. There were circular landing pads for choppers and Disks and landing strips for jets, cross-hatched with black skid marks. Most of the Disk sites were empty. There were three or four executive jets and a half dozen fighter jets. The landing zones were bordered by buildings that looked like offices and barracks. There were service vehicles parked in various grouping. Ground vehicles moved slowly around the perimeter with flashing yellow lights. The base was built alongside the lip of the canyon, on a wide shelf about a hundred feet below the rim of the land, where a forest of small trees extended away into the night. Antenna and laser canons overlooked the area. We took mental snapshots of all this to relay to the Siddhe in rote later.

We slowly flew all around the perimeter of the base but saw nothing that looked like what could lead to a wormhole. While there was some activity around the barracks buildings and the ground vehicles moving at the perimeter, not much seemed to be going on.

Suddenly, lights began flashing near the cliff. I thought maybe they'd spotted us and I was about to make us shoot away. But then we saw movement in the wall of the canyon. The sandstone cliff cracked open revealing a dark space. The crack widened and I realized that doors were opening outwards in the sandstone face. In a moment, two Aeron disks hovered out of the darkness, rose up above the canyon rim and then dropped down onto landing pads. The doors in the cliff then closed seamlessly.

We flew over to the doors and up over the canyon rim above them, then dropped down through the ground. We came out in a tall, wide tunnel carved through sandstone. It was illumined with no clear source of light.

We glided down the tunnel, which kept going and going in a straight line until it widened into the huge cylindrical space that we recognized immediately. It was the Draco Council Chamber! Of course! The Human and Ovvalan members of the Andrr-Ka would meet in the middle between the two dimensions! The Siddhe didn't know this! When we had penetrated the Draco Council, we had only found it by homing in on the Draco Vrryl energy broadcast by so many Homosaurs being together.

The immense cavern was empty and still now. We crouched cautiously against the wall, ready to activate our escape modes. We were barely breathing. But there was no movement or noise or any sense of a presence anywhere. This central chamber took on a new significance to us. It was fascinating to consider that this tunnel created a meeting place between our two different species, imprinted for millennia to remain ignorant of one another. Bludgeoned by lies, the scar tissue of the mind had locked out any other conception of things. A naturally transdimensional people, we took for granted that we were one-dimensional while reality was entirely different.

We cautiously touched down on the floor of the chamber and assumed walking postures, advancing towards the center of the room.

'Quick! Against the wall!' Llueve hissed and pushed against me. I edged up against the wall with her at my side and looked at her to see what had set her off. Bright little lights came on along the base of the tunnel. She pointed across the chamber to where the tunnel continued. In the hollow of the ongoing tunnel, an almost imperceptibly small light appeared to be moving. Then we heard a low, rhythmic, grinding. As the thing advanced it got louder and louder until it was thundering in the echoing cavern.

Three jet-propelled black helicopters were moving single file towards us. As they passed the middle of the chamber, they slowed to a hover. At this point they became vaporous - like looking through barbecue fumes. Then they became normal again, sped up, and passed on down the tunnel towards Kovrro.

So - the chamber itself was where the transubstantiation between Earth and Ovvala took place! Either a natural, or synthesized force field, caused the shift from matter to anti-matter. Or something like that.

As the sound faded, we calmed down and walked along the floor down the middle of the chamber - now looking forward and backward along both arms of the tunnel to see if anything was coming. I noticed techno devices hooked to the wall, high up near the ceiling, that I figured were motion sensors or video cameras.

As we continued walking, I felt strange - dense and queasy and kind of throw-uppy. This passed and then I felt a wave of dizziness but nothing appeared to be different. I reflexively reached for Llueve's hand as we approached the far side of the cavern to enter the tunnel on the other side.

It was when our hands touched that we both stopped and turned to each other in shock. We had become physical! We stood there - still holding hands, turned towards each other, and realized we were naked and in the flesh, standing on the sandstone floor of the cavern.

Two things struck me at the same time; one was that she was a tall woman. I'm six feet two and she was only a few inches shorter than me. The other thing was that her skin was blue and her nipples an iridescent violet. Since most of our time together was spent either flying or making love, I had never really noticed her height. And in the astral there is so much color and energy perception generally that I never once had thought that her skin color could be different than mine.

In the astral, her physical features were an extension of her spirit and personality and I related to them as energy. Suddenly she was really physical and the full impact of her presence - her otherworldliness - gave me the shivers. Her feminine beauty was all the more accentuated by her physicality. In the astral she was like touching a dream. Suddenly, in the dim lights of the tunnel, and fully naked, her oval breasts, girlish shoulders, and her hips with their uniquely long Ovvalan curves, and her glistening, faintly writhing hair, was all shockingly exotic.

She told me later that my physical presence at that moment made her completely forget where we were or what we were doing. My body was so much denser and muscular than she had imagined and my skin appeared to her at first to be made of stone. And the thought that what was down below was made of some kind of living stone had been distracting to her.

Our recent alienation, because of our conflict about going to the wormhole, was suddenly overwhelmed by a mutual desire for tenderness. The physical reality of one another suddenly renewed our attraction. The experience of having, what in essence had been a dream lover, suddenly now become flesh before my eyes - and inside my hands - was staggering.

The long lines of her arms and her elegant, pendant breasts, just intoxicated me. I reached out - completely forgetting where we were, and what we were doing, and cupped my hands on her hip as she put her hand to my cheek. Unable to resist, I cupped a breast as she leaned out to kiss me when we heard a huge, echoing metallic crash behind us.

Something was coming! Complete fear shattered the sense of awe glowing between us. We started running down the tunnel away from Kovrro into the depths of the tunnel.

Llueve stopped suddenly and grabbed me by the arm, speaking in rapid fire Ovvalan.

'Irreliaaeven tae dah lio-sieh ventaalnish kiendiord!' I realized that we had lost telepathic communication! She tried to pull me back toward the Ovvalan side of the tunnel. She was in a panic, her pupils dilated wildly. She was terrified of leaving the Ovvala dimension!

I didn't know what to do. Neither of us had ever been physical in the other's dimension. We had always been in the astral. This vortex made us physical, and I assumed, human type physical, because my skin looked normal even if hers didn't. If we went back to the center of the vortex would we become anti-matter? Ovvalan physical? Or would we return to the astral? If we had to physically exit the tunnel at Kovrro, we would be captured in minutes - fifty sensors would be activated. Inside the tunnel there was nowhere to hide.

Meanwhile, a sound like soughing wind passing through a wha-wha pedal was coming from the Ovvalan side - and we were physical - we could be seen!

I pulled her in the direction we had been headed but she insisted on going the other way, hissing wildly and writhing in my grip, all the while talking in rapid Ovvalan. Then she put her hands above her head and pushed up on her toes frantically - she was taking the position we used to take when we first flew up into the sky together. Tears smeared her face as she tried to communicate to me that she thought we could get back to the astral by going back across the center of the tunnel. But this possibility was an unknown, and there was no time to find out. We couldn't make a mistake and be found in the physical in the middle of the chamber. Our physicality could have set off sensors already and the noise we heard could be the Skandrr military police coming at us. We knew what was behind us and there was no place to hide. Perhaps ahead there would be...

Llueve was crying hysterically now. I held her by the shoulders and looked deep into her eyes and said in as calm a voice as I could – 'we're together - I'm with you - we've got to stay calm!' Then I grabbed her wrist in a grip she couldn't break and yanked her down the tunnel away from Ovvala. She stumbled after me not knowing what to do, but I gave her no choice.

We ran. The sounds were not getting any dimmer as we ran and ran seeing only more and more tunnel. Then the tunnel ended in a riveted, black steel wall. This was another set of doors like those at the other end, but seen from the inside. Then I saw a stairway cut into the sandstone wall. We ran up it. It led to a low ceilinged hallway. We were gasping for air now. I really felt my nakedness. The hallway took a couple of turns and came to a small steel door like a bank vault with one large wheel in the center that moved bolts in every direction. There was a shelf in the wall where there was a black rectangular instrument that looked like a very sophisticated remote control. I picked it up wondering if it would open the door while Llueve wildly turned the wheel on the door. The door opened out. It led onto a sand stone shelf partly lit by the light coming from the tunnel behind us, and partly by the incredible amount of stars in a moonless night sky. A wave of fresh air hit us as we gasped at the cold of it. The sandstone shelf was actually a shallow cave. Beyond the cliff-edge, we could see a sheer drop into the darkness of the canyon below.

The pulsing and throbbing sounds were nearing the bottom of the stairs as we went through the door. Crashing sounds echoed up at us as the large metal doors began to open outwards. Simultaneously, the sound of the door we had just come through closed with a deep thunk that left us standing outside, in the dark. As the larger doors opened below us, light from the tunnel lit up three, sleek, silver Aeron ships, silently hovering out over the dark chasm. High pitched, whirlwind sounds came from their engines. Llueve pulled me back into the shadows of the cave, as the ships floated silently down into the canyon and were swallowed by the night.

The band of light from the tunnel where the ships had emerged narrowed and went black. Then we heard the grate and boom of the big doors closing and locking. I looked behind us at the door we had just come through but there was no chink of light anywhere. I ran my hands over the surface where the door had been and felt an irregular sandstone surface. It was camouflaged. I pushed against the rock face but it was rock solid. Then I saw the crystal blue glint of a video lens hidden in a recess above the door. We had to get out of there.

It was possible to climb along the natural ledges on the face of the Canyon. We hugged the face of the cliff and felt our way through the darkness. The only light now came from the stars. Warm wind gusted up out of the canyon below, comforting because otherwise it was really cold. I could feel goose bumps on Llueve's skin when our bodies touched. I had them myself. There was no easy way to climb up the canyon so we crept laterally along the sandstone cliff. Little, hysterical animal noises came out of Llueve as we edged along through the darkness. We were both hyperventilating with fear.

We were in a part of the canyon that had nearly vertical walls. There were shelves and crevices and we climbed from one to another. The air was getting colder as our warmth evaporated. The sandstone scrapped our knees, hands and feet. We came to a wide shelf of some kind where our feet sank into cold sand. I dug into the sand and found it was fairly warm a couple inches down. So I hollowed out a trough and laid down in it and got Llueve to lie beside me. We scooped the warm sand over ourselves and hugged each other for warmth. There was no sign of dawn in the glittering sky. We lay silently next to each other looking up at the stars feeling each other's warmth, both of us taking fast, shallow breaths.

After a while we calmed down. A sense of the powers of the universe, of the unknown was vibrating inside me. A sparkling, diamond like flickering caught my attention and I looked at the horizon. A star had risen - it was easily four times bigger than any other star in the sky. Shafts of liquid light peeled off it to glow in the night before fading. This must be Venus, I thought. The Morningstar. I became entranced as I experienced the star pulsing in a rhythm that matched my own thoughts. Questions, doubts and fears rose up in my mind in exact time with the shafts of light peeling off the star; each pulsation returning the star, and my mind to that perfect, diamond brightness in its center. It was like the star was speaking to me, saying that the diamond light in the center was the answer to each question. At one point I stopped breathing, I was so completely enchanted. Llueve I think became nervous and nudged me in the ribs to see if I was still alive. In perfect calm I turned to her and smiled.

My normal reality softly crashed inside me and a greater identity took over. Until now I had been relating to out of body experiences as a dream state. Anything can happen in a dream. But as I lay there with Llueve pressed to my side, and her feet pressing against mine for warmth, and felt her short, nervous breaths against my cheek, the incredible became credible, my sense of a fixed reality dissolved. The fluid intelligence I saw in the star became my own mind. I started to re-digest what was happening. It was overwhelming but it matched the miracle of creation. The miraculous was normality. All is one.

At first, lying there next to her, Llueve was a complete stranger. The exotic desire I had felt for her just moments before had been overwhelmed by danger. But alieness had always been in the air between us. We'd never really faced it. I knew she was sensing similar things. Seeing the star shifted the energy, my heart opened in ways I had no idea were possible. A sense of courage and greater purpose electrified my senses. A calm confidence in forces greater than ourselves, and that we were a part of, and which were aware of us, replaced my fear. When I smiled at her it was as though the star was smiling through me. My state of mind touched her. We regrouped as we lay in the warmth and quiet. The solid, ancient walls of stone and the trusty, starry night, were our friends. Two people from different dimensions suddenly finding themselves nipple to nipple, buried in the sand, was then not scary, but thrilling and affirming of something great coming closer.

I got a photographic image of UFO's swooping down along the canyon walls with spotlights. This was no time to relax. I was in a state of cosmic overload and it started a fire in me. I was running on some other energy now. I forced myself to breathe deeply and slowly and to think soberly and practically.

It was impossible to sleep. We were too close to the tunnel. I felt the first impulses of thirst and realized that Llueve, being pregnant, was going to need water... and food! And soon!

Llueve tried to speak a couple of times but then burst out crying. After a while - who knows how long - the sky in the east began to get light. The Morning star continued to pour out shafts of that diamond light. But as it got lighter the star was absorbed into the dawn.

The lighter it got the more dangerous it would become for us. It was damn cold when I stood up and brushed the sand off myself. The moisture on my skin quickly turned cold, but my sense of mission was overwhelming so I just ignored it. I've never felt more focused and determined to survive and protect my own - more human – than I did when I stood up like that in the dawn light.

I indicated to Llueve to stay in the sand while I looked around. I climbed around a big sandstone outcrop and saw that above us, and a little ways along the Canyon wall, the indentation of a side-canyon showed, with what looked like pinon pines growing along its floor.

With no time to loose, I went back for Llueve and motioned for her to come. She dusted herself off, her swollen, bluish belly making her look so biological and vulnerable.

We climbed up the canyon wall to the mouth of the side canyon and saw a little pool of water formed by a trickling stream sinking into the sand. Both of us drank. I was intensely aware of Llueve's need to eat. But even more, I was aware of the possibility of enemies appearing any minute. Looking back from where we had just come, I could see into the main chasm of what I knew now was unmistakably the Grand Canyon.

The canyon floor rose as we climbed heading south. The walls of the little canyon framed a cloudless sky. A million years of flowing water cutting down through the rock and spilling into the Canyon was written in the different sediment bands and outcroppings in the stone that rose around us. Sparkling gold, blood red, crystal white sandstone surrounded us. The knobs and shelves, creases and columns all spoke of time, ancient, soulful, time. The time it had taken us to become people.

A raven flew overhead, each down stroke of its wings whooshing clearly in the silence, punctuated by a small eternity of perfect stillness before the next stroke. The green, tangy smell of pinon sap colored the air. Stunted, wizened bristle-cone pines grew out of the crevices of rock and sand on the ridges. The place felt as though no human had ever walked there before.

The large trees were definitely pinons. I remembered once harvesting pinon nuts with Yvonne in New Mexico. I now ripped off a couple of the dried cones from the branch of a tree and sure enough there were some brown shelled little nuts inside. I cracked one open and ate it. It was sweet. I cracked another and gave it to Llueve. She liked it. I ripped off a few more cones and we ate them as we walked along.

Wide pools of water appeared in the stream-bed as we ascended the canyon. The light grew radiant in the East. We walked along munching the nuts. The stars faded. Warm air drifted up from the canyon. We came to a crevice in the eastern face of the little canyon where we could see the sun rising above the mesas on the horizon. The blinding, liquid light of the sun crested over the mesas, infiltrating the blue shadows, its rays so warm and welcome, so full of life. In that moment, filled with wonder, I held Llueve's hand as she watched her first sunrise on Earth.

Tears flowed down her face as she looked down at her rounded blue belly as the first rays of the sun touched her body and sparkled on the wetness of her tears. I surrounded her belly with my hands and I too began to cry, my tears dripping on her belly. We looked at one another, our hearts in our eyes, our bellies touching as the sun rose, watery and distorted through our tears. I closed my eyes and said a prayer to the sun and the universe - 'please protect us!' I don't think either of us expected to survive till noon.

The sun cleared the horizon and it got hotter. We came to our senses and started walking, stepping from rock to rock along the stream. In the pools of water, mica and quartz reflected sunshine up through the water. A tuft of cottony lavender moss floated underwater between two sandstone rocks. Llueve leaned down to look closer. I had never seen Ovvala in the flesh and I wondered what all this looked like to her, what it felt like. I was standing behind her, looking down at her radiant auburn hair spread across her faintly blue shoulders. I pulled her hair into a long ponytail and let it slide luxuriously through my hands. She reached down and cupped water to her face and washed. She stood up, gave me a brave little smile and we continued walking.

We had just cleared a tall boulder, passing between it and the canyon wall and were about to walk into the open beside the stream, when a flash caught my eye. I recoiled and pulled Llueve into a crouch behind the boulder and put my fingers on her lips. A silver disk was moving silently up the canyon. It hovered just above the tops of the pines as it approached. It was moving very slowly. As it got closer we could hear a high pitched warbling bleep sounding every few moments. It glided down next to the stream, hovering a couple of feet above the ground. All the hair on my body stood on end. A silver ramp slid silently to the ground. Three little, gray Annanokian clones, their black eyes shiny as the backs of beetles, dropped clumsily to the ground, followed by a tall Skandrr soldier in a black body suit and a short gray cape. The soldier carried a weapon. The Grays had the transparent glass-like rods I had seen used on the Annanokian spacecraft. We were naked and completely defenseless. I looked around on the ground for rocks, a stick, anything to use as a weapon but there was just sand. My chest felt it would burst with the tension. I thought quickly, wondering if we had left wet foot prints but our feet had only touched rock. Llueve had washed over a pool.

The clones walked up the canyon on the other side of the stream. The ship followed close behind them - beeping regularly. I wondered if the sound might be a kind of heat seeking sonar or motion sensor. As they passed the boulder they were about thirty feet away. We edged carefully back to keep the boulder between them and us and they continued slowly on up the canyon. When they were out of sight I stood up and looked around. They might come back. We could climb up the crevice in the canyon wall where we had seen the sunrise. So we went back to where the side canyon started - both of us drinking as much water as we could hold and then climbed up the little canyon. At least there would be miles of pinon nuts.

In minutes we were walking in a pinon forest on a level plane. We walked in silence feeling the warmth of the sun on our naked skin, keeping a continuous watch for the silent disk. We were fully exposed to the sky. I tried to think where there would be a road, a campsite. I had been to the Grand Canyon a few times since living in New Mexico but I had no Idea what part we were in. We could be miles from civilization. Then I noticed footprints. They were very lightly impressed in the sand and fresh. They led to a low boulder to the south. A clutch of fear went through me and I motioned to Llueve to crouch down under a pinon tree. We crouched very still, our hearts pounding.

A wrinkled, old, very dark skinned Indian man stepped out from behind the rock. He wore a white loin cloth and held what looked like blue parrot feathers in his hands. He looked at us with shinning black eyes then pointed with his face towards the east, pursing his lips and jutting his chin out. He looked back at us, then turned and started walking in the direction he had indicated.

He was leading us somewhere. His look and manner told me we could trust him. So we followed. Llueve was uncertain and I tried to reassure her. The old man walked fast in a semi crouch. We went around some outcroppings of sandstone and through a couple of washes that drained into the Canyon. We must have walked for an hour. Every once in a while the old man looked back and our eyes locked. His eyes were like shiny black stones on fire.

I was so nearly delirious with the intensity of being with a physical Llueve, and the lack of sleep, and the fear of discovery by these unknown agents of darkness, that the presence of the Indian was for me, very reassuring. The fact that he didn't run up to Llueve and investigate her, the fact that he didn't talk but just walked at a fast, even pace made me feel like things were under control somehow.

We heard a semi gearing down and I knew we were near the South Rim road and cars and phones. There is only the one road along the south rim of the canyon. There was an arroyo with large boulders exposed. The old Indian stopped next to one of these and lifted his chin in the direction of the sound holding his parrot feathers to his chest. Magnetic waves of light vibrated out around him before he suddenly disappeared behind one of the boulders. He knew all about the transdimensional tunnel. He knew about Ovvalans. He had been prepared to meet us. How? From a dream? ESP? Was he Havasupai? Hopi?

I followed his footprints until they came to a large boulder with a cave-like hollow at its base. A perfect hiding place. The footprints reversed themselves right there. I looked back and saw the dark old man retracing our steps on the other side of the arroyo, swishing the sandy ground with a long pinon branch. He was erasing our footprints. He didn't look up. We walked on to until I saw the parking lot of a truck stop.

Keeping well inside the cover of the trees, we squatted in the shade of a pinon and looked over the station. There was a set of diesel pumps for the trucks and another set of gas pumps. There was a large building with a convenience store, maybe a cafeteria and showers. And pay phones. I could call Spencer or Yvonne.

In daylight there was nothing I could do. It would be impossible. Walk up to someone fully naked and ask for money? We could be reported and that would be the end. We would have to wait until dark. I could see two full size RV's, a truck with a camper, three cars with luggage-boxes on their roofs. Somewhere in all that were clothes, food, money. I considered stealing a car. Suddenly I heard the thwacking of a helicopter. Llueve and I looked at each other with fear.

We ran back through the trees to the boulder with the space beneath it and started crawling in when I had the thought that snakes or scorpions could be in there. I quickly broke a branch off a pinon and raked the edges with it as the choppers got closer and closer. I watched in ongoing disbelief as Llueve's blue breasts swung and bounced and her limbs disappeared under the overhanging rock.

Three black helicopters came on flying so low over the trees that the branches whipped around and clouds of dust rose in the air. My heart was in my mouth. They were about a hundred yards apart as they circled the truck stop and then headed back towards the Canyon. I figured this meant that there were going to be carloads of agents of one kind or another scouring the truck stop soon.

After the choppers were gone I stood up and collected fallen chunks of sandstone and stacked them to create a little wall along the edge of the boulder. I broke off a couple pinon branches and went back to the parking lot and retraced our steps, brushing away our footprints as I'd seen the Indian do. Twilight came and it got cold again and we dug ourselves into the warm sand in the cavern. Every once in a while Llueve's whole body trembled like a panicked animal.

When it was fully dark I went back to the truck stop and watched and listened, huddling behind a large pinon. A semi pulled in, its bright yellow running lights lit up the whole parking lot. It came to a stop. The lights and engine went off. Then the lights in the cabin finally went on then off. After a while I heard the thud of a man's feet jumping down from the cab and heard the slam of a door. I saw the man's silhouette as he walked into the lights of the buildings carrying a gym bag. Once he had gone inside the building, I ran across the parking lot and jumped up on the running board of the truck. I tried the door. It was locked. But a little triangular vent was ajar. I pushed it open and felt around for the lock and got the door open.

I was looking for anything I could find and what I found was a suitcase opened in the sleeping loft. There was a Levi jacket lying on the passenger seat. I pulled the suitcase towards the door. Something shinny caught my eye and feeling out for it I found a dip in the dashboard with change in it. I grabbed all of it and stuffed it in the suitcase. There was a pair of sunglasses on the dash and I took those. Looking out the window I could see nothing moving out by the station. There was a half full bottle of water in a holder on the dashboard and I stuck this under my arm. I tossed the suitcase to the ground, pushed the door closed, and jumped down.

I ran across the lot and into the trees. In the dark I walked about the distance to the rock outcrop but missed it and hooted to Llueve. She hooted back and I found her dusting sand off herself outside the cavern. I gave her the water to drink.

I opened the suitcase. There was a pair of gray alligator leather boots on top of a folded gray, western style suit with rhinestone studded buttons, a few shirts, some clean boxer underwear, a wool sweater, a baseball cap, some muscle T-shirts, a sweatshirt and a gray, rubber raincoat and a couple pairs of jeans. In the side pocket of the suitcase there was a pair of flip-flops, rolled up socks and a half bottle of Ten High whisky. I was shivering uncontrollably from the cold by now. So I took a pull on the whisky for some anti-freeze. I offered Llueve the bottle. She took one sniff and stuck her tongue out with a sneer.

The T-shirt, a dress shirt, the suit jacket and pants more or less fit Llueve. I fit into the boxers and a sweatshirt but couldn't get into the pants or the boots. But they fit Llueve. The wool sweater stretched almost to the ripping point but I got it on. The flip-flops fit with my toes hanging over the edge. Llueve pushed the last of the water at me and insisted I drink it.

'Uudualeh!' She unconsciously spoke in Daag.

If the trucker discovered he'd been ripped off, we were in trouble, but probably not for a while. We needed more water. And food.

We were still freaked out but sitting there - dressed – we both felt more in control for the first time since becoming physical.

Llueve spoke softly. She was looking at me intently with a half smile on her face.

'Meow…' she said, and grinned nervously.

'Meow,' I said back shyly and we laughed.

I counted $3.75 in quarters. I took the empty water bottle and walked back through the woods and across the lot into the station. The tight navy blue sweater ended before it got to the boxer shorts and my toes hung over the flip-flops but I was dressed. Besides being bloodshot, my eyes were probably spooked looking, so as I approached the brilliantly lit up convenience store I put on the sunglasses. I pushed open the glass door acting sleepy, yawning and noisily flip-flopped my way back to the men's room. There was a guy at the cash register with a small TV going. A fat couple with two little boys were tearing open some cellophane packages at some tables. They didn't pay any special attention to me as I passed by. I was aware that I could bump into the trucker any minute and that while he might not recognize his sweater and shorts, as soon as he got back to his truck he'd be looking for me so I wanted to get out of there as fast as I could. I looked through the trash and found two quart soda bottles. I rinsed them out and filled them and the empty water bottle I'd brought at the sink. I took a long drink and then re-filled the bottle. I'd also found a plastic shopping bag and carried the water bottles in it.

I got two big Planter's peanut bars and walked up to the counter. I'd pushed the shades to the end of my nose and looked at the attendant stupidly over the tops of the sunglasses, like I was half asleep. He looked back at me with the same expression.

'How far's the Village?' I asked him in a sleepy drawl, putting the candy bars on the counter.

'It's about four miles,' he pointed vaguely over his shoulder. 'That's two eighty nine,' he said in a monotone, and quickly glanced at the TV. I paid him and it left me only thirty six cents. I felt robbed.

I knew the basic layout of the Grand Canyon Village on the South Rim - the highway that headed south to Williams and the motels along that road. I made like I was reading the ingredients on the candy bar.

'Oh,' I said, looking down. 'Are we north or south of the Village here?'

'Grand View is about four miles *east* of here,' he said sarcastically.

'Oh.' I said and walked out still trying to look stupid.

There was a pay phone stall at the front of the store. I called Yvonne collect. It was Sunday evening and she was home thank God.

'Yvonne, I really need your help!'

'Hmm. You liked the way I helped you last time huh?' Yvonne was winding up her sarcasm in case it was needed anytime soon.

'No,' I didn't even try to fake a laugh. ' Really. I - need -you - to – pick -me -up. It's an emergency!'

'Did you have an accident? Where are you?' She started catching my panic.

'No I'm OK. I'm at a gas station West of Grand Canyon Village.'

'You're at the Grand Canyon! That's like ten hours from here! What are you doing there?'

'My uh truck broke down - I uh came to camp out.'

'Joseph you are lying to me!' Silence. 'Are you with a woman?'

'No. I came alone.'

'You sound like you're not really sure Joey.'

'Yvonne - this is a matter of life and death!' I hissed into the phone. She could tell that I really meant it.

'Joe, you're scaring me. What's going on?'

'Yvonne,' I said, trying for a calmer tone, 'you have to come now. For real. I can't explain it over the phone. Please you've got to believe me!'

'You better explain.'

'I can't. I need you to get here as soon as it is humanly possible. Please. Please. Please trust me.'

'Jesus. - O.K.! - I'll come. But - you're paying for the gas!'

'O.K. Fine. And bring some food - like cheese and uh peanut butter - some fruit.' What did Llueve eat?

'Don't push your luck! I'll be there as soon as I can.' I made sure she had the directions. And told her to park on the edge of the lot near the trees.

'Thank you sweetie. Really hurry, huh?'

'Sweetie yourself!' she said and clicked off. I made it back to Llueve as fast as I could. Yvonne would take all night to get there. That was good because there would be less activity during the night and I could keep an eye out for the lights of patrol vehicles.

I went back to Llueve. She devoured the candy bar. I ate mine between sips of the whisky. I sat with my back against the rock listening to the forest. It was too eerie to lie in the dark with an alien and it was impossible to sleep.

The helicopters returned. They flew to the East of us, their spotlights raking the Canyon rim. Later, a bunch of emergency vehicles passed through the gas station. We saw flashing red and blue lights through the trees. It was a long night.

Toward dawn it got really cold and I crawled in next to Llueve. When I saw first light I went and sat under a tree on the edge of the lot watching for Yvonne. I felt terrible. My mouth was stale and puckered. I was in a near stupor from lack of sleep and cramped from sitting and hung over when I saw Yvonne's old tan Volvo station wagon pull into the lot.

I walked up and got in the passenger seat. Yvonne's eyes were bloodshot from driving through the night. She squinted at me suspiciously, her eyes taking in the foreign, ill fitting clothes, my blood shot eyes.

'Joe - tell me you're not on drugs,' she said in a dead serious voice.

'Yvonne - something's happened.' I'd been trying to put together a sort of opening statement that led into Llueve but I just couldn't find any place to start. There was nothing I could say to prepare her. My pupils must have been little pinholes by now. I was repressing the urge to just push Yvonne out of the driver's seat and take over, aware of the deadly forces searching for us right then. My eyes must have been popping out of my head with the stress. With her showing up, the tension I'd been in released and my head started shaking. 'No. I'm not on drugs,' I said. Yvonne stared at me with complete distrust.

'Would you please pull over there, I pointed. 'I have to show you...'

'Oh my God Joe - you're scaring me the way you're acting!' She drove carefully to the edge of the lot.

'No. It's O.K. Here. Stop here. You'll understand everything in a minute. I'll be right back.' I got out and then turned around and said - when I come back we have to get out of here O.K.?'

'Joe!?' Yvonne was freaked already.

I went back to Llueve and motioned for her to come with me. When we walked out of the trees she hesitated seeing the car with someone inside it. She was carrying the yellow raincoat in front of her. The cowboy suit was pretty tight under her arms and the dress shirt was a bit stressed by Llueve's tits and belly. With the baseball cap and the sunglasses on and her hair hanging down, not much of her blue skin was showing. Even so, the way she moved, everything about her said 'different'. This would be her first contact with a human other than me and she was stiff with fear. I tried to reassure her but still had to almost physically drag her along. I opened the rear door and pushed her in. I got into the front and said "Yvonne - drive! We've got to get moving." Yvonne was frozen, stunned, staring at Llueve. 'We have to drive Vonnie,' I said fiercely.

'Holy shit!' she said in a high squeaky voice, staring at Llueve 'It's her isn't it!?' Yvonne said. 'Ooooo Jesusy Joe - I'm getting goose bumps all over!'

'I know,' I said, 'but you've got to drive.' Goose bumps were crawling all over me too. She drove out of the parking lot in stunned silence. I turned in my seat and extended my hand back to Llueve who was staring in a catatonic freeze, first at me and then at Yvonne and then out the window and then back at Yvonne and then back at me. Here was your stranger in a strange land. She wouldn't take my hand so I put my hand on her knee saying 'It's all right sweetie.

'Does she speak English?' Yvonne asked.

'No she doesn't and she's really scared,' I said.

'So - how did - this - happen? Oh my God Joe!!' Yvonne adjusted her rearview mirror so as to see what she could of Llueve.

'We were out of our bodies and were investigating this place in Ovvala that disks - UFO's - use as a base. We saw these doors in the side of a mesa and went in there. It led to a tunnel. It's some kind of dimension changing tunnel. We saw military helicopters go through it...'

'Through the tunnel...?' Yvonne stole another glance at Llueve through the mirror.

'Yeah. It's huge. When we were in the middle of it - in this big cavern we...became physical. She wanted to go back to where the change took place to try and change back again but there were disks coming and we had to run. We came out in the Canyon and got locked out of the tunnel. They're looking for us - there's been helicopters flying over and sirens going by...'

'Who's looking for you?' Yvonne asked in a deadpan voice.

'The cross dimensional police ...fuck! I don't know!'

'Oh Jesus,' Yvonne said fully grasping all the implications of getting caught. I didn't realize until that moment that if we got caught 'we' could be killed and 'we' now included Yvonne.

'Vonnie...you don't have to be in on this. The people looking for us are evil, deadly people. You could get out and take a bus back to Santa Fe...'

'Shssh,' she said. 'Don't tell me, I'll get scared. This is too incredible to miss.' She kept driving.

'There was roadblock stopping all the cars going south from the Canyon. It's her they're looking for isn't it?'

'Her and me. They probably got pictures of us coming through the tunnel. There were cameras on the walls,' I was feeling like I couldn't take any more stress. I was thinking about how I'd been asleep in my bed when I met with Llueve in Ovvala. And now she was in the back seat of Yvonne's car. Was I still asleep in my bed?

'We've got to go around them.' I said. 'Do you have map?'

'There's a pocket on the back of your seat.' I grabbed some maps and found Arizona. 'There's, ah, let's see ...the rim road... here is 64 and it joins 89. We go left to 160 and then there's what looks like a back road that goes through a place called Shungopavi and then keeps going into New Mexico. How much gas've you got?' I asked trying to see the guage in the recessed dash.

'Three quarters,' Yvonne had caught all the paranoia. Having Llueve in the back of the car was sending out waves of unreality. My ability to make connections about Yvonne's reality and Llueve's reality was too much. I tried to just focus on the traffic. I felt little pops and squirts going on in my brain and in my body. Being on a mind altering drug was one thing. Having reality flip on you...

'She has to lay down so no one will see her,' Yvonne said.

'Right,' I said and turned to Llueve and tried to communicate lying down. I patted the seat and gently pulled her head down .

'Meow...meow.' I said softly.

'What are you doing?' Yvonne burst out.

'It's the only word we both understand!'

'Give me a break!'

While we drove I told Yvonne in more detail the stuff that had been happening in dreamland that I had avoided telling her the other night. About Stonehenge and the crop circle and the UFO. Making love and becoming physical. But I couldn't bring myself to tell Yvonne Llueve was pregnant. The raincoat hid her bulge when she came out of the woods and I felt weird talking about that with Yvonne right then.

I tried to explain what I understood about the planned Terrorization to bring the rest of the planet into globalization. I had to talk. I was so glad to be able to tell her these things with Llueve right there - it helped me integrate what had become two me's. I'd never really considered all this stuff as 'real'. It hadn't been 'real' it was just realistic dreaming. Now - it was real. And Yvonne was in it with me. This set off a whole new series of changes.

We got to Shungopavi where there was a combination grocery store, clothing and hardware store. Llueve and I sat in the car while Yvonne shopped.

All they had in clothes were jeans and cowboy shirts. She got some for each of us. She also got us tube socks and cheap sneakers. She picked up some oranges and bananas and cheese. She got a huge straw hat and the biggest sunglasses she could find for Llueve. And she got a compact of skin tone makeup. She also got some spray cans of weird, colored hair dies. We filled up the gas and hit the road.

I gave Llueve her clothes and immediately started changing into mine. When we both had all the trucker's clothes off I told Yvonne to pull over - we were in the middle of nowhere - I bunched all the clothes up and dropped them behind a big rock on the side of the road. At the time it seemed like a pretty 007 thing to do, but then I realized that getting rid of the evidence of having ripped off the trucker wasn't going to go far at a roadblock with a blue extraterrestrial sitting in the back seat.

Yvonne was seeing double so I took over driving. Yvonne sprayed purple and yellow streaks in Llueve's hair - this made her look more normal right? And she put the tan cosmetic on Llueve's face, which made her look like she had leprosy. I took the back roads East from Grants to avoid Albuquerqui. We passed by Chaco Canyon and came out at Abiquiu, north of Espanola. From there it was an easy drive to Jaconita. This route added an hour to the drive but we avoided the main arteries.

What a relief to pull into my driveway. It really helped to see familiar surroundings - Neutron and my kitchen, the piles of adobe bricks out the window. First thing I did was check the bedroom for my sleeping body. The bed looked slept in but it was empty - thank God! Now all I had to worry about was if I was wandering around somewhere - a vegetable without a soul - in sweat pants. Neutron was more interested in Llueve than in eating. He sniffed Llueve's shoes a few times while she petted him passionately. She seemed to find this comforting. Neutron himself seemed fascinated with her.

Llueve had liked the oranges and cheese Yvonne had bought. I was just glad she'd eaten and not vomited up some weird purple alien glop. I got a Sam Adams out of the fridge and tried to relax. Yvonne was making a big effort to buddy up to Llueve - galactic sisters. She took her in the bathroom and showed her the shower which Llueve understood - and immediately used - they do have showers in Ovvala. Yvonne sat on the toilet seat talking to Llueve as she took her shower and then Yvonne took one. Then they went into the living room and dried each other's hair with towels.

I had an inspiration and put my DVD of The Sound of Music on. Llueve was still definitely in a kind of trance. She felt safe with us all right, but the weirdness of being out of Ovvala was still a shock and that, coupled with her extreme tiredness must have made her feel like she really was dreaming. And who knows maybe the air was different or gravity or the ions or just everything. Eventually she fell asleep, curled up in the corner of the sofa covered with one of my wool blankets. After three beers and a frozen pizza I started nodding off on the other end of the couch.

Yvonne stayed with Llueve in the living room while I went to bed in my room. Neutron lay down next to Llueve. I got up to pee later and, half asleep, stuck my head in the living room. Yvonne was sitting on the floor wrapped in a blanket. She stared at me with owl eyes. Llueve was asleep on the couch. Yvonne looked at me with such a deep look as I'll never forget. I think she stayed awake all night - in pure wonder.

I was too tired and stressed to go out of body but I had vivid dreams of Isult and Djagda. When I woke up in the morning and remembered this - I felt they and the Siddhe were close, that we weren't alone in this. If Llueve was real so were the Siddhe. They would help us.

Chapter Nineteen

5/9/05

The sound of car doors slamming made me jump up out of bed and run to the window. It was about nine in the morning and my brain was still full of sleep endorphins.

'It's them!' I thought, as I leaped across the hall into the junk room, which looked out on the street. But it was only an electric meter checker and a trainee reading Dona Lucia's meter. It was just a normal Monday morning and the work-a-day world was getting into gear.

But the secret police were heavy on my mind. We wouldn't be trailed by the NSA, FBI, CIA - those were legal policing forces. Whoever had military helicopters flying through the transdimensional tunnel to Ovvala were undercover beyond any radar going. But what did I know? Half of Congress and the Senate could Draco possessed zombies who after putting up a flutter of pretended outrage, did whatever the Dracos told them to. Were first term Congresspersons escorted to a plush room, deep in the basements of the Congressional building, where a Draco in a black cape formally sucked their blood and said 'vote for more nuclear reactors or we'll kill your children?' Why were they so spineless? As I turned away from the window I remembered - Llueve!

In the silent, darkened living room where Yvonne had pulled the curtains shut, Llueve was a long, sleeping lump under blankets on the couch. She was buried under the huge multicolored patch quilt my Grandmother had made me. A feeling, almost of fear, pulsed in my chest at the thought of looking in Llueve's eyes. We were family! I wanted her to just stay under the quilt and not upset this illusion of normality that such things as she didn't exist. Being in her presence was like being on drugs. For one blessed moment things were normal in my mind. As soon as she sat up that would be over.

Yvonne was asleep next to the couch tangled up in the covers from the bed in the junk room. Her fine red hair was tussled over the flower petal pillowcase. Neutron was sitting up next to the couch, breathing through his mouth, wondering what was up. He has a doggie door in the kitchen so I knew he didn't need that. Neutron is one of those dogs with human eyes. He flicked a serious look at sleeping Llueve, and then back at me, as though to say, 'she's an extraterrestrial isn't she?' He's an Aussie collie, and they're sharp.

I put on the teakettle and took a quick shower. I got a pair of my own jeans and my lucky blue T-shirt that says Maine on it with my lucky plaid shirt over it. I needed to feel as normal and as lucky as possible. I'd left the whistle up on the kettle so as not to wake everyone. When I heard the water thundering in the pot I made my usual soup bowl of black tea with four bags and sugar and sat down to pull myself together ,and started typing. This has become a way to get myself collected. The familiar look of my kitchen, the fridge with my magnetic, cross-eyed Guadalupe holding down a pizza menu, the paned windows looking out on the back yard, the solid maple table with its homely, dark green, spotted and frayed table cloth, my antique manual toaster on the counter. I looked at all these as though at the memory of the deceased. I wanted to indulge in the plainness and boringness of the scene but something was pulling at the edge of my mind. What was it? Oh yeah! Fear!

I'd gone to sleep thinking about how they could track us. The only information they had was pictures of us from the video cameras in the tunnel. Were super computers right now trying to match my features to photos on driver's licenses all over America? I'd heard this report on Democracy Now about insurance companies and the NSA buying up all these photos from motor vehicle departments in order to track people down. That'd make people pay their library fines! I wondered about the astral encounter with the agent from BATS. Could he track me just by having seen my face? Had satellites photographed Yvonne's license plate when she entered the Grand Canyon? Would they make a connection to me through her phone records? Maybe they'd alert the normal police of Santa Fe or even the National Guard to check every lead. Was I just being paranoid? No.

Yvonne stumbled to the bathroom in light blue, cotton panties, hugging herself and giving me a wide eyed look and a sour little wave as she closed the door. A moment later, Llueve walked into the kitchen. Her eyes sought mine out uncertainly. It was hard to read her emotions through her puffy, exotically beautiful blue face. I had to remember that Llueve was in even greater shock than me. She was in the wrong dimension!

I stood up - it seemed too much to hug her - I barely knew her! When we were in the act of escaping from the tunnel there had been a clear basis of alliance. But who were we to each other really? I guess I felt insecure - as in trans dimensionally insecure. I took her hand sort of formally - apparently up to that moment she'd had similar reservations about touching me, because at the touch of my hand she threw her arms around me and sobbed out her tension and fear in Daag.

'Souqroiat lei'm seetleia aap kien neiell...'

The quilt slipped aside and I felt the full voluptuous length of her against me and this gave me courage. She looked at me through tear filled eyes and stood back to put her hands on her belly and look mournfully into my eyes. Her hair was a lovely rat's nest of auburn tangles and she was smiling crookedly through her tears - saying things in Ovvalan that she knew I couldn't understand - telling me of her concern for our multidimensional baby, of her love, of her fear. I held her and felt my heart convulse.

She was so beautiful it made my heart ache to look at her. Her hair was like no substance I have ever felt - like thick strands of living silk. It was shiny and alive, supernaturally healthy. I brushed tears from her blue cheeks while with my other arm I pulled her belly-first into me. Ovvalan nerves and muscles are different than ours; she has a different, more liquid elasticity. A different kind of electricity goes through her. My arm was singing at the touch of her waist. She pressed herself against me and hissed through clenched teeth. I looked in her eyes and for a second we got swallowed up by the hunger, fascination and fear of each other. It's that strong that it made me momentarily forget the reality of our situation.

I got a dark green bathrobe off the back of my bedroom door and wrapped her up in it. Then I sat her down in a chair and filled a bowl with Cap'n Crunch and poured some milk on it. She took one spoonful, her pupils dilated in horror and she spit the whole mouthful out onto the linoleum floor making a betrayed face. Too sweet? So I cleaned up her little mess with paper , and gave her corn flakes with milk, and stood back. She took one hesitant little spoonful and smiled radiantly. She liked corn flakes!

Neutron, who had slept by her side all night, had come into the kitchen earlier, before Llueve came in. He'd licked my hand and then gone back to the living room. He returned now to sit at her feet and she stuck her bare feet in his fur. This seemed to comfort her and his eyes rolled up in his head like he'd become enlightened.

My thoughts went back to what to do next. Could the Siddhe physically take her back? How could we contact them? Should we try and sneak back in the tunnel to Ovvala? Impossible. If the Siddhe showed up in a saucer could I go to Ovvala with Llueve? Could Llueve even survive in this atmosphere? She looked O.K. at the moment, just a little blue. Was there enough oxygen for her? Too much? These were the kind of questions going through my mind as I watched her eat.

When she finished her corn flakes, Llueve came around the table to stand next to me, placing a hand on my neck and pressing her belly against my shoulder. I reflexively sat her on my lap.

'Meow,' she said into my ear in her low, quivering and fluid voice, which was so continuously exotic to me. Maybe she was naturally shy or quiet? Or was she loud and demanding and only now repressed by fear? We only knew each other in the astral as energies. Were our personalities different in physical reality? I felt so intensely shy as I looked in her luminous alien green eyes. She smiled at me hesitantly, a smile that revealed love for me but a smile that couldn't hide how odd she felt sitting on the lap of an alien - me. She tossed her hair in a really cute way.

'Meow,' I said, sort of formally, mostly out of an intense admiration for her courage as I stroked her hair and looked into those almond eyes. I felt the silky skin in the hollow of her spine, the weight and density of her breasts against me - probably swollen to a bigger size than they would ordinarily be. I couldn't help but wonder what it would be like to make love to her now - in the physical and fell into that thought pattern as I felt my heart bend to every pout of her Turlington lips. I vaguely heard the soft padding of feet enter the kitchen and looked up to see Yvonne standing there, bare footed in an old blue and gray flannel shirt of mine she'd found in the bathroom, my comb in her hand. I had completely forgotten that Yvonne was in the house! She was staring at Llueve, sitting on my lap, wearing the green bathrobe Yvonne had given me for my birthday and which, I guess, she considered her personal intimate connection to the house. Her eyes were widening in shock. As the speechless silence grew, flames began shooting out of her eyes. Yvonne turned on her heel and stomped into the living room.

Llueve spun her head around to look at me - auburn hair whipping across my face, as she pushed herself away from me, her eyes now acid green with anger and stung with nitro glycerin tears. Giving me as equally an evil and betrayed look as Yvonne, she leaped up, and not knowing where else to go, stomped into the bathroom and slammed the door.

I got half way to the bathroom door and stopped not sure what to do. Yvonne stalked up and stared at me, hands on hips.

'So - now the dream girl gets to sit on earth-stud's lap eh? So now I'm just the chauffeur! I drive all the way across the fucking state, hold your Luuvies goddamned hand all night, miss a day's work and have to make lame excuses to half a dozen customers so I can watch you replace me on the great lap?! And I thought our necking on your kitchen chair was our special little thing!' She burst out crying. 'You baaastaaard!'

'Yvonne - I'm sorry! I didn't think - I'm kind of stressed out you know and ...well...it just happened - I mean she is pregnant and...'

'Pregnant!?' How could that possibly be?! I thought she was just fat! Until last night she was only a figment of your imagination! You mean you were bonking in the tunnel of love that night and now you think she's pregnant? My God Joe - and to make me a part of this...' She wailed out loud, her mouth a big O.

'Vonnie - not now...you've got to cool it ...she's in the bathroom freaking out and she's - from – another... planet!' Yvonne's eyes lost their glassy look and she looked towards the bathroom door, her expression completely changing to concern.

'My God, you're right!' she sniffed, wiping the spit from her lips. She went to the bathroom door and knocked softly. 'Llueve - honey - it's me - it's all right - let me in O.K.?' Yvonne opened the door cautiously and looked inside.

Llueve was sitting on the toilet, hugging the bathrobe tightly around herself, obviously shocked to have suddenly realized that Yvonne wasn't just a friendly earthling but some kind of intimate, while she, Llueve, was the future mother of my child. Her shocked eyes met mine for a second, a steely burning heat flashed out of them and I saw betrayal added to all the other emotions pulsing in her eyes before Yvonne closed the door and started talking to her.

I needed some room. I put my desert boots on, whistled for Neutron and walked out the door. We got in my truck and drove to Spencer's. The familiarity of the drive down the pock marked highway, the old abandoned gas station just past Jaconita, and the sight of certain familiar pinon pines growing on the flattened hills across the highway helped me to stabilize. I knocked on Spencer's bus door.

'Cummon in,' Spencer yelled. He would have heard my truck pull in on the gravel. I could tell from his muffled holler that he was way in the back of the bus, writing in his book probably. His book is about how trees transmit pheromones and share global information about weather patterns across the continents in order to balance the atmospheric gasses of the earth. It's sort of about whatever is obsessing Spencer that month, the history of proto-biology transferred to human life through food. But it's also about half a dozen other things all at once, and he can never describe what it is he'd aiming at, and it's never finished. Lena and I joke about this. Whenever we find ourselves discussing some weird subject that has no conclusion we'll say – 'that's what Spencer's book is about!' and burst out laughing.

'Hi Joe,' Spencer looked up smiling and then saw my face. 'Wo! Man! What's going on with you? You look like you've seen a ghost.'

I gazed at his ignorant, innocent face for a moment before I told him.

'She's at your house!? With Yvonne?' I let him look at my own sick eyes and let it seep in. 'Let me get this straight - this woman you've been having dreams about is in the flesh - in your house - with Yvonne - and they're both mad at you for two timing both of them!?' I nodded. I was very close right there to beaming up.

'I've got to see this!' Spencer started getting up. I put a hand on his shoulder.

'Not right now man...give them a little room - they need to come to terms with each other. And I need a break... really bad.'

'Right,' he said slowly, taking a closer look at me and starting over. Then he laughed uncontrollably. 'My God!' he said, 'I thought I had problems!' When I didn't smile he got serious.

'Ahem - Joe you look really sick...' I brushed that aside and said;

'So you going to Cancun to that or what?' I desperately needed to have a normal conversation. Another World Bank, IMF, mega wealth, New World Order meeting was happening in Cancun, and a busload of demonstrators and videographers was passing through Albuquerque on their way there. Spencer and Lena had raised funds over the Internet for the trip and were anticipating their coming and thinking of going along.

'Lena won't let us go,' Spencer stared at me really hard as he got that I was trying to change the subject. I think he saw I was about to snap and played along. 'She says we did Seattle and that if we got busted or killed or had our heads bashed in who would run the web site?'

'You had any news from Brazil?'

'Jesus Joe! I've got to see her!'

'I know Spencer,' it was useless. 'Look,' I said and filled him in on the accident in the tunnel, the night spent under the rock, driving through Hopi land to avoid the roadblock. 'I've been with her over forty-eight hours - the secret police of her world and ours are looking for us. Just talk about something normal....just for a little bit...fake it!' I yelled. Spenser was silent a moment.

'A Korean farmer killed himself in protest of what the World Bank is doing to farmers,' he said deadpan.

'Jesus,' I said. There's just nowhere to hide.

'It's a heavy business mate. It's the little farmers who really know the value of things. It's them who see the land actually dying from the salting of chemical fertilizers and with the dying of the farm land, the farmer himself feels like he dies and becomes one more 711 drone. People who just buy groceries at the supermarket have no idea what agribusiness is doing to the soil, or how GMO's are spreading to traditional crops. When global warming really gets going, in about ten years, this Korean guy will be remembered like Nathan Hale is remembered in the American Revolution.'

'Was he the guy who said 'two if by land, three if by sea'?'

'No. That was Benjamin Franklin. Nathan Hale was 'Don't fire until you see the whites of their eyes!'

'Oh. Right. So, will this Cancun get like the 'Battle of Seattle'?'

'Who knows? Lena's on the horn now,' the horn - that's what Spencer calls the Internet - 'It's a caravan of three buses. Many of the same people from Seattle. A lot of the independent videographers are going. Just - what does she look like?'

'She's blue, tall...green eyes.'

'I've got to tell Lena this.' Spencer called Lena on a walkie talkie they both carry at home. I went out and poked around in his garden. I kicked at a hump of dirt. Looked at the buds swollen to bursting on the pear tree I'd planted. How could Yvonne be pissed at me for being with someone from another dimension? It was so unfair, I was thinking. And it's not like we had a steady thing going...it was just like before. We'd just been experimenting. I just felt guilty. And I admired Yvonne for pulling herself together so quickly for the sake of Llueve. And I was sick with worry that I'd hurt Llueve's feelings. I still hadn't slept enough. My brain was buzzing. After a bit Spencer came out.

'Lena wants to see her too - I mean - how could we not want to see her Joe?'

'Yeah - I know - it's mind blowing. My mind is blown right now can't you tell? Well, get Lena. Let's go, I should get back. Wait, let me call Yvonne and see what's going on,' I said.

'Are you serious Joe?' Lena said, walking across the yard. I just stared at her. 'My God Joe,' was all she could say. My eyes seem to carry more information than they did before. I saw right there how this was going to happen from one person to another - cosmic fever. I got Yvonne on her cell. She said things were O.K. That we were all in this together and that it wasn't like a normal betrayal and that she herself had encouraged me to astral travel so that she was just as responsible as me. She asked me if I knew if Llueve had a brother and I said ha ha.

I told her Spencer and Lena wanted to see Llueve. She thought it would be better if that happened later - maybe over dinner - that the three of us should get grounded first. I told this to Spencer and Lena and took off.

When I got back to the house they were sitting on the living room floor drawing pictures on perforated printer paper as a way of communicating while 'The Sound of Music' looped on the video, with the sound down low. Llueve had her new jeans on, and a sweater of mine over her cowboy shirt. Yvonne was back in her own slept in clothes. They had pages and pages of drawings scattered all over the floor made with crayons and colored markers of mine. There were stick figures and houses, cars, UFO's and jet fighters. A big black doughnut picture of the Mothership. The rows of caskets. A very accurate likeness of Llueve's house and of the Saala skyline. Planters on the sides of buildings. She is an architect after all. And knows how to draw.

I was really nervous wondering what was going to happen but they both smiled at me with real sweetness - Yvonne took my hand and then Llueve took my other hand. I sat down on the rug with them and we all hugged, laughed and watched the movie. Jesus. How long would this go on? I made pop corn and we all made drawings. After a while Yvonne led me into my bedroom. We sat on the bed and held hands.

'She grew up in suburbia. She studied architecture or something. She had a thing with a guy but they split up. She was a competition swimmer. She's worried about her cat.'

'So you learned all that from drawing pictures?'

'I think I got it across to her that you and I don't live here together. I think that's what she thought earlier.'

'Oh,' I said

'Yeah. And honey,' Yvonne said scootching closer and putting her arm around me, 'it's O.K. I realize we have to be really focused on her needs and realistic about you and me - I mean - we aren't really in a real relationship right?' she said this so tenderly as she played with the buttons of my shirt.

'We were just playing footsie with it, and taking care of her is much more important than anything else right now right?'

'Whew. I'm so glad you see it that way,' I said. Yvonne moved closer and we hugged. 'I feel so weird Vonnie. We're pregnant, so I have to really stay close to her and not let her freak out about that, along with everything else.'

'I know baby. She thinks she's pregnant by you too though of course that's impossible. You are both a little mixed up right now that's all.' Yvonne kissed me on the neck and then I kissed her on the cheek and then she slipped her hands up the back of my shirt and then I slipped my hand up the front of her blouse. She fell back on the bed and pulled me with her while we're applying suction at which point I freaked and jumped up.

'Vonnie! Not now! Are you crazy?!'

'I just wanted to see if I could compete with Loovy there!' Yvonne snickered with satisfaction, sat up tucking in her blouse in a businesslike way and stood up. I stood up too, straightened her hair out, and tucked my own shirt in, and we went back into the living room.

As the sun went down, I took Llueve out in the cactus garden, Neutron shadowing her, and showed her around. We held hands and walked from one rock and cactus island to another, me telling her all about the adobe wall that was going to go up and the fountain that would be in the middle and the flagstone terracing. She smiled humbly and took it all in good humor because she didn't know what the hell I was talking about anymore than me she.

About two hours later Spencer and Lena showed up. Yvonne had managed to communicate that this was going to happen so that Llueve wasn't too shocked. The dinner they brought included a huge bowl of fresh mixed greens from their greenhouse. This totally won Llueve over. I'd forgot about the salad angle.

Llueve had one of my belts on over the sweater, with my ten inch hunting knife in its scabbard, and with the safety snap in place. So much for her being wilting and shy.

'It makes her feel more secure,' Yvonne told me.

We sat at the kitchen table and ate. I had some beers in the fridge and we shared them. Spencer and Lena didn't know how to act and since they couldn't talk to Llueve, they just stared, which made everyone uncomfortable.

'Oh! Joe! I forgot to tell you,' Yvonne said. 'Llueve plays the violin!' Yvonne got up and went into the junk room. She came back with the fiddle made by my great great grandfather, in the middle of the eighteen hundreds, in Connecticut. I keep it hanging on the wall and try and play some notes on it once in a while.

Yvonne handed the fiddle to Llueve who checked the tuning - which was a different tuning than standard. Odd sharp and flat notes. She smiled and played the weirdest music I've ever heard. It hung together; you could tell it was from a definite style, and was a composition with repeating parts and all, but way different than our music. It had Balkan kind of feel. When she finished, we all clapped softly.

'Oriegielket raie neufluds oodriodokly fleueedwie smawie vurruru!' Llueve said and looked around uncertainly at all of us - knowing full well no one understood what she'd just said. Then she smiled and handed the fiddle back to Yvonne.

Lena stood up and put her arm around Llueve, who had stood next to Yvonne during the whole performance. A profound and silent exchange happened between the three women. While Llueve never really came out of shock, she knew she was safe here among us. The presence of two women, and two such bright women as Yvonne and Lena, I think, was really comforting. Spencer then stood up and formally shook Llueve's hand.

'My name is Doctor Spencer Holbrook. May our worlds thrive in Peace and Prosperity!' he said and then turned beet red and boomed -'well - *somebody* had to say it!' My smile at Llueve was a little sickly.

We had Thai rice noodles. Llueve made faces and played with hers like it was alive. Do they not have noodles in Daag? Yvonne and I watched Spencer and Lena going through the same changes we had already got a head start on. Their eyes would go out of focus as the full implications went deeper and deeper into them. Llueve's presence made us see each other - and ourselves - differently. We suddenly had unknown depths to one another. The world is not what we've been told.

'So you saw fighter jets over there and U.F.O.'s over here. And some military force over here is in contact with the Ovvalans over there... What the hell is going on?' Spencer was starting to ask the same questions I had been asking myself for months.

'What do the flying disks run on?' Spencer asked me.

'I don't know. They make a high, spinning, whooshing sound. It was only in the tunnel that I could hear them.'

'If the evil Ovvalans can fly UFO's over here, then these Siddhe people may be able to as well. Do you think they'll come and get her?' I had no Idea. We discussed the different possibilities and then Yvonne decided Llueve needed to quiet down.

Spencer and Lena left and later Yvonne went home. She had to go to work in the morning. I wrote her a check for five hundred dollars to cover her expenses and the work she'd missed and just to say thanks for saving our lives...and risking her own. So Llueve and I were left alone in my house. I drew a picture of the two of us sleeping, and of Isult in her black pointy hat, flying on a broomstick, in a bubble over our heads.

'Meow,' Llueve said with emphasis, pushing the drawing aside carelessly, her eyes sparkling. I laughed. She kissed me and I meowmeowed happily back. The curve of her hips, the life force in her belly, her blue skin and her meaty, oval breasts - none of your business. I slept great.

I woke up around midnight. Llueve was sleeping away. I quietly went to the bathroom and then got back in bed and went right back to sleep. And then right out of my body where I found Llueve waiting for me.

'At last I can talk!' she said, her aura rippling with red and yellow vibrations of released frustration and alarm.

'Are you O.K.?' I asked her.

'Yeah. I'm fine. Just nervous. Come on! Let's find them!' Of course I knew she meant Isult, Djagda and the Siddhe. Llueve wanted to see that her cat in Saala was all right before we went to Logaana, so we headed for her house. As we approached her neighborhood, Ilsenaad and Silvaan suddenly blocked our way.

'Red alert! Red alert!' They flashed an intense warning beam at us. 'Llueve your house is surrounded with Adrrik agents. They've set a trap! Go back. Go back where you came from. Go back! Go back! Right now!' They radiated such an intense force against us, with such total alarm-vibrations that we bounced off it. We tuned in the frequency of my house and shot back through the sea of Loosh with Silvaan and Ilsenaad on our heels.

When we'd gone through the hole between the worlds they stopped us.

'That's far enough!' Silvaan beamed. The four of us made a circle and created a sphere of unity as the waves of Loosh crashed down through us. We created a rote-sphere and poured our information into it. Intelligence agencies of both physical worlds, as well as psychic police in both dimensions, were concentrated around Saala and Llueve's house, and in the Southwestern states on earth and were hunting for us. They were also scouring the desert around the Kovrro base and its counterpart at the Grand Canyon, which I learned was called Area 52, and trying to follow us through time with the BATS remote viewers, which was the first I'd heard of as being possible.

We also learned that while the Siddhe could get a saucer to Earth, they could only do it through Ireland or Brazil. To travel to Santa Fe and back to either of those locations was too dangerous. So we might ourselves have to get to one of those places, so that Llueve could get back to Ovvala. But for now, they told us, we had to get away from my house as soon as we woke up in Jaconita. They felt the remote viewers could track our trail to my house and inform physical agents at any minute.

They said that the physical dimension of earth wouldn't hurt Llueve at all which was a relief.

I felt all my worries and fears vaporizing as I breathed in the Loosh. The timeless cosmic viewpoint that had come to me the morning before, at the Grand Canyon, came back to me again. A vast intelligence and benevolence surrounded us each and by sensing it, breathing it, that intelligence would create a way forward. This was the resonance. The sea of Loosh-waves around us became very vivid as the soft shushing and crashing of the waves enveloped us.

From deep within my sleeping state Ilsenaad's voice reached my ears.

'I am near your sleeping body. We know where you are. We are with you. We know where you are Llueve. Be careful. Follow the instructions. Don't get distracted. Remember the Say; Contemplation of the One is Creation of the Self. All of the Siddhe and the Atlanteans on Terra are aware of what is going on and will help. We love you.'

When I woke up early this morning I felt calm and collected and began to plan our escape. I realized that any minute there could be screaming sirens screeching to a stop on the lawn - running boots - crashing doors and windows...time to haul.

Llueve lay sleeping beside me as I thought about how I would put my camper on the truck and we could go to a national forest and then try and come up with a plan. First I had to get Llueve out of the house and over to Spencer and Lena's at the back of the arroyo in Chimayo.

I got dressed made tea and poured Llueve some corn flakes with chopped up banana - she liked that - and got all the drawing stuff from the living room floor and burned it in the fireplace. While she ate, I put the camper on the back of the truck and loaded up some blankets, cooking stuff and clothes, Neutron's bowl and leash.

We got three blocks away when the full weight of it all hit me - I might never be able to go back to the house. I drove back.

I filled a suitcase with more clothes, sheets and some expensive wool blankets my cousin Carole had given me and that we might need. I got my laundry bag and filled it with towels and sweaters and jackets. I basically dumped my clothes-drawers in the suitcases. I checked to see the windows were all locked, front porch and kitchen lights on the timer, and doors both locked. When we got to Spencer's I explained the latest to him. I needed to leave Llueve there while I got groceries and propane and went to the bank.

'No one can see her Spence. Not a kid on a bike - no one.'

'Right. Don't worry,' he said.

We led Llueve to Spencer's library in the bus and I got some paper and colored pencils for her. Lena came out and I gave her a short hand version of what was up.

'I've got to get to the bank,' I said and got back in the truck. Lena went to connect with Llueve and I drove to the main branch of my bank. I needed to take all my money out - about $7,000. It all went pretty smooth except that. I was so antsy I felt like I was going to throw up. I got most of it in Traveler's Checks.

While I was in the bank I thought of Yvonne and worried she might try and pop over to the house just when the G men were closing in. That's when I realized that calls to Yvonne and Spencer were linked to my phone number.

I called Yvonne on my cell. She was still at her office.

'Oh good I got you,' I said when she answered. 'Look Yvonne - it's serious time again - '

'Uh oh,' she said.

'Look. We both went out last night right?'

Pause. Then -'Oh Yeah!'

'And our friends over there told us we are the target of a huge intelligence operation right?'

'Oh boy.'

'So -I just moved out of my place and took all my money out of the bank. She's at our friend's house right? Anything could happen Vonnie. I mean...they could get hold of my phone record and trace my calls and you're on there'

'Oh my God you're right!' I could tell her mind was in tenth gear now. 'What are you going to do?' she asked.

'I'm going to just get away from the house for starters. Her uh friends can get her back but only from out of the country.'

'Is this as serious as I think it is?'

'Yes!' I said. 'This is full on serious Vonnie.'

'Joe - Should I get out too?'

'We should all get out of here Vonnie. Your cell number and Spencer's are in the computer connected to my number see? For all we know they photographed your license plate at the Canyon from a satellite!' There was silence. She got it. 'Keep your cell phone on,' I said. 'I've got mine and we'll keep track of things.'

'Oh Joe!' Yvonne was feeling scared.

'I know sweetie - hey - do you know how fried I am!? This has been going on for days! '

'Me too!' she said in her personal private voice and I remembered why she was so hard to get away from.

'Yeah. You too.'

'Well so much for my business.' Yvonne sounded baffled and bewildered.

'I'm sorry Vonnie - I guess Armageddon always catches you by surprise.' She snorted.

'Call me as soon as you can,' she said. 'I'll go to my sisters - oops!'

'Yeah. Don't say anymore. Take your special stuff.'

'Right. Bye.'

Right away I called Spencer.

'Spencer - if they find me they'll get my phone record - you're on it.'

'Oh Jesus.' Long pause. 8th , 9th, 10th gear. 'We could go to ...' as Spencer started to say where we could go to I spluttered nonsense syllables loudly into the phone.

'Oh, right.' Spencer said.

'I'll be there in an hour,' I said and clicked off.

I stopped at a mall and got Llueve a thick, wool charcoal sweater and some hiking boots I hoped would fit, socks, a windbreaker, a really good sleeping bag. I steeled myself to go into a women's department and buy her underwear and a dress. When I was sure no one was looking I cupped my palm on a bra to see if it would fit. I was mostly thinking of disguises but I was also thinking we might end up hiking through the woods. My sense of urgency was growing stronger as I imagined what sorts of resources these secret police might have at their command. Probably everything.

I bought some pale rouge that maybe Llueve could disguise her skin with.

The camper had a working fridge, a stove and a heater. There was a ten gallon propane tank that sat in a rack on the back of the camper. I got this filled and then bought one full shopping cart of groceries with a lot of organic greens for Llueve. I bought a box of drinking water bottles. I could fill the truck's water reservoir for washing at Spencer's.

I got back to Spencer's about an hour before sundown. Everything was calm. The sun made long shadows of the fence posts up the face of the hill and across the vegetable gardens where Lena was packing clothes in a box. She looked at me excitedly. Her eyes said 'Adventure!'

'I haven't had this much fun since the Chicago Convention!' She said, her eyes gleaming.

Spencer was hauling more boxes and bags into the bus, and boxes of tools out of it while the bus idled and smoked. When Spencer looked up I could see that he'd been infected with the same sense of cosmosis I had. We both thought we knew quite a bit about the covert operations of the shadow government. Now we were targets. The idea of a staged, global 'Alien Invasion' indicated an incredible amount of organization between agencies and a huge plan. And a deadly intelligence.

'Llueve's in the house,' he said struggling with a box of books he was taking out of the bus.

Llueve was sitting in a sofa chair watching another video - something with Bruce Willis and a statuesque blond who spoke bad English that Lena had put on for her. She looked up as I came into the room - her eyes haunted. God but this must be intense for her - I thought. I didn't think the video was such a good idea. There were too many cops and explosions. I took her out to the big rock to show her where I'd planted the pear tree. We stood on either side of it and I knew she was thinking of her own fruit tree planted in her garden. She smiled at me with big, sad, wet eyes. Just then, a wind devil whipped up around us and we laughed as it moved off up the arroyo.

For another three hours I helped Lena and Spencer unload and then re-load the bus. At one point we had to fill some gas cans for the bus from the station in nearby Pojoaque in my truck. While we were gone Yvonne had arrived in her Volvo. We had agreed we should only take the bus and my truck and camper. Three cars seemed like too much of a convoy. Our basic plan was to hit the road and look back later.

Lena called an Indian friend at San Juan Pueblo who lives in the town of Nambe who would keep an eye on the birds and gardens while they were gone. Lena and Yvonne decided they would call in sick from the road. Around eleven that night, tense from expecting vans full of covert operatives to pull up with guns drawn, we finally burned rubber out the driveway and headed north.

Chapter Twenty

5/10/05

Sunshine Valley, New Mexico is a collection of scattered homesteads on a flat sage plain that extends nearly to the horizon to the west and across rolling sage plains up to and across the Colorado border to the north where the White Mountains drop down from the clouds like a vision of Shagrila. It's only a little over three hours going straight north from Santa Fe. This was good, because Spencer's unregistered bus was coughing smoke and not running so great. He and Lena had loaded enough materials including dried and canned food, to live in the bus for at least month.

Spencer had called ahead to warn his friends who run the Plantation, as he calls the farm, that he was dropping in for an unexpected visit. Without telling them any particulars, or that there were more people than him and Lena involved; to expect them at about three in the morning, and to not bother getting up.

We followed the two lane highway past Questa, the last town of any size in the high desert country north of Taos and before Sunshine. I remembered how remote the area was from visiting David, an old friend who lives in the area, a few times over the years.

Once off the asphalt we drove straight into the sage land on a sandy, deeply rutted dirt road, for about a half mile, took a few turns, and pulled in at a driveway with an entry made of two telephone poles with a bright, gold and green rectangular sign hanging from heavy, rusty chains. The headlights of the truck picked out the words on the sign - 'BEYOND THE END'.

I remembered what the area looked like from my previous visits, but there was powdery green glow in the air from the endless sage, now dark and sleeping. Spencer owned the twenty unfenced acres of it. There was a fence enclosing a full acre of land for a garden, with a straw bale and stucco, one story house next to it. Behind that there were two small adobe casitas with their own fenced garden areas and chicken runs. At the very back of the fenced land was a little sdobe dome where an older man, a strange fellow named Raven lived, wrote poetry and did what ever outfielders do.

The whole farm was irrigated from a well that ran on solar. There was a long, circular bird run of hooped fowl fencing growing currant bushes, and dwarf cherry trees, strawberry plants, and grape vines inside it, where quail, guinea hens and wild turkeys ran around. This hoop had curved, corrugated tin roofing collecting rain and snow-melt in gutters that fed plastic barrels from which micro tubing irrigated the caged plants and birds. The birds were alternately harvested and either eaten or sold to the tourist restaurants up in touristy Red River; in Questa, and at the Taos Farmer's Market in the summer.

There was a fenced orchard on the north side of a small barn of dwarf apricot trees, apples and pears and grapes for raisins. There were two - thirty something couples with kids in the adobe houses. I'd met the couple that lived in the main farmhouse before - Vince Johnson and Lisa Klein. They had been friends of Spencer and Lena's in Berkeley and were now involved in the web site tracking the World Bank and IMF.

Vince and Lisa had taken in their dogs so that except for some distant barking, it was a silent night. Spencer led us to a remote area of the farm where we wouldn't be disturbed in the morning, then he and Lena bedded down. Pretty soon all was as quiet as a toomb on Venus.

Yvonne went to sleep in Spencer's bus, so Llueve and I had the camper to ourselves. We weren't so disturbed by one another by now, but we still couldn't communicate, which made being together awkward. She had discovered frozen grape juice and was eating it out of a can with a spoon, along with cheese and crackers. She tried to tell me something about the juice that excited her but I didn't get it. The tension of the day finally lifted and we laughed off not being able to talk. He he, me and the extraterrestrial can't communicate.

The immediate danger of 'them' finding us was at least delayed. We were in control, and doing something, and had the endless expanse of the New Mexico back country to escape into.

As Spencer had been telling me for some months now, everyone in the valley was paranoid about the BLM blowing up the local artesian spring that people around here had used since the turn of the century. When it was tested recently, they found one or two parts per million of arsenic which is normal for local groundwater. But by BIA standards, it made the water impure for human consumption. So the BIA was planning to blow up the well to comply with their technical regulations. Litigation to stop this from happening had been going on for months because people far and wide in this remote area, had depended on the well for so long. But the BIA was determined to robotically comply with their guidelines. Any day there could be a loud boom and then scores of people would be out of water.

The upshot of it was that a big meeting of all concerned was to take place the next morning so that hardly anyone would be around to discover Llueve.

About forty people were prepared to try and block the blowing up of the well, taking turns camping out by the road, day and night. While they were concerned with the immediate sabotage to their land from beurocratic robots, we were concerned with exposure to the Black Riders from Hell!

Our greatest fear was that someone in the area would spot Llueve and start asking questions. She just didn't look or act human. If some yokel saw her and told others about her, she could become the second coming or something even worse. And that just wouldn't stay under wraps. I was worrying that the psychic intelligence operations from the Skandrr and the Bats could possibly spot some kind of unusual disturbance in the airwaves and sense her. The Dracos themselves, and who knows who else, were supposedly in the astral all over the South West looking for Llueve's Ovvalan vibratory field. Could you hide from such beings? I knew we had only bought time. I was considering taking Llueve over to David's place across the highway in El Rito. Another plan was that Llueve, Yvonne and I could go up into the mountains and make a campsite. At least there, Llueve could walk around in the day and we would hear any cars coming before they could see us. Yvonne and I could pose as a couple camping and hide Llueve. I tried sleeping in the camper with Llueve but it just got too weird with out not being able to talk so I moved a sleeping and a camping pad out between some sage bushes and slept outside. In the morning we started organizing all the junk we'd thrown in the vehicles. The rest of the day dragged by.

Spencer and Lena had gone to the well meeting that morning to avoid suspicion, since it was such a big local deal, and also because they were concerned with the issue. It had been decided by the local group to block access to the well with cars and trucks beginning that night. I stuck with Llueve in case anything happened. She was so strange a presence to be near and was also so beautiful that I was practicing a lot of yoga breathing to keep my cool. Once it got dark we all had dinner together.

'Let's get some sleep. If you're going to move over to David's place you can do it in the morning.' Spencer said. Lena and Yvonne hugged Llueve goodnight and she said something like;

'Geaeduvriea shien-niella.' Then we were alone. She, Neutron and I went for a walk in the sage.

The first night at Sunshine, Llueve had seemed to calm down somewhat but now her eyes were glassy again and her pupils dilated. She still had the knife strapped to her waist. Silvaan had said that her being blue was a normal reaction for an Ovvalan to our atmosphere and that it wasn't dangerous for her. So I had a clue that her growing hyper state wasn't due to lack of oxygen. We walked for a while and then got back in the camper. It was hard for me to get to sleep sensing Llueve's tortured state and we lay nervously in the camper bed. It felt cruel to leave her in such a state so we lay in complete estrangement until she finally took some blankets and lay down on the floor to be in her own space.

I forced myself to relax and concentrated on going out of body and after what seemed hours I started to buzz. I'd become so accustomed to turning around to go out the back of my head to go to Ovvala, so that when the buzzing feeling came, I almost did it that night. When I'd almost exited through the top of my neck, I remembered Llueve was on this side of the astral passage and I rolled sideways out of my body, as Monroe and Peterson describe doing. Llueve was already out and was impatiently waiting for me in her astral body and pacing impatiently back and forth in the camper's little hallway.

'Finally you come!' she nearly yelled. I guess she had got out long before me and had been waiting. 'Jwo! I think I'm going to die!' she shrieked. 'I feel so sick with worry. The Adrrik are merciless and could not only force me to reveal where my physical body is but threaten to torture my parents if I don't reveal where Logaana or Inxalrok are and I don't even know!'

I tried to comfort her but she could see in my aura that I was just as freaked out. You can't hide anything in the astral. We headed for the opening to Ovvala. Asaalen was there.

'Come. We must go to Logaana,' He commanded us.

Djagda, Kaelaa, Avaala, Elsinaad, Seshena, Bodiccea, Oorden and Granvold, some of the top commanders of the Siddhe Guard, were waiting for us. The entire Siddhe were concerned for our safety and were keeping watches posted. Siddhe agents from Venezuela and the Caribbean were physically traveling to New Mexico. Both of the captured Aeron disks were en route, through dimensional wormholes, to try and get to us. Llueve has become a kind of Siddhe princess and retrieving her and protecting us both was the greatest priority among the Siddhe. We made a circle with Assalen and exchanged rotes.

We learned that Llueve's house was still surrounded by Adrrik agents, but the Siddhe had managed to capture her cat by luring it from within the astral, as cats can see the astral. Isult had created an image of Llueve in the cat's mind and lured the cat through the neighborhood hedges and gardens to Elsinaad who had a disk parked on a side street. The cat was then transported to the cottage in Inxalrok where Llueve's new home was. Knowing her cat was safe had the most soothing effect on Llueve.

The office of the Suura, the environmental group Llueve, Elsinaad, Seshena and Kaelaa belonged to had been raided by the Skandrr. Its papers were confiscated and its members warned by the Siddhe not to go near it.

Fighter jets had flown over Inxalrok as direct warning to the Siddhe concerning Llueve and me trespassing their wormhole. The heat was on and the Siddhe were on full battle alert. Earth side Siddhe posts in the West from Vancouver Island to Venezuela were on full alert.

The Siddhe have successfully hidden out in the vast mountain regions of Inxalrok for centuries. There are extensive underground caverns behind the walls of the river gorge and are well mapped by the Siddhe and unknown to the Skandrr. The underground communities are mobile and can be quickly shifted from one area to another in case of prolonged conflict. One lone Ovvalan woman like Llueve could be hidden there indefinitely. But then again the Siddhe know that the planned 'Alien Invasion' and terrorization of Earth and Ovvala has begun and the Siddhe have no Idea to what extreme the Dracos will now go.

'We may move to the mountains nearby,' I told Asaalen. He told me we were being tracked in the astral and that if we moved anywhere, we would be kept track of. He told me that agents of the Siddhe are watching my house in Jaconita but they haven't seen any activity in either dimension as of the moment.

'The Draco Council is set to meet again tonight, so they will probably act on what is decided in the next forty eight hours. We should have Siddhe agents in the physical in your area within twenty-four hours,' Elsinaad told us when we separated.

Seeing the Siddhe responding so energetically to her situation really lifted Llueve's spirits. As we flew away from this encounter, I realized she had regained a sense of confidence enough to be playful when she manifested herself dressed in flowing, dark red silk pants and an elegant, Daag style, hemp blouse and red boots, and rode sidesaddle on her broomstick. She smiled a wicked smile at me as she carefully applied lipstick with a pretend applicator. I decked myself out in a dark brown, three-piece Harris Tweed suit with a Derby hat and a Colt 45 as I pictured Pinkerton agents wore in the Wild West. We were both very energized, and instead of going straight back to the camper in Sunshine Valley, Llueve detoured us to the Grand Canyon which we had seen only under severe stress. We were both curious what the area we had walked in would look like in the astral, and zoomed across New Mexico to the Canyon and dove in.

The towering buttes and mesas, alight in the star glow, the purple and blue canyons stretching into the distance were as you can imagine - otherworldly. We made love in the sand of a little stream that drained into the Colorado River. It was sweet. The stress and fear of the last few days lifted as we sat up looking at the stars making moonshadows of the buttes across the sandstone mesas and cliffs. We both felt a renewed confidence knowing that the Siddhe were near. It was only a matter of hours before we would be safe. Perhaps it was this over confidence that led Llueve to her inspiration.

'Jwo, what we are experiencing is bizarre. Ever since it began happening I've been living in a state of disbelief. Somehow you and I were destined to play a special role to stop the Dracos from taking over our world. Somehow we are linked to this Ea from the time we were born - we are a part of her and she of us. We are Siddhe - you and I - we planned all this. None of this is an accident. We have a power that has allowed us to already be instrumental in upsetting the Draco plans...'

I knew what was coming. She wanted to penetrate the Draco Council Chambers. But I had a new sense of purpose since being forced to run away from my home. And I had a new, more solid sense of identity since experiencing Llueve as physically real. Also, I felt we both understood much, much more about dealing with danger in the astral. We knew how to read the topography of light vibrations around us, and sense intrusions. We understood cloaking and evasion better now. We understood fighting. The Adrrik and the BATS were much less subtle than the Siddhe in doing these things.

'I feel that this life within me is talking to me,' Llueve said passionately. 'If this really is who they say it is - the ancient Ea - then she sees what is happening, and she wants to act! Now! Through us! I feel she is telling us to go to that Council Jwo.' What a tricky girl!

But I had been feeling strange promptings myself from within the force between us. I felt like we existed beyond life and death. Death didn't seem to matter now. Nothing mattered. Only exposing the Dracos and freeing people from their deluded slavery mattered. I agreed with Llueve. It was important to act now, to feel now, to be here now! It was now that the alien invasion was beginning to cause terror and subservience to the New World Order of corporate control - it was now that genetically modified plants were being forced on humanity – it was now that aluminum and barium chemtrails were being sprayed across the skies causing autistic births and emphesima, and it was now that the redwoods were being cut down never to regain the grandeur of old growth forests. It was now that mountain top removal to expose coal seams was taking place in the Appalachias. Global warming or climate change or whatever could be stopped now but later? It may already be too late. So what did it matter how long we lived? If we didn't act now, the tragedy that was coming was like the Nazi Holocaust to the tenth power. The sense of impotence to defy our controllers was deeply inbred into our collective mentality, yet the idea that it was possible to introduce an entirely different social order overnight to meet the emergency of global warming, was only as far away as imagining it. If the televisions were turned off and the anti-depressants flushed, if people would leap over their inbred need to have someone else define the nature of God and love, love itself could awaken as direct action for the common good *now*. The psychic glop that prevented these realizations must be what the Ouroboros of the Dracos produced. That was the gobledegook of what Djagda had called the Negative Mystery. I threw caution to the winds.

'Well, it's the last place they would think to look for us!' I said. Llueve laughed and her aura shimmered with defiant happiness. I felt her love for me like a sugary kiss.

We shot up into the sky and searched for the truck stop that led to the side canyon that led to the Earthside door to the Draco wormhole. I recognized the intersecting canyons and we followed this to the canyon's rim.Staying close together and moving very cautiously, sending out sensors ahead of us, we floated down the face of the Canyon.

Inching forwards into the enemy vibratory field, we were aware, unlike the times before, that they were expecting us and that we were on their most wanted list. I wondered if Rexxon would 'smell' me or sense Ea inside Llueve. But we were intensely focused. And we were really pissed.

A needle of awareness hit me in the third eye. Llueve had spotted something. It was an astral guard outside the smaller entry into the tunnel that we had exited. We touched hands amplifying our invisibility and altered our approach. The guard was alert, staring into the dark. He sensed us but didn't know just what it was he was sensing. Silently, Llueve and I agreed on our tactic. We each made a pentacle of reflective silver Lexl-light.

'Now,' I signaled her and we slammed the pentagrams together sandwiching the guard's head inside a double mirror of crystal light. He slumped over catatonically. This would leave him cross-eyed for hours.

We slid through the little door and hovered down the tunnel emerging into the already crowded central chamber positioning ourselves near the ceiling but well away from the central crossing point that would make us materialize.

A deeper, older identity became very strong in me at this point. This time, it was more than a vague intuition of a greater and more complex identity. This might seem extraordinary - though at this point what could seem extraordinary? I could *see* that I have been with the Siddhe through many lives and that this fight with the Dracos has been part of my soul purpose before. I understood that the Ixtellar technology is the pursuit of many lifetimes and that there is a me aware of the many lifetimes I've practiced it. I know that I have been Ovvalan and Atlantean and that Llueve and I have been relatives before. I discovered something else. I like fighting!

My ability to move in the astral and communicate mentally has grown in leaps and bounds which is not unusual once the veil of material delusion is pierced. Spencer and Lena have told me that I seem different to them; that all of this has had a noticeable effect on my personality, even on my appearance. They said I have a powerful presence now. So before I'd been a whimp?

Once we were in position, we remembered what was about to happen - the strangely burning dark vibrations, the energy depletion caused by the Vrryl force, the sense of psychic horror, the sick feeling of the robust naked woman selling her soul to darkness and then the shocking presence of Rexxon. Because we knew the program, we were more prepared to stay focused. Also, our astral attention span was longer now. I understood the use of colors and textures of camouflage and the deflective power of psychic geometry. And I understood the unique power of my love for Llueve and Ea differently, more soberly. This love included my friends in the Siddhe and the things that I treasure in nature. All of this was joined in me. I was just one point in a vast field of the creative force of the Ixtellaria.

We wrapped one another in layers of geometry and love, asserted in our hearts our commitment as universal brethren to the service of Mahaala and the Ixtellar. We both understood death differently now. It doesn't matter. How long you exist doesn't matter. Existence without a sense of purpose is a burden. There is no death. We were in a stream of such powerful circumstances that no trivial death could come to us now. We were prepared to die during the next hour but we were positive, both of us, that this was our role to play - that this is what love is for. I remembered a phrase of Che Guevara's that had always puzzled me - that to serve the people by engaging the oppressor was the greatest act of love. I was a little nervous that I would again leave Llueve's side so I made her agree to constructs that would prevent that - if I were to leave her side we would be withdrawn from the astral and physically wake up. But my revulsion for Rexxon and the Dracos was so powerful by this point that I doubted he could affect me as before.

Our arms around one another, cloaked to the max, energy shields in place, we locked into the stillness and became Watchers.

Already the room was full of the Homosaurs in their black and red robes. They were milling excitedly around the edges of the white crisscross bands on the ground. The tall guards walked around distributing the fluted glasses of fresh blood with little sprigs of watercress dangling on their rims. The robed participants tossed these off and impatiently threw the crystal glasses in the canvas bags the giants brought around. A sense of urgency and rabid lust arced off the assembly in jagged waves of menace and aggression. I noticed the deathly calm man with the waxy complexion, surrounded by bodyguards. I recognized him now from the occasional pictures of him in Vanity Fair. It was xxxxx xxxxxxx. Next to him were five or six others, males and females, all old and well preserved and with a similar pasty look. They were members of the original fourteen Andrr-Ka. Xxxxx entered the circle and stood next to the naked priestess, intoned the magik words and cast his geometry at the ceiling.

The naked priestess in her golden slippers and bikini held her arms up and exuded the golden energy that rose up inside the triangle to the ceiling. The murmur of voices suddenly became more intense as flashes of black lightning cracked and purple clouds pulsed and throbbed down from the top of the chamber. A broiling, malevolent thunder cloud twisted, tornado-like, over the congregation, trying to come down. Everyone looked up expectantly in awe and adoration.

The tall ushers appeared leading a large, very muscular man, a bodybuilder, who was wearing only black Speedos. He seemed uncoordinated or drunk as he was jerked along like a baby by the giants. He was pushed inside the red band of the circle where he stopped and stood mindlessly, transfixed and swaying in place. Someone shouted and pointed upwards where the scaly, ectoplasmic haunches of the Tyrannosaurus were already descending through the evil black storm.

The naked man's head hung limply as his eyes stared vacantly ahead. This, I realized was a soulless clone from the Annanokian ship.

The Reptilian descended further, malleable like dense smoke. Blobs of pale ectoplasmic slime dripped from him making loud plops as they hit the sandstone floor. The priestess nervously held up her arms, quickly calling out the last of the invocations. The assembly answered more and more impatiently. Then Rexxon's head came into view.

The black tornado surrounding Rexxon's form lengthened and became very defined and pierced through the back of the neck of the clone which threw its head and arms up and back in a convulsive seizure and screamed with terror. In the crowd of Homosaurs I again saw senators, media owners - famous world figures - Noriega, Saddam Hussein, Bin Laden, former American Presidents, English and French Prime Ministers. I saw former presidents of Chile and Spain, Israel and Syria, China and Russia. But I had to stop searching the crowd. What was happening in the center was intensifying.

The writhing smoke that had been the tyrannosaur entered the breath of the clone. Rexxon had entered the muscle bound man who started bucking and flinging his arms around wildly and shouting out spasmodically as the energy of Rexxon possessed him.

With a roar from the clone's opened mouth, a hush fell over the assembly. The clone stood to his full height, chest out, with clenched jaws. His eyes radiated black light as menacing waves of power coming from him visibly possessed the assembly with his primacy. His muscles rippled rhythmically as the reptilian face became superimposed upon the clone's and possession became complete. Looking down along its arms, the clone flexed its muscles with self-admiration. The figure seemed to swell with power, bucking every now and then, as it stood barefoot and virtually naked in the middle of the silenced assembly. It looked all around the chamber, its head quivering with Reptilian spasms. Finally it spoke in the now familiar voice but with an impossible force of volume that filled the entire chamber as before and made the veins stand out on the clone's neck. Every syllable echoed clearly off the chamber walls.

'THE SIDDHE HAVE BROUGHT TOGETHER AN OVVALAN WOMAN AND A HUMAN MAN!!' The muscle bound clone roared accusingly. Everyone gasped and looked shocked. Evidently they knew the significance of this.

'HOW COULD YOU LET THIS HAPPEN?!

'YOU HAVE THOUSANDS OF TRAINED AGENTS ON THE GROUND IN BOTH WORLDS! IN THE GOVERNMENTS OF EVERY NATION ON TERRA AND OVVALA - IN POSITIONS OF CONTROL IN MOST MAJOR INDUSTRIES AND BANKING ESTABLISHMENTS IN EVERY MAJOR CITY IN BOTH WORLDS AND IN THE ASTRAL DIMENSIONS - ON THE MOON! ON MARS! AND STILL YOU LET THIS HAPPEN!!

'DO YOU REALIZE YOU HAVE ALLOWED OUR PLANS TO BE ENDANGERED?' Individuals struck themselves on the chest or stomped their feet in rage.

'SILENCE!! Rexxon roared through the voice of the clone, making fists that extruded droplets of blood from the bone crushing intensity applied. The assembly became breathlessly, unwillingly still, dominated by Rexxon's anger.

'THESE TWO MET IN THE ASTRAL AND WALKED THROUGH THE TRANSUBSTANTIATION TUNNEL!' Gasps. 'THEY WALKED RIGHT ACROSS THIS GROUND YOU ARE STANDING ON RIGHT NOW! THEY WENT OUT THAT WAY,' Rexxon pointed down the tunnel towards Ovvala but the Priestess pointed in the other direction, correcting him.

'WHATEVER!!' Rexxon screamed, and pointed in the other direction. REXXON shook his jowls Hitler like and hushed, fearful murmurs rippled uncertainly through the crowd.

'THEY ARE IN TERRA NOW. IN THE FLESH! OBVIOUSLY THE SIDDHE ARE FAR MORE ORGANIZED AND KNOWLEDGEABLE THAN YOU HAVE INFORMED ME! HOW COULD YOU LET THIS ESCAPE YOU?! OR IS THERE A SECRET PLOT AMONG YOU? IF THIS IS SO, WHO EVER IT IS THAT IS PLOTTING AGAINST ME WILL WISH THEY HAD NEVER BEEN BORN!! IF YOU THINK YOU CAN PLOT AGAINST ME AND MY FAMILY - THINK AGAIN! TO SAY WE WILL TEAR YOU OUT OF YOUR PHYSICAL BODY GOES WITHOUT SAYING! WE WILL INCARCERATE YOU IN KRUAAL AND SLOWLY SUCK YOUR BLOOD FOR A CENTURY! WE WILL EAT YOU ALIVE!

'THEY HAVE EVEN SENT AGENTS ON TO THE ANNANOKIAN MOTHERSHIP WHERE THE CLONES ARE MADE!' Horrified gasps. Rexxon whacked himself in the chest and almost fell over from the force of the blow. WHERE THIS BEAUTIFUL SPECIMEN CAME FROM!

'FOR CENTURIES WE HAVE TRAINED YOU TO SERVE US, GIVEN YOU ALL THE GOLD AND WEAPONS YOU DESIRED, SLAVES AND ACCESS TO POWER! I MADE IT POSSIBLE FOR YOU TO BECOME MASTERS OF YOUR PLANET AND THIS IS HOW YOU REPAY ME?!' A perfect, fearful silence hung in the air as the Reptilians cast stealthy glances at one another.

'YOU MUST KNOW THE COLONY OF HEAVEN ON MARS IS NOT FOR EVERYONE!' He paused and slowly looked around the room. There were gasps of pure fear from the assembly. Rexxon had been pointing at the Assembly with an outstretched arm and at this point he sniffed this naked arm. He breathed in a long intake of breath and his face contorted and his lips twitched. He licked his arm and then, with a visible effort, he slammed his arm against his side and jerked his head up to look at the crowd. The Priestess edged away to the extreme side of the central circle staying as far away from the clone as possible as golden light continued to radiate out of her.

IT IS FOR THE ELECT ONLY! FOR THOSE WHO SERVE US AND AID IN CONTROLLING THESE OVVALAN AND HUMANOID MICE! EACH OF YOU IN THIS ASSEMBLY IS HOST TO A DRACO ENTITY - TO THE DRACO BLOOD YOU ARE FOREVER IN ALLEGIANCE. BUT THIS DOES NOT GUARANTEE THE TRANSPORTATION OF THE HOST! I FORGOT TO TELL YOU THAT DIDN'T I!?

'YOU CAN BE REPLACED! DO YOU KNOW HOW MANY THOUSANDS OF YOUR OWN STAFFS WOULD TAKE YOUR PLACE IN A MOMENT IF THEY WERE GIVEN THE WORD?! WHAT YOU DO IS NOT SO UNIQUE! IT IS THE POWER OF THE DRACO THAT LETS YOU CONTROL YOUR SUBORDINATES AND THIS POWER IS MINE TO GIVE AND TAKE!' Again he smelled his arm and gave it a little lick.

'WE ONLY NEED ONE MORE WAVE OF ECONOMIC REORGANIZATION. ONE MORE INDUSTRIAL THRUST OF THE MIGHTY MACHINE THAT DRACO HAS BUILT AND WE WILL HAVE CONTROL OF THE GLOBAL ECONOMY!! AND OF OIL - THE ANCIENT PRECIOUS BLOOD OF OUR FOREFATHERS!' The crowd roared, desperately wanting Rexxon's approval. Rexxon looked at his arm distractedly, sniffed and licked it again. Suddenly his chest expanded and his bulging muscles rippled wildly. In spasms and convulsions, the clone bucked and thrashed as Rexxon's reptilian face grew even more defined out of the clone's physical face into a terrible, scaled snout with its rows of white pointed teeth protruding through bleeding gums until the Tyrannosaurus Rex face had morphed completely out of the human face. The muscular human body was now topped with a Tyranosaurian head with its huge, green, Reptilian eyes.

'IF THE FULL IMPACT OF GLOBAL PHOTONIC WARMING BECOMES FULLY KNOWN OVER OUR MEDIA OUTLETS ON OVVALA AND EARTH, A GLOBAL ENVIRONMENTAL MOVEMENT WILL BEGIN THAT COULD UNDERMINE THE MASTER PLAN! The volume of the clone's voice was supernaturally piercing, guttural, terrifying.

'TIME IS SHORT! THE FIRST CLONES WILL BE DELIVERED TO SOUTH AMERICA, AFRICA AND MONGOLIA THIS MONTH. THE SIMULATED EXTRATERRESTRIAL LANDINGS WILL NOW BEGIN. YOU HAVE THE RESOURCES, THE TECHNOLOGY, THE MAN POWER, THE WEAPONS! IF YOU FAIL US NOW YOU WILL BE DISPOSSESSED. YOUR WEALTH AND POWER WILL VANISH IN A HEARTBEAT. YOU WILL BE DELIVERED TO THE MASSES WITH NO HOPE OF RE-ENTERING THE RANKS OF THE ELITE! YOU WILL HAVE TO GET A REGULAR JOB!!' Rexxon laughed maliciously - The entire audience shuddered. A few of the Homosaurs gagged. 'GAK GAK GAK!' Rexxon laughed.

'TODAY ARRAGLOCON HAS DEMANDED THE FIRST OF THREE TRILLION DOLLARS TO PROP UP THE CORPORATE ECONOMY. WE GOT A LITTLE GREEDY DOWN THERE EH?! There was general abashed laughter. 'WE WERE TRYING TO GET THE GOLDEN GOOSE TO LAY EGGS FASTER! NOT HEMORRHAGE HERSELF TO DEATH!!' There was now loud and relieved guffawing. 'SO YOU THINK THIS FUNNY!!' The laughter stopped suddenly. 'LET ME TELL YOU SOMETHING! THE WORMHOLE LINKING THE NEPTUNIANS TO BRAZIL ALSO COMES OUT IN VENEZUELA. A BRANCH OF THAT WORMHOLE LEADS DIRECTLY TO KRRUAL!!

'OUR SACRED HOMELAND!!

'IF THIS ENTIRE WORMHOLE IS NOT CONTROLLED BY US - AND QUICK! THE SIDDHE AND THE ATLANTEANS WILL BE ABLE TO PENETRATE TO SKARROR DIRECTLY!' Gasps from the assembly. A hushed terror overcame the group. Rexxon shook his jowls and glared menacingly around the room. Llueve and I froze and intensely concentrated on our invisibility mantras. 'WITH NO KRRUAL THERE WILL BE NO MARS! WE MUST GET ALL THE AVAILABLE GOLD! WE MUST CONTROL THE PORTALS IN BRAZIL AND VENEZUELA! WE MUST DESTROY THE SIDDHE AND THE ATLANTEANS!! AND YOU MUST CAPTURE THIS OVVALAN WOMAN AND HUMAN MAN WHO ARE SPYING ON US!'

'EVERYTHING DEPENDS ON KEEPING OUR HUMANOID AND OVVALAN PIGLETS DISTRACTED BY THE ALIEN INVASION. SKANDRR DISCS AND TERRAN JETS HAVE BEEN FLYING LOW OVER THREE CONTINENTS IN BOTH DIMENSIONS DROPPING INCENDIARY BOMBS ON USELESS GOVERNMENTAL BUILDINGS AND BOMBING A FEW DOMESTIC RESIDENTIAL INSTALLATIONS PREPARING THE PEOPLE FOR THE LANDING OF THE EXTRATERRESTRIAL CLONES.

GO BACK TO YOUR PRECINCTS AND DEPLOY THE ALIEN INVASION! WE WILL GO TO MARS!! WE WILL LIVE IN THE PARADISE OF THE NEW WORLD ORDER. WE WILL BREED HUMANS AND OVVALANS AND EAT THEM FOR BREAKFAST, LUNCH AND DINNER!'

'REXXON, REXXON REXXON!' Lusty bellows rose up out of the subdued crowd. But most of the Reptilians were in shock, like children who have been scolded.

'TWO LITTLE PEOPLE YOU HAVE LET GET BY YOU! TWO LITTLE PEOPLE THAT COULD UNDERMINE THE WORK OF TWO HUNDRED MILLION YEARS!' Rexxon's eyes were continuously searching all around the cavern as he made glancing eye contact with each person in the crowd. Every once in a while he took deep sniffs of his extended arm and licked his bicep. He suddenly seemed to have a fit. His head began to shake and his jaws to masticate and he bit into his right bicep with his extended Tyranosaurian snout and gnashed at the skin and tissue with his fangs until blood was spilling on the floor and tendrils of muscle were hanging between his jaws and his bloody arm.

Rexxon quickly swallowed the bicep and then licked and sucked at his mangled arm making obscene gurgling noises, which only seemed to make him more frantic and wild. His thoughts distracted he began yelling as he slurped the blood dripping from his lips, his flapping Reptilian tongue spraying blood on the nearest of the devotees in front of him who stood expressionless with dread. He bent down and sniffed at the huge muscle of one of his thighs with his gargantuan Reptilian head and then ripped into it with razor sharp teeth so that blood and tissue spilled down on the floor. 'YOU MUST NOT LET THE SIDDHE GET A HEAD START ON YOU! YOU MUST NOT LET THEM DISCOVER THE ENTRY TO KRRUAL IN THE MOUNTAINS OF PARAGUAY!'

'YOU MUST USE YOUR SUPERIOR INTELLIGENCE TO MAKE THESE LITTLE PEOPLE KNOW THAT WE ARE THE MASTERS AND THAT THEY ARE OUR SLAVES FOR THAT IS ALL THEY ARE CAPABLE OF BEING!' He yelled, looking up for a moment as he chewed on the muscles dangling from his snout until he fell over against his weakened leg.

'WE ARE THE LEADERS. THEY ARE THE FOLLOWERS!! THESE LITTLE PIGLETS IN THEIR PENS, THESE STUPID LITTLE GNOMES THAT THINK ABOUT NOTHING BUT SEX GOLDEN

OLDIES AND HOLLYWOOD AND COCA COLA!' He was writhing on the ground and snapping at himself anywhere he could get his jaws to close, licking his own blood with his rasp-like reptilian tongue until the bones of his legs began to protrude.

'REXXON REXXON REXXON,' the crowd seemed to be begging. Their own bodies had become swollen with power, passion and anger. Their clothes were bursting as their bodies swelled before our eyes. Snouts of toothed jaws morphed out of their faces. Their teeth had become gnashing fangs violently expanding in their bleeding gums and they were looking at each other with the same blood lust of the writhing Rexxon, squirming in a bloody heap in their center. But when one Draco possessed Reptilian looked at another with the bloodlust the other slashed at them with their teeth and screamed out a warning roar. Fights were breaking out everywhere.

Suddenly REXXON sat up, the limbs of his clone in bloody shreds. The sudden stillness among the Assembly made it look like they were playing 'Freeze'.

'AND ONE MORE THING! ALL OF OUR POWER OVER OUR PREY IS BASED ON ONE THING! THAT THEY CONTINUE TO BELIEVE THEY NEED OIL TO RUN THEIR ECONOMY AND THAT FEAR IS THE ONLY RESPONSE TO A HOSTILE UNIVERSE. IF ONE SINGLE COMMUNITY STARTS GROWING ITS OWN FOOD, RAISING ITS OWN CHICKENS AND FOR VRRYL'S SAKE, RIDING BICYCLES! WE WOULD LOOSE ALL POWER OVER THEM! IF NEWS OF SUCH AN EVENT GOT OUT OVER THE INTERNET, CITIES WOULD START DIGGING UP THEIR OWN STREETS! PEOPLE WOULD STOP GOING TO WORK! - THIS WOULD SPREAD LIKE WILDFIRE!! PEOPLE MUST FEAR CREDIT CARD DEBT! THEY MUST FEAR THE DRACO!! YOU MUST CREATE THE NEWS EVENTS THAT WILL PARALYZE THEIR MINDS OR THEY WILL BEGIN POPPING UP OUT OF OUR CONTROL LIKE PRAIRIE DOGS!'

The Assembly seemed to nod in unison and then with a roar go back to happily lunging and gnashing at each other's throats.

The Priestess had replaced her robes tightly around herself and was motioning to the guards to come get her. The giant guards themselves were cowering by an entry in the tunnel wall. Suddenly they rushed through the crowd clubbing and zapping and kicking the rabid Reptilians. They grabbed the Priestess, lifted her off her feet and ran back to the doorway with her on their shoulders.

Some of the wild hoard, lizardy snouts protruding from their faces, gums bleeding from the swelling of their fangs, momentarily awoke out of their rage and lust for one another and tried to claw at the Priestess and were electrocuted by the batons of the tall guards. A few of the robes were in flames. A roar above all the others screamed out -

'THERE!' Rexxon screamed and pointed right at us where we were hovering near the ceiling, but got distracted by his bleeding thigh. Everyone turned to look where he had pointed. Two astral Pterodactyls, their eyes like lumps of smouldering coal and their bat wings like thick, polished leather, were shooting at us like arrows a pulsing, black, ragged hatred came out of their auras.

Rexxon screamed through the blood and gore choking him and somehow sunk his jaws onto his own neck and killed himself. His astral body leaped up out of the dying clone in a black tornado. In a clap of thunder and purple black light, and with a deafening Tyranosaurian scream. Rexxon vanished up into the ceiling of the chamber screaming 'WE ARE THE MASTER RACE!'

'Home. Home. Home.' I yelled in Llueve's ear. She was in a trance from looking at Rexxon covered in blood and still chewing on himself. I shook her and she stared at me dumbly. I embraced her and for some reason the image of the boulder in Lena's garden flashed clearly into my mind, the quartz hump on it appearing like a bull's-eye on a target.

'YES!' I mentally shouted. With a jolt of energy we zoomed out of the Draco chamber and snapped into focus next to the boulder.

Still stunned from our sudden discovery, and as we were still coming into definition in Lena's garden, I saw the Pterodactyls coming into focus right behind us. Massive, nine foot tall monsters with the long thin jaws lined with barracuda teeth, the Pterodactyls stared at us with soulless eyes. They landed on extended claws and bent leather wings and skidded to a stop. I pushed Llueve behind me so that she could escape towards the boulder and as I did this we backed right past the apricot tree. I wasn't sure whether we were at Lena's garden or in Llueve's front yard.

The Pterodactyls lunged towards us snapping their jaws. Suddenly, what had been a faint glowing aura around the tree lit up into a bright flash of intense blue-white light and lightninged into the Pterodactyls with an explosion like the shot of a gun.

The Pterodactyls screamed in their guttural lizard voices and imploded. Out of their eyes, intense, purple, blue-black stars of some kind of atomic fire flashed in perfect crosses. An angelic hum filled the air and the two sets of blue crosses shot away into the sky.

Then everything was still and silent. Llueve and I looked at one another amazed that we were still alive. The encounter had been so brief and the energy force that had come out of the tree so unexpected and powerful. The sky, glowing with galactic waves of stardust shimmered gently as we looked at our brave little tree. We began to fade and immediately woke up in the camper and turned to look at one another. From the horror of Rexxon eating himself to the terror produced by the Pterodactyls confronting us we had become completely empowered when the blue stars shot off into the night. We had won!

I slowly became aware of various kinds of sparkling lights circling around us in the darkness of the camper. There were whorls of disturbance in the air getting pierced by red bursts and white slashes. A thunderous battle seemed to be going on around us. Llueve got up, stumbled out the door and threw up. She then went into the little stall in the camper and took a shower.

When Llueve got out of the shower, she started putting on some of the new clothes I'd bought her. I got up and showered and also put on fresh clothes. The sense of being covered in scum after seeing Rexxon had been disgusting. Llueve flung open the door of the camper, jumped down and walked away into the sage. It was very frustrating not being able to talk about things once back in the physical. I put some bud in my little pipe and took a couple hits while keeping an eye on her. This helped lower my blood pressure. Then I joined Llueve.

We stood in the moonlight, sickened and in wonder all at once. When we looked back at the camper we could see different colored lights circling around it searching for us. After a while the lights went away and we went back and fell asleep, exhausted.

Chapter Twenty One

5/10/05

The locals involved in the blockade of the artesian spring have set watches along the dirt road skirting Ute Mountain, where the spring is. They are expecting BIA agents to attempt blowing up the spring late at night while everyone in the neighborhood is asleep. They're preparing to camp out on the seats of two dozen old station wagons and pickups hidden among the trees along the route until something is resolved. A lot of them have cell phones with which to alert the rest of the group and will call up Vince and Lisa at the farm here if there's any action.

Yvonne and I chatted with Vince and Lisa this morning as they were loading up to go into nearby Questa and Red River to deliver pheasants to some restaurants. They were too preoccupied to pay us much attention.

Llueve is getting really antsy having to stay cooped up in the camper drawing crayon pictures all day. She's a strong limbed athletic girl and the inaction is killing her. We've moved the vehicles as far out on the property away from the house as possible. Supposedly to not crowd Vince and Lisa.

I feel depressed and am really worried that the flickering lights circling around the camper last night were BATS or Skandrr agents and that they've found us. The psychic tension is at a fever pitch. My hands are practically shacking so that I'm having to type with two fingers to get the letters right.

In mid afternoon two unmarked black helicopters that strangely made very little sound flew low over the valley and disappeared going north. It could have been the enemy - or just you're every day black helicopters on maneuvers. Llueve and I reinforced our cloaking. We're ready to leave at a moment's notice. Spencer reported that the locals believe the helicopters were BIA operatives casing the joint and talked to one of the locals camped out along the road who are now on high alert. Sure. We'd better leave tomorrow morning.

Lena and Yvonne waited for dark to cook dinner so as to include Llueve and give her some distraction. While they made dinner in the bus, Spence and I walked to the fence line to look over the route the demolition team is expected to follow. There was a light breeze blowing through the sage so that an odd sound we heard at first blended with the wind. But then the sound got louder. It was like a low whistling.

'Look over there Joe,' Spencer said pointing vaguely into the sky over Ute Mountain towards where the trucks and station wagons were hidden in the trees. I only saw the hump of the mountain looming against the stars and the gray haze of sage vanishing into the distance. When I didn't react Spencer said;

'Look at how the stars disappear,' and then I saw what he was looking at. A large moving black area was displacing the stars about a quarter mile away. It was headed north, moving silently along the Rio Grande Gorge to our west.

As we watched, feint Helicopter sounds began thwacking from the opposite direction then, suddenly, brilliant halogen lights cut across the valley from the behind us, as a car turned into Sunshine Valley from the highway, sweeping brilliantly across the entire community. We turned to watch as the car's painfully bright beams whipped across the sage and then began bumping along the dirt road directly at us.

The car lights turning off the highway seemed to set off a panic. Everything seemed to happen at once. The trucks and cars hidden in the trees turned on their headlights to expose what they thought were the BLM bomber helicopters. This lit up the hillside like it was daytime and revealed the two black choppers from the afternoon flying south and just above the tree tops at the base of the mountain. Simultaneously, the shadow Spencer and I had been watching was illuminated by the headlights showing the underbelly of a huge, black, Skandrr disk flying just above the ground - and it was right on top of the choppers. In the blinding lights, we watched the choppers veer away from each other to avoid the disk that was right on top of them, but too late. Each chopper caught a glancing blow from the edges of the huge disk's rim and spun out of control to crash in two separate balls of flame. The saucer, illuminated in the headlights, turned off to the west, wobbling and listing sideways as it arced down towards the Rio Grande Gorge.

The women all tumbled out of the bus with the booming explosions of the choppers. We were all so stunned watching the disk ship wobble away that we'd forgotten about the car that had set the whole thing off, and that now swept through the darkness into the farm. We turned as a group as the car skidded on the turn through the gate, the lights catching us full on, standing in a little group, with Llueve right in the middle of us. The car bucked to a stop and honked its horn a couple times. Spencer went to see who it was and Yvonne and I pushed Llueve behind us and out of sight behind the bus. I was just about to take off into the sage with Llueve when Spencer called out.

'Joe!' He came running up. 'It's a man and a woman who say they know you! She says her name is Solange? She says she's a friend of yours from Santa Fe? How does she know we're here? She has a French accent...?' Yvonne was holding Llueve's hand where we were hidden in the shadow of the bus. Llueve's eyes were like the eyes of a cornered, terror stricken deer.

'If this gets weird,' I told Yvonne, go that way,' I pointed west into the sage. 'Hop the fence and lay down in the sage until we come to you O.K.?' Yvonne nodded. I touched Llueve's arm, looked in her eyes and turned to Spencer.

'What's she look like?' I hissed at Spencer.

'A babe. Sort of anemic looking, long red hair, shades. Looks like an heiress from an old Hollywood movie.' he said, impressed.

'Spencer - I don't know anyone named Solange. Who's with her?

'A mean looking dude... he didn't say anything.'

I walked cautiously up to the car - a pearly new, white Subaru - and there sat Silvaan in the driver's seat with a goatee and pancake makeup, wearing a black leather jacket. His eyes darted around trying to pierce the darkness. He had one hand on the wheel and the other plunged into the inside of his jacket. Isult was taking off her sunglasses. She was ghostly white and shockingly intense.

'Isult!?' I was dumfounded.

'Jwo! So neeice to say you again!' She said in a theatrically chatty way. Then she added in a stage whisper - 'But right now eye yam Solange. He's Gilles,' she said hooking her thumb at Silvaan. The incredible intensity of Isult that I knew in the astral was five times stronger in physical reality. She was like flesh on fire. 'What the yell was all that? It looked like a Skandrr battleship just hit two heliocopterres.' The precision of her voice seemed to slice right into my brain.

'Yeah - I think that's what it was,' I said, still confused. 'But how did you get here?' Evidently there was a way to come over from Ovvala. Isult popped open her door and walked around the back of the station wagon. Silvaan opened his door and leaped out.

'We flew into Alcuberkaay!' She yelled and headed towards where Yvonne was hiding with Llueve. Silvaan was right behind her.

'Thees place is going to be crawling with agents een about twentay minootes,' Isult said. Evidently having already seen Llueve, she sang out 'Karo-olia seshena!' To which Llueve in an uncontrollable explosion of passionate relief to hear Ovvalan spoken and recognizing Isult's unmistakable voice, called back in a rapid fire stream of Ovvalan. It sounded like -

'Mehellia sturuadekeia shanaet iell leascion curbaraetain bearstia!' to which Isult screamed with relieved laughter.

'Hello Jwo,' Silvaan nodded gravely at me. 'Are you ready to gwo? We'll have to gwo *now*!' He spoke with an accent that seemed a mix of Irish and Eastern European.

'We'll gwo north into Cowlorado,' Silvaan said. 'On thee map there's road going along the Rio Garandy Gorge. The traffic will be coming from north and the swouth on this highway,' he twitched his lips towards the direction from which they had just come. 'So we gwo west.'

We walked towards the bus. Spencer, Lena and Yvonne were standing around Llueve. 'Theese are you friends? We trust them?' Silvaan asked, his hand inside his coat, always suspicious.

'Yes,' I said. 'They're friends.'

'We have to giet out of hear neow!' Isult said generally and with an irritated grimace.

'Do you kneeow how to feeind bridge in west of here?' Silvaan asked us all, jutting his chin towards the west while pointing a little flashlight at a map.

'Yes. We can get there from the dirt road that goes along there,' Spencer said, pointing back along the road from where Silvaan had just driven in. Unable to take his eyes off of Isult, Spencer was going into hyper mode at the realization he was fully engaging with extraterrestrials - or aliens or...whatever Ovvalans are.

'You kneeow way to get aycross river from hear?' Silvaan asked him, thrusting out his jaw like a challenge.

'Yes.' Spencer's eyes were two moons of astonishment.

'You show Jwo!' Silvaan said. 'We wiell follow. We need to go *neeow*!' Silvaan said with a quiet viciousness. By the look in Llueve, Isult and Silvaan's eyes - they did not stop being aware for a minute they were on the wrong side of the fence. Their sense of desperation was catching.

'Lena, let's get what we can out of the bus,' Spencer said and started backing toward the bus while he stared at Isult and Silvaan. Lena, who hadn't said a word, began to run. 'Joe, open the camper door and we'll throw in some stuff,' Spencer yelled at me. I opened the back of the camper. In a nook in the wall I saw the gizmo I'd picked up in the UFO tunnel and grabbed it. A moment later I gave it to Silvaan. Out of the habit of sending thought waves to Silvaan, I relayed a mental picture of the sandstone room at the end of the transubstantiation tunnel where it had come from. Silvaan nodded acknowledgment and turned it over briefly and then stuffed it inside his leather jacket with a grunt.

Lena was struggling towards the back of the camper with some clothes, her handbag, and a briefcase. Spencer came running behind her stuffing a wad of papers from the bus's glove compartment into his jacket pocket. He also had a pile of clothes, a small metal box and a leather bag.

Neutron sensed something was up and was sticking close to me. Silvaan saw him and said - 'We cannot briang daog - too dangerous.' In the general intensity of what was going on, this warning got the best of me and I ran to lock Neutron in Vince and Lisa's house thinking he'd have a better chance there than wherever this was leading. I hated to do it but there seemed no choice.

'Jwo - you drive ahiead,' Isult shouted cheerily at me as she backed towards the Subaru. 'Llueve can come with us – to speak Daag for a while O.K. yes?' I saw the sense of what she said but I suspected Isult really wanted to protect Llueve. If it came to a fight I knew that she and Silvaan had weapons and could get Llueve back to Ovvala, which I sure couldn't do. Isult tossed off a bunch of Ovvalan words to Llueve who immediately turned to stare at me with a haunted look in her eyes. There was no knowing if at any minute we would be parted forever. We both knew this.

'Meow babby,' she said in a serious tone and with a new fierceness, tossing back her lustrous hair and smiling bravely. In that toss of her head was the defiance of a Queen. Llueve was definitely reassured by this change of events.

'Meow scred~eulfsah,' I said. I think this meant something like 'you-who-are-so-fine!' in Ovvalan. I smiled with more confidence than I felt. She was smiling the first real smile since we had come through the tunnel. Isult pulled her away from me towards their car, breaking our hand hold. We locked eyes and she paused so that Silvaan unceremoniously grabbed her by the shoulders and stuffed her into the back seat of the car. This galvanized me back to action. Llueve and Isult were a greater priority for the interplanetary cops than even hiding the crashed helicopters and recovering the Skandrr disk. If Llueve had been spotted psychically, they would hit the farm first. Capturing Isult would also be a major coup. Someone somewhere had already got the news that a Skandrr disk had just crashed into two helicopters so that there were undoubtedly carloads of operatives speeding our way at a hundred miles an hour with lights whipping around and sirens screaming through the night.

Lena and Spencer got in the cab of my truck with Yvonne and me and I turned the key.

'Go right and then right again,' Spencer said. I headed west as fast as I could drive on the deeply rutted road that cut through the sagebrush. Silvaan was right on my ass. Everyone in the community was still up at the crash site. The flames from the helicopters had ignited some trees and lit up the side of Ute Mountain. Some of the lights from the cars were still blazing across the sage. We saw no movement around the few houses we passed. After about two miles on the deeply rutted road we turned right going north along the Gorge. As we drove, the ruts got worse and worse and I had to drive on the rims of the ruts, hitting sagebrush so as to avoid bottoming out on the high middle hump.

Juggling the ruts forced us to go slower than we wanted and after a while I saw Neutron in my rear view mirror lit up by Silvaan's headlights. I slammed on the breaks thinking if Silvaan has a problem with this then too damn bad. I opened the door and Neutron leaped in over me and landed on Spencer and Lena. I gunned it and we were off again.

We couldn't see that far ahead because we were sort of encased in sage growing above the sunken, eroded road so that I had to slam on the breaks to keep from hitting the crashed Skandrr disk blocking the road. The ship was huge and surreal, lying tilted at an angle with smoke rising from one side of it. Pieces of what looked like thin, shiny metal cloth were scattered everywhere and a deep ditch had been plowed right through the sage and across the road. I stopped to see if we could drive through the ditch but was unable to stop looking at the crashed disk. I opened the truck door to get out and then a number of things happened all at once.

I heard the crackling of sage brush as Silvaan's car accelerated off the road to my left, sage snapping, his headlights jumping wildly, when a hand grabbed me from the back of the neck and threw me hard to the ground. A foot tried to kick me in the face but this foot got caught in the sage and I rolled out of the way. I looked up to see somebody pulling Lena violently out of the passenger side of my truck as Neutron leaped out at them snarling. Then Silvaan's car shot alongside my truck and hit two Skandrr soldiers wearing black body suits and the short gray capes. Silvaan and Isult were out of their car before it finished lurching to a stop and then six or seven men wearing capes were on us. Silvaan punched one guy in the throat and he fell down choking. He kicked another in the thigh and when he fell down, he kicked him in the stomach and then turned and punched a guy who was strangling Isult who had opened his face with her nails. I'd gotten up but was immediately grabbed from behind and was getting strangled in a half nelson so I deliberately fell backwards to make my attacker fall too and then I turned around and just started punching and kicking.

I heard Llueve's screams and turned to look into the halogen beams of the Subaru and saw that a Skandrr soldier had pulled Llueve out of the Subaru and was dragging her by the hair through the sage towards the crashed disk. I ran at him and tackled him as hard as I could. He let go of Llueve and turned on me. I saw the exaggerated widow's peak of his black hair, and cold black eyes in blue skin by the glare of the halogen lights, and knew right away that it was the Skandrr officer who had groped Llueve at the cafe in Saala .

He kicked me in the stomach but I was tensed up so it didn't get me. I caught his leg and pulled him off balance. But he hit me in the side of the head as he fell and before I could recover he was strangling Llueve. She was choking with rage as she pulled my hunting knife out of its sheath and stuck it through his thigh. He screamed and fell and we stood over him as he writhed on the ground clutching at the knife. Llueve whipped around to face me, lifting up her blouse to exposed her tits and screamed 'karoolia dnaeg slaih enhoat!' then, lowering her blouse, whipped back around and spit at the Skandrr as he stared up at her with pain and rage in his eyes. I reached down and yanked my knife out of his leg. It's an expensive knife my dad gave me and I've had it for years. I wiped the glistening red blood with the Skandrr's cape and the bastard turned even bluer and glared at me with focused hatred and I am sure, memorized my looks. Isult yelled for us to come.

We ran back towards the others when four or five arcs of electric force crackled out of Silvaan and Isult's Tsaat weapons and zapped that many Skandrr who collapsed and lay still and smoking in the sage. Silvaan jumped in my three quarter ton truck and rammed it into the rim of the disk ship, which was teetering, on the edge of the Gorge. He backed and rammed the disk until it began tilting over the edge of the Gorge and then accelerated, the wheels kicking up dirt and sage roots until the disk started sliding. We heard booming and crashing as it flipped over boulders and rock shelves. An arc of electric fire glanced off the side of my truck and Isult whipped around and shot the shooter. With a few of the Skandrr still moaning and writhing in the sage, we jumped back in the vehicles, crossed the plowed ditch and took off down the dirt road.

One of my headlights was gone but I could see fine. In a couple of minutes we crossed an old bridge and hit the highway going north into Colorado. In forty-five minutes we were on the outskirts of Alamosa passing motels and stores. I pulled down a dark side street for a conference. Silvaan pulled up beside me.

Chapter Twenty Two

'We don't wiant to be on the roads in the dayetime becouse they will have agents on the roads,' Isult spoke through the open driver's window. 'I look like a Geisha,' she said freshening her lipstick in the visor mirror. 'And he looks like a corpse,' she said, hooking her thumb at Silvaan who scowled. 'And she looks like bleu cheese gone bad!' she nodded back at Llueve. 'It is too reesky. Find us a hotel Jwo,' she then addressed Silvaan and Llueve in rapid Ovvalan ululations.

'We need food first.' I said to Isult, aware of just how pale Llueve looked. 'I'll find a grocery and then we can find a motel.' Isult nodded and we drove on. We found a convenience store. Silvaan parked next to my truck. I went over and asked Isult what to buy.

'No cans! No meat, pasterrie or sugar or things in cephollane. Try cottage cheese and uh peanut butter... froots!' she said.

I got a bunch of different kinds of cheese, bread, fruits, juice drinks. The only meat they had was that permanently preserved baloney and some Kraft cheese slices that a builder once told me in a pinch you could use as roofing shingles.

As we passed a Motel 6, I remembered that they let you keep a dog in your room and had Wi-Fi, so I pulled into the parking lot. I went in with Yvonneso that the night clerk could get a good look at us and not get curious later. I asked for two rooms on the backside of the building, away from the road so as not to be disturbed by traffic. But the guy could have cared less. He wanted to go back to his video. I looked up and saw staggering, bloodstained ghouls stumbling through a burning industrial plant.

'I got two rooms side by side but they're on the second floor,' he said, bored.

'Fine - long as we're away from the traffic,' I told him and paid with Traveler's Checks.

So we holed up in two rooms, right next to each other, each with two queen size beds, bathrooms and a connecting door in between. The Ovvalans vanished into their own room and us Humans went into the other so that Yvonne and I were contemplating sharing one of the twin beds.

Lena immediately turned on her laptop, to search for news about the crashed UFO. There was nothing. But she found two video clips of UFO disks flying over Ireland and Germany during the last forty-eight hours. We all watched the shaky footage of a black disk as it hovered down vertically over a large, burning, expensive two-story house, in a well to do neighborhood in Koln before the disk rose vertically into some clouds.

In the other clip, a black, streamlined disk was flying low over pastures separated by flinty stone walls. It was visible for a long time - for miles - as it flew slowly over the countryside in what the narration said was County Mayo. As the disk passed over a large factory like building with twin towers, a white projectile shot out of the disk and the towers collapsed. And then the large building behind them, that hadn't even been touched, imploded and collapsed as well.

With the lap top screen flickering out images, Isult came in with Llueve and Silvaan and sat on the beds with us and watched. We tore open the groceries. Silvaan had his streamlined silver weapon openly exposed in a shoulder holster.

This was the first calm moment since the crash and we all sat in silence for a moment chewing.

Being in the presence of Isult and Silvaan was nerve wracking all by itself. Her piercing awareness, the speed and depth of her mental penetration of situations and environments is continuously beyond my expectations, as her mind seems to work ten times faster than you are ever ready for. There is no small talk with her. I had to continually control my mind from being overwhelmed by her presence. Silvaan was less intense but so deadly serious.

Lena's laptop landed on news about the imposition of GMO crops in Iraq by multinational agricultural firms. The woman narrating the piece mentioned two American chemical fertilizer companies whose stock had begun a meteoric climb on the NASDAQ.

Silvaan reached out and tapped a long URL into the laptop and a video came on. He manned one of the characters in the game and made him walk through a wall into an artificially lit stone cavern about the size of a normal room in a house Inside there were transparent Plexiglas boxes with curved lids. Inside the boxes were naked Human forms encased in different colors of what looked like Jell-O. There was a John McCain in cherry, a Dick Cheney in lime, a Barak Obama in apple, an Arnold Schwarzenegger in grape, a Hillary Clinton in strawberry and Hanna Montana in vanilla. The camera swept slowly over the scene. The faces of the clones farther away were out of focus so I couldn't identify them.

'These are from Annanokan sheep,' Silvaan said. 'This is rooms where gthey row at Inxalrok.' He typed in a new URL so that the screen went to some black disk ships flying in formation on either side of a 747 airliner.

Isult's eyes never rested in one place and as she spoke her eyes roamed around the room, across the ceiling and then, as she continued to speak, her opened eyes would go blank and I knew she was looking into another dimension for intruders and whatever it was she looked for. She snapped into present time and lit some candles and placed them on the floor.

'The electric lights hurt my skin,' she said. She had changed into a heavy, midnight blue silk dress with a short calfskin jacket and designer sneakers. She still wore the stockings that were all torn up from the fight. She drew us into a circle on the floor to concentrate our forces and create a single protective aura and guided us in a group visualization to center ourselves and stay alert and focused. I felt magnetic impulses weave through my brain.

Llueve spoke in Ovvalan to Isult and Silvaan for a long time. I watched Llueve in awe. She was so beautiful and strange and we were going to be parents. What would our child look like? I hoped more like Llueve than me. Llueve was wearing the new blue jeans I'd got her and a green plaid shirt of mine over a green T-shirt I'd bought her. The knife was again in its sheath around her waist and I felt there was no better place for it. The luster of her auburn hair, the movements of her face, her shoulders, and the expressions of her hands ,were all so elegant. I see the snake-like fluidity, and electric impulsiveness of Ovvalan motion that I could also see in Isult, and to some degree in Silvaan. It's a sense of viewing human bodies that have become liquid. The thought that Llueve and I are lovers, that we are pregnant together just poleaxes me.

When Llueve finished, Silvaan and Isult asked her questions then Isult turned to me.

'Llueve has just told me about the incident with the Draco birds exploding into stars Jwo. Were these stars four directional - like crosses or like starbursts in all directions?' I brought back the moment. The picture of perfect, four directional, luminous lines of electric blue light shooting out with geometrical, gemlike precision came to me. I didn't bother to say 'yes' because I could sense Isult reading my mind. Silvaan made some comments to Llueve and Isult in Daag. Isult turned to me.

'We will have to study theese more, but zat particular geometry of the blue light usually means the atomic transmogrification of the soul - ees disintegration on one plane and to birth into another. If this is what it appears to be - that trees planted in both worlds causes the Draco beings to transmogrify – this whole thing with the Oonda trees is Ea communicating something to us about how to deal with Dracos.' She didn't explain this but paused in deep thought for a while.

'There has been a very curious development,' Isult said quietly. 'The Siddhe keep track of the flight patterns of the Skandrr disks over Daag in order to keep records of where they are spying so we can tell if they are aware of any of our installations.

'Radar records from the last two years show, that in the northeast area of Daag, in the Aarrten Valley, the flight paths of Skandrr disks elliptically veer around one particular area. A Siddhe agent was sent to investigate why this happened. By using an orgone accumulator that reads levels of Aa-vitality, she centered in on a particular area and discovered a strange object.

'The Aarrten Valley is an old farming area famous for its apple and pear orchards. It is interspersed with large farms separated by small forests.

'The Aa-meter displayed high vitality radiations from one specific area in a forest next to a large farm.

'The object found, was a two story glass pyramid greenhouse about the size of a small house. The energy radiations from this pyramid extended for miles in every direction around it. Not only were the radiations powerful but also the wavelength structure was identical to Ixtellar wavelengths. These wave lengths are twelve strand braids of a bioenergetic code, only found in particular places - untouched virgin forests and marine grazing grounds, the linear pathways between stars and the radiations left in Arcturian Crop Circles, for instance.

'We sent a team of our people to investigate and discovered that people in the area are drawing ancient Aaltandaev symbols on rocks and trees with an ink made from chlorophyll and copper dust.' Isult drew the design in the rug with her finger. It was a spiral inside an oval surrounded by little triangles pointing in the four directions.

'The copper dust in these designs, some of them twenty miles from the pyramid, extend the radiations from the pyramid and create a stellar resonance that appears to link the trees together to create a force field that alters the atmosphere. The Skandrr ships are definitely avoiding this airspace, but whether this is a conscious or unconscious action, we don't know.

'The food produced in the pyramid - common vegetables - squashes, potatoes, kohlrabi, cabbages, carrots - are sold in the area and eaten by individuals for miles around the pyramid. There is no evidence of the Faal in the entire area! There hasn't been a Faal suicide there for two years in a population of a quarter million people!

'Twenty-seven Arcturian crop circles have appeared in the area since the pyramid was made. Arcturians tend to gravitate to areas of high positive energy content.

'The pyramid was built by a young Ovvalan woman who lives on one of the large old farms in the valley. She says she had a vision in which she saw what she called 'Star People' - tall beings made of sparkling energy standing around a glass pyramid with radiant vegetables growing in it - so she made one! It was probably Andromedans she saw.

'The woman, whose name is Sabelle, gave us a bucket of the soil from her pyramid with which to inoculate the soil of a pyramid we are building in Inxalrok.' Isult suddenly sat bolt upright and closed her eyes. Her aura shimmered.

'I will go in the other room and be alone for a little time,' she said getting up suddenly. She rattled off something quickly in Ovvalan to Silvaan and returned to her room through the connecting door.

We all ate cottage cheese and oranges and watched the laptop images. I was sitting on the floor with my back against the end of one of the beds. Yvonne was sitting on the bed, her leg pressed tightly against my side. Llueve and Silvaan sat on the floor at the foot of the other bed. They were both on a level of alertness that made Llueve seem unapproachable to me. She had an awareness that didn't include me just then.

To be exposed to the Ovvalans for this length of time and to the events that were unfolding as relentlessly as they were, had me feeling like an electric fire was burning in my nerves. It was too intense and there was no way to shut it down. Lena must have felt it was time to slow things down too because she shut down her laptop and tuned the TV to a nature show about migrating geese. It really helped seeing something simple and familiar. The touch of Yvonne was also reassuring to me. We didn't move an inch away from each other. I think we were all craving the familiar.

After a while Isult came back, closed the door and started to speak, looked at the TV and spit out an Ovvalan phrase and the TV blinked off.

'We are being followed - the Adrrik are in the rooms with us now. They will inform the Skandrr and their watchdogs will soon be arriving. They are going to stick with us so we have to be sharp!' A twinkle of pleasure shined in her eyes as she said this. This was exciting to her. 'I have made contact with the Siddhe and they too are around us now and will try and block the Adrrik from within astral space.' She looked at Silvaan sharply. His eyes were maniacal pinpoints of concentration. His weapon shined brighter than tin foil. 'Figuring out a physical location from seeing it in the astryal can takes a while because the energy patterns match up not exactly and our people in the astral can reconfigure the patterns to further throw them off.. . Jwo - why don't you take that dog of yours and go for a little drive - park your truck somewhere where it looks like it belongs, then, when you come back you'll just look like you're walking your dog. The camper is a giveaway.' I started to do this as she spoke quietly in Ovvalan to Silvaan. Llueve looked at me with a sad expression. This could be it. For all of us. Our last minutes of life and Llueve and I couldn't even talk to each other. I reached out my hand and we slid our fingers through each other's.

'I'm going with Joe honey,' Spencer said to Lena. He then turned to face Silvaan and said 'O.K.?' as in, if that's all right with you Mr. Blue. Silvaan nodded, trying to smile.

We went out. The street was quiet, the night still. We walked down the stairs and got into the truck.

'I feel like I'm frying inside - the intensity of that woman...' I said. I couldn't find anything to compare it to and just stopped talking. Spencer didn't even try to talk. I started the truck and drove like a zombie.

A week ago we both used to live outside Santa Fe and have somewhat normal lives - I mean as normal a life as can be had as the ice caps melt, nations play footsie with nuclear Armageddon, antidepressants are showing up in the ground water, people are eating genetically modified animals and our government is blowing up its own buildings and spraying the population with poisonous chemtrails.

Being around the Ovvalans could lead to a kind of religious worship - at least where Isult was concerned. Silvaan was just very serious but fairly calm by comparison, though he sometimes came across something like an enlightened psycho. Llueve was different than the Siddhe. Though they were all Ovvalan, Llueve was more like a human in the level of her energy and was no more fanatically intense than Yvonne or myself. But she was scared and this showed. Scared doesn't describe it. She was in a state of prolonged panic at being in the Earth realm and she continually turned to Isult and Silvaan for a reassurance of her sanity. She was also beginning to burn at Isult's intensity and it made her feel like a stranger to me. What am I saying? She was a stranger to me. I think that being pregnant by me - a human - and this talk about Ea made her feel like a Siddhe Virgin Mary about to give birth to a divine elf or something. Everything was just so intense.

'We're in the soup now Spence,' I said as I turned down a side street.

'Yeah. Whoever this crowd is that is doing this shit - I don't want to meet them.'

I could only agree. Except that I'm meeting them - just not in the flesh. Yet. My chest still burned at times from Rexxon slicing me. I was catching glimpses of Reptilians and Skandrr with a kind of second sight that was growing in me. It made me nervous about closing my eyes. I found an all-night grocery store and got a six-pack of Sierra Nevada Torpedo. We drove around a bit until we found a likely place for the truck in a working class neighborhood with cars parked on the street. I tuned the radio to KRZA, the local public station and we drank beer for a while. Then I got my laptop and a few things and locked the truck up.

We walked back to the motel drinking beer. There was zero traffic, a clear, black sky, sparkly stars, and silence down below. Things looked so normal, and quiet, walking through that suburban neighborhood. Yet we were in a completely different reality now. Never would the appearance of things now represent the same thing they had before. I could see flashing whorls of light, which were probably Adrrik or BATS remote viewers checking us out. I used a key to pop a Torpedo. Spencer puffed his pipe.

When we got back, the Ovvalans had gone to their room. Yvonne and Lena were happy to see us. Yvonne took a beer and we all sat in the dark lying on our beds watching another nature show - this time it was otters.

Lena was sitting on the floor in a corner of the room, tented inside one of the motel blankets meditating.

I kept seeing the whorls of lights flickering in the dark corners of the room and knew we were being watched. I intensified the silver shroud around me - as we were all supposed to be doing.

Siddhe and Adrrik agents must have been chasing each other, not just all around the Motel 6 but all up and down the neighborhood. It made me so nervous I had another beer, trusting that if Isult had survived for 900 years so as to develop these powers of awareness, that she knew what she was doing. I spooned into Yvonne on the bed, propped up on the pillows and we watched the otters.

I got sort of abstracted when I felt a bug land on my cheek and swatted it off only to realize there were no bugs in the room. I put the bottle of beer down on the night table and felt my exhaustion cover me like a blanket. I thought about the sea of Loosh - the huge crashing vapor waves and cuddled into Yvonne and fell asleep.

The next thing I knew was when I felt Silvaan shaking me by the shoulder. I sat up still half asleep.

We had left the TV on the nature channel with the sound off. A mini camera on a flexible snake extension was looking at a full screen close up of a beaver in its den looking right at me, the fisheye lens making its teeth curve into a crazy smile framed in huge whiskers. Adrrik! I thought and sat bolt upright but then heard Silvaan's voice -

'Taxi service now here,' Silvaan was grinning crazily. 'Come quick!'

Silvaan stood there smiling and holding his silver phaser and motioning us into the other room. Spencer and Lena were already grabbing things and heading towards the door. Silvaan pointed into the other room where I could see Llueve being pushed out the second story window by Isult.

Ilsenaad's head then stuck in through the curtain. Was I dreaming? Silvaan was pushing us each forward by the shoulder. Neutron was staring at me and sticking close.

When I stuck my head out the window I saw a huge, black disk-ship fixed rock slid in mid-air outside the window with no lights on. It was completely motionless and solid as a building. It had an open oval porthole from which a dim blue light glowed. Isult was pushing Llueve ahead of her up a ramp into it and Yvonne and Lena were following. There were three Siddhe soldiers in silver suits standing on the disk's rim, holding Tsaat weapons at the ready. Ilsenaad smiled at me as I pushed Neutron into her and Spencer's arms and then climbed out. Silvaan came through last. We all ran into the interior of the ship with the pod carrying guards right behind us. The ship started to move laterally away from the motel as the porthole closed. It passed over an empty field behind the hotel and swept up into the sky as the door closed on whooshing air. When we were about twenty blocks away from the motel, and a few hundred feet above the town, the disk jolted into high speed and shot across the sky in a long arc like a shooting star.

A Glossary of Ovvalan Words and Names

Aa - Creative Force. Prana.

Aaltare - The dimension above Ovvala and Earth

Aamaat - A Feminine Bodhisattva existing in astral time

Aan – The prana - vitality found in plants that Ovvalans crave

Aarrten Valley - Northwest of Saala where first garden-pyramid found in Daag Asaalen - A Siddhe Commander

Aeron Disk Ships - New, ultra fast Skandrr flight disks

Adrrik - Skandrr astral police

Adriaana - Wixxal healer

Aetlan - The Daag name for the continent of Atlantis.

Aldhe - Forest of evergreens around Inxalrok

Altandaar - Galactic oceanic currents of star frequencies that can be read and traversed with the SkaTaal meditation techniques and that have weather patterns felt in Mahaala, Ovvala and Earth.

AndrrKa - The 14 traitor magicians – Meaning Chosen Ones to themselves.

Anikaa - Siddhe Wixxal Woman

Altaandaev - The vocabulary of the Yoga of Ska Taal.

Aouvwhuaalla – Phonetic spelling of Ovvala.

Aran-Skaala - the continent from where Skandrr Royal lineage and military operate from and where the region of Daag is. Relative to North America.

Arraglocon - Draco Prince

Asaalen – A Siddhe officer.

Assembly Of One True God - The name for the central council of the 14 AndrrKa fallen magicians on Earth. The Skandrr Royalty is its Ovvalan counterpart.

Ouroboros - Negative Draco Linguistic. The Ixtellar linguistic reversed

Avaala - Siddhe Wixxal woman

Balatek – Skandrr technological/agricultural ministry

Barndoltd - Llueve's father' name

Biolova – Biosoul – the organic basis of astral nature

Bodiccea – Siddhe Commander

Crop Circles – The video I saw at Spencer's came from Stardreams-Cropcircles.com

Daag - An ancient and dominant region of AranSkaala. Compare to Europe. Also the language the Siddhe speak.

Djagdaa - A Human Incarnation of one of the original 19 Counsuelaars. High officer of the Siddhe.

Draco Webs - Negative thought constructs and discontinuities to baffle, confuse and deplete energy; counterpart to the Ixtellar strings.

Druiddaal - A monastic order at Kalkaava near the Inxalrok Valley where astral constructs are maintained.

Duraam - Llueve's brother who committed suicide

Ea - One of the original 19 Counsuelaars. Ea was also one of the original Co-creators of Mahaala - the Solar System. A Very Ancient Soul.

Elsinaad - Siddhe leader

Faal - The sadness disease on Ovvala that leads to suicide

Falkrr - Skandrr secret police

Muurial - Name of the Hekate healer at Wixxal

Fiellistr- Ovvalan white spruce trees

Gala-Bala - a Daag expression meaning 'Wow'

Homosaurans - Humans with a dominant conduit to the reptilian brain and whose logic is the obverse of mammals

Hunamunan - Old Daag word for Human

Ideema - An incarnation of one of the original 19 Counsuelaars.

Iduuna - the small moon that fell on Aetlan (Atlantis) to end the Jurassic Era.

Ildrevva - An acknowledgement of a magikal occurrence.

Ilaan - a river valley in the Inxalrok wilderness

Illum - The Counsuelaar who incarnated as the author Paul Twitchell of Eckankar; Author of 'The Tiger's Fang' 'Key To Secret Worlds' and other books. Now transcended.

Illuva - The single name for the dimensionally polarized planet that contains both Earth and Ovvala

Iluun - the valley where the Kalkaava monestary is

Inxalrok - Siddhe settlement - in Ilaan River valley. Relative to Siberia

Inxol - a region in Ovvala

Isult - Reincarnation of one original 19 Counsuelaars and Siddhe Commander.

Ixtaal - A yogic activation command that vertically conjoins Uma, the SxtraJiel (Self-Jewel) to Aaltare - the Higher Octave. Vertical ascension.

Ixtellar – 1. The Yoga of the imagination. 2. Fibers of an Intelligent substance constructing the Universe that respond to creative designs.

Janosians - A race of Humanoids who destroyed their home planet with greedy environmental abuse and who arrived in our solar system looking for a new home. Having lost the ability to procreate because of eating artificial foods, they mastered the science of cloning themselves and other life forms.

Kaelaa - Siddhe Wixxal woman

Kadoka - ?

Kabakadak - Draco Prince.

Kalkaava - A monastic order of 'imagination gardeners' at Inxalrok who use sacred geometry to grow and sustain an astral garden.

Karoolia! –A declaration of female ardor.

Kavra - 'Crystal force' an anti-gravity energy that flight disks run on

Kovrro - Flight base dimensionally across Draco wormhole from area 52. It is in the Glaan sector of AranSkala

Krrual – The capitol of Skarror, the Draco reincarnational vortex in the Qlipothic underworld

Lavaana - Siddhe Wixxal Priestess

Lexl – A command in SkaTaal Yoga that activates a construct with light from Aaltare. A high frequency of Light.

Llueve Anaalia - Llueve's full name

Logaana - Underground Siddhe colony

Loosh - the Ovvalan word for Shakti - Soul Force; a term originally discovered by Robert Monroe

Maggan-da – Ovvalan women's ceremony at Wixxal Canyon

Mahaltaar - The Great Work. Mahaala's ascension into Aaltare

Mier - Llueve's mother

Monroe, Robert; author of three concise books on his out of body experiences over 35 years. 'Journeys Out Of The Body', 'Far Journey', and 'Ultimate Journey'. monroeinstitute.com

Oonda - Daag for Pear

Ostrad and Vologa – Areas of AranSkaala where there are concentrations of Skandrr supporters

Oorden - Siddhe Wixxal Priestess

OvaSapiens - A word used in the Blue Stone transmission to indicate Ovvalans and Humans collectively

Ovvana - the Ovvalan side of a wormhole to Renne Le Chateaux in France bombed during the Inquisition

Pachycephalosauri (25' tall) - Underling Draco souls who serve the Tyranosaurian Draco chieftains

Peterson, Robert -Author of 'Out of Body Experiences'.

Pterodactyl - A winged Reptilian from the Jurassic era

Qlipoth - the underworld where disintegral beings and demons exist

Remote Viewing - a method of controlled, out of body experiences, used by military agencies for spying.

Rote - a concentrated set of memories and pictures of an event or conversation, relayed Astrally. A process discovered by Robert Monroe.

Saala - Ovvalan city in the region of Daag. Very stylish and liberal. Paris.

Sahasrah-dal-Kanwal - An astral city created millions of years ago by unknown beings. Mentioned in 'The Key To Secret Worlds' by Paul Twitchell – author of 'The Tiger's Fang' and also by Monroe in 'Ultimate Journey'.

Seshena - Siddhe Wixxal

Siel - Demonic astral females from Qlipothic underworld. (Uoluan are the males)

Shenella - an Ovvalan endearment; 'sweet girl'; 'darling girl'

Silvaan - High ranking Siddhe Commander

Skaalin - Ovvalan for disk ship

Skandrr - Draco possessed Ovvalan royal Lineage started on Ovvala by the AndrrKan magicians who defected

Skarror – The Draco astral planetoid in the Underworld.

SkaTaal - 'Star Talking'. A part of the Altandaar Yoga involving reception of galactic frequencies with the astral jewel of the self - the SxtraJiel - within the heart, and then projecting the produced vibration into the higher self in the next octave of being in Aaltare. Self Birth. Self Creation.

Suudilve - The Creative Intelligence of Love. The essential, core energy in the universe. Activated through Co-creative intent. The confluence of Loosh (Shakti) and Aa (prana)

Suura - environmental group in the city of Saala that Llueve belonged to

SxtraJiel - A crystal fluid, diamond construct, to house imaginative constructions; the aura construct of the body; a malleable shape - micro to macro; the basic building block of the Universal Ixtellar Continuum

Tantaala White Buffalo – An Atlantean Counsuelaar

Terrulia - Human Female in Daag mythology. Equates to a troll.

Tovro - a Terran or Earth male. A denigrating expression. A troll.

Tsaat - the silver weapons used by Siddhe

Uma - The Deity of Mercy in Darkness; the virgin, universal darkness, that exists below the Qlipothic Underworld

Uul - A large river that runs through the city of Saala

Uralaam - country where a suspicious fungus destroyed crops causing famine

Velociraptor (6ft tall) Another of the underling souls who serve Draco Tyrannosaurs

Voluan - demonic astral males from Qlipothic underworld (Siel is the female)

Vrryl – The predatory energy of fear and violence in the core of Dracos. Anti-Love.

Wixxal – Ancient female magikal sect among Siddhe Women.

Made in the USA
San Bernardino, CA
21 June 2018